"I MAY NOT BE A PROPER LADY, BUT I'M NOT A FOOL," KATE SAID.

Alexis folded his arms and smiled at her. She was glaring at him with her hands on her hips, which gave him an excellent view of her figure.

"You've been gone from the others for a long time. So have I. The whole castle knows we're missing by now, and you can bet one of your precious gold mines they'll never believe we spent the whole time talking."

"I don't care if they think I entertained a whole regiment. Anyway, you said yourself there's nothing I can do."

"There is one thing. Do me the honor of betrothing yourself to me, my dearest," Alexis bowed over her hand and kissed it.

She snatched her hand away. "Toad."

"Only for a few months. For your reputation."

"A few days."

"Months," Alexis said.

"Six weeks," Kate said.

"I bow to your wishes."

"Somehow I find that hard to believe. What are you doing?"

Before he kissed her, he spoke. "I'm sealing our bargain."

The kiss went straight through his body. He'd been trying so hard to keep from watching her all evening. He was done with looking.

Lady
Hellfire

Suzanne
Robinson

BANTAM BOOKS

New York London Toronto Sydney Auckland

LADY HELLFIRE

A Bantam Fanfare Book / published by arrangement with
Doubleday

PRINTING HISTORY
Doubleday Loveswept edition published March 1992
Bantam edition / June 1992

ISBN 0-553-29678-7

Published simultaneously in the United States and Canada

Bantam Books are published by Bantam Books, a division of Bantam Doubleday
Dell Publishing Group, Inc. Its trademark, consisting of the words "Bantam Books"
and the portrayal of a rooster, is Registered in U.S. Patent and Trademark Office
and in other countries. Marca Registrada. Bantam Books, 666 Fifth Avenue, New
York, New York 10103.

PRINTED IN THE UNITED STATES OF AMERICA

OPM   0 9 8 7 6 5 4 3 2 1

To Brian O'Doherty,
with my love.
When my spirits are dark,
or I feel alone,
Thoughts of you bring a smile—
and give me courage.

Lady
Hellfire

Chapter One

England, February 1854

The death ride beckoned to him. Alexis kicked his stallion from a canter into a gallop. Leaning forward, he shortened his reins and rose out of the saddle. Valentine was taken by surprise, and Alexis laughed when he heard Val shout.

"Alexis, no!"

As his friend grabbed for him, Alexis swerved. "Don't try to stop me, old chap. You'll get hurt."

Alexis bent over his horse's neck. Standing in the stirrups, he let Theseus go. The animal stretched into the gallop. Hooves dug into frost-covered soil; legs contracted and sprang out until the horse seemed to claw the earth and then leap from it with each stride.

Alexis heard Val's voice calling to him from far away, but the speed was flowing in his veins. He tore through the wet dawn. Racing faster and faster, he strove toward that unattainable quarry—peace.

Devils and sins, they rode with him. Theseus sensed them, too, and strained to leave them behind. Shrieking taunts, they flew beside him, lurid pennants to the staff of transgression on which he was impaled. Dirt and pebbles thrown up by the flying hooves hit him in the face. His heart raced with the stallion's, and his lungs heaved. Still the devils and sins kept pace with him, but now he couldn't hear their screaming. The pounding of his blood drowned all other sounds.

On he rode through the open fields. He urged his stallion over fences and icy streams, bushes and wagons. With each leap he risked death. He beckoned it, reached out to it, but in the end Theseus pulled him away from it. Of his own will, the horse slowed to a canter, broke stride and began to trot. The demons settled down to their usual drooling murmur, and Alexis collapsed on Theseus's neck, shivering in reaction.

He let the stallion take him back. Lacking the strength to lift his head, he rested his cheek on Theseus's mane and blew white clouds of air from his aching lungs. The long walk passed in a blur for Alexis. When he raised his head, the castle was within sight. It was the size of a small town, his home. Towered and battlemented, dominating the nearby river and its valley, Castle Richfield was both his refuge and his prison.

As Alexis rode nearer, he could make out the gold of Val's hair. The young man was waiting for him astride his own Thoroughbred. Alexis pulled out his handkerchief and buried his face in it. By the time he neared Val, he was calm. He guided Theseus alongside the other man's horse and inclined his head to his friend.

Val held his body rigid, controlling his nervous horse with one hand. "Damn you!" he almost shouted at Alexis.

"Yes," Alexis said. Valentine Beaufort was the only person outside the family ever to witness the death ride, but Alexis wasn't going to relinquish mastery because of it.

"Why don't you put a gun to your head? It would be simpler."

"But not nearly so fascinating for you."

Alexis listened to Val's curses while they crossed the bridge over the drained moat and walked the horses between the gates and into the outer ward. Grooms ran up to them. Alexis slid from the saddle, and his knees buckled. Valentine was there to catch him.

Alexis shoved at the younger man, but was forced to allow Val to help him as they passed into the inner ward. It was a long walk. He began to shiver, feeling alternately hot and cold as their boot heels clicked and echoed on damp paving stones. He was taller than Val, and heavier, so he had to listen to his friend's complaints along the way.

"You're a hulking idiot," Val said between puffs of breath. "A black-haired and damned heavy madman."

"Is that any way to talk to an old school fellow? And it's not me who's too big, it's that you've got the build of a salamander."

"Close your mouth and try to walk, will you?"

Alexis glanced down at Val and almost smiled. His friend had the temper of a cock robbed of his hens, and had had since they'd first met at Oxford. A good bit of his time there had been spent rescuing the fool from scrapes of his own making. Slender and volatile, with the face of a baroque cherub and a grudge against fate because of his illegitimacy, Val could start a row among a flock of doves, much less a hoard of upperclassmen.

Ahead the doors that led into the great hall swung open, and Alexis looked up. As he expected, his mother and his cousin Fulke appeared. Walking out into the morning sunlight, Fulke lent his arm to Lady Juliana. She stopped at the top step, tugged her shawl around her shoulders, and gazed down at Alexis. About her skirts lurked three cats and a golden marmoset. Juliana's mouth curled up at one corner. Her gaze swept her son, from his tousled black hair to his muddy boots.

"He survived again," she said. "The Almighty has not answered my prayers."

Alexis bowed. "I tried to answer them, Mother."

Beside him Val stiffened, and his hold on Alexis's arm tightened painfully. Alexis tried to stop the laughter that trickled out of his mouth, for he knew it would further enrage Val. He couldn't help it. The low, bubbling sound came out of its own accord. Only he heard Val's curse.

"My lady," Val said. "Providence has shielded your son, and I pray it will continue to do so. There are many who admire him."

Juliana waved a hand. "Lazy tenants, dissolute regimental officers like you, and beggars."

"Juliana," Fulke said in what Alexis called his clergyman's tone. "Alexis has great Christian charity. Without his aid many folk in the county would go hungry."

Alexis had managed to control his laughter, but he was still smiling. "Spare us the accolades."

"But it's true," Fulke said. "And she should acknowledge your virtues."

Another laugh burst from Alexis's lips. Val poked him with his elbow.

"Mother has studied my character for years." Alexis surveyed the woman standing before him amid her pets. "She sees me more clearly than you know, Fulke. Her vision is perfect. Is it not, my lady Mother?"

There was no reply. Juliana turned, skirts swaying to reveal another cat beneath them, and walked back into the hall.

Fulke came down the steps and grabbed Alexis by the arm. As the three of them walked inside, Alexis was spared more lectures. Both men were too angry to speak.

Val left them at the top of the staircase. "I tried to stop

him," he told Fulke. "It was impossible. A devil riding a comet, and both too fast for their own good." He scoured Alexis with his gaze, then addressed Fulke again. "You do something, my lord. I cannot."

Fulke thrust Alexis into his bedroom and into the care of Meredith, his valet. Without a word he stalked from the room, giving Alexis privacy for bathing and changing.

By the time Alexis had pulled on his trousers, his arms and legs had stopped shaking, mostly. He walked into his bedroom, a towel draped around his neck, while he tried to make his fingers negotiate buttons and buttonholes at his waist.

The effort cost him all of his recently restored strength. Collapsing on the edge of the bed, he sat there and contemplated the drops of water that rolled from his hair, down his neck and shoulder to his arm. He hadn't really meant to launch into the death ride with Val along, but the doubts and suspicions had invaded his mind without warning.

Burying his nose in the towel that hung over his shoulder, Alexis squeezed his eyes shut. If only he could remember more of what happened the day his father and sister were killed. If only he knew for sure . . .

But perhaps it didn't matter. He'd been so young, and God forgave children much, or so Fulke said. And since then he'd tried so hard to be good, when the demons weren't torturing him, as if to assure himself that he could be. Alexis rose and scooped up the shirt Meredith had laid out on the bed. The movement cost him a stabbing pain in his shoulder, and he winced. He was staring at the white wave of fabric when Meredith came back into the room to help.

He wasn't surprised that Fulke returned while he was still dressing. Holding still while his valet straightened his cravat, Alexis glanced at Fulke as the older man stood before Alexis's desk, foot tapping as he flipped through the pages of a book, each sheet crackling as it was turned.

At last Alexis took pity on his cousin and decided to dismiss Meredith. After all, one owed one's ex-guardian respect. Indeed, he owed Fulke Sinclair a debt it would take ten lifetimes to repay. Sixteen years ago Fulke had given up a successful political career to take care of a brain-fevered widow, her distraught son, and the de Granville estates.

On that nightmare day when his father and sister were killed, Fulke had rescued him from terror. As always, Alexis's thoughts veered away from those memories. He considered Fulke again, and his sacrifice. Fulke had been the conservative comer, one of the Queen's rising Tory favorites. Yet Fulke's affection for his first cousin, Alexis's father, had compelled him to take up the guardianship of his cousin's son once it was clear that Juliana's nerves had been permanently damaged. Now Fulke was within two years of fifty, and discontented. Alexis couldn't blame him.

Yes, he owed Fulke gratitude, and there was fondness —no—love between them. When Fulke wasn't on one of his religious tirades, that is. Lately they'd been growing worse, plunging Alexis from gratitude to guilt, from fondness to frenzied irritation, from admiration to cynicism. There was no middle ground with Fulke now, any more than there was with his mother.

Alexis heard the snap of a roughly turned page. Annoyance surfaced, and he tried to rid himself of it. The effort proved useless, so he settled for trying to hide it. He nodded at Meredith, who departed with a look of relief.

The moment the door shut behind the valet, Fulke slammed the book he'd been abusing down on the table. "By God, you cost me much, sir."

Alexis grabbed a handful of letters from a silver tray. Collapsing on the window seat, he began going through them. A hand slashed down and sent the envelopes flying out of his grasp. Alexis watched the papers drop to the rug, then raised his eyes to Fulke's.

Fulke glared at him, but Alexis's stare possessed all the detachment of a field surgeon's in battle. Fulke drew back, his mouth compressed to a thin ribbon, and lifted a hand.

"Forgive me," he said, "but I thought joining the regiment would rid you of this madness."

Alexis twisted and sprang up. He gathered the letters to the accompaniment of verse.

" 'My life has crept so long upon a broken wing/Thro' cells of madness, haunts of horror and fear,/That I come to be grateful at last for a little thing.' "

Kneeling at Fulke's feet to pick up the last envelope, Alexis looked up and smiled. "Ophelia Maitland's ball is tonight. I vow I'm the fox run to ground by the mighty huntress."

He waited for Fulke to decide which was worse, his death rides or Ophelia Maitland.

"You haven't run from that Maitland harpy at all," Fulke said at last.

"You're the one who keeps telling me I should stay home and get an heir."

"As Marquess of Richfield it's your duty to care for the estates and to breed."

"How do you know I haven't bred already?"

Fulke darted at Alexis before the younger man could say more. He shoved Alexis back into the window seat. Alexis stayed where he landed, for Fulke placed a knee in his chest.

"Since you were a stripling that face has made you prey to women. I tried to protect you. God loves chastity and purity, not beauty, Alexis."

Moving so quickly that Fulke lost his balance, Alexis wriggled free and stood up.

"I tried your way," he said. "But my sins are such that to play the monk would make the angels laugh. I'm hungry. Let's go down to breakfast where we can fence over tea and the china. Please, Fulke. You know I hate quarreling with you."

Fulke managed a smile, and they fell in step together. Outside his chambers they met Val, who was escorted by Alexis's dog, Iago. Alexis watched the two men exchange glances as would two exasperated physicians. Fulke took leave of them, and Alexis held up a hand as Val opened his mouth.

"Be still," Alexis said. "I'm between mistresses and the boredom affects me."

"Ass." Valentine made fists of both hands and turned on Alexis. "You enjoy setting me off. Is that why you used your influence to get me a place in Cardigan's regiment? So you would have someone near to devil? Someone beholden to you who couldn't escape? Lord St. Maur's bastard—under your thumb."

Alexis sighed and stroked Iago's head. "Yes, I needed another pet. Oh, shut up, Val. After all, you're in the Light Brigade and I'm in the Heavy. Plenty of opportunity for you to escape me. You should be worrying about the Tsar and his appetite for the Crimea instead. If there's war, we'll be in it. Then you can use all that ire to fight Russians."

"You tried to kill yourself."

"What imagination," Alexis drawled. " '*La mort ne surprend point le sage; il est toujours prêt à partir.*' "

Valentine stared at him for a moment, then translated. "Death never takes the wise man by surprise; he is always ready to go."

"Well done. You were always clever in school, but you needn't scowl at me. I'm done riding for the day."

They started toward the stairs, Iago taking up his position at Alexis's left.

"Do cheer up," Alexis said, clapping Val on the shoulder. "It's not dying that I'm concerned with, but the lovely Ophelia Maitland."

"Be careful with that one. Her merchant ancestor is only three generations back, and Lady Juliana won't approve of a daughter-in-law so tainted any more than she approves of my illegitimate self."

Alexis laughed and led the way to the passage that would take them to the small dining chamber. "That's why I'm thinking of going to Maitland House and making an offer after breakfast." He looked at his friend's open mouth and laughed again. They were at the dining table before Val regained enough of his composure to close it.

At Maitland House, Kate Grey perched on a chair in her sitting room. Her gaze was pinned to the pages of *Othello* in case anyone should come in, but she was fuming like an overstoked boiler. She couldn't do it. She couldn't be a Lady like Mama wanted. What was she doing here, an American used to frontier towns and clapboard houses? It wasn't her fault Mama wanted to relive the past by making her daughter into a fussy, simpering Lady. She was plain old Kate Grey, with a papa who was a gold miner and a mama who never should have given up Society for him.

Besides, Ladies couldn't do anything interesting. They sat around making doilies and reading Improving Works. She didn't have time to be a Lady. There was real work to be done now that they were rich, but Mama had insisted that Kate go to her relatives in England to be Ladyfied. Mama had wheedled and taken all over faint until Papa finally surrendered. So here Kate was, planted in Maitland House, surrounded by her widowed aunt, cousin Ophelia, and Great-aunt Emeline, surrounded and pinned down without hope of escape from that dreaded entity Mama was always talking about—Society.

Trouble, that's what she was in all right, and it was all

because Papa had found gold almost two years ago. Kate remembered that day well, for she'd been working just before Papa came home with the news. Working at a chore no Lady would undertake. She'd been washing clothes.

Five washtubs sat in the yard behind Grey's Boardinghouse in San Francisco, attended by Kate and four Chinese women. Kate had been rubbing cloth up and down the washboard until her fingers and palms tingled. Suds splashed into her face. Water sloshed onto her chest. She neither looked at the other women nor at the setting sun. She had to get her wash finished before the evening chill set in.

A shirt slipped from fingers numb from constant rubbing. She bent down over the washboard to search for it.

"Please, Lord," she prayed to the soapy water, "don't let Mama see me."

A skein of her hair fell forward over her face. Strands of bright copper and darker cinnamon ran through it. She tossed the lock back over her shoulder. Before she could straighten up, something wrapped around her waist and she flew backward. A beard stuck itself in her left ear, and two arms squeezed her ribs.

"Jesus," a male voice said. "Jesus."

Kate found herself tossed in the air. When she came back down, the man caught her to him, chest to chest, cupped her buttocks, and ground his hips into her. Too furious to yell, Kate pulled her arm back and rammed her palm into the man's nose. He dropped her.

"Jesus!"

Backing up to the washtub, Kate snatched her revolver from the stool beside it. She turned around as the man took a step toward her, and cocked the gun.

"Stay back."

The man blinked at her. Judging by his appearance, he was another prospector just in from his digs. Tired, dirty,

and peeled clean of manners by months of isolation. His
beard was long, and he smelled of horse, mule, and week-
old sweat. He eyed the gun, then grinned at her.

"Now little girl, I ain't hurt you. Put that old gun
down." As he talked, the man eased closer. In another
three steps, he'd be within reach.

"Hellfire," Kate said. "I hate it when men talk to me
like I'm a two-year-old."

The barrel of the gun dipped. It spat, and a bullet tore
open the ground less than an inch from the man's boot.
For a big man, he hopped quickly. He danced back, repeating his blandishments all the while. Suddenly, he
lunged at her, and she fired a second time. The prospector
yowled and clutched his upper arm. He yowled again,
turned, and galloped out of the yard like a spooked mule.

The back door to the boardinghouse slammed open.
Kate looked over her shoulder to see her brothers. Robbie
came charging down the steps with a rifle in his hand,
Zachary behind him, and last came Mama.

Sighing, Kate wiped the perspiration from her forehead. She winced at her mother's shriek.

"Oh dear! Oh dear, oh dear, oh dear."

Robbie slid to a halt with his rifle aimed at the retreating prospector. Zachary pointed at the man's churning legs
and laughed. Kate tried not to grin herself. It was hard
because her mother was babbling and fluttering helplessly
even as she maneuvered her eight petticoats and bomba-
zine skirt through a door never meant to accommodate
them. Kate's admiration increased when Sophia squeezed
through the opening and down the steps without revealing
so much as an ankle.

Kate sighed again as her mother floated toward them.
Zachary trotted around to stand beside her and cast up a
glance of sympathy. Robbie hadn't moved, and Kate knew
he wouldn't until he was sure his family was no longer in
danger.

Sophia glided to a stop between her daughter and the washtub, in the only spot not covered in mud. After pressing trembling fingers to her lips, she threw her hands out toward Kate.

"You're at the washtubs again. The disgrace. After all my care in teaching you proper conduct, miss. We're not in the goldfields any longer. I won't have you grubbing about."

"Mama, one of the Chinese ladies was sick."

"And your dress." Sophia curled her lip and shuddered. "To go out without the proper dress."

"You mean not wearing twenty petticoats and a corset?" Kate paused while her mother gasped and put her hands to red cheeks. "How can I wash clothes if I can't bend over to reach the tub? I have too much chest as it is without pushing it up with lacing."

"Ohhhhhh. Be quiet, miss. You're eighteen years old, a young woman. If you'd been dressed as a Lady, that—that gentleman would never have—have . . ."

Kate handed her revolver to Zachary and put her hands on her hips. "Don't worry. I'd have shot him between the eyes first."

"Ohhhhhhh." Sophia put the back of her hand to her forehead.

Hunching her shoulders, Kate struggled not to cover her ears. Mama could shrill like a train whistle when she was distressed. Calling to her sons, she swirled away in a cloud of petticoats and disappeared into the house.

One of the laundresses silently took over Kate's washtub. Kate smiled her thanks and trudged toward the building that housed the kitchen. She had eighteen miners to feed, and one of the cook's helpers had burned her hand. Rolling up her sleeves, she stepped into the kitchen. Soon her hands were buried in sourdough and flour covered her damp gown from chest to thighs.

It had been almost four years. Four years since Papa

had dragged Mama from his family's plantation in Virginia to seek a fortune in the goldfields of California. Ever since they'd come west, Kate knew she'd been a disappointment to Mama. But there hadn't been time to be a Lady. Not on the wagon trip over desert and mountains where endurance saved your life, not delicacy. Not in San Francisco where earning a living mattered more than the fact that Ladies weren't supposed to know there was such a thing as men's underwear, much less touch it.

Kate lifted her sourdough into a pan and looked around for a towel to wipe her hands. It had been her idea to run a boardinghouse when it became obvious that Papa wasn't going to strike gold before their savings and Mama's inheritance ran out.

Kate found a towel and carried it to the washbowl. She dipped her hands in the bowl, and the water turned white. Sometimes she wanted to scream at her mother.

When faced with their financial crisis, Mama had only fluttered her hands. An English gentlewoman wasn't supposed to know about money or business, and it was Timothy Grey's fault that the subject had to be mentioned at all. If he hadn't sought independence from his wealthy Virginia family, Sophia and her children would be safe and comfortable instead of grubbing in a frontier town.

Kate had been wiping dough from the front of her dress and trying to think of a way to assuage Mama's ire, when Papa had burst in with the news of his gold strike. The whole boardinghouse had erupted in jubilation, and Kate's world had changed.

"Hellfire."

Kate snapped her book closed and tried to shake free of the irritating memories. Sometimes Ladies had to do things that were lacking in gentility, and washing gold-prospectors' laundry was one of them. Mama had wanted her to be a Lady, but Mama had also wanted food on the table. Kate had learned years ago that sometimes you couldn't have both.

Glancing around the sitting room brimming with dust-catching lace and flounces, Kate sniffed in disgust. To Sophia, the daughter of an English Gentleman, the only proper places for young Ladies were rooms like this, in England.

Ever since Kate could remember, Mama had talked of her English heritage as if it were second only to saintliness. She would tell stories about how she was a Maitland. She would natter on about the Maitland Heritage and Maitland House, near Castle Richfield in Sussex. To Mama, all that was refined and noble was epitomized within the confines of Maitland House. Her brother, his wife, and their daughter Ophelia inhabited a fairy-tale world called Society.

Kate suspected Mama should never have left Society, because not a day went by that she didn't mourn some aspect of her life that wasn't at all what Society would require. Sometimes, when Mama was droning on about Maitland House and Society, Papa would look so sad. Once they became rich, Mama's lament took a new turn. She began insisting that Kate be sent to England, to her brother's family. Kate resisted, and the battle was joined.

One victory fell quickly to Kate because Papa and she loved to read. Once Timothy gained wealth, he resumed the lessons with his children he'd begun long ago. Robbie and Zachary suffered through them. Kate fell in love with them. She immersed herself in Voltaire, Aristotle, Herodotus, and Euclid. Together she and her father devoured books faster than Robbie gobbled up apple pie. Then Timothy discovered how time-consuming being rich was. Kate watched him struggle under the burden of managing the family wealth and offered to lend a hand. They became business allies, their partnership a natural consequence of their shared interests.

Yet what seemed a sensible solution to their difficulties was anathema to Sophia. Timothy was burdening their daughter with tasks that could strain her delicate female constitution. Kate pointed out that her delicate constitution had survived the Rockies, the deserts, and the goldfields. Mama dismissed this argument with a wave of her lace handkerchief. Kate grew to hate that handkerchief. Every time Mama found something of which to disapprove, the handkerchief was waved like a banner on a battlefield.

Unsteady footfalls beyond Kate's sitting room door signaled the progress of her great aunt Emeline down the hall for her morning nap. For Kate, breakfast had been another trial, what with Aunt's light-mindedness and Ophelia and her mother's tizzies about the ball that night.

She dropped her book on the floor. She must count herself fortunate to have escaped being Ladyfied for so long. If it hadn't been for Mama discovering her friendship with Patience, she wouldn't be in England now.

A Fallen Woman, that was what Mama had called Patience. Kate had known the girl for over a year, so she understood that Fallen Woman meant whore. She didn't care. Patience had saved her from being raped when she'd wandered down the wrong street in San Francisco, and there was nothing that would make Kate give up the girl's friendship.

Besides, she learned so many interesting things from Patience. Like why men jumped on a person for no reason, and how babies were made, and why men didn't seem to have any discipline below the waist. In return Kate taught Patience to read and gave her advice on how to save some of the money she earned. But it was the discovery of Patience that lost her the small war she'd been carrying on with her mother for so long.

"Hellfire."

Kate caught her lower lip between her teeth and

looked around. Good. No one was there to hear. That was another thing she had yet to accustom herself to, the surplus of people who felt obliged to do things for her. More so than in America, the English had people to do for them. There were persons to open doors, persons to take one's cloak, persons to conduct one hither and yon, persons to help one dress and undress. There was someone to make up fires, someone to fetch water, many someones to prepare and serve meals. No wonder this small country was so crowded.

She should write Mama. She'd promised to do so once a week, but every time she took up her pen, Kate realized how much she missed her mother. Mama might nag and fuss, but the pestering was all due to love. And Kate did enjoy some of the Lady things she'd had to learn, like dancing and music.

If only she weren't so nervous. She was to go to a ball that night. Cousin Ophelia said it was a disgrace that Kate was almost twenty and hadn't come out or been to a ball. The affair that night was just the thing to introduce Kate to the intricacies of the dance. Ophelia was adamant that Kate couldn't possibly be presented during the London season in the spring without a few practice balls to break her in.

And etiquette. How was she to remember the proper forms of address, the rules of precedence? Kate got up from her chair, nearly tripping over her skirt in the process. She lifted the yards of material above her ankles— something she knew she shouldn't do—and walked to the window. Her room overlooked the front entrance, and she spotted a carriage pulling up. It was one of the prettiest she'd ever seen, all shiny black with polished brass and colorful gold, red, and white armorial bearings on the side. Ophelia would jump out of her corset with excitement at receiving a call from such a noble visitor.

Kate placed her elbows on the windowsill and pressed

her forehead to the glass. She'd allow herself a few minutes looking out the window, then she'd study cousin Ophelia's list of important people who were to be guests that night.

As she rested her head on the windowpane, Kate saw the occupant of the carriage alight. Her rooms were in the east wing of the house, so she looked down at an angle upon the visitor. From her vantage she could see him clearly, though, for she was only one floor above him. Whoever he was, he must be important, for the butler was out to assist him, and so were two footmen.

The visitor stepped toward the house and removed his hat. The sight of him made her press close to the windowpane and flatten her hands against the glass.

It was impossible to put into words a feeling she'd never before experienced. Kate knew a great many serviceable words. Her collection of words was so large, in fact, it frightened the young men to whom she was introduced. Yet upon seeing this man, she couldn't call up a single one to help her understand her own reaction.

If he hadn't removed his hat, she never would have known. But he did, and she saw him and the very air around him suffused with magic. It was impossible for her to say why it was so, but it was. For the first time in her life she wanted to touch a man.

Perhaps the magic was his physical beauty, for indeed there was plenty of it. Glorious black hair. The contrast between his skin and sunlit hair made the black locks brighter than any fair color could ever be. His face was a set of Euclid's wonderful angles, but his lips curved in a low arc that made Kate purse her own for a reason she couldn't identify. Before she could do more than take in the fluid movements of his body, he was gone. With him he took the magic.

Kate looked down at her hands. They were clasped together, damp and cold. Without thinking, she raced from her room and along the hall to the corner of the landing to peep down into the entry hall. She couldn't see him. He was already being led to a drawing room, but she could hear his voice. Faint as it was, the sound shot arrows of fire and ice through her body. She could feel them strike with each word he spoke. Then a door shut, and she heard no more.

She walked back to her bedroom. Going to one of the armoires, she reached up high and brought down a heavy book. It was full of engravings of the works of Michelangelo and da Vinci. Her cold hands turned the pages, one after the other, until she came to the last. She snapped the book closed. Just as she thought. Those elegant clothes concealed a mighty fine set of muscles, if either artist was at all accurate in his portrayal of the male anatomy.

Still, there was no explanation for her own behavior. She'd seen men of great beauty before. But none of them made the air brighter by coming near. None of them made her skin tingle merely by speaking. It was a wonder; there was no doubt.

Chapter Two

As he had threatened to Fulke and Val, that morning Alexis waited on Ophelia Maitland with the intention of offering marriage. The drawing room at Maitland House was bright with sunlight and the sprinklings of Ophelia's accomplishments. Accomplishments were necessary to young women. They were the epaulets and badges of rank by which a Gentleman could recognize a Lady.

He picked up a piece of intricate embroidery from the settee and tossed it aside. He wandered to the piano where he leafed through works by Chopin and Mozart. Ophelia was indeed accomplished, but what recommended her to Alexis was that she had neither the rank nor the wits to make his past an obstacle to an alliance.

But that wasn't all that recommended her, he admitted. Though he'd never say as much to Fulke or anyone else, he actually liked Ophelia. As soon as that thought formed, a burning lump settled in his chest, born of edginess and fear. What if he was in love and didn't know it? After all, Ophelia, in spite of her pretensions, exuded a lighthearted goodness and humor that gave him hope. He needed hope, and the idea of losing it scared him as nothing else could.

He might as well confess his real reasons for being there, if only in his thoughts. In spite of the distrust with which he protected himself against females who wanted him only for his position or for his appearance, Ophelia's goodness had drawn him. For if Ophelia was good, and Ophelia loved him, then was he not also good? If she wanted him for himself, he might be able to fight the demons, build a life with Ophelia, and find peace. He might even be able to give his love again.

Who would have thought he'd find redemption in a Maitland? The Maitlands were social athletes. Since their rise from obscurity a few generations ago, they had climbed the social ladder with all the tenacity of mountain goats and the agility of monkeys. They grasped at each rung, each niche and rock of respectability with agile claws and toes.

The Maitlands' ambitions were well known to the de Granvilles. For almost two centuries the Maitland holdings had sat in the middle of the Richfield domain like a gap in the battlements of an otherwise secure castle. One of Alexis's ancestors had been convinced by a Maitland to sell the lands. On those lands sat Tower Richfield, the original fortress of the first Baron Richfield. Its loss festered into a canker upon the family breast. Ever after, the de Granville seller had been vilified by his successors.

Year after year the de Granvilles watched the Maitlands scratch off a little more of the mud of plebeian descent while slowly marrying their way into gentility. Alexis didn't mind having people near him who claimed weavers and tanners as forebears; he minded like the devil having a hole in his battlements. For over five hundred years the de Granvilles had lived and fought at Richfield, and he considered it his duty and his honor to guard the family heritage.

His family had fought with the Yorkists against the Lancastrians in the War of the Roses. But they'd twisted and wormed their way into the affections of Henry VIII and Elizabeth the Great, and survived Cromwell to reclaim their titles and lands during the Restoration. The place where this fight for greatness started was in the keeping of people who might tear it down to put up a pinchbeck castle of their own in their ceaseless hopping from social rock to crag of rank.

Ophelia, however, had not devoted herself to the family occupation. He detected nothing of the mountain goat in her. It was Alexis who had first sought her out, and he who had pursued the girl. He liked the way she made friends with anyone who seemed out of place. He'd seen her take a plain girl under her protection and turn her into a success during the course of one dinner party. And—since he was being so bloody honest—he might as well admit that if he hadn't thought he might love her, even the possibilities of obtaining redemption and regaining the Tower wouldn't have brought him here. Yes, he had hope, for the girl had made it clear over the past year that she loved him.

He was imagining the fury of his mother and Fulke's wife upon hearing of his offer, when Ophelia was ushered in by her mother. The two looked as if they would burst from the effort to hide their excitement, and it took little inducement to get the mother to leave. The inanities of conversation took up a few minutes, and as he waded through them, Alexis tried not to expose his impatience.

"It is so kind of you to call upon Mother, my lord," Ophelia said.

"It is my honor," Alexis said.

"And we look forward to seeing you tonight as well."

He'd had enough. Slipping from his chair, he crossed the room to the settee and sat beside Ophelia. He paid no attention to her scandalized look. She'd let him come a lot closer on several occasions. Ophelia wasn't a prig, and he'd become more and more familiar with her over the last weeks. He took her hand and kissed the palm, then pulled back her cuff and brushed his lips across her inner wrist.

Letting his tongue slide over her white flesh, he whispered, "Do you know what I want?"

He silently cursed the idiotic question. He couldn't believe his courage was failing him at the last moment. He wanted to be poetic.

"Of course I know." Ophelia was breathing rapidly, and her neck and cheeks were flushed. Pleased by her obvious delight, he prepared to make his declaration, but she chattered on.

"Oh, my lord, this has been my greatest wish, and—and think of it!"

"Mmmm. What I wished to say was—" He stopped, noticing that her gaze was directed at a point over his shoulder.

"Plain Ophelia Maitland and the Marquess of Richfield," she said. "Why, a marquess ranks above every peer except a duke."

Alexis glanced down at their joined hands, then looked up and found the girl biting her lip and watching him. He closed his eyes against the apprehension he saw in her face. The small sparrow of hope that had been fluttering inside him caught fire and burned to ashes. Feeling empty except for those ashes, he opened his eyes.

"Agile claws and toes," he murmured to himself.

"What?"

While he stuffed his pain into a deep pocket of his mind, Alexis got up and locked the drawing room door.

Both of them knew that neither her mother nor anyone else would dare disturb the marquess unless summoned. He pulled the curtains closed, walked back to Ophelia, and sat beside her.

Drawing on the arousal that still simmered within him, he let it loose in his stare. Until she made her blunder, he hadn't been serious about his physical pursuit. Now he touched his fingertips to her lips and deliberately drew her attention to his own with a soft whisper of her name.

It was the opening tactic in a campaign he never lost. He used no other words. They would make her think. He used his body—as he would a saber—and the girl responded. By pressing close, he could feel her chest rise and fall. Putting his hands on her hips, he held himself back from her and ran his tongue from her lips, down her throat to the flesh above her breasts. He kissed her there once, twice, a third time. After stroking his tongue over the places he'd kissed, he whispered her name again.

His breath made her wet skin goose bump. Ophelia muttered something. To his surprise, she pushed at his shoulders and brought him down beneath her. Once he was supine, she attacked his lips.

Still more unexpected were her breathless words. "It's been so hard to wait for you."

His eyes widened, and he tried to ask how long she had been stalking him, but she drove her tongue into his mouth. He submitted until her hand began to steal down his chest. It fumbled with the buttons of his trousers, then moved toward his groin. At that moment he ground his teeth until his jaw hurt, summoning the will to thrust her from him and rise. She toppled aside, her crinoline swinging up to bump her nose. Grinning, Alexis began to straighten his clothing. It was a mean grin, mostly because he was in pain. Unshed tears made his eyes sting. Furious at himself for his gullibility, he willed the tears away as he always did. Why couldn't she have been different?

He'd been wrong to take this risk. His gaze wandered to a Chinese vase. He should never have forgotten that he was different—condemned to feed his starving soul on the stale water and moldy bread of sensuality. He'd learned young that no banquets of true affection existed between men and women of rank.

Alexis shook his head. The morning's ride must have addled him. All he really wanted was to swim along the surface, not to dive deep and be swept into an undersea current. Yet this revenge against Ophelia was leaving him feeling soiled and disgusted with himself. He couldn't seem to stop, though. He needed to escape the hurt, and anger burned it away.

"Alexis."

Something in her voice, a change in timbre, a faltering, caused him to glance up from buttoning his trousers. She had straightened her clothing. She rose and put her hand on his cheek.

"What's wrong? Alexis, you are so beautiful."

"Thank you." He turned away, not wanting to hear, but she pursued him.

"How chivalrous you are to wait for me."

He picked up his coat, then drew back the curtains. Ophelia hastened to finish buttoning her collar. She came to him as he fastened his coat.

"How long shall we wait?" she asked.

"Wait for what?" He brushed the hair back from his brow.

"To make the announcement of our betrothal."

He lifted his eyes to hers. His brows shot up. "Ophelia, my dear, you said you knew what I wanted, and then you gave it to me. Part of it, that is."

The air shot out of the girl's lungs. She stepped back and opened her mouth to scream. He fastened a hand around the back of her neck and pulled her to him.

"If you bring them down on me, I'll call a physician to examine you for proof of virginity."

"Oooooh!"

He released her, smiling at her ladylike outrage.

"I could kill you."

"If I'm dead you can't marry my title."

To his surprise, Ophelia's fury disappeared. If a face could become an accounting ledger, hers did in the second before her self-control reasserted itself.

Mountain goat to the bone. Alexis's shoulders drooped. It served him right for being such a bloody fool.

Ophelia began to indulge in tears. He wanted to slap her, but even now he couldn't bring himself to do violence to a woman. So he stopped the tears by pressing his mouth against her neck. The sadness always went away for a while if he took physical solace, so he sucked at the base of her throat while his thumb rubbed over the material that covered her nipple. As desire built, hurt faded enough so that he could almost ignore it. He spoke with his mouth grazing her skin.

"We mistook one another. That doesn't mean we can't make the best of what's passed between us."

"But you have to marry me."

"Hush." He nipped at her lower lip. "You'll learn not to try to force me, and then we'll get along much better."

He kissed her once. As he walked to the door, she remained standing in the middle of the room smiling at him in a self-satisfied way that he knew meant she hadn't given up. He left her to think of ways to subdue him. He was used to women who spent most of their time away from him doing just that. One more would make no difference.

It was time for Kate to dress for the ball. Ophelia's latest Improving Work was transforming Kate Grey into a belle, so it was Ophelia's fault that dressing had become a tactical nightmare that lasted for hours. Kate was at the mercy of two maids because of this terrible ball, and her cousin was turning out to be a benevolent bully. Ophelia sat in a chair in her dressing gown and personally directed the transformation.

Underthings. They weren't so bad. Then came the corset. A skirmish over how tight to lace it. Kate won. Next, the camisole and the hated stiff petticoat. Then another petticoat. And another, and another, and another, and one more. Finally the dress. It was hefted overhead by means of long rods and dropped like a net over an insect. When it was in place, the buttoning started.

At last Kate was able to turn and look at herself in the mirror. The gown was white, all lace and pearls. If she hadn't been so squashed and loaded down, she would have gasped. Even with her hair mussed, she looked so different, not herself at all. Kate looked down at her breasts. If these low-cut gowns were the fashion for balls, she was lucky her waist was so small. The difference in size between it and the rest of her would keep the dress from falling off.

Ophelia floated over to the mirror while Kate was gawking at her reflection. "Didn't I tell you that gown would do wonders?"

"I don't know," Kate said. "What do you think?" She turned around in a circle.

"Oh, lovely, lovely. Only . . ."

"Something wrong?"

"Well, yes. You see, it's your hair." Ophelia pursed her lips and looked at Kate's head. "I've been meaning to tell you. In your own interest, of course. I mean, well, the color is what you might call garish."

Kate put her hand to her hair and blushed. Ophelia rushed to her and gave her a hug.

"There. I've said it and I'm glad. Now I can tell you

what to do about it. A chignon." Ophelia turned to one of the maids. "Minnie, a chignon. And Jane, bring that spray of white flowers for Miss Kate's hair."

It didn't take long to subdue the unfortunate curls into a ball at the back of Kate's head. The flowers were brought and afixed around the knot. Kate gazed at the results and tried not to be hurt. She had forgotten about her hair. It was like wearing a fireball on her head. Ophelia was kind to have thought of it, even if Kate couldn't help the ache it brought to her throat to have it described with a delicate grimace.

Ophelia put her cheek to Kate's and hugged her again. They stared at each other in the mirror, and Ophelia whispered, "And now let's take care of those spots."

Kate felt the heat rush to her face. "What do you mean?"

"Well, we want to cover up as many of those little freckles as we can."

Kate tried not to turn red, but it was no use. She concentrated on making her face a blank so that no one would notice the tears she was holding back. She hadn't known that other people were disgusted by her freckles, and Ophelia was too much of a Lady to say so. Kate swallowed hard and allowed Ophelia to apply powder papers, one after the other, until her face was almost as white as her gown. As she worked, Ophelia chattered.

"You'll never guess who called, never." She didn't wait for Kate to guess. "It was the Marquess of Richfield." Squirming with the effort not to jump up and down, Ophelia paused and watched Kate as if she expected her cousin to swoon at her news.

Kate nodded politely. She put her hands behind her back to hide their fidgeting.

"Officially he came to visit Mother, but it was on account of me." Ophelia waved a powder paper and beamed at Kate. "I mean to have him. Oh, you should see him. His eyes are the most brilliant green and his hands—Kate, he's tall and—and everything!"

"That's nice."

"Nice? Indeed yes he's nice. Didn't you hear what I said? He called on Mother, and he's the Marquess of Richfield. The Richfield lands take up most of the county. Kate, I'm talking about Alexis Phillipe Charles Michael Carlyle de Granville."

"All of them?"

Ophelia tapped Kate's forehead with the powder paper. "No, silly chit. There's only one. Those are his names. And there are three or four more titles, but I forget them all. The important thing for you to understand is that he sees the Queen and he owns half of England."

Kate smiled and let Ophelia natter on. Her glance strayed to the book of engravings lying on the table beside her bed. She would put it away along with her thoughts about the Marquess of Richfield. Both were scandalous for her to possess. Kate knew a staked claim when she saw it, and Alexis de Granville was well marked.

After powdering Kate's nose one last time, Ophelia stepped back to judge her work and smiled.

"Got most of them. I must go, but I'll be back to take you down. Don't muss your dress."

With that, Ophelia was gone. Kate turned her back to the mirror. With the help of the two maids, she stepped into her dancing slippers, then they left, too. Kate stood still in the middle of the room, feeling chilled. She couldn't sit down for fear of wrinkling the gown. Walking across the room, she leaned her forehead against the window as she had that afternoon. The pane was cold, but she paid no attention.

It wouldn't do to cry. A veteran of the American frontier didn't cry over garish hair and freckles. Besides, the tears would spoil the powder.

Much later Kate was standing beside Aunt Emeline,

who dozed in an armchair. Before her was the polished
ballroom floor, and across it swept a blur of skirts and
trousered legs. Standing with her was a young man whom
Ophelia had introduced as Mr. Arbuthnot. Kate clenched
her gloved hands together and searched her mind for
something else to say. Each time she tried to begin a conversation, something went wrong. Perhaps Englishmen
weren't interested in the argument between the Northern
and Southern states on slavery, or in the beauty of San
Francisco Bay. Of course. She must talk about England.
Fixing a smile on her lips, she tried again.

"I have read some of the stories of Mr. Charles Dickens lately."

Mr. Arbuthnot was watching a group of laughing cavalry officers. Kate glanced down at her hands, then looked
up and smiled again.

"Are you interested in history, Mr. Arbuthnot?"

The young man dragged his gaze away from his friends
and looked down at her. "History? Can't abide the stuff.
Ah! Here is Miss Maitland. I'll leave you two ladies to rest
after all this dancing, shall I?"

Without waiting for her answer, Mr. Arbuthnot bolted
away. Kate saw him rejoin the officers he'd been with before Ophelia made him talk to her. As she watched, Mr.
Arbuthnot made a comment, and several pairs of male
eyes glanced at her. There was a round of smirks among
them. Kate turned her back.

"Really, Kate, what did you say to Weedy to make him
rush off like that?" Ophelia patted her upper lip with her
kerchief and smiled at a gentleman passing by.

"I don't know. I asked him—"

"Shhh." Ophelia grabbed Kate's arm. "Don't turn
around. Keep looking at me and smiling. He's here. It's so
late, I thought he wasn't coming."

"Who?"

"The marquess. You can turn around, but don't let him

see you looking at him. He's the one talking to Lord
Bunton and Mother." Ophelia giggled. "He's so much
taller he has to bend down to hear old Bunty. No, over by
the doors. See the one with the black hair?"

Kate saw him, and there it was again, that feeling of
magic. The world grew fantastical. Colors suffused with
brightness, and her spirits lifted as though she'd discovered her own gold mine.

She stared at Alexis de Granville until Ophelia nudged
her. The marquess wasn't looking their way, however, for
his progress about the room was hindered by friends. He
took a step, then was stopped by a couple. After exchang-
ing a few words, he began to move again, only to be
brought up short by a pack of young officers. She couldn't
hear what he said to them, but the whole group closed
around him, quiet and attentive for once. Alexis laid a
hand on one man's shoulder, gave him a sweet look, and
said three words. She started when every officer in the
group burst into laughter, including the young man who
was the brunt of the marquess's comment.

He left them before they'd recovered and ran into a
blockade of skirts. Beside her, Kate heard Ophelia growl
as a mama and her two daughters cooed at him. By this
time, however, Ophelia's mother had decided to rescue
Alexis, and the blockade evaporated under the attack of
this worthy battleship. He was captured and towed to port
in front of Kate and Ophelia.

As he came closer, Kate could feel the tug of the
magic. She was sure it was real now, because she'd seen it
work on a roomful of people. She wasn't imagining things.
People fought for his attention; they claimed him as they
would a prize. Yet she sensed a hesitancy in those who
sought him out. It was as though they approached an un-
predictable deity who might favor them or strike them
dead according to his whim. And in a few eyes, she per-
ceived wariness.

He was standing in front of her. She was aware Ophelia and her mother were talking, and she was sure he was introduced to her, for he took her hand. The warmth of his penetrated to her innermost self, and she couldn't keep from staring at him. He wasn't looking at her, though. He was looking at Ophelia, who had put her hand on his arm as though he were a wayward child in need of guidance. Ophelia's mother was gushing. Ophelia was purring.

Then he spoke. Kate let the deep sound flow through her, but unfortunately, Ophelia interrupted him.

"Mother and I were just telling Kate about how the de Granvilles used to own the old Tower, my lord." Ophelia snapped her fan open and waved it slowly, disturbing a curl that cascaded to her breast. "Kate didn't know that the Maitlands have acquired quite a bit of de Granville land, and we were saying how fitting it would be if the ancient holdings were united again, somehow."

Hearing so many lies at once, Kate could only stare from Ophelia and her undulating fan to the marquess. Ophelia's mother bobbed her head in agreement.

"Yes indeed, it would be fitting," Ophelia said. "And of course, Lord Alexis is so clever as well as handsome, we're all sure he'll be able to find a way of solving such a little problem. Don't you think so, Kate?"

Flushing, Kate nodded. Such blatant fawning clearly annoyed the marquess, and she was embarrassed for Ophelia and for herself. Oblivious of her error, Ophelia continued.

"Kate is a stranger to England, and I've taken her under my wing." Ophelia moved closer to the marquess. "I know everyone would like her if you were to take her up, my lord."

Kate could feel her cheeks redden even further. She wondered what they looked like under all the powder, but it couldn't be too awful, for the marquess only flicked a glance down at her before returning an increasingly frigid stare to Ophelia. Ophelia plunged on, while Kate tried to quell her own discomfort.

"So I'm sure you'll do my cousin the honor of dancing with her. Kate would like that, wouldn't you?"

Kate nodded again, but the marquess was still examining Ophelia as though she were a frog on the toe of his boot. A few moments went by during which Kate kept a smile tacked on her face and willed herself not to blush again. Finally de Granville let his gaze drop to her, but it quickly flitted away to survey the dancers.

"I regret that I am unable to avail myself of such a great honor. I pulled a muscle while riding, and it is only with the greatest difficulty that I walk without limping."

Kate said nothing, for Ophelia began to scold the man before she could open her mouth. It was evident that the marquess rode too much for Ophelia's convenience, and his recklessness displeased her. Kate offered her own sympathy. The marquess bowed to her, and she made up the excuse of fetching water for the dozing Aunt Emeline that got her away from the two.

She had to restrain herself from racing toward the refreshment room. Hellfire. That man must have traded his soul to the devil for a wagonload of male allure that would have gotten him accused of witchcraft two centuries ago. She would have loved to dance with him, even if Ophelia's claim was staked.

She obtained a glass of Aunt Emeline's special mineral water and went back to the ballroom. Balancing the glass carefully, she skirted the edge of the dance floor. Shining black hair caught her eye, and she stopped. The Marquess of Richfield swept past her with a young woman in his arms. Violins filled the air with the strains of a waltz.

He was dancing. Kate tightened her fingers around the water glass while her heart skidded to a halt, fluttered, then began to pound. Her hands went cold. Her fingers were numb, and the numbness spread to her legs and feet. Someone almost tripped over her. She stumbled backward into a corner beside a table and set the glass down. Looking around her, she saw that no one was paying attention to her. She had to get away, because there was a pain in her chest, deep down inside. Her lungs tightened, and her eyes hurt from tears that were working their way to the surface. Soon she wouldn't be able to stop them.

If she were an English girl, someone would have noticed her going. Since she was that odd, ill-bred American, she wasn't important enough to cause comment by her leaving. For that she was grateful.

Kate picked up her skirts and walked toward the sweeping great staircase that would take her to her room. She reached the foot of it before her vision blurred. She thanked the good Lord she was in the dark hallway when her tears fell, and that she was in her room before she began to sob.

Why was she hurt so badly? Horrible, dirty men had tried to do things to her, and she hadn't cried. It was only that she hadn't expected the cruelty. He was a stranger, and he was supposed to be a Gentleman. She couldn't understand why he would want to humiliate her.

She sank into a chair, leaned on its arm, and cried. She pressed her hands over her mouth so that none of the servants would hear her and investigate. As she tried to control her sobs, her corset creaked with the movement of her body, making her feel ridiculous, and she cried harder. Eventually she was too tired to cry. She leaned back in the chair and stared at the flames in the fireplace. The fire was the only light in the room.

There must be something wrong with her. She hadn't realized it, but it must be so. That was why Mr. Arbuthnot didn't want to talk to her, and that was why Alexis de Granville lied so he wouldn't have to dance with her. Both men were ashamed to be seen with her. Perhaps it was the way she looked. After all, Ophelia had almost said straight out that Kate's coloring was freakish. She must be right.

Kate pressed two fingers to the bridge of her nose and dragged them beneath her eyes. They came away covered in powder.

It hurt too much, this trying to be a Lady. She wanted to find a woodpile and dive under it. Standing up, she reached behind her back and tore at the fastenings of her gown. More material ripped when her fingers dug into the corset lacings. Soon she was nude and shivering. She climbed over the pile of discarded clothes, found a night-gown, and put it on.

Climbing under the covers, she tugged at the bell cord beside her bed. She would tell a servant to let Ophelia and her mother know that she was sick. Then she hopped back out of bed and retrieved two handkerchiefs from an armoire. She might need them. Huddling beneath blankets and sheets, she felt something at the back of her head. The spray of white flowers. She tore them from her hair. Her fingers twisted and shredded the petals. Faster and faster they worked, until there was nothing left of the blossoms. She gathered a fistfull of petals and hurled them to the floor.

"Who needs dancing anyway." Her voice was barely audible to her own ears.

She didn't need dancing. If she didn't go to dances, she wouldn't be hurt anymore. And the way to avoid dances was not to become a Lady. Kate settled back among the pillows. She was going back to America. She didn't need dancing at all, and the next time a man turned her world into magic, she would shoot him.

Chapter Three

Maitland House, April 1855

She'd promised herself never to return, and yet here she was, plumb in the middle of English Society again after little more than a year. Kate stepped over the threshold of Maitland House, past a bowing butler, and onto the white marble floor of the entryway. She caught her lower lip between her teeth when she heard Mama burst into tears as she threw herself into cousin Ophelia's arms. She wasn't going to cry. There was unpacking to be seen to, letters to write.

What an odd coincidence it had been that she'd convinced Mama to let her come home last February. If she hadn't, she might not have been there when Papa took ill. His heart, the doctors had said. There had been something wrong with his heart, and now there was something wrong with hers.

Papa was gone, and he was never coming back. Never. There was no one to depend on now, no one to share with, no one to turn to. Last May Papa had started out for one of the gold mines, and he'd never come back.

That was death. Someone was alive, and then they weren't, and there was nothing you could do to bring them back. You were left with a hole in your existence. You felt all broken inside, but you still had to go on living. You had to get up in the morning, get dressed, eat, and work, even though you'd much rather follow Papa so you could be with him instead of all alone and lost. But someone had to take care of Mama and Zachary and Robbie. Someone had to manage business while the boys were in school.

Mama couldn't. Mama hadn't left her bed for three months after Papa died, and that was why Kate had to do all that getting up in the morning, getting dressed, eating and working. It was also why she was standing on this cold white marble floor when she'd promised herself she'd never have to stand on it again. Mama was more broken than she was, and Kate was hoping that coming home would mend Mama. Anything was worth seeing Mama smile again, even returning to Maitland House.

A week later, Kate was waiting for Ophelia on the stair landing, scuffing her boot on the carpet. Her hopes for her mother were rising. Ophelia's own mother had died a few months after Papa, and Sophia had been able to find comfort in shared grief. Mama was getting better.

Unfortunately for Kate, Society hadn't changed in the time she'd been away. There just wasn't much for Ladies to do, not much that was interesting. So Kate chafed even as her mother improved.

Yes ma'am, here she was—in the land where Ladies dwelt, damn them. If Mama hadn't had her poor grieving heart set on returning to her old home, Kate would still be

in San Francisco with her brothers. Busy. With no Ladies
to put up with. Kate was trying to keep from wishing Papa
was with her when Ophelia flounced out of her room,
chirruping a hello.

Kate followed Ophelia down the staircase, almost
laughing at the contrast between their progress. Ophelia
glided along in her cage composed of crinoline, petticoats,
and skirt, while she, crinolineless, stumped down each
step with a violence that revealed her lack of enthusiasm
for another afternoon carriage drive in the cold English
sunlight. Kate had to admire her cousin. This year's wider
crinoline made her look as though she were a child's toy
rolling along on oiled wheels.

Ophelia sailed across the entry hall. The butler opened
the door. Ophelia oozed forward—and stuck. Kate was
right behind her cousin and rammed into the edge of the
silk cage. The hoop swung down in response to pressure
from Kate's own skirts. The front half of the crinoline
tilted. Ophelia shrieked and rammed her arms down to
stop the whole edifice from rising up, while Kate hopped
backward and reached out to steady the wayward hoop.

"Sorry," she said. "Here. You hold it down in front,
and I'll squish it so you can get through."

With the butler averting his eyes, Kate helped Ophelia
maneuver through the door. On the porch, they paused to
straighten mussed hair and dresses. As a groom opened
the door to the carriage, Kate couldn't resist whispering to
her cousin.

"Told you that would happen. How are you going to
get into the carriage?"

Kate grinned and pretended to adjust her mantle while
Ophelia appeared to behold a carriage door for the first
time in her life. The carriage was an open vehicle with
doors made to accommodate ladies' wide skirts, but its
designer had never envisioned the advent of hoops.

"If the hoop tips—" Kate began.

"I don't intend to embarrass myself," Ophelia said. "You'll have to steady the hoop while I get in."

"How did you manage before I came?"

Ophelia flushed. "With the help of a maid, but these new skirts are wider than ever. I've never had this much trouble."

With the groom assisting from the other side of the carriage, Ophelia was levered into place. Kate climbed in, swatted a bowed portion of the crinoline down beneath her own skirts, and sat on it.

"You'll wrinkle me!"

Kate got up again. It took another few moments to dispose of Ophelia's skirts to her satisfaction. By then what was left of Kate's good humor had evaporated.

They set out at a quick pace. For once it wasn't raining, and the sun made the dew on the grass and leaves sparkle silver and white. Unfortunately, a line of black clouds was amassing over the trees at the horizon. Kate groaned when she saw it. Resting her arm on the side of the carriage, she drummed her fingers. She noticed the shiny black of her sleeve and the snowy froth of the under-sleeve. Mourning. She was in mourning for Papa. Hellfire, she was going to cry. No, no she wouldn't. She wouldn't think about Papa.

She glanced at Ophelia. She and her cousin had corresponded ever since Kate had gone home after her first visit, and their friendship had strengthened. Underneath all that blond hair of Ophelia's was a head full of ideas. Like Kate, Ophelia was interested in books and politics. She simply never let anyone know about it, and all her practicing at appearing not to have any intelligence had withered some of her natural sense.

Also like Kate, Ophelia wore mourning, but for her recently dead husband as well as her mother. Ophelia's heart was in the grave now that she was a widow. Kate knew that because Ophelia kept repeating it, usually with an accompanying dab at a tearless eye with one of her black-bordered handkerchiefs. How anyone's heart could be buried in the same hole with the red-nosed, corpulent Earl of Swinburn mystified Kate.

She was equally mystified as to why Ophelia had rushed into marriage with the old bore so soon after declaring her quest for the dark and serious Marquess of Richfield. Yet she'd betrothed herself and married within a few months of that cursed ball, only to lose the earl, wrinkles, red nose, and all, in January of the new year.

Ophelia's grief was as artistic as it was voluble. She languished. She fluttered and kissed her husband's picture, especially in the company of any gentleman who called to express sympathy. Her mourning clothes were in the latest styles from Paris, her ornaments of the costliest jet. Kate had merely had all her dresses dyed. Wearing mourning wouldn't bring Papa back, and she didn't care if she was fashionable.

"Turnpenny," Ophelia said, tapping her parasol on the floor of the carriage. "Turnpenny, do hurry. I want to get to the Tower before I lose this marvelous light for my painting."

"Yes, mum."

Kate eyed the ribbons and netting of Ophelia's bonnet before speaking in a low voice. "Afraid we'll be late and his high and mighty lordship will bolt?"

"Shhhh!"

"I think you're as daft as the girl you're named for. He didn't marry you the first time."

"You little squit, keep your voice down." Ophelia opened her parasol and positioned it so that they were concealed from the backs of the coachman and groom. "You said you didn't mind. All you have to do is drive about for an hour and then come back for me."

"I don't mind, but I think you're a fool. My maid says that since he recovered from his Crimean wounds, he's spent most of his nights somewhere else besides his own bed."

"With maids and kitchen girls, I'm sure. They probably throw themselves at his feet or drag him into haystacks."

Kate couldn't see the difference between entertaining Alexis de Granville in a musty old Tower and allowing him liberties in a haystack. She didn't say so, however.

"You don't like him because you and Aunt Sophia have been here a whole week and his mother hasn't called," Ophelia said. "It's most unkind of you to mock him when he's only now recovered his health. He nearly got his arm blown away rescuing Mr. Beaufort when the poor man got shot off his horse in the war."

Kate cast a sidelong glance at the righteous Ophelia. "That was six months ago, and his arm wasn't nearly blown off. You're always exaggerating. He probably got a bad case of dysentery and still suffers from the runs."

"Katherine Ann Grey!"

Kate grinned. "Did I turn your stomach? Sorry."

"Oh, hush. You're just angry because Lady Juliana won't call."

Kate sighed and shook her head. "Mama wants to be invited to the castle, not me. I told her what you said about Lady Juliana not having anything to do with Americans and that she considers Mama an American."

Ophelia leaned closer to Kate. "I have to have him."

Her cousin's voice quivered, and Kate was surprised to see tears glistening in her eyes.

"He thought I wanted his title," Ophelia said. "I did, and that's why I lost my first chance with him. But I don't care about that anymore. After all, I'm Lady Swinburn now. But his mother hates me. I think she suspects that I've given myself to him. If she ever finds out for certain, she could ruin me. Please, Kate. Don't make trouble."

Kate grumbled, but shrugged when Ophelia besieged her with pleading looks.

"If it was me," Kate said, "I'd rather be stranded in Hangtown on a Saturday night with a bunch of miners who just struck color. But if you want him, you can have him. Just don't expect me to bathe him in that melted-sugar flattery like you do."

The fierce hug she got for her compliance pinched her shoulder blades together. Their talk turned to the Crimean War again; it looked as if it would never end, and the British government appeared stalled in its own incompetence while young men died by the thousands. Then they went on to discuss the latest attack against slavery in the American Congress. When Turnpenny drove the carriage down the path to the old Tower, Ophelia ended the conversation abruptly. Kate leaned back against the cushions, aware that her cousin didn't want the marquess to catch her discussing politics.

They arrived at the deserted Tower, and Ophelia made a great show of having the groom place her painting materials in the right spot. She and Kate climbed the interior stone stairs of the ruin to look at the view from the top. The Tower was on a bluff that commanded a lookout over the valley that lay between the lands of the de Granvilles and the Maitlands.

As they stood shivering in the cool April breeze, a figure shot down the valley toward the Tower. Kate's eyes widened as she beheld the speed of the horse and rider. The stallion swept through a stream as though it weren't there, hurled himself over a hedgerow, then plunged headlong down a steep gully.

"You'd think he'd have had enough of that after Balaclava," Ophelia said.

Kate winced as horse and rider jumped a fence everyone else in the neighborhood rode around. "As we say in San Francisco, the marquess is a ripsniptious rider. I'd better go before he gets here. But remember, I have to be back to meet with Mr. Poggs about the railroad shares I'm buying."

Alexis dismounted from Theseus and led him to the old keep. He'd walked the horse up from the valley to cool him. Removing blanket and saddle, he began rubbing the animal down using handfuls of the long grass that grew at the base of the Tower. He knew Ophelia was waiting for him inside, but he was in no hurry to join her. She'd wriggled her way back into his good graces and his bed for her own reasons, and she knew he hadn't wanted her there to begin with.

"Alexis?"

His hand stilled on Theseus's flank, but he didn't answer her. What was he doing there? He shouldn't have come again. It still hurt too much just being home. Home was too green, the air too clear and fragrant. It hurt for home to be so beautiful when inside he was still on a battlefield sodden with mud and blood, stinking with burning flesh, gray with smoke from artillery that chopped men into bits of flesh-covered bone.

Crumpling a fistful of grass, Alexis hissed under his breath. "Stop, damn you. Don't think about it. God, don't think about it."

That was why he was there, because Ophelia would help him not think, and because if he didn't keep busy, he might give up. Sometimes he felt so dead inside he couldn't even hear the shrieks of his old devils and sins. Their quiescence was Fate's ultimate insult. A shared horror had silenced his private demons. Dear God, he craved peace at almost any price, even the price of nonexistence. He couldn't give up though, for Val and the others needed him. He may have given up on himself, but he couldn't abandon them.

"Alexis, what are you doing?" Ophelia appeared in the doorway of the Tower. "Alexis."

Only Ophelia could contrive to plead and scold at the same time. Wearily he resumed his swirling motions with the makeshift brush. He needed time.

"I'm busy."

She floated over to him. Theseus gave her a contemptuous snuffle and shook his head. She watched Alexis groom the horse for perhaps forty seconds before she put her hand on his to stop him.

"You'll get all smelly from doing that."

Alexis looked at his mistress and raised one eyebrow. "It never stopped you before."

She touched a damp lock of hair that clung to his forehead. "No."

He shoved the hair out of his face with the back of his forearm, then led Theseus to the stream that ran behind the Tower. Ophelia tripped after him. Her presence annoyed him. What did she know of the real world, the atrocity that was his own life?

"You might at least speak to me," she said.

Feeling guilty for his rudeness, Alexis glanced over his shoulder and tried to smile at her. Her response was all out of proportion to the amount of enthusiasm he had to offer. She fluttered and almost danced as she came to him. Standing on tiptoe, she offered her lips. He kissed her lightly and stepped away to tie Theseus to a tree. She was waiting for him when he finished. He took her hand and started walking toward the Tower while she chattered to him.

He was used to her empty conversation, used to ignoring it, and he let his own thoughts wander to the wounded men under his care back at the castle. Val and the others had suffered more from the incompetence of the high command than from the enemy. One man had gone without water for two days before someone bothered to help him.

He shouldn't be thinking of the men. There was Ophelia to consider. Alexis forced his mind away from the wounded waiting at home.

"Alexis, you aren't listening," Ophelia said.

"I'm sorry. What did you say?"

"I said that your mother hasn't called. You know how much it means to me that she approve of me. And until she calls, I can't come to Richfield. What must I do to gain her approval? After all, every leading family in the county receives me."

Alexis bowed before the door to the Tower and allowed her to precede him up the stairs to the roof. He found himself smiling as he listened to her. At least she was a consistent little blight. As she informed him of how high she stood in the estimation of the social paragons of the neighborhood, he leaned against the wall that topped the structure and surveyed the landscape.

"Alexis, answer me."

He took a deep breath and let it out. "My mother and I have little in common, but one trait we do share. We dislike being used."

Ophelia put her hand on his arm, and he looked at her for the first time since gaining the roof. Her usually bright expression had vanished.

"I'm not using you," she said. "Or if I am, I allow you to use me in return."

"I know what you want from me."

"Perhaps, but you don't know it all."

"Oh?"

"Do you know what a pleasure it is merely to look at you?" she asked. "If a magician turned your Theseus into a man, he would look like you, all black fire and vibrancy. I revel in the possession of that fire."

"You're more believable when you harp about my

mother calling on you." He watched her lips. The lower one was caught between her teeth, and she was chewing on it.

She suddenly threw her arms out wide. "I do want you. It's not my fault that I need other things as well."

"No." He was speaking more to himself than to her. "I shouldn't complain. What you want is no more than I deserve."

He turned his back to the wall and fully faced his anxious mistress. "Show me. Show me how much you want what I can give, and I'll speak to Mother."

Upon returning to Maitland House with Ophelia, Kate found her mother and Aunt Emeline entertaining old friends, the ladies of Gresham Priory. She was forbidden by good manners from attending to Mr. Poggs at once. She sat in the drawing room with them, stirring sugar into her tea while Mama chatted with the women. Mama was happy. Kate knew her mother loved Emeline and Ophelia, and Maitland House, and the elegant life she was leading once more. She moved gracefully from lady to lady, dispensing refreshment and sincere compliments.

Seeing her mother amid the lace curtains and brocaded furniture of Maitland House brought a memory back to Kate. The desert. They'd lost their way and been caught at sunrise. Papa had stopped the wagons, and they'd broiled beneath the fireball sun until nightfall when they could travel again.

Kate woke drenched in sweat to feel a cool breeze on her skin. She stumbled out of the wagon into the welcoming night. When she saw Mama, she almost climbed back into the wagon. Sophia had dragged a crate from one of the wagons while the men were hitching the oxen. She was smoothing a lace tablecloth over the box. The cloth was one she'd brought from England.

She bent to the ground, picked up a silver candelabra, and placed it in the center of the cloth. Kate eyed the silver piece with dismay. Papa had said they must cast off all their heavy possessions. Kate backed up and slid around the wagon, then peered around the corner at her mother.

Sophia was pouring tea into a china cup when Timothy Grey walked by with a harness. The harness dropped. Timothy stared at his wife. Sophia paid him no attention as she set a small box beside her makeshift table. Seating herself, she lifted the china cup to her lips and sipped.

"Sophia," Timothy said.

"I must have my things about me, husband. I must have my linens and my silver. I may be in the devil's wilderness, but I'm still a gentlewoman."

Timothy shook his head and picked up the harness. "We have to go. Now. The oxen will die if we don't get them to water. If they die, we'll be next, and you waste water on tea."

Sophia's lips trembled. She took another sip from the china cup. "It's probably teatime back home."

"Dear Lord." Timothy closed his eyes for a moment before turning away from his wife. "We're almost ready. You can bring the china or the silver. Not both."

Sophia bit her lip, then drank more tea. Kate watched her father walk away from her mother. Tears made her eyes sting, so she wiped them away. Sophia remained seated, drinking from her china cup while about her men and women prepared to battle the desert for their lives. Weary and frightened, Kate slipped out from behind the wagon and over to her mother.

"Mama. Mama, we have to go."

"I know, dear. Just a few more minutes. You know how I am. After my tea, I can face anything."

Kate had been fourteen years old, but that night she learned that courage was a mutable thing. Some people shouted to stoke up bravery, some quietly endured. Mama clung to her gentility. Kate would spit in death's face; Mama served tea. And because Kate understood her mother's loneliness and bravery, she was willing to put up with stuffy English gentility and boredom. But she wasn't sure how long her endurance could last.

The meeting with Mr. Poggs took most of the afternoon. Conducting business across an ocean was cumbersome and frustrating to Kate, but she'd promised Mama to stay in England at least six months before declaring it a second Hades and settling permanently in San Francisco. Since they'd arrived initially in London more than a month ago, she'd managed the family business affairs by correspondence. Control of the Grey fortune had been left in Kate's hands in accordance with her father's will. She had to oversee investments in a shipping firm, in ranches in California, in a New York bank, and now in a railroad. If there was one thing her father had believed in more than the value of learning, it was that wealth should be spread around. Kate remembered his lectures.

"My family in Virginia raises cotton and tobacco, Kate, with the labor of slaves. That's why I left. I couldn't live with slavery, and my family couldn't live without it. We're going to put our money in different places so that no matter what happens, we won't be dependent on one or two sources. There's a fight coming, Katie Ann, and it's going to be a bad one, because the South has put all its eggs in one rotten basket."

Kate sat behind a cherry-wood desk while Mr. Poggs finished his notes on the railroad purchase. The only crack in his dignified façade she had detected in the weeks they'd been acquainted was on the day they met. Kate had shaken hands and immediately started reeling off instructions about correspondence with her lawyers in New York and San Francisco. When she finished, the man gawked at her, openmouthed. Then he closed it and burst into speech.

"I assumed that there would be an advisor," he said.

"An advisor?"

"A gentleman to take the burden of business from you, Miss Grey."

"Mr. Poggs, I have advisors in New York, San Francisco, and London, but I make all the final decisions. If you have difficulty with that fact, say so now so I can get somebody else to do your job."

The threat of losing so rich a client nearly sent Mr. Poggs into a faint. Gentleman advisors were never mentioned again. After a couple of weeks of working with Kate, Poggs treated her with respect instead of polite tolerance.

Mr. Poggs was to dine with them and then stay the night at an inn before departing for London in the morning. Dinner was therefore pleasant for Kate. When Mama complained too often about being slighted by Lady Juliana, Kate could talk about her latest clipper ship with the solicitor. Unfortunately, Mr. Poggs left early, and she was doomed to another evening in the drawing room with the ladies.

Of the three, Ophelia was the most trying, for she flitted from sofa to chair to window like a demented nuthatch. Usually, after a morning spent in the arms of her marquess, she was dreamy and disgustingly self-satisfied. Now she twisted her giant handkerchief like a washrag, chewed her lip, and paced. As she walked, Kate kept expecting a collision. Her cousin's skirt pushed at a Chinese vase on a pedestal. It veered toward the Meissen tea set. It attacked a bronze andiron in front of the fireplace. When Ophelia swirled around in one of her abrupt changes of direction, the hoop bobbed. Kate thrust her teacup onto an end table, dived from the couch and swatted at her cousin's skirt as it touched the flames. Ophelia jumped and made a squawking noise.

"Kate, what are you doing?"

"Saving you from being burned."

Mama and Aunt Emeline joined in a chorus of "Oh dear." Ophelia scooted away from the fire, thanked Kate, and began her flitting again. Half an hour later she was still at it, so Kate excused herself and retreated to her room.

In a short time she was curled up in bed, maid dismissed for the night, a book cradled in her lap. It was *Romeo and Juliet*. Heroes and love were safe as long as they were on paper. Outside, the storm clouds that had been moving in all day dropped their load of rain. A rumble of thunder made the window shutters clatter, and the wind whipped raindrops against the panes. They sounded like pins thrown against glass. The last words she saw before falling asleep were appropriate for the stormy night. "These violent delights have violent ends,/And in their triumph die."

Kate surfaced from an unremembered dream with something poking her in the ribs. Fishing the book out from the covers, she lowered it to the floor. Outside, the storm had grown more violent. Water hurled itself in sheets at the windows. Kate was hauling the blankets up over her head when she heard a loud squeak. It came from the warped floorboard directly opposite her door. She knew that because she had to step over it when she was sneaking around trying to avoid afternoon callers.

Curious about who would be up in the middle of the night, she wrapped a blanket around herself and tiptoed to the door. She opened it a crack and fitted one eye to the opening, but all she could see was a hooped skirt—a darker, swaying blob in the darkness of the hall—as it headed for the front staircase and disappeared.

Kate shut her door and hurried back to the warmth of

her bed. Ophelia was prowling about, and it didn't take much imagination to guess why. A few minutes later, Kate's suspicions were confirmed by two separate squeaks of the floorboard.

"No more sense than Hamlet's Ophelia," Kate muttered to herself. "I suppose it's too much to expect." She punched her pillow several times, but her annoyance kept growing. "Sneaking about, bringing him here with Mama and Aunt Emeline just down the hall." She shoved her head under the pillow and rammed it against her ears as though it could keep away thoughts of the man and woman next door. "She'll pay for it, sure as eggs."

The ticking of the porcelain clock by her bed and the wind-blown rain kept her awake for an hour before she finally drifted back to sleep. It was two o'clock when the floorboard squeaked again, jolting her awake. This time she groaned and jerked the covers over her head, then turned on her stomach and made herself recite from the *Iliad* until she dozed.

In her dream she was smothering. Kate gasped and coughed herself awake. The feeling of smothering became terrifyingly real. Smoke, gray and hot, curled and billowed into the room from beneath her door. Leaping up, she shoved her feet into slippers. As she pulled on a dressing gown, she scurried to the door and pressed her hand to it. Cool. After all the fires in tinderbox San Francisco, she knew better than to open a door without testing it.

Opening the portal a crack, Kate choked on the smoke that swirled around her. She slammed the door shut and raced to the commode where she wet a towel and tied it around her nose and mouth. By the time she opened the door again, she could hear shouting from below stairs. Giving herself no time to panic, she dropped to her hands and knees and crawled into the hall.

Breath-clogging smoke engulfed her. Snapping and hissing sounds came from the right, the direction of Ophelia's room, as well as heat and the dancing light of flames. Kate turned to her left and inched toward her mother's room. She could hear screams above the steady crackle and hum of the fire. She caught sight of Mama huddled in the doorway of her room trying to keep Aunt Emeline on her feet. Kate pulled on her mother's arm.

"Kate! Thank God."

"Get down and help me with Aunt Emeline, Mama. There's not much time."

Sophia coughed, but managed to choke out Ophelia's name.

"The fire is in her room," Kate said. "We have to get out. Hurry!"

Kate tugged, and Sophia had no choice but to follow. Together they crawled down the hall, half-carrying Emeline through the growing miasma. On the landing the air was clearer, and they could stand. They met the butler and Turnpenny racing up the stairs. Nightcaps askew, white nightgowns sodden with water splashed from the pails they carried, neither stopped.

Plunging down the staircase, Kate was almost tripped by more men hauling water. When she and her mother and aunt reached the front door, maids threw blankets around them and they were rushed out into the chilling rainstorm. They were quickly drenched by sheets of rain as they ran around the house to the stables. Servants took charge of Sophia and Emeline. All three of them gagged, choked, and shivered for long minutes.

Finally, with her lungs and skin burning and her blanket trailing behind her, Kate went back to the house and ran upstairs, holding her wet towel to her nose and mouth. In the hall the smoke was so thick she had to crawl again. She'd been cold in the rain, and now she felt the heat of the fire on her wet skin. She bumped into Turnpenny making his way down the hall checking each room. The coachman steadied her.

"Miss, I can't find Lady Ophelia. I fear she's still in her room."

"You keep looking," Kate said. "I'll see if she went outside."

Ophelia wasn't outside. Drenched servants rushed past her carrying silver, paintings, and furniture. Maids wept or helped lift water, but no Ophelia. As Kate searched, her dread grew, and pictures of her cousin burning alive kept leaping into her mind. Her stomach roiled and her legs grew weak, and she bolted back into the house and upstairs.

Turnpenny had given up. He was throwing buckets of water with the rest of the menservants, and Kate could see a wall of flames where Ophelia's door used to be. Turnpenny yelled at her.

"It's no use, miss. We can't get to Lady Ophelia's room."

Kate screened her face with her hands and coughed. *Oh God. Oh God, no. Dear Lord, please no.* Feeling her strength drain away in the face of horror, Kate made herself leave the inferno.

Stumbling over the skirt of her gown, she lurched out of the house and across the lawn to fall against the side of the stables. She doubled over, her hand clamped to her mouth. Trembling and sobbing, she huddled against the wall and finally dropped to her knees. She could feel a great wail building inside as she imagined Ophelia burning. Desperate, she clamped both hands over her mouth to muffle the sound, and let it out.

The scream filled her mind, tore at her throat. She gulped in air as another keening sob gathered from deep inside her body. They kept coming, one after the other until she lost count.

Some time later, a gust of wind whipped a lock of wet

hair across her face, and she dragged it out of the way. Her cheek pressed to the wall, she pounded the brick with her fist. The impact scraped skin from her hand, and she caught her breath. She couldn't stay there whimpering. Ophelia was dead, but there were others who needed help.

Clawing the wall, she managed to stand. She took several breaths, wiped her face on her gown, and picked up her blanket. Hands shaking, tears still falling, she joined the Maitland House staff in filling water buckets.

She didn't know how long she stood in the rain and pumped water. All she did know was that her hands were as numb from the cold as her feelings were from shock. She kept her attention on the repetitive motions of raising and lowering the pump handle, until the clatter of hooves and wagon wheels broke her concentration.

The storm was passing when several men rode into the stable yard, followed by a wagon carrying more. As a stable boy took her place at the pump, Kate gathered her sodden blanket around her and ran to meet the newcomers. The lead man hauled back on the reins of his horse and bent down to her.

"Is everyone safe? Where is Lady Ophelia?"

It was de Granville.

Kate wiped the sweat and rain from her face and clutched her blanket to her neck. "She was caught—caught in the fire." Her voice sounded dead and far away. She turned and headed for the house.

De Granville swung off his horse. He ran past her without a glance and disappeared inside the house. Kate kept her attention on putting her feet down and picking them up, putting them down and picking them up. The rain had faded to a drizzle when de Granville reappeared. His face was blackened, and the moisture made tracks through the smudges on his cheeks.

The marquess called to someone named Fulke. As

Kate reached the front steps, the marquess and another man were talking hurriedly with the Maitland butler, Crossthwaite. Kate stood on the porch in a daze watching the Marquess of Richfield try to save Maitland House.

At last she gathered her wits and crept back inside and upstairs. Quick work and the help of the rainstorm had confined the fire to the area around Ophelia's room, but the flames had burned through to Kate's room before the servants and the marquess's men could completely subdue it.

The hall past her room was a charred, black cavern. Kate passed several men on their way out, carrying jagged pieces of wood. As she walked, the floor got warmer and warmer, but she kept on, her gaze fixed on the hole where Ophelia's door used to be.

A white silk wall loomed in front of her. She looked up at the Marquess de Granville. His face was smeared with grime and sweat, and the shirt, soaked by perspiration and rain, clung to his chest. In the light of a nearby candle, his eyes took on the luster of the green in a stained-glass window. Kate stepped to the side, intent on finding Ophelia, but the marquess put his arm across her chest.

"It's not safe. But we were lucky. The fire burned through the roof and the rain helped put out the flames."

She shoved his arm away. "You went in." She took another step, but her arm was clasped by long fingers.

"Your mistress is dead. There's nothing left that a woman should look upon."

Kate yanked her arm free. Tears started and wouldn't be stopped. "I know she's dead. She didn't come with my mother and Aunt Emeline and me. I've known she burned to death ever since we got out of the house."

Ignoring the marquess's apologies, Kate hurried back down the stairs and out onto the porch. Sophia and Aunt Emeline were there. As she approached, her watery vision revealed the marquess talking to her mother. Kate stopped in confusion, then realized that the man before her wasn't de Granville. He was older than the marquess. She wiped her eyes and took in the upright posture, silver strands in the black cap of hair.

Behind her she heard the thump of a boot. Those tensile fingers gripped her arm again. She was about to object when the older man spoke.

"Alexis, I have offered the hospitality of Castle Richfield to the Maitland ladies."

The fingers on her arm tightened. Kate looked up at the finely etched brows that drew together, the slightly squared chin. Down-curved lips formed words.

"Damn and blast you, Fulke."

Chapter Four

Alexis stood motionless, his hand clamped around a strange woman's arm. Wind blew in his face, but it didn't cool the flush in his cheeks. He released the lady while he battled for control of his temper. Ophelia was dead, and he couldn't find within himself anything resembling grief. The war had taken it all, and he was ashamed.

His control was little better than it had been in those horrible days of weakness after he first returned from the Crimea, and now Fulke stood in front of him and openly invited this family of social mountain goats into his home. He wanted to shout at all of them that the dead woman was one of his lovers and he didn't want her family and its sorrow invading his already somber domain. Instead he inclined his head and murmured an apology. Fulke jumped in to save him.

"My cousin has only recently recov-

ered from wounds and illness gained in the war." Fulke
bent over the snuffling Emeline and patted her hand. "I
fear his strength has been taxed and that makes his manners less than they should be. With your permission, I will
see to having you moved."

During Fulke's speech Alexis noticed that the young
woman in front of him was shaking her head. He should
apologize for mistaking her for a servant, he told himself.

"Miss, I don't know your name."

The lady turned, and Alexis found himself being examined by a pair of brown-gold eyes and with all the thor-
oughness of a headmaster.

"My name is Katherine Ann Grey."

"Yes. Miss Grey. Lady Ophelia mentioned that you
and your mother were staying with her. I'm sorry about
your cousin."

"Indeed."

Why did she look at him as if he were one of those
wriggling insects one found beneath dead logs? "My
cousin is right. Maitland House will be uninhabitable for
some time."

"My lord, grimy and charred as it is, this house is far
more comfortable than the Carson Desert or a canvas tent
in San Francisco in the winter rains. I'll manage."

Her unexpected coldness made Alexis really look at
the woman for the first time. She was a small thing. She
barely reached his shoulder, and her hair was plastered to
her head and back. Even wet, even in darkness, he could
make out its polished copper tint. She clutched a sodden
blanket, twisting in the fabric around her neck. He could
see thin blue veins in the pale skin of her hands.

As they studied each other like two angry cats, Alexis
found himself growing curious. Where the devil was the
Carson Desert? What had this young lady been doing
there? And most important, what did she look like when
she wasn't drenched and covered with black soot?

"What did you say?" he asked.

"We'll go to that place in the village."

"You mean the Queen of Scots Inn? It hasn't been improved since the Restoration. And anyway, it's no place for ladies."

"You'd be surprised to what places ladies go when they have to."

Alexis straightened his shoulders and gave the troublesome little person before him one of his lord-of-the-castle smiles. "Permit me to know what is due a lady under my protection. You and your mother and Lady Emeline will be my guests."

He bowed and slipped away before she could object. He heard her take a step after him, so he lengthened his stride. Walking into the house, he joined the crowd of men salvaging the Maitland possessions before the determined Miss Grey could say anything else.

Moving the ladies took some time, and it was near dawn before he got to his own bed. His body ached from lifting buckets and his lungs hurt from breathing smoke and ash, but he slept without dreams of blood and dead men. It was an unlooked-for blessing.

He woke to late afternoon sunlight. He was sitting up in bed with his head in his hands when Meredith came in with tea. He'd given up trying to discover how the man knew when he woke. He kept his eyes closed as Meredith set the tray beside the bed.

"Tea, my lord Colonel."

"Meredith, please. I resigned my commission weeks ago."

"I'm sorry, my lord. Habit."

Meredith held the cup and saucer out so that Alexis could smell the tea he'd poured. Alexis breathed deeply and became human. Almost. He fished blindly for the cup. Meredith put it in his hand and guided it toward his mouth. Alexis downed the hot liquid.

"Thank you. I can talk now."

The valet knew this was his signal to help Alexis begin the day. He held out a dressing gown of striped silk.

"Those women," Alexis said.

"Lady Emeline, Mrs. Grey, and Miss Grey."

Alexis nodded and faced his shaving mirror. For the first time in many months he thought he might look forward to something besides duty, even if it was only the irritating task of foiling the matrimonial plots of a young lady and her mama.

"Is she up and about?" he asked.

"Which, my lord?" Meredith whipped the shaving cream with a silver-handled brush.

"Miss Grey, of course."

"Miss Grey has been up for an hour or two, my lord. She asked the housekeeper for a tour of the castle, but at the moment I'm not sure where she is."

"I think I'll wear that new morning coat. And the black silk cravat, and whatever goes with them. You know Lady Ophelia died last night."

"Yes, my lord. Permit me to offer my sympathy."

"Thank you. She was a mountain goat, but she was a kindhearted one. Once I almost believed . . ."

Alexis allowed Meredith to apply a hot cloth to his face, grateful that the man said nothing. Meredith had a sensitivity to his moods that had kept them together since Alexis was a youth. Alexis knew the man understood him. There was no need to resort to the embarrassment of putting uncomfortable emotions into words.

Washed and partially dressed, he stopped in the middle of putting on his shirt.

"The mountain goats have invaded, Meredith."

The valet held the shirt off Alexis's arm so it wouldn't wrinkle. "Yes, my lord."

"Miss Grey and her mama probably want a title."

"No doubt."

"Then I should be busy today, and every day they're here. Ask Major—Mr. Beaufort to be ready to go to the Dower House with me. That will keep me away long enough. And don't let them come after me."

Meredith took the opportunity of Alexis's pause to slip the shirt into place. He nodded.

"She's probably lurking in the dining room," Alexis said, "poised to strike, crouched on a branch ready to pounce."

"I'm afraid you're in for a great deal of maidenly admiration, my lord."

Alexis closed his eyes while Meredith pulled at his coat and arranged his cravat. "What I hate the most is feeling guilty. Ladies seem to have nothing to do but wait for one to appear. It doesn't matter what one does—hunt, arrange business, read—when whatever it is is complete, there they are, hovering, anxious to please. And they hardly ever do, you know. Please, that is. How many times can I listen to gossip about the Queen, or whether it's more fashionable to carry a bouquet or a scent bottle to a ball?"

"Ladies have delicate minds," Meredith said. He stepped back to survey the results of his work with a pleased look.

"Delicate? I don't know. Not Mother. I sometimes think their delicacy is like the fine net on a bonnet. The frothy stuff covers framework much sturdier than one would think. And some ladies' minds are lined with gutter bricks. Don't have a fit, Meredith." Alexis drew in a deep breath. "I'm ready. Thank you."

He headed for the small dining room, not surprised when Iago didn't meet him on the way. The dog only waited for Alexis a short while before he gave up and went bird hunting. Alexis paused before opening the door to the dining room. Sparks of excitement shot through him. The prospect of eluding Miss Grey wasn't as annoying as he'd thought it would be.

He opened the door, stepped in, and frowned. She wasn't there. No matter. She'd be along any moment. The girl had probably set her maid to watch for him so she could appear after he was seated. Alexis rang for tea. He worked his way through cold roast, Welsh rarebit, fruit salad, scones, and more fruit salad. He had the servants leave the door open. No one came. He called for more tea.

Scowling at the empty doorway, he stirred his tea. *The Times* lay unopened by his plate. He drummed his fingers on it. He dug his fork into the fruit salad, but couldn't bring himself to eat any more. He'd be bloody damned if he'd slouch about while she frittered time away doing fancywork or making seaweed albums.

He shoved his chair back from the table. As he did so, the door opposite the dining room opened. It led to the library, and out of that room came Kate Grey and a man.

Alexis scowled. The girl had been closeted with a man this whole time. Alone. He looked at her companion. All nose and Adam's apple, and the dress of a professional man.

Somewhat appeased, he next glared at Miss Grey. His rebuke was wasted, for Miss Grey was still talking to the professional man. Rich bronze curls were pulled away from her face to fall down her back. He grew impatient. He wanted to drag her over to a window and watch the sun turn her hair to fire. She moved, and he noticed the freedom and grace with which she did so. She wore a black gown with lace at the neck and sleeves, but she didn't make him queasy as some women did by swaying their skirts like church bells. She wasn't wearing one of those damnable crinolines, he realized. A lady with sense. And one whose body was worth plowing through twelve petticoats to reach.

She was still talking to the Adam's apple. Irritated, Alexis shoved his chair back under the table with as much noise as possible. Miss Grey glanced at him, but continued to talk without smiling. Alexis stalked toward the two and heard what she was saying.

"Since all of the family but Great Aunt Emeline are dead now, I'll have to arrange things myself. I believe she left Maitland House to my mother, so I'll have to take care of the repairs and the servant arrangements. Now, about those railroad shares. I want to get them on their way back to New York as soon as possible, so you'd better leave today."

The professional man said something Alexis didn't catch. He bowed to Miss Grey, nodded respectfully in Alexis's direction, and left.

Alexis's stalking took him directly to his guest. She gave him a nod that was much less respectful than the one Adam's apple had given him.

"Good afternoon, Miss Grey."

"Yes, good afternoon."

She was staring at him. Alexis smiled. She kept staring at him. It wasn't like the concealed stares of appreciation he was used to. It was an honest, what-are-you? stare. She must have realized her gaffe, for she dropped her gaze to the sleeve of his coat.

"Please excuse me," she said. "I must go to Maitland House and see about repairs."

Surprised, Alexis spoke before she could move away. "I was going to walk in the gardens."

"Enjoy yourself."

His eyes widened. It was he who stared now. She hadn't jumped at the chance to accompany him. She hadn't even sounded interested in where he was going or what he was going to do. She really was going to Maitland House. And she didn't call him "my lord." She didn't call him anything at all. Perverse little barbarian.

"There's no need," he said.

She was turning from him and stopped. "I beg pardon?"

"My cousin and I will arrange everything for you, Miss Grey. There's no need for you to overset yourself with details best left to others more fit to deal with them."

Alexis was distracted by the sight of Miss Grey putting her hands on her hips. It was a gesture well-bred women of his acquaintance avoided, yet Miss Grey seemed at home using it.

"Thanks for the offer, but if I can manage a gold mine, a shipping firm, and all the other family interests, I think I can direct the reconstruction of one house."

With that, she walked away. Alexis stood and watched her. She was actually going to leave him standing there like a dismissed servant. Three long strides brought him even with her.

"I'll escort you, Miss Grey."

"I have a maid."

He grasped her elbow and turned her toward the stairs. "I'll have the carriage brought round."

"My lord." Meredith came toward him followed by Valentine Beaufort. "I've found Mr. Beaufort for you."

"Why?" Alexis asked. He tightened his grip on Miss Grey's elbow so she couldn't get away.

"The Dower House," Meredith said. "Your lordship said you—"

"I'll be going to Maitland House first. Have the carriage brought around."

Meredith gave him a confused look and hurried away. Alexis turned to Val and introduced him to Miss Grey. Val balanced on his cane and bowed. Taking advantage of the presence of a third person, Alexis sent Miss Grey upstairs to get a wrap. He guessed—rightly—that she wouldn't be rude to him in front of Val.

Once she was gone, Val turned on him. "You know I don't want to go to the Dower House. Quit trying to make me."

Alexis took Val's arm and guided him toward the library at a slow pace. Val limped beside him in silence.

"You can't keep avoiding the men," Alexis said.

"Most of them are dying because of that bloody war. I won't go."

"You had the courage to charge a battery of Russian guns, but you can't face men wounded in the same war?"

Alexis helped Val sit in a chair next to the glass doors that led to the terrace.

Val laughed unsteadily. "The famous charge of the Light Brigade." He looked up at Alexis, his eyes bright with an inner fever. "I can't believe it. The whole country is in raptures about how Cardigan led us on a ride down the valley of death. What do the people care if the Russian guns blew whole sections of the Lancers out of existence? You saw."

"Val, don't. You know the doctors said you'll never get well if you torture yourself like this."

"All of my men were killed. Blown apart. It rained blood." Fallen deep into his memories, Val talked more to himself than to Alexis. He wiped his hands on the shoulders of his coat, back and forth, as though it were soiled. "My clothes were soaked with the blood of my men." The hands stopped moving, and Val looked out past Alexis to the terrace and the woodlands in the distance. "I wiped someone's eye off my sleeve."

Alexis stepped in front of his friend. "Val."

He got no reaction. He knelt and shook his arm. "Val."

Val met his gaze.

"Remember when we were at school and you tried to fight half the rowing team?" Alexis asked.

"I don't care."

"Listen. Old Percy Cheswit was sitting on you trying to flatten your face."

Val almost smiled. "I'd lost my grip on his fat neck. I was strangling him for calling me a bastard." He looked at

Alexis. "You pulled him off me and kicked him down the college stairs. I never saw anyone frighten two oarsmen with a mere stare before."

"It wasn't the stare. It was the idea of having me for an enemy that sent them skipping. And you, you touchy devil, you laughed so hard I couldn't get you to stand. You just lay there hiccuping and guffawing. I spent the next three years trying to persuade you not to be so quick off the mark about your birth."

They looked at each other, neither smiling.

"Would you do something for me?" Alexis asked.

"Of course."

"Would you go to the garden and cut some flowers for me."

"Me? Flowers?" Val sounded as if he wasn't sure what a flower was. "Why?"

"I want to give them to someone."

"But you have dozens of servants to do that."

"A servant wouldn't be as careful. I want you to choose the most perfect flowers. No flaws. They're for Miss Grey."

A transitory smile crossed Val's pale face. "That hair."

"Yes, and while you're at it get enough for the Dower House. Now listen. You must promise to take your time and choose only the best. Study each flower."

Val sighed. "Is this a de Granville remedy for crushed souls?"

"I'll bet you a new hunter that you feel better after doing it. But you have to promise to try."

Gazing at the garden that stretched out below the terrace, Val nodded. "I'll do it. But only because I know you'll make me go to the Dower House with you if I don't."

"You do know me well," Alexis said.

Meredith appeared again. "My lord, Miss Grey is getting into the carriage. She wouldn't wait."

"The coachman will. Damned impertinent little midge."

He took his time getting into his topcoat. After settling his hat on his head, he strolled outside, tugging at his gloves. She was annoyed. He could tell because she sat up too straight and stared at the coachman's back.

Sliding into place opposite her, Alexis eyed her while addressing the coachman. "Maitland House, please."

They rode in silence. It seemed to him that the young lady would be content to peruse the scenery and not talk to him the whole way. Didn't she know how to engage a man's interest?

"Losing your cousin is a terrible tragedy."

Miss Grey jerked her head around in his direction so quickly he could hear the ribbons of her bonnet rustle against her cloak. She regarded him for a moment before speaking.

"Ophelia was a loving woman, and young to die, like her namesake, only instead of drowning, she burned." Her lips trembled, and she pressed them together.

Alexis shook his head. "Don't think about it. Besides, she would have died from the smoke long before the flames consumed her."

" 'I thought thy bride-bed to have deck'd, sweet maid,/ And not have strewed thy grave.' "

"Do all Americans quote Shakespeare, Miss Grey?"

"Don't sound so incredulous, my lord. She didn't scream."

He lifted his brows and leaned back. "What?"

"Ophelia didn't scream. I would have heard her."

"If she was asleep when the smoke overcame her, she wouldn't have awakened."

She was looking at him oddly again. It was that look that made him feel like a diseased rodent. Lovely women shouldn't make a fellow feel like a diseased rodent.

"Last night after dinner I noticed that Ophelia was

nervous," she said. "She bounced about so much her skirt got too near the fire and caught the flames. I had to put them out."

He shook his head. "Ophelia was always careless."

Miss Grey hadn't left off her Lord Justice's stare. "She also prowled around the house after everyone was asleep. What do you think kept her awake?"

"I don't know." Alexis grew uncomfortable under the young lady's scrutiny, and it was a new experience. Women looked at him often, but he had a feeling Miss Grey's reasons for doing so weren't the usual ones. He stared back at her, and she finally transferred her attention to the coachman's hat.

The drive continued with Alexis studying Miss Grey and Miss Grey ignoring Alexis. The more she ignored him, the angrier he grew.

"You're from America, Miss Grey."

"Yes, but Mother is English. She was Ophelia's father's sister. Mother married a gentleman from Virginia."

"I vaguely remember people talking about it when I was young, but you mentioned San Francisco, which is supposed to be in California."

"It is in California. We took the Overland Trail in '49. My father struck gold a few years ago, and Mother wanted to come back to England."

"You must be grateful."

There it was again. That look.

"Miss Grey, I feel it my duty as a host to warn you not to look at gentlemen as if they were insects. It's off-putting and unladylike."

He smiled, then caught his breath at the firecracker sparks that went off in her eyes as she lost her temper. The sheer excitement of it caused him to toy with the idea of evoking an explosion from her. Unfortunately, the coach was stopping before battered Maitland House. He watched in admiration as Miss Grey got out of the carriage by herself. She opened the door, gathered her skirts in one hand, and swung herself down the steps before the footman could reach her. She faced him.

"You're right."

"About what?" Alexis asked.

"I was looking at you as if you were an insect."

Leaving him red-faced and bereft of a retort, Katherine Ann Grey walked up the steps of Maitland House with the clear implication that he was of no further interest to her.

Alexis stayed in the carriage and gawked at her back. He couldn't believe it. She just got up and left. She wasn't worried that he thought she was unladylike. She didn't cower at his displeasure. He wished she were a boy so he could thrash her. He wished she were one of his men so he could have her put under close arrest.

Alexis jumped out of the carriage and strode quickly toward the house to catch up with the savage Miss Grey. This young lady needed to be taught a lesson. Respect was what she should give him. Politeness and respect.

He ran her to ground in the drawing room. She was standing beside a plain wooden coffin with her head bowed. His steps slowed. He came to rest beside her and heard her draw in a ragged breath. Restraining the urge to wipe away the tear that slid down one of her cheeks, Alexis forgot his anger.

She spread out her gloved hands on the top of the coffin. "I'm afraid to look."

He pulled her away and headed for the entryway.

"There's nothing to see," he said. "And no reason for you to look."

When they were in the front hall, he stood with his body between Miss Grey and the servants scurrying back and forth in their cleaning chores. She wiped the tears from her cheeks, then twisted a crumpled handkerchief so violently, he thought it would rip. Just when he thought she would ask to be taken home, she whirled and walked past him to the stairs.

"Wait." He caught up with her.

"I want to see her room."

"Why?" He stepped over a piece of charred wood and turned to give his hand to Miss Grey. She took it and hopped over the obstruction.

"I want to know how the fire started."

"It was probably a spark from the fireplace, or an over-turned candle."

Miss Grey continued on her way upstairs. "I want to know."

Crossthwaite was directing the removal of furniture and met them on the landing. He led them to Ophelia's room. The floor was burned, but it remained intact in the area around the threshold. Alexis looked in at the black hollow cave. Skeletons of brittle charcoal were all that was left of the furniture. Last night he'd only been able to see flames.

"Do you know what caused the fire?" Miss Grey asked Crossthwaite.

"We think an overturned candle, miss, one on the table beside the armchair near the fireplace. Lady Ophelia had fallen to the floor in front of the chair."

"But I didn't hear her scream."

"She must have fallen asleep in the chair and knocked the candle over," Alexis said.

"That is my theory, my lord. Lady Ophelia was fully dressed." Crossthwaite hesitated, then lowered his voice. "We found the remains of a hoop and some jewelry."

Miss Grey shook her head. "I warned her about that stupid hoop."

Alexis took her arm and drew her away from the room. "There's no need to feel guilty for not hearing her. She obviously slept while the fire smoldered and never woke.

You could see the remains of a glass. She may have had a glass of milk and nodded off."

"Perhaps," Miss Grey said. "Crossthwaite, you know the arrangements for Lady Ophelia's body. Also, we'll need to move the stable animals and the servants. I'm sending for drapers and furniture merchants from London. Lord Sinclair is sending carpenters. You may tell everyone that the staff of Maitland House will not be changed. All your people will have wages through the time it will take to repair the house. When the repairs are completed, Mrs. Grey will be living here with Lady Emeline. They will keep the staff unchanged."

"Yes, miss."

As Alexis listened to her giving instructions, he soon felt like unnecessary baggage. At the end of her conversation with the butler, Miss Grey made ready to leave, and Alexis followed her to the carriage, like a page attending the mistress of a medieval castle.

The drive back was spent in polite conversation. He would offer a tidbit and sit back to see if Miss Grey accepted his offering. They eyed each other like a cat and a dog stuck together in a closed railroad car. At last his irritation got the better of him.

"Really, Miss Grey, all this activity is quite unnecessary. I'll be happy to manage everything while you're so stricken with grief for your cousin."

He must have heard wrong. Surely no lady knew the word he thought she'd muttered as she turned on him.

"No thank you. I don't want your help, marquess. And did it ever occur to you that some women can't afford to fall apart when bad things happen? Not all of us have big strong men to take care of us. Not all of us need them." Her voice broke, but she swallowed and continued. "Do you think I want to sit in a dark room and cry all day? No thank you, sir. Now, since the carriage has stopped, do you think you could open the door so this poor weak simpleton can get out?"

As soon as her foot touched the ground, Miss Grey excused herself, saying she needed to go to her room to sort out the wreck of her papers and wardrobe. Alexis got the feeling she was more concerned about her business correspondence and legal documents than she was about her clothing. Inside the castle, he followed her progress up the stairs. He couldn't decide what to watch, the sway of her hips or the play of sunlight and shadow on her hair. Since most of her hair was covered by a bonnet, he settled on her hips.

Once she was gone, he was able to think more clearly. The more he thought, the more irritated he became. Nothing had gone as he'd expected that afternoon. Furthermore, a beautiful woman had just abandoned him for legal papers. And she had as good as called him an insect and accused him of insensitivity. It must be her American upbringing. Miss Grey wanted manners. What she needed was to go into Society so that she could see for herself how a lady treated a gentleman. If she could see how Carolina Beechwith behaved toward him, or Fulke's wife, Hannah, her shortcomings would be obvious to her.

Chapter Five

Kate charged through the great hall, her footsteps echoing off the stone walls. The room was more cavern than anything else, and halfway down she stopped and looked around. She'd been so furious with that stuffy peacock of a marquess, she'd forgotten which door to take out of this place. One, two, three, four, five. She stopped counting doors. Recessed behind identical pointed arches, any could be the one she needed. Over her shoulder she spied what the housekeeper had called the musician's gallery, high above floor level. That wasn't the way.

Feeling her insides begin to shake, Kate gripped her skirt with her hands. The presumption of the man, to assume she didn't care that Ophelia was—No, she couldn't start down that path again or she'd end up on the floor crying, and everyone would hear her. She had work to do, work that would keep the hurt at bay.

"You're one of those Americans."

Kate started and whipped around, scanning the various alcoves for the origin of that booming voice.

"Ophelia is dead, I hear."

This time Kate spotted the owner of the hunting-horn voice. A woman in black stood in a window recess beside a suit of armor. Sunlight from the window behind the speaker made Kate squint as she approached the woman.

"Yes, she's dead. It was horrible."

Kate stopped a few paces from the woman. She was looking down at her, which made Kate uncomfortable. Abruptly, she realized she was looking at another de Granville. There was the familiar tall, long-limbed body, a female version of that square chin, and the air of dignity that reminded her of royalty on its way to the guillotine.

The woman didn't reply. Kate waited, but the woman was distracted by a wet black nose that thrust itself from beneath her skirts. She bent and picked up a white ball of fur that seemed to have consumption. Too fat for its legs, it wheezed and snorted and grunted while the woman talked to it.

"My little poppin is testy today. Yes he is. He's a little testy sweetpea, he is. His Papa will be most annoyed with my little poppin." The woman tucked the dog under her arm and glanced at Kate. "My husband detests hearing Terrence breathe. That's why we're walking in the hall. We're quite old now, and can hardly see or hear, but we still enjoy our little walks. You're one of those Americans, and I am Juliana de Granville. You will address me as Lady Juliana. You may shake my hand."

In a fog, Kate did as ordered. "Lady Juliana—but I thought your husband was—"

"Off to the city this morning. I do so tire of doing without him when the King summons him for consultation. Who are you?"

"I'm Katherine Grey, Ophelia's cousin." *This woman*

talks about her dead husband as if he's alive. And she thinks King William is still on the throne.

"You don't keep a grizzly bear for a pet, do you?" Lady Juliana asked.

Kate's eyes opened as wide as they could. "No ma'am."

"Or wear a pistol in a holster?"

"Not in England."

"And you don't keep any Red Indians about you?"

"They don't like white people much," Kate said. "No."

"Then you may stay." Lady Juliana shifted Terrence to her other arm and cooed at him while he wheezed, then she surveyed Kate. "You're a polite and sensible young woman. No Red Indians, no bears. I have decided to like you."

"Thank you, Lady Juliana."

"And that means I have to warn you about my son." Juliana darted glances at various corners of the hall before continuing. "Alexis is, well, not a boy of even temper. The marquess and I have quite a bit of trouble with him. Not to put too fine a point on it, Miss Grey, Alexis can be deceitful. In the past he's done some shameful things, so beware."

"Thank you for the warning, my lady." Kate backed away as Lady Juliana moved past her toward the musician's gallery.

"You want the third door from the left at the other end, Miss Grey."

"Thank you," Kate called after the woman.

There was no answer. Lady Juliana disappeared through another door, leaving Kate once more alone in the hall.

A castle full of snobs and lunatics, she thought. Ripsnitious. Wonderful. She pressed her palms to her temples and groaned. Poor Ophelia was dead, dear Lord, and she was cast in the midst of strangers. Poor, pretty Ophelia. Kate cursed as tears spilled over her cheeks once again.

She couldn't bear to think that Ophelia had suffered. *Dear God, please make it true that she was asleep.*

Ophelia might sometimes have been as annoying as a starving mosquito, but she'd had a good heart. It wasn't her fault she'd been raised useless and trained to silliness. Poor Ophelia. Poor, poor Ophelia.

Kate quickly brushed the tears from her cheeks, irritated with herself. This whole day was one long frustration. When she'd first awakened she had asked for a tour of this damnable maze, but it hadn't kept her from getting lost.

Castle Richfield sat on a hill in a patchwork plain of fields, streams, and clusters of trees. One side of it backed on a steep cliff overlooking a river. The night before, they'd ridden over a bridge that spanned that river, but only in daylight had she seen the truly massive proportions of the castle.

It was roughly rectangular in plan, and she'd counted at least six drum towers overlooking an enclosed courtyard larger than some California mining towns. Within that courtyard rose the oldest building in the castle, the keep. The drum towers were connected by great rampart walls, and, the housekeeper had said, over the centuries the de Granvilles had added room after room within the confines of those walls.

Which led to the problem that had baffled Kate. Too many wings, too many apartments. She needed a map to find her room. She walked through the doorway indicated by Lady Juliana and up a passage, only to stop in confusion at the foot of a staircase. A serving man with a tray passed by.

"Oh, miss. Tea?" He opened a door, revealing a salon of liveable proportions. Unfortunately, there were people in it. She started to back away, but . . .

"Miss Grey."

Caught. Kate summoned a smile and entered the salon. Fulke came to her, taking the hand she offered and kissing it.

"Time has passed quickly," she said. "I didn't know it was so late."

"It's only natural," Fulke replied, leading her farther into the room. "Your mother, Lady Emeline, and Lady Juliana preferred tea in their rooms." He stopped before a woman who appeared to be in her mid thirties and who was decked in one of those gowns that so annoyed Kate— all flounces held up by bouquets of flowers, edged with lace, poofed and padded, fussy and unmanageable. "My wife, Hannah, Miss Grey of San Francisco. Dear Lady Ophelia's cousin."

Kate had to lean forward to hear the woman's greeting, so quietly did she speak. Hannah was the kind of woman Kate had often envied. She had skin that had never been touched by the rays of the sun and thus bore no blemishing freckles. As oval as a picture frame, her face boasted a cupid's-bow mouth and those light blue eyes men wrote poems about. And most enviable of all, she didn't have garish hair. It was a nice, ordinary light brown, like old beech wood. Kate shook Hannah's hand and told herself not to commit the sin of jealousy.

"And Alexis of course," Fulke continued.

Almost scowling, Kate nodded at the silent figure leaning against the white marble mantel. He probably posed there on purpose, she thought, so that she would notice the contrast between his hair and the snowy marble. She allowed Fulke to seat her while Hannah poured tea and offered tidbits of food.

By looking at Hannah, Kate could pretend not to see the marquess and yet watch him at the same time. As the door was opened by a servant, he knelt down and opened his arms. A blur of white and black spots rushed past Kate, and seventy pounds of English springer spaniel landed on him. While Fulke muttered a reprimand and Hannah shrieked, he greeted the dog.

"Hello, Iago, old fellow." Alexis laughed and shoved Iago's face away from his own before the dog's long tongue could bathe him.

The dog burrowed his head against Alexis's pant leg. Alexis caught the wide shoulders. Iago tucked his head between his front legs and tumbled into a somersault. Jumping to his feet, he barked once and sat still.

"Tea, Iago." The marquess handed the spaniel a hard biscuit.

The dog gulped down the biscuit and settled in front of the fireplace. Alexis sat beside Fulke on a settee opposite Hannah and Kate as the older man began speaking again.

"We were discussing," he said to Kate, "Alexis's last visit to court. My cousin was honored with a private audience because Her Majesty had heard of his sheltering wounded soldiers at the Dower House here. How did you find Her Majesty?"

"As moral and disapproving as ever," Alexis said. "Victoria worships Prince Albert; he worships learning. And they're both so painfully upright. I'm not with them ten minutes before I'm tempted to do something ruinous like ask the prince to a whorehouse."

"Alexis." Fulke scowled at the marquess, who grinned at him.

"Goodness doesn't have to be boring," Fulke said.

"But sin never is, dear cousin."

Hannah chirped disapproval while Kate tried not to yawn. She resorted to starting to count the tiny bouquets on the flounces of Hannah's gown. The marquess attracted her attention again, though, by rising and lifting her hand to his lips in apology for his ungentlemanly behavior. He continued to look at her as he resumed his seat, but she kept her gaze on her teacup.

Fulke spoke again. "And did Her Majesty have anything in particular to say to you?"

Alexis placed his own teacup on a side table and ran a finger across the rim of the saucer. "The regiment has been the making of me, according to the Queen. Suffering has ennobled me as my heritage could not. Our Victoria loves martyrs and showers them with favor. Oh, don't bristle, Fulke. I told you I'm not political, and I'm not going to swim in governmental ink for the rest of my life. That's your bit of work, not mine."

The sound of Hannah's breathy voice floated in the air. "I think Fulke is conscious of your duty to Richfield. He wants you to stay home—for once."

The marquess touched Hannah with the wisp of a glance before looking at Fulke. "I am home."

"Hannah, my dear, we have a guest," Fulke said with a gesture at Kate.

Waving her cup and saucer, Kate said, "Pay no attention to me."

"You see," Fulke continued to Kate, "I've been asked to run for election again, and my wife is concerned that Alexis isn't well enough to manage on his own yet."

Kate eyed the apparently healthy marquess and raised her brows. He lifted one corner of his mouth, met her gaze briefly, then transferred his own to Iago.

"Why keep everyone in suspense, revered guardian?" the marquess asked Fulke. "You wouldn't want to miss the opportunity of telling the whole kingdom how to run its affairs, would you?"

Fulke turned red. "Service to queen and kingdom is hardly meddling."

As far as Kate could tell, the marquess was the only one in the salon comfortable in the silence that followed. Evidently Hannah felt obliged to smooth over what she considered a breach of manners. Kate had learned that, to the English Lady, any departure from inane conversation was a breach of manners. Hannah turned to the marquess. The curls of brown hair at the base of her neck fell over her shoulder. The fingers that held her teaspoon pressed into the silver so hard, they were almost blue.

"Your reputation as a hero is the talk of London, Alexis. General Abercrombie's wife was telling me how wonderful you look in uniform, how dashing the cavalry looks on parade."

Kate had learned a little since she was last in England, and she didn't miss the sudden tension in the marquess's body at the mention of the general's wife. Hannah missed it, though. Kate could tell because the woman was too busy covering whatever real message she was trying to convey with a theatrical smile.

The marquess leaned back on the settee, lifted his cup to his lips, and met Hannah's gaze over the rim. She blushed and looked down at her plate.

Alexis directed a cherub's smile at Kate. "When one is commanding men, it's so important to look sharp. Don't you agree?"

"Don't see how shiny buttons and a pretty uniform could do anything but help the Russians see you better."

The marquess inclined his head in a salute to Kate.

Fulke raised his eyes in the direction of the God he so often consulted, sighed, and addressed his wife. "My dear, for an officer to command obedience from his men requires the ability to dominate through personal authority and military expertise."

"Of course, Fulke."

Kate's already tried patience snapped under the burden of enduring all this family sniping. She hated veiled messages and crooked talk. She would have left earlier if she hadn't been sure the marquess was waiting for her to retreat, but Hannah's gushing flattery continued and Kate gave up.

Pleading exhaustion, she fled, leaving the three in the

salon to their so-called tea. To her it felt more like a Society version of the Battle of Balaclava. She wasn't sure what was going on in this family, but it was as intricate as the layout of the castle. She headed up the stairs in search of her room, praying that she could get there without meeting Terrence and Lady Juliana again.

After tea, at the Dower House, half a mile from Castle Richfield, Alexis sought to escape his irritation with Miss Grey and his family. He was growing more and more impatient with Hannah's verbal traps. She'd wanted him to know she knew about Abercrombie's wife. He was lucky she and Fulke wouldn't be staying much longer, for he hated being ripped to pieces between the two of them, a scrap of meat tugged at by two wild dogs. The only consolation was that their games took his mind off the war, for a while.

Alexis paused in the alcove that sheltered the front doors to the Dower House, gathering his courage to enter. The war, after all, was never far away. In the Crimea the army had been mauled not so much by the enemy as by its own inefficiency. Stranded in a primitive country, it had suffered from lack of food and medical supplies. Alexis and his fellow cavalry officers of the Heavy Brigade had tried to supply their men out of their own pockets, but there was little food or medicine to be bought. Cholera and dysentery rampaged. By winter, men would be walking in the snow barefoot. After Balaclava, the wounded lay for hours alongside the dead without medical aid, without water.

It was at Balaclava that Val and the Light Brigade were destroyed by a bungled order that sent the cavalry charging a battery of Russian guns. They rode one and a half miles down a valley under fire from the hills to either side. Alexis could still remember the consternation among his comrades in the Heavy Brigade as they watched the suicidal charge.

Over six hundred men began the attack. Less than three hundred returned. In the confusion that followed the slaughter, Alexis searched for Val. He found his friend half buried under the body of a headless horse. His uniform was wet with blood and draped in the entrails of men and horses. He pulled Val from under the carcass and onto his own horse and rode for safety, only to get in the way of debris from an artillery blast himself. At least he'd been able to ride in spite of the holes in his shoulder and arm.

That was in October. Two months of horror followed. He had Val transferred to his own yacht along with as many men as it would hold, and turned the craft into a hospital. If he hadn't been wounded himself, he'd still be there watching men die because of the stupidity of fools like Val's commander, the Earl of Cardigan.

He'd been home since January, and Val had come with him since Val's father was too old and uninterested to care for him. Not that Alexis would have allowed his friend to be under anyone else's care. It was only in March that the doctors assured him that Val would live. Alexis's happiness at the news soon turned to apprehension, for the atrocities Val had endured wounded his soul far more than his body.

Inside the Dower House Alexis walked past rows of beds containing injured men. It had all started with his yacht full of wounded. Most of the men couldn't afford good medical treatment, not the kind that would get them well instead of kill them. After the Crimea, Alexis hadn't trusted the government to take care of them, so he'd brought them home. His fellow officers had heard about the Dower House, and begged to send their own wounded.

Soon Alexis was hiring doctors and attendants, cooks and household staff. He wrote to Miss Florence Nightingale in the Crimea, and kept writing when her letters returned precious, hardheaded advice. He needed an administrator, and he needed more room. The newest invalids were housed in the cellar.

Climbing down into that candle-lit room, Alexis stumbled over the bed of an infantryman. The man was unconscious, and a doctor was bending over him. As Alexis straightened up, he saw the physician pull a sheet over the man's head and rise from his chair.

"Gone, my lord. We got him too late to do any good."

"I only wish his last days had been spent in sunlight," Alexis said.

"He wouldn't have known. But we do need room."

"I can add on to the house," Alexis said. "But it will take so long, and the noise and mess would be unpleasant for the men. I need a bigger house. All these candles and lamps are dangerous. There was a fire last night." He stopped, remembering Ophelia and her burned house. "Maitland House."

"My lord?"

"I know where I can get a larger house. Excuse me, doctor."

He cut short his visit and hastened back to the castle. As his carriage clattered over the permanently lowered drawbridge, he calculated what amount to offer Miss Grey for Maitland House. He might as well offer for the whole estate, if she owned all the land. He would get the Tower back too. Then he wouldn't have a hole in his lands anymore, and he'd rid himself of mountain goats. He wished her solicitor hadn't left. What was his name? Poggs? He could have talked to Poggs and arranged the sale efficiently. Instead he was going to have to explain the whole process to Miss Grey and hope she understood the complexities.

Of course he couldn't find her. She'd gone off by herself on foot, and no one knew where. Alexis had to content himself with writing to his own solicitor.

His secretary was handing him the letter to sign when Fulke paid him a visit. Alexis finished his signature and dismissed the secretary. Fulke promptly set a stack of papers in front of him.

"Sign," his cousin said.

As Alexis read and signed, Fulke took a seat in the armchair in front of the desk.

"I see my revenues have gone up," Alexis said without looking up.

"You needn't thank me," Fulke said.

"I wasn't going to. Why am I paying Badger Snead an allowance?"

"Broke both legs thatching one of the tenant houses."

"Drinking again?"

"Yes. Alexis . . ."

"Mmmm."

Fulke waited until Alexis looked up from the papers. "I've invited someone for a visit."

"You know you're free to ask whomever you wish."

"I know, and I have consulted Juliana. She agrees that no matter how we feel, it is our duty as Christians and as subjects to help."

Alexis put his pen down, then walked around the desk and leaned on it with one arm.

"When you start talking about Christian duty I almost get a recurrence of dysentery. Out with the wormwood and gall."

"The Earl of Cardigan."

Alexis didn't move. To hear the name hurt physically. "Not if the Queen herself asked."

"She does," Fulke said. "That is, His Royal Highness does on her behalf."

Alexis turned to the cabinet where he kept liquor. He poured two whiskeys and held one out to Fulke. As he bent to hand the glass to his cousin he whispered as if in church.

"If you bring him into my house, I may throw him in the oubliette."

"Charity, Alexis." Fulke stood up and walked over to the fireplace. "There have been threats upon Lord Cardigan's life."

"Good," Alexis said. Fulke scowled at him, and he grinned and lifted his glass in a toast. "To James Thomas Brudenell, the Earl of Cardigan. May he take up residence in hell."

"Don't blaspheme."

Alexis drained his glass. "Cardigan is a permanent scandal. He's been involved in more duels and lawsuits than anyone else I know. He is simultaneously arrogant, unintelligent, and fearless. Did you know he spies on the officers under his command? Has adjutants hide in closets and take down their conversation? If he weren't so brave I'd call him a weasel. As he is brave and a damned good horseman, I'll call him a selfish idiot. He's not coming here."

Fulke took a folded letter out of his coat and handed it to Alexis. Alexis glanced at the Royal Seal, then tossed the letter on the desk and shook his head.

"He's arriving tomorrow," Fulke said.

"Is that so? Then I'll put a canon on the battlement and he can charge it. I won't miss like the Russians did. God! Fulke, the man tossed away the lives of hundreds of men in a useless charge." Alexis felt his control beginning to shatter. His voice rose with each word until it almost echoed throughout the room. "Useless, dammit. And Val lives a bloody waking nightmare. You weren't there. You didn't see the headless bodies still riding horses. Damn you, Fulke. Damn you for bringing that monstrous fool where I can reach him."

"Alexis!"

Fulke was beside him holding his wrist. Alexis looked down. He'd broken his glass with his grip. Whiskey and blood dripped from his hand. Fulke pried his fingers loose and removed the pieces of glass. Shoving Alexis into the armchair, he wrapped the hand in his handkerchief before summoning the butler.

Alexis studied his hand while Fulke dabbed at it with the handkerchief. "It's too late to stop him, isn't it."

"I'm afraid so. You must practice forgiveness. The Lord has a grand design, and you cannot know what he intends by bringing him to you."

"God told you to inflict Cardigan on Val and me? It's all right for you. You'll be going home in a few weeks, but I'll still be here with him, may God shrivel his—"

"I told you not to blaspheme. I'll try to keep him from you as much as possible. The idea is to remove Lord Cardigan from his usual haunts until these threats are proved false or a malefactor is caught." Fulke pulled another shard of glass from Alexis's palm. "I am sorry, Alexis. When the Prince mentioned the problem, I volunteered without thinking."

"You can make up for it by getting the bastard to help my invalids. Some of their families have no income. And keep him away from Val. Keep him far away from Val."

Chapter Six

He was watching her, the bastard. He was watching to see if she knew which fork to use. The pig. No, he was too slender to be a pig. He was a snake. An arrogant, pretty snake—black and poisonous.

Kate let her hand drift toward the dessert fork just to tantalize the Marquess of Richfield, then picked up her soup spoon. She nearly snickered. His face fell the way Zachary's did when one of his practical jokes failed. A familiar sadness welled up at the thought of her brothers. She missed them. Zachary was in San Francisco with his governor, and Robbie was at Harvard. Even long letters didn't ease the pain of being apart from them.

Letting the conversation go on without her, Kate alternated between her sorrow at the several deaths in her family that year and fuming at the marquess. She would hurry the repairs to Maitland

House so she could get out of the reach of de Granville's condescending patronage.

He didn't remember her. She could still feel the scarifying humiliation of that night when he had publicly rejected her, and when she returned to England, he thought they'd never met. And how dare he treat her as though she were addled simply because she was a woman?

A servant offered bread. Kate shook her head and tried to shake her foul mood as well. All she had to do was see Mama established in Maitland House amid the Society of her dreams; then she could go back home. San Francisco might be full of gamblers, sailors, and Australian convicts, but it didn't have any English aristocrats.

"Miss Grey, how is Lady Emeline?"

Kate smiled at Fulke Sinclair. He was a kind man. It wasn't his fault he was so unbearably upright. Perhaps having served in the government made him so tired he couldn't help ignoring his wife and preaching at people.

"Aunt Emeline finds it hard to take in what has happened," Kate said. "I have to keep reminding her where she is and why. I hope to get her back to Maitland House as soon as possible." She would have said more, but Lady Juliana's annoyed voice overrode all others.

"My dear Mrs. Grey, I don't concern myself with the doings of King William's unfortunate offspring."

Kate made a fist with the hand that rested in her lap. Fulke had taken her aside before dinner and explained that Lady Juliana had "bad spells," but that this evening she'd improved enough to come down to dinner. Unfortunately, Juliana and Mama hadn't taken to each other. Mama loved gossip about royalty, and the illegitimate sons and daughters of Queen Victoria's uncle were among her favorite topics. Lady Juliana, however, didn't gossip. At least, not with ladies she considered her social inferiors.

Why did Mama provoke the woman? Juliana was one of the few people who intimidated Kate. It wasn't her "bad spells." Kate had recovered from her encounter with one of them. From what she could understand, they weren't very frequent. Perhaps it was Lady Juliana's height. She was almost as tall as her son. Perpetually dressed in mourning for her dead husband and daughter, she nevertheless dominated county society by virtue of her birth and force of will.

Juliana put down her spoon. Kate knew it was the signal of an impending set-down. Fulke came to Sophia's rescue before Kate could.

"Miss Grey, didn't you say your father was from Virginia?" Fulke asked the question in a voice raised to attract everyone's attention.

Grateful, Kate nodded and smiled at him again. "Yes, but we traveled west to California when I was a girl."

"Virginia," the marquess said. He slouched in his chair and raised a brow. "Ah, no doubt the Grey family were gentlemen planters—gentlemen who owned slaves. Tell me, Miss Grey, did you take your slaves west too?"

The attack was so unexpected, it took Kate a moment to respond. She felt like throwing her soup at his face, but Mama would have died.

"No, my lord, we didn't take slaves. Let me enlighten you. My father conceived an abhorrence of slavery that got him kicked out of his family. We went west with him because he was forced to leave Virginia. Not that he could have stayed much longer, feeling the way he did." Kate clasped her hands in front of her and batted her eyes at the marquess. "Slavery in my country is as bad as the plight of the English poor in cities like London, where children work in rat-infested workhouses for fourteen hours straight."

De Granville gave her a stare she was sure intimidated many a young miss.

"It's hardly the same," he said.

"Oh," Kate said. "Forgive me. I didn't know you approved of working children to death." Kate turned to Hannah. "Lady Sinclair, I dearly love history, and the castle is fascinating to me. Could I persuade you to show me about?"

Hannah cast a fearful glance at the marquess. "I-I—"

"Excellent!" Juliana's voice almost made Kate drop her wineglass. It was deep and filled the long room with its near roar. "Excellent, Miss Grey. I shall call you Kate."

Kate regarded Lady Juliana with distrust.

"It isn't often that I meet a young lady who can see past my son's attractions to the flaws in his character. And it's more rare for such a young lady to be honest enough to express her distaste for him."

No one moved. Juliana smiled and lifted her glass to Kate as though she were discussing the quality of their meal rather than humiliating her own son. In the silence that followed, Kate couldn't help looking at the marquess.

His cheeks were flushed. The hand beside his plate was clenched so tightly, the knuckles were white. He stared at his mother without saying anything. Slowly, with care, he uncurled his fist until his hand lay flat on the linen tablecloth. Oblivious to everyone else, he continued to stare at his mother, who was feeding scraps to a cat and a monkey at her feet. Kate felt the intensity of that stare. Nothing and no one existed for the marquess except his mother. Finally thick lashes swept down over his eyes, hiding whatever emotion might have escaped his control.

Around him the carousel of conversation began to spin once more. Fulke treated Sophia and Hannah to a lecture on the Great Exhibition of scientific wonders of a few years before. The marquess kept his eyes lowered.

Kate wanted to say something to take away the hurt. She could barely imagine the pain he must be feeling. Such a proud spirit to be so cruelly shamed before others.

He moved abruptly. Resting his elbow on the table, the marquess downed his wine and shifted his gaze to

Fulke. Gone was the flush, the withdrawal. His lips curled in amusement at his cousin's stilted conversation.

"But Fulke," he interrupted, "you haven't told the ladies about my friend Mr. Darwin's views on the evolution of life. Or about geology. Do tell Mrs. Grey about how the earth has been proved to be much older than the Scriptures make it out to be."

It was Fulke's turn to blush. "You're improper, sir, to bring up such subjects in the presence of ladies."

Alexis laughed and teased more. Kate stabbed at her roast beef in disgust. She was a fool to have felt sorry for the man. Lady Juliana knew her son better than anyone. Alexis de Granville was flawed all right. As far as Kate could see he was a master of verbal torture, and she wasn't about to become one of his victims.

After dinner Kate sat as long as she could in the drawing room with the women, listening to her mother chatting with Hannah. Without warning, Sophia looked up at Kate and flashed a smile so filled with contentment, it brought tears to Kate's eyes. After Papa died, Kate had been afraid she would never see that smile again. She smiled back and resigned herself to an evening of tedium. Her participation would please Mama.

She tried hard. She tried awfully hard. But when the conversation turned to Ophelia's tragic death, Kate had to leave. Her sorrow was too raw for her to share it with others. She slipped out into the hall and gathered her skirts in both hands, preparing to race up the stairs before someone saw her. In the back of her mind was the disturbing thought that she was avoiding the marquess. She didn't trust the man. After the way he'd humiliated her when they first met, she found herself on guard in his presence, dreading another insult. Besides, he'd been Ophelia's lover.

"Miss Grey."

She gasped and whirled around. It was de Granville.

"Hellfire. Do you have to sneak up on me?" She pressed a hand to her chest in an effort to still the thudding of her heart.

The marquess strolled over to her from the threshold of the dining salon. The door was closed, and he'd been leaning there watching her progress. Kate mounted the first step to put more distance between them.

"Hellfire?" he said. "What an expression for a gently reared young woman to use."

"I've used worse," Kate said. "What do you want?"

"I would like to discuss something with you. Don't start shaking your head, Miss Grey. It's a matter of business. I would have approached your Mr. Poggs, but you sent him away."

She folded her arms in front of her. "What?"

De Granville held out his hand. It was obvious he wasn't going to converse on the stairs. Kate unfolded her arms. She had no intention of giving him her hand, but he took it anyway, and it disappeared in his. Seeing the hand she took for granted being swallowed up by his warm flesh gave her a start. He wouldn't let go, and the feel of his hand was so good, she was distracted into letting him take her into a sitting room.

He must have planned this meeting, for a fire was already lit. He escorted her to a chair. She was sure he chose such a large one to make her feel small. Her feet didn't touch the floor, and to make things worse, he knew it and brought an ottoman for her. The snake.

A servant came in with a tray. Coffee. What was he up to?

"I don't like coffee," she said.

"You like weak coffee with lots of cream and sugar," the marquess said. He poured cream into a cup until it was half full.

"How did you know, and why do you care?"

De Granville handed her the cup and stood by her while she took a sip. It was perfect. She sipped some more. He dropped to his haunches beside her chair. Her cup clattered against the saucer.

"Miss Grey, you're doing it again."

"What?"

"Looking at me as though I were dung clinging to your shoe. I am at a loss. I barely know you, yet you abhor me."

He rested his arm on her chair. She glanced at it, then shifted her gaze to his face. Somehow his eyes had changed. They looked almost sleepy, yet glittered with vibrant life. Bottle-glass green, torrid and heavy-lidded, they were lodestones that caught and held her own gaze. She forgot to be angry. Indeed, she was concentrating so hard on the brilliance of his eyes, she failed to notice that he was leaning toward her. When she did, his mouth was close, and she was too late to avoid him. His tongue darted out. It touched her lips and feathered over them. She blinked, and during that blink, he replaced his tongue with his lips. No, his tongue was still there. It was inside her mouth.

It felt so good, she decided to forget her distrust. She wanted to feel his mouth and his tongue, even if he was a snake.

He pulled back so that their lips barely touched and breathed his words at her. "Little savage." He pressed close and delved into her mouth again. There was a clatter, and he jerked away.

Kate was still holding her cup and saucer, and it had finally begun to shake along with her hand. Breathing heavily, she clutched it with her other hand too. The marquess took it from her and set it on the small table between her and the fireplace. Then he rose and stood by the fire with his hands behind his back.

Of all the actions she might have expected, his kissing

her would seem the least probable. She pressed her hands together in her lap. Hellfire. Her breasts were tingling, and other places too. She much suspected that she was experiencing arousal. Patience had explained the feelings to her long ago, but her descriptions had been inadequate.

"I apologize, Miss Grey."

She turned even more red than she already was. "You're sorry you kissed me. I don't know why you did it, but—"

"I'm not sorry I kissed you," he said. "I was apologizing because as a gentleman I shouldn't take liberties."

"If you're not sorry, don't bother about the rest. I'd rather you were honest instead of polite."

De Granville cocked his head to the side. His smile revealed his confusion. "Miss Grey, you are unlike anyone I've ever met."

"What did you want to talk about?" She was fast becoming edgy. The longer they were together, the more she regretted the kiss.

Taking the armchair opposite her, the marquess poured himself coffee from an urn separate from the one containing Kate's weak concoction.

"I wanted to speak to you about Maitland House. Long ago the estate was the property of my family, and I'd like to purchase it from you."

"I'm sorry, but I can't sell it. Mama wants to live there. You see, ever since she married my father she's regretted leaving England. It's always been her dream to come home and be in Society again. Now that Papa is dead, it's all she cares about."

The marquess set his cup down. Leaning forward, he rested his forearms on his thighs. "I understand your concern, but I want the place for a reason. I've undertaken to care for some of the wounded from the war. Right now they're in the old Dower House, but the building is in poor condition, and there's not enough room. Surely you see the importance of caring for them."

"Of course," Kate said. "But you can fix your old building. I can't replace Mama's childhood home."

"Miss Grey, I'm having to put some of the men in the cellar."

"Adding to the Dower House will take less time than the repairs to Maitland House."

The marquess stood and scowled at her. Kate lifted her chin and refused to be intimidated.

"I'll offer you twice what it's worth," de Granville said. "The land contains an old tower that is a part of my family's heritage. I want the land and the house, Miss Grey."

"You can't have it," Kate said. She thrust herself to her feet. Now she understood the cozy room, the just-right coffee, and the kiss. He thought she would be so frazzle-brained once he touched her that she'd agree to anything. "You don't really need the house, and it's not for sale." She marched to the door with the marquess glaring at her the whole time. He muttered something, and she spun to face him. "What did you say?"

"I said 'mountain goat.'"

Kate's voice was low and calm. "What?"

"Your mama wants to climb the social mountain, and you're going to see that she gets her chance at the expense of mutilated and dying men." De Granville walked past her and opened the door for her. He bowed. "Mountain goat, Miss Grey."

So furious she wanted to roar, Kate didn't settle for cussing at the man. She doubled up her fist and rammed it into his stomach. Caught off guard, the marquess doubled over with the breath knocked out of him. Kate swept past him. Outside, she passed Valentine Beaufort.

"You looking for the marquess?" she asked.

The young man stopped and nodded.

She pointed to the open door behind her. "He's in there, the snake."

Alexis was still bent over rubbing his sore stomach. A pair of shoes and the tip of a cane walked into his line of sight.

"Have a row with the little American, old fellow?"

"She hit me." He sounded ridiculously like a ten-year-old bully who had gotten a black eye. "She hit me."

"I'm sure you deserved it," Val said. He limped over to a chair and sat down. "Fulke and I both think you'd be better behaved if more women hit you instead of spreading their legs for you."

Alexis eyed Val. He quit rubbing his stomach and took the chair opposite him. "Hmmm."

"I know that look. Don't," Val said.

"I want Maitland House for the men."

"It's cruel, and you want revenge for the punch." Val poked Alexis with the tip of his cane. "You're fizzed because she doesn't pant after you."

"I'll make her pant. It will do her good. All she thinks of is poking about in affairs that should be left to men. Uppity female. Someone has to teach her why God gave her that body. And when I have, she'll sell me her house and anything else I want."

Val scooted to the edge of his chair, grimacing, and placed his hand on Alexis's arm. "This isn't like you. You're never deliberately mean, Alexis. At least, not to innocent girls."

"I won't be mean. Miss Katherine Grey needs reforming, and I'm going to do her the favor of undertaking the challenge."

"Ah!"

"What do you mean, 'ah'?"

"It's your pride, and the excitement of the chase. How

cliché. I'm going to give Miss Grey some of those flowers you made me gather and get to know the lady."

"She's mine, Val."

"That doesn't mean I can't make her acquaintance."

"It means I'll chain you in the dungeon if you do more than that. Now explain why you weren't at dinner."

Val looked away. "I was tired from hefting all those flowers."

Alexis slipped out of his chair and stepped over to Val. "But you've had plenty of rest. Come." He took Val's arm.

"Where are we going?" Val halted as they started across the room. "I told you I'm not going to the Dower House."

"You're needed there. You need to be there."

"I won't look at any more men without arms and legs."

"It's not that," Alexis said. "You're afraid."

"Don't you call me a coward, you bloody ass." Val turned away from Alexis and limped to the door.

"You're afraid to know them and then see them die."

Val faced Alexis and clamped a shaking hand on the doorknob. "At least I'm not afraid of my own dreams. And I'm not the only one who hides from the past."

"I'll send for a carriage," Alexis said. "We'll take some of your flowers to the Dower House, and you can meet the new physician."

Alexis approached Val again, took his arm, and led him away from the door.

"You were jealous of your sister, Alexis, and you can't forget that. You told me how she used to get you in trouble, blame you for things she did, and you took the beatings she deserved."

Alexis jerked Val's arm. The cane slipped, and he was forced to catch Val before he fell.

"You're trying to distract me, and it won't work. I need help with the Dower House. Someone has to see that supplies are ordered and the servants do their jobs. I can't do it all and manage the new wounded too."

"Your sister is dead, and your father," Val said as Alexis pulled a cord to summon the butler. "Let the past go."

Alexis said nothing. When the butler came, he ordered both carriage and flowers, then waited for them with a furious Val. He helped his friend into the carriage and remained silent until they drew up to the Dower House. Through the windows he could see the yellow glow of lamps and the shadow of a nurse as she walked past. He glanced at Val. His friend was sitting amid baskets of flowers. He held a rose and was studying its petals as if the flower were a map.

"Do you suppose they've learned not to send cavalry against artillery yet?" Val asked.

"I don't think so. Val, Russell is telling the country what's going on. The generals, the Horse Guards, they can't hide the disaster because Russell is printing it in *The Times*."

Val laughed then, a laugh filled with pain. "What is the old saying? Something about evil hating the light?"

Alexis got out of the carriage. Holding out his hand, he waited for Val.

"It takes a different kind of courage to face life than to face death," Alexis said. "You've shown me the second, now show me the first."

Val threw the rose at him. "I won't play the slave to your Caesar."

"Very well." He dropped to his knees. "Will you get out of that carriage if I kneel in the dirt and beg you?"

Lurching out of the seat, Val peered at Alexis. "Get up, you fool. Get up, I said, and help me out of this bloody carriage. You always were too damned dutiful. You'd have been better off becoming a curate."

Together, arms loaded with flowers, they entered the Dower House. Inside the doorway, they stopped to unload the blossoms. As Alexis shoved the last basket into the arms of a nurse, he heard a scream. Beside him, Val stiffened. His eyes widened and his face drained of blood. Alexis caught him by the arm and headed in the direction of the scream. Val hung back, causing him to stumble. A doctor rushed past them into the room from which the screams came.

"We're going to help, Val. Nothing will be as bad as the Crimea. Val."

His friend wasn't listening. His eyes grew unfocused, and he suddenly hunched his shoulders and began rubbing his coat sleeves.

"I can't stand it," Val muttered. "Get it off. It's flesh, his flesh."

"Bloody Hell." Alexis held his breath and slapped Val hard across the cheek.

Val jerked and thrashed, but Alexis held on, shaking him roughly. This time Val cried out and turned on him. "You frigging ass, you hit me."

"Much better," Alexis said.

"You won't think so for long." Val drew back his fist.

Alexis held up both hands. "Don't you think we've seen enough fighting, you and I?"

Lowering his arm, Val was quiet for a few moments, then he sighed and wiped his brow. "God, it happened again. I knew it would. I was back there, in that valley of blood. God, I should be locked away."

"Then you'll never face the fear." Alexis held out a hand. "Come on, old school chum. If you can survive a beating by the rowing team, you can do this."

"I'd rather take the beating."

Alexis chuckled as they walked together into the sickroom. Inside were two rows of beds. The doctor was sitting beside the first bed on the right, in which lay a sobbing man.

"It were like I was back there, Doctor," the man was

saying. "A laying in mud watching me blood drain away. I'm going mad, I am. They'll put me in one of them lunatic places."

Val quickened his pace with every word, until he passed Alexis and arrived at the foot of the bed. As the doctor quieted the wounded man, Val leaned toward him.

"You have those waking nightmares too?"

The man, with the red nose and unshaven cheeks of a Dickens character, nodded his bandaged head. "Yes sir, and they're going to put me in one of them lunatic places."

"No they won't," Val said. "Will they, Doctor?"

"I don't think so."

"I won't let them," Alexis said to the patient. "After all, Val and I both have had them. Mine are going away. Aren't they, Val?"

"Yes, and—and mine are fading. A bit. If so many of us have these spells, perhaps it's the mind's way of telling us it's had enough."

"Really, sir?" the man asked.

Val nodded.

Alexis waited quietly while the two conversed. Val was tense and white the whole time, but his own suffering seemed to fade as he talked. Finally, color flowed back into his face, and Alexis was able to relax his vigil. By the end of their stay, Val had promised to come back the following day and write a letter home for the wounded man.

When they returned to the castle, they both headed for the drawing room and the liquor cabinet. Alexis poured a whiskey and handed it to Val.

"Drink," he said. "Think of it as a reward for good behavior." When Val downed the whiskey in one gulp, Alexis knew his friend was in need of distraction. "Have another, and do me a favor. Help me think of ways to entice Miss Katherine Grey. I'm going to enjoy disarming my barbarian quarry."

Disarming people was something Alexis had been doing for a long time. When he was a boy, Fulke had chastised him for trying to make people like him. The criticism had confused him, for he never meant anyone harm. He was a youth of fifteen when he finally figured out that his cousin thought charm akin to seduction, and that seduction was a sin. Alexis had finally told Fulke not to try to make him into a saint, for he only had tainted material to work with.

He remembered his own father saying that Fulke's father had been so religious, he went to church three times a day each day of the week. Fulke never talked about him, except to say that he'd been almost a saint, with an abhorrence of "fleshly weakness." He used to warn Fulke daily about the evil brought into the world by women and would support his opinions by quoting Scripture. The older Fulke got, the more like his father he grew. Alexis considered himself fortunate that the worst godliness hadn't taken hold of Fulke until the last few years.

That night Alexis fell asleep contemplating what he called his Miss Grey Strategy, after getting little cooperation from Val in its planning. His next awareness was of someone shaking him. He bolted upright, shooting a fist toward his attacker, then heaving to throw the body off him.

"Bloody hell!"

Alexis stopped fighting. "Val?"

Fully dressed and with a bleeding lip, Val pulled himself off Alexis. He sat on the bed and touched the back of his hand to his mouth.

"I was on my way to get a book from the library and heard you moan," Val said. "I don't sleep at all; you sleep but get no rest. We're a pair."

Alexis sat still, his chest heaving. He flexed the hand that had hit Val. At his silence, Val got up and started to leave.

"Val."

The young man turned around.

"*Merci, mon ami.*"

"*N'importe,*" Val said as Alexis stood up. "Where are you going?"

"It's almost dawn."

"Alexis, no."

"Rotten luck that you're not well enough to come along."

Val limped back to Alexis. "Don't go. You haven't done this since we came home. Don't start."

Alexis was already pulling on trousers. "You once told me I was the best horseman in England."

"When you're not trying to outrun sunlight."

Alexis concentrated on tugging on a boot so he wouldn't have to answer. He stuffed his shirt into his trousers and called to Val's retreating figure. "Don't try sending someone after me. It won't do any good, and I'll make you pay afterward."

A slammed door was the only response he got.

Chapter Seven

Kate had found what she called the "back gate" to Castle Richfield. Not a gate like she was used to, of course, but a massive thing flanked by two defensive towers and stopped up by a drawbridge. It led to a path that in turn led to the stables. After the previous night's quarrel with the marquess about Maitland House, she wanted to escape high walls and gilt paneling. He'd given her a new worry.

Mutilated, mutilated, mutilated. The marquess's description of the men at the Dower House kept rattling around in her head like acorns shaken in a cardboard box. It was his fault that she was going to have to change her mind. And what made things worse was that she couldn't detest him nearly so well now that she suspected him of having a heart. A generous, caring heart didn't belong inside a snake.

Late the night before she'd visited the marquess's invalid home. Unwilling to admit he'd impressed her, she had walked into the house unaccompanied and introduced herself to a nurse.

"Most of the cholera cases don't make it back to England," the woman told her. "His lordship says that so many died so quickly, they had to throw the bodies in the harbor. He says that his men had to keep their horses saddled and their clothes on for days at a time." The nurse gestured to a gaunt man resting in a chair. "That's why disease takes them so quickly. They're worn to nothing before they even get sick."

"But why?" Kate squeezed her hands together and tried not to look at a man being brought in on a stretcher. He had no legs.

"Why the waste, do you mean?" The nurse smiled. "His lordship told us the army hasn't been reorganized since Wellington fought Napoleon. Inefficiency is rampant. He said the officers had only biscuits and salt pork, and little of that, to live on. And they had to use doors and furniture for firewood. The men's food was worse, and that was before they were wounded."

"How many?" Kate asked. Her mouth was dry from shock. "How many dead?"

"I don't know, miss. Thousands and thousands. All I know is that his lordship said that the Russians made a point of shooting officers, all that gold and the brilliant uniforms, you know. And the officers ride in front of their men. They're mounted, and they're in front, so the Russians have good targets. His lordship told me that Debrett's is being wiped out."

"Debrett's?"

"The roll of peers, miss. The officers, the young noblemen. Soon we won't have any left."

Kate had quitted the Dower House feeling as small as a tick, and as admirable. So now she had to change her answer to the marquess, and she was certain he'd gloat.

Oh well, Mama and Aunt Emeline would enjoy a house full of soldiers to mother.

Kate felt relieved of guilt, too, and her reward was a ride. Not a Lady's ride. A real bone-jarring, sweaty frontier kind of ride. For that she was dressed in a split skirt, her jacket was unbuttoned at the throat, and she wore no silly hat that would fly off. She'd tied her pesky hair at the nape of her neck. She was going to have fun this morning.

As the stable buildings came into view, Kate heard a sound behind her. *Crunch crunch tap. Tap crunch crunch.* Hard-soled shoes on the sandy surface of the path. She looked over her shoulder, veered back the way she'd come, and latched onto the arm of that troubled young man, Valentine Beaufort.

"Hold up, Mr. Beaufort. You're going to fall if you don't get below locomotive speed."

Beaufort leaned hard on his cane and panted. Kate noted the pallor of his skin and the perspiration that coated his forehead and cheeks.

"I'll—damn. Pardon." He breathed in deeply. "Never make it."

"What's wrong?" she asked.

"It isn't a matter for your concern, though I thank you, Miss Grey."

"Must be pretty important for you to risk breaking your neck on this grit." She fished in her pocket for a handkerchief. Finding one, she dabbed at Beaufort's forehead.

Val submitted for a few moments, then pulled away. "Never in my life has a lady wiped my face for me. Is this an American custom?"

"Sorry. I've done it again, haven't I? I have an excuse. I have two brothers who used to need a lot of cleaning up. You aren't listening."

He inspected her skirt and boots. "You were going riding." He chewed his lip and studied Kate. "Someday he's going to tease the Devil once too often. This could be the day. Miss Grey, could I beg a favor of you?"

Kate listened to him, but found Val's concern hard to credit. If the marquess wanted to jump fences no one else took, that was his prerogative. However, she was going to be out anyway, and the poor man looked so distressed that she promised to take the route he'd outlined and watch for Alexis de Granville. She didn't tell him she already knew part of the way from her excursions with Ophelia.

Reassuring Val that, yes, she could ride quickly, Kate set out to hunt down a snake. Judging from his head start, she would be able to intercept him in the valley below the Tower. If she rode at a gallop, she could stop him before he took that impossible leap across Fleet's Ditch. She took a shortcut over the hills to the next valley and cantered out onto flat land in time to see a black shooting star race past. She was already at a gallop by the time she moved into position behind the flying figure. Standing in her stirrups, she whistled to her gelding. He was a quarter horse, a "quarter miler" with a little Thoroughbred in him, and he was going to run down the marquess's hunter like a stampeded heifer.

Ahead, all she could see was a black tail and a lithe, straining man's body. Closing in, Kate pulled to the left, whistled again, and felt her gelding surge forward. She drew even with the marquess and shouted at him.

"Morning."

He didn't answer. His face was dripping sweat. Dark hair streamed back from his face and his eyes scoured the ground ahead. There was a light in them she didn't like, and a lack of color to his flesh. He rode as though he and the horse were the same beast, but she could see his muscles straining. She shouted again, louder.

"Morning!"

His head jerked in her direction. Until that moment she wouldn't have believed him oblivious to her. Yet he had been. It was obvious from the way he loosened the tension on his reins. At once his horse began to slow. The marquess abruptly looked away from her to watch the ground in front of him. They slowed to a trot without speaking. Finally they were able to ease into a walk. Over her own labored breathing, Kate could hear him gasping for air. He was drenched, and his horse was too.

"What are you doing here?" he managed to ask.

"I was riding and saw you. I thought I'd tell you I changed my mind."

"Who told you where I was? Was it Val?"

"Oh, of course. I've got nothing better to do than chase all over the countryside for a demented man who thinks it's exciting to risk his horse's life for entertainment."

She pulled her horse to a stop because the marquess had. He was gawking at her.

"You're riding astride, like a man."

"I'm riding astride like a woman."

"We're going back before someone sees you," the marquess said. He nudged her horse with his knee and herded her along. "I can't believe it. I just can't believe it."

Kate lifted her eyes to the sky.

"It's so unmaidenly, so improper."

"You're mad 'cause I caught you," she said.

She looked down her nose—a short distance—at the marquess. He was studying her. His gaze slid from her face to her chest, to her hips, and back to her chest. She snorted and stared out at the hills they were approaching.

"You did catch me," he said. "I've never been caught before. What is that you're riding?"

"Quarter horse."

"Ride him sidesaddle from now on."

"No."

"That was a command, Miss Grey."

"I know, Mr. de Granville."

She could hear him grind his teeth. He was madder than a caged raccoon. She grinned.

"No one," the marquess said. "No one has ever addressed me as 'Mr.' before."

"Don't like it? All right, I'll think of something else. How about 'stuffy' or 'prude'? They fit with your high-minded objections to my personal habits."

"Prude!"

The marquess made a grab for her. She dodged him and kicked her horse. He chased after her all the way back to the stables. She was lucky his horse was tired, or he would have caught her. She could tell he was still angry when she handed over her mount to a groom. De Granville dismounted and hurled his reins at an attendant, then stalked around his horse toward her. Another groom waylaid him with a question, and Kate left. She walked down the path to the castle without bothering to see if she was followed. She had rounded a bend when she was hauled off the path and into the bordering grove of trees.

Stumbling along in the wake of the man who had captured her, she caught a glimpse of bright black hair. It was the marquess.

"Let me go," she said.

He paid no attention. He pulled her after him into a clearing, and she saw the tree stump he was heading for. A suspicion flitted into her mind, and rebellion exploded when she heard him snap at her.

"The little savage needs some respect whipped into her."

De Granville reached the stump, sat, and hauled her over his lap. Kate was ready. Instead of resisting, she plunged over his knees with her head down. When the marquess brought his arms down across her back and thighs, she kept going. Before he could stop her, she bent close to his thigh, opened her jaws, and bit.

His yowl was quite satisfying. It was worth the embarrassment of the attempted spanking. De Granville yanked at her hair, then shoved her off his lap and onto the ground. Kate landed on her bottom and bounced to her feet, ready for his next attack.

It never came, for the marquess was sitting on the stump nursing his thigh and cursing. He lifted furious eyes to her.

"You almost drew blood, damn you."

"Stupid man." She put her hands on her hips to conceal their trembling. "You should think about the consequences of your actions. When I was a girl I faced the dangers of the Overland Trail. Indian ambushes, drunken miners, besotted gamblers. Do you really think I'd let you abuse me? That's what you'd have to do, you know, to give me a spanking. You'd have to hold me down so hard you'd turn my skin black and blue. And I'd fight. You'd be the one to draw blood. Or is that what you wanted all along?"

De Granville stared at her, rubbing his thigh absently. Without warning he stood up and captured her hand. She tried to pull free, but he brought the hand to his mouth. It was the merest brush of warm lips to cold skin.

"I am ashamed," he said. "I beg your forgiveness, for your distaste for me falls immeasurably short of that I have for myself."

To her own surprise, Kate believed him. She could see the unhappiness in his eyes. She didn't like to see those eyes full of sadness.

Freeing her hand, she rubbed her upper arms and shrugged. "I'm sorry I called you a prude. From what Ophelia said you're certainly not— Oh!"

His soft laugh did nothing to lessen her chagrin. Kate tried to bolt. He dodged around to stand in front of her, grinning.

"Miss Grey, being with you is like downing shots of whiskey one after another. Shall we forgive each other, then?"

What was different? Kate wondered, confused. Perhaps it was because he was standing so close. Her vision was filled with long legs and muscles that made subtle curves in his thighs. She focused on the warm skin at the base of his throat, revealed by his open shirt.

She wet her lips. "Yes, forgiveness is a good idea."

"You shouldn't have done that," the marquess said.

"Done what?"

"This." He lowered his head and touched his tongue to her lips. He whispered to her, "You shouldn't have done it, but I thank God you did."

She had plenty of warning. He gathered her in his arms slowly, and she could have avoided him. She didn't want to.

He put his mouth against hers and proceeded to try to swallow it. She loved the warm wetness, the softness of his lips, the way he sucked rhythmically like a small pump at the tissues of her mouth. Then she realized the significance of that rhythm, for his hips were repeating it against her own. A hot stinging sensation built at the juncture of her thighs. She was hot, and her breasts were tingling again. That was when her brain, what was left of it, went to sleep. As her mind dozed, her body woke, and she pressed her hips to those that teased her.

He quit trying to devour her mouth and ran his tongue down her neck. Kate had never held a man before. It didn't matter. Her hands knew what would feel good. She slipped them under his jacket and rubbed his chest through his damp shirt. In response, he grasped her buttocks and ground their hips together.

Crunch crunch tap.

The marquess lifted his head. Kate rested her forehead on his chest and groaned. In mid groan he pulled her chin up and covered her mouth once again. Then he set her away from him and swiftly brushed curls away from her face. He pulled the ends of her jacket together and arranged his own. Taking her arm, he ushered her back onto the path and started walking.

His calm, the way he reacted to the approach of a witness, brought common sense lumbering back into Kate's head. She had no idea why this man wanted to kiss her. That is, she knew why men wanted to kiss, but she didn't know why this particular man wanted to kiss this particular woman.

As they approached Valentine Beaufort, she began to fidget mentally. The marquess must think she was pretty, or he wouldn't want to kiss her. But it hadn't been that long ago that he hadn't wanted to dance with her. He thought she was entertaining, but he disapproved of her behavior. He liked her, but he didn't like her. He insulted, then he kissed.

"Miss Grey," he said softly, "my worried friend is coming. Before we reach him, I'd like to ask that you call me by my given name and beg the same favor of you."

"Very well, Lord Alexis."

"No. Alexis, plain Alexis."

Kate smiled at Val, who was almost within hearing distance, and he smiled back.

"Careful," she said. " 'And the Devil did grin, for his darling sin is pride that apes humility.' "

She heard a sharp intake of breath followed by a wondering laugh. "You little beast."

She pulled ahead of the marquess and looked back over her shoulder. Disheveled sensuality caught her off guard. He was bathed in it; he emitted it in heat waves that rolled over her. And he wasn't doing it on purpose. That was evident by the way he smiled at her like a saint and expected her to join him in laughing at himself.

Turning to face Val again, Kate hurried away from Alexis de Granville to the safety of his friend's company.

. . .

He'd never had a young lady insult him with poetry. Alexis stopped walking to enjoy the view of Kate Grey from the rear. A bluestocking with hair that burned with a sunset glow. Such a gift for verbal jousting must mean she'd had plenty of men tilting their lances at her. She had reached Val and the two were talking. Kate flicked her boot with her riding crop. The black stock swept up in an arc and cut the air.

The simple motion was all it took to bring the memory roiling back into his mind. Alexis tensed, but it was too late. In an eye blink he was twelve, alone and furious. He sat on his horse watching his father and his sister gallop toward him. Jealousy expanded in his heart. He was puffing from the exertion of beating them to this point on the race path, and rankling, snarling offense churned inside him. Father was holding his mount in check so Thalia would win the race. Pampered, lovely Thalia came hurtling toward him. He could see the veil on her hat flapping madly.

Alexis gripped his own reins with sweaty hands. As he sat there nursing his rage, Thalia plunged between the two giant oak trees that marked the finish line. To Alexis it looked as if she jumped off her horse on purpose. Her hands flew out, and her body jerked backward. Red water appeared out of nowhere, and somehow, Thalia came apart. Her head went toppling away from her body. Alexis froze in his saddle. His eyes took in what his mind could not.

A high screech and the hollow thud of hooves followed. Alexis screamed along with his father's horse. The hunter stumbled over Thalia's body. Its great forelegs buckled, and horse and rider tumbled over each other. Alexis kicked his own horse, but the animal wouldn't run.

He shouted to his father. He dug his spurs into his mount, but the horse ignored him and walked. He couldn't get off and run himself. He could only sit and watch his father's horse roll and thrash, crushing his father beneath hundreds of pounds of flesh.

A giggle made the blood and the bodies disappear. Alexis shook his head. He couldn't have been standing in the middle of the path as stiff as a Maypole for long, or Val and Kate would have noticed. He stuffed his hands in his pockets to hide their shaking.

He'd dreamed about Father and Thalia again last night. If Val hadn't shaken him awake, the nightmare would have continued on through the shock of death, his own hysteria, the numbness and loss of the threads of memory, until it ended with him kneeling in the chapel asking God if it had really been he who tied the fishing line between the oaks so that it would behead his sister and cause his father's death. Val had interrupted the horror, but the desperation and need for escape remained. There was only one method of exorcism. He'd used it immediately, only to have a redheaded elf pop into his path and shout "Morning" at him.

Alexis smiled. Then he stopped smiling because he was surprised he could smile. He waited. There it was again. He was smiling. Where was the oppression that engulfed him after a death ride?

He wasn't foolish enough to go looking for it. Val called to him, and he joined his friend and Kate Grey.

"A guest has arrived," Val said. "Fulke sent me to find you."

"Lord help me," Alexis said. "I hope it isn't Sir Eustace. He wants the living of Heppleton for his son, and his son is a boring dispenser of cant. Though, come to think on it, such qualities make him the perfect churchman."

Alexis took his place on the other side of Kate and offered his arm. She took it, and the three of them walked toward the house. He was proud of himself for going the whole way without sparring with her. They stopped just inside the great hall. Through an open set of nearby double doors they all could see a man talking to Fulke.

"Bloody hell." Val took a jerky step forward.

There was no time to make a polite excuse and turn around. Alexis shoved Kate aside and leaped for his friend. "Bloody hell" expressed his own feelings accurately. He'd forgotten Cardigan. There he was, curling hair, elegant mustache and all, unaware of the danger. Alexis grabbed Val's arms. Val jerked free and kept heading for the earl. Alexis swooped after him and snatched the cane from his friend. Val tottered, and Alexis hauled him close by the neck of his jacket agilely, dodging a fist.

Hands full, Alexis tossed the cane to Kate. The girl caught it as he'd expected and kept out of his way, as he'd also expected. He wrapped his arms around Val from behind. Ignoring the barracks curses hurled at him, he lifted the lighter man off his feet and half carried, half dragged him toward a side door.

"Well done, Miss Grey—Kate. Val is overexcited and needs to lie down. Uh!" Alexis squeezed harder on Val's arms and lifted him higher. For a sick man, Val's blows were powerful. Alexis shook his head as Kate hissed questions at him. "Please, distract those two until I can come back. Please?"

"I'm staying in a castle full of demented squirrels," she said. "Oh, all right. I'm going."

Alexis shoved Val back out of the great hall and slammed the door shut. Val caught hold of a chest sitting against a wall and propped himself against it.

"You're too weak to fight me," Alexis said.

"I'm going to kill him. I'll tear out his heart with my hands."

"You can hardly walk. Look at you. You're trembling like a newborn calf. There are blue smudges under your eyes, and your skin feels as cold as pond ice. The doctors have told you and told you that you won't get well if your mind doesn't give your body peace."

Val lunged for the door. Alexis caught him as he fell. A heavy weight jammed into his shoulder. It was Val's head. Dragging his friend's arm across his shoulders, Alexis bent and lifted Val.

"Put me down, you bastard."

"You've had a busy time, haven't you? Prowling the castle all night. Routing me out of bed. Hunting down Miss Grey and launching her at me. Attempted murder. I think I'll lock you in your room. Quit fighting me or I may drop you down the stairs."

A few minutes later Alexis joined Fulke, Kate, and the Earl of Cardigan in the drawing room. He hadn't taken the time to change, but Cardigan was a fanatic horseman and wouldn't balk at Alexis's riding clothes. Not that he cared. He was too busy lecturing himself not to call the man out. It would annoy the Queen.

He needn't have given his apparel a thought, for Cardigan didn't seem to care where his host was. His whole attention was on Kate Grey. As Kate poured him a cup of coffee, Alexis listened to Cardigan, and he tried not to hate.

"Would have faced the cowards myself," the earl was saying. "No way to find them out, you see. They send anonymous threats full of abuse and accusations. Her Majesty asked me to come down here while the authorities investigate."

Alexis nodded without speaking. Fulke plunged into the hole in the conversation.

"What do the notes say, James?"

Cardigan flushed and twirled his mustache. Alexis was hurled back six months to a day of blood. Cardigan had sat on his horse at the head of the Light Brigade and twirled his mustache while he argued with the Earl of Lucan. If the two hadn't been locked in a prima donna battle for command, both would have asked for clarification of the order that sent hundreds of men to slaughter.

"And they accuse me of lying," he heard Cardigan say. "Lying! They claim I never asked Lucan to question the order."

Kate set her cup down and eyed the furious man. "Why didn't you refuse to do it, my lord?"

Alexis nearly choked on his coffee, but the earl turned sky-blue eyes on the girl and went from a boil to a simmer.

"My dear Miss Grey," he said. "Of course a lady does not understand a soldier's duty. A soldier obeys his commander."

"You said this commander-in-chief, Lord Raglan, was a desk general. The last battle he fought was against Napoleon at Waterloo. Nobody would have blamed you for refusing to kill yourself and a whole brigade, would they?"

"Yes, Miss Grey, they would."

"Well, it seems to me that a man who can't supply his own men, who lets them starve and suffer from wounds without medical treatment—"

"Miss Grey," Alexis said.

He couldn't help the strain in his voice, or the whip-crack way he lashed out at her. She exposed unhealed wounds. Cardigan had that distant, haunted look he'd seen on Val's face too many times. He only hoped his own countenance wasn't so ravaged.

Bless Fulke for smoothing things over.

"May I show you to your rooms, James? Juliana put you in the state chambers. You'll be honored to know you're sleeping where Henry VIII did, although considering his bloodthirsty reputation, you might not rest easily."

Alexis got up with the others, but didn't follow the earl and Fulke. That was why he noticed the exchange of glances between Cardigan and Kate. The earl looked over Fulke's shoulder and scrutinized her body with the thor-

oughness he used in a full-dress inspection of Prince Albert's Own Hussars.

Kate did what no other young lady of Alexis's acquaintance ever did. She stared back with open interest, ap-
praisal, and appreciation. Damn her. The door shut,
cutting off contact between the two.

Alexis jerked the silver pot off its tray and poured more
coffee into his cup. "Miss Grey." He was too angry to call
her Kate. "I must insist that you observe a semblance of
decorum with my guests. Perhaps in a backward country
like the United States young ladies are allowed to conduct
themselves with the boldness of a waterfront doxy, but in
my house I expect a superficial adherence to the rules of
polite society."

She got up. His anger was fed by the sight of her split
skirt, the open neck of her blouse, the curls that rioted
about her face.

"What was that word you used?" she asked calmly.

The urge to send her fleeing from him in embarrassment was too great. "Doxy."

"Are you calling me a whore?"

As had happened too often with Katherine Ann Grey,
he found himself gaping at her.

"I said, are you calling me a whore?"

He shook his head in denial.

"That's good, because now I won't have to call you a
gutter-minded, tight-assed fool."

She stalked out of the room and slammed the door
behind her.

Alexis picked up a spoon and stirred his coffee without
looking at it.

"Tight assed?"

He squirmed uncomfortably on the aforementioned
body part.

"We'll see whose ass is tight after I'm through with
you, Kate Grey."

Chapter Eight

Kate tramped down the hall muttering to herself.

"I can't believe I said that. I called a nobleman tight assed. Mama will vapor to death if she finds out, but I don't care. He is tight assed."

A door to her left opened. A golden marmoset scooted out from behind a fan of black satin skirts. Kate stopped, distracted by the tiny creature.

"Miss Grey." Lady Juliana beckoned to her from the doorway of yet another drawing room. "Kate."

The marmoset climbed up Kate's skirt. Kate snatched the monkey from her waist and carried it into the room with her. Lady Juliana was smiling at her. Juliana seldom smiled, and Kate had never seen her laugh.

Juliana took the marmoset from her. "My dear, I heard that unfortunate exchange with my son."

"I'm sorry, ma'am."

"Don't be." Juliana stroked the long fur of her monkey. On a sofa behind her slept three Persian cats. "I've been watching you, and my son deserves your contempt. He is the opposite of his father, who was perfection among men. You see, Miss Grey, Alexis preys upon women the way a tiger hunts antelope. You are the first girl I ever saw get the best of him and the only one who ever judged him as he should be judged."

Kate experienced the sensation she would get when she first tried to read a foreign language. "I don't understand, ma'am. Your son and I don't get on well, it's true."

"Ah! But you don't realize that Alexis always gets on. He gets on well with any woman at whom he takes the trouble to snap his fingers." Juliana put the marmoset down and laid her hand on Kate's arm. "I admire you. Thirty years ago girls had your kind of wits and courage. Today they act as though it's a crime to have either."

"Thank you, ma'am."

"I shall take you up."

Kate furrowed her brow. "Take me up?"

"Introduce you to Society." Juliana picked up a fat, cream-colored cat and began stroking it. "Frankly, Kate, I can't abide your mother. She has no backbone, and she simpers. I hate simpering."

"Don't talk about my mother like—"

"Hush, child. You feel the same way about simpering. I've seen it in your face every time Sophia flourishes her smelling salts. It's best to be honest."

"Still . . ." Kate said.

"She's your mother. Let's not touch upon the subject again. I shall take you up. We didn't go to London for the season because of Alexis's and Val's injuries, but I can put together a few small parties. Much better for you anyway. I can invite young men of character."

After describing a few of Kate's potential suitors, Juliana shooed her out of the room. "Run along, my dear. I have plans to make."

Kate found herself gently shoved over the threshold. She turned around to object, and the door shut in her face. She heard a cat whine and the marmoset squeak. Swallowing, Kate lost her nerve and hurried on her way. As short as her acquaintance with Lady Juliana was, she knew that arguing with the woman would be useless. Once she made up her mind, Juliana was apparently as stubborn about changing it as Queen Victoria herself.

"Take me up," she said to herself. "That's all I need, being taken up and shown off to a bunch of leering snobs. What in . . ."

Someone was banging at a wall or a door. The noise was faint and accompanied by a muffled shout. Kate followed the sound. The castle had bedrooms on several levels. She located the source of the racket on the second floor, in the wing used by the marquess and his family. As she walked down the hall, the banging got louder. She found the door behind which it emanated and stood before it.

"Alexis!" a man shouted. "Alexis, you bloody bastard, let me out."

"Mr. Beaufort?" Kate said.

Val called to her. "Please, let me out."

Kate examined the lock on the door. It was empty. She backed up and surveyed the floor. Nearby lay a brass key. She picked it up and unlocked the door, which sprang open and slammed against the wall. Val stood before her balancing on his cane. He was flushed, his chest heaving. He glared at her as he snapped out a thank-you.

"Where is he?" he asked.

"You mean the earl? He's being shown his rooms. Now don't go trying to find him. You know you're too weak to do anything." Kate took Val's arm and started pulling him down the hall. "Mr. Beaufort, you're going to have to control this hair-trigger temper of yours. Back in San Francisco we have a lot of thugs, the Sydney Ducks, waterfront riffraff and such, that need cleaning out. You think the earl is your Sydney Duck and you're itching to string him up the way our vigilantes do the Ducks. The trouble is, vigilantes aren't judges, and neither are you."

"Yes I am."

She yanked on his arm. "Don't argue with a Lady. And don't you go telling me I don't behave like a Lady. I've heard enough of that from Lord Alexis."

Val smiled. "Don't pay attention to him. Alexis is always looking for the Perfect Lady. When he finds this paragon, he's going to marry her. She's supposed to lend respectability to his tarnished name, you see."

"Tarnished? I didn't know he was tarnished. So far I haven't seen anybody making a sign against the evil eye at him."

"And you won't. One doesn't offend rich, blue-blooded noblemen who happen to be related to the Queen. One simply takes care that one's eligible daughters are warned away from him. Unfortunately, warning away daughters makes them want to throw themselves at the feet of the aforementioned nobleman."

"I'm confused."

"And I, Miss Grey, have said enough to get me put to the lash if Alexis finds out."

"Then why did you say anything?"

"Revenge, Miss Grey. Nasty, sneaking, soul-satisfying revenge. Have you ever read *A Midsummer Night's Dream*? I have the feeling you are going to turn Alexis from a dignified Theseus into a bewitched and confused Lysander."

She stopped, for they had reached the stairs that led to her own rooms.

"You've made a mistake," she said. "His high and mightiness has already transformed himself. Only he didn't change into Lysander. He changed into Bottom. And if you remember, Bottom spent a lot of time as an ass."

Afternoon was fading when Alexis went in search of Kate again. He'd spent the intervening time trying not to think about her. He'd never tried not to think about a woman before. Never had to. It didn't work, and so he'd made the mistake of allowing himself to remember that she'd smiled upon that colossal sausage-wit Cardigan.

As soon as he did, he felt as if ants were swimming in his blood. He wanted a fight, and not just any fight, but a fight with Katherine Ann. Katie Ann. Mouthy, presumptuous, succulent Katie Ann. He found her in the kitchen garden stabbing at weeds with a trowel.

"Why are you digging in the dirt, Miss Grey?"

The blade hit a rock. Dirt flew in Kate's face and she swore.

"Hellfire. Do you have to sneak up on people and shout at them?"

Alexis studied one of his immaculate white cuffs before letting his gaze shift to the dirt on Kate's small nose. He grinned when she sputtered, discarded the trowel, and began wiping her face with the apron she wore to protect her dress.

"I asked why you are playing in my cook's garden."

"I used to take care of our garden at home. I miss it."

"Are you finished?" He held out his hand without giving her a chance to say no.

Taking Alexis's hand, she rose. "I guess I am." She placed her hands on the small of her back and leaned backward, groaning. "Oh, my. I haven't gardened in a while. What are you laughing at?"

"I don't think I've ever seen a lady pull her arms back and stick out her chest before. Not in my whole life." He laughed again at the confused look on her face and glanced pointedly at her breasts. "Your posture, Katie Ann. Gentility and maidenliness seem to be lacking across the Atlantic."

She scooped up the trowel and poked him with it. "I don't need you to tell me what maidens should or shouldn't do or talk about, Alexis de Granville. And stop grinning at me. And don't call me Katie Ann. My father is the only one who called me that."

"He must have been a brave man." He captured the hand that held the trowel. "A brave man to raise such a lightning storm of a daughter as you, Katie Ann."

He let her snatch her hand away. She rounded on him, and he watched her ire grow. She was mad enough to spit bullets. Her cheeks were flushed, her eyes bright with unladylike wrath. And he felt more alive than he had in years. Alexis couldn't help laughing again.

"You ass," she said.

"Please." He held up both hands in mock protest. "My sensibilities, Katie Ann. I shiver to think what body part you'll mention next."

"You can take all your body parts and go to hell," she said. She turned her back on him and marched across the garden to the kitchen door.

"Come back, Lady Hellfire," he called after her. "You've yet to speak of the most interesting body parts."

Several days passed after her conversation with Lady Juliana, during which Kate felt as though she were a condemned prisoner waiting for the hangman to come to town. Even Ophelia's funeral, held on a disturbingly sunny day, did not deter Juliana from her plans for a house party. Kate was to be her guest of honor. It was hard for Kate to carry on with business when she knew that soon she'd be surrounded by polished young men and women who were bound to think she had the grace and deportment of a gopher.

Sophia was transported with rapture. Although she had been deeply saddened by Ophelia's death, especially since she'd just gotten to know the younger woman, being in England among her own people gave her the strength to rally more quickly from this latest sorrow. She also had the comfort of calls on childhood friends with whom she'd been renewing friendships. Sophia drew great solace from their company.

Kate didn't. Spending time with Mama's friends only made her more jittery. Kate was scared. She didn't know a thing about house parties, and one loomed, as terrifying as King Lear's storm, on the horizon. What frightened her the most was talking. She had never learned frivolous conversation. Banter was more mysterious to her than the workings of a steamship. Other girls could bat their eyes at a man and mew asinine flatteries. When Kate tried it, she felt so ridiculous her face turned red and her mouth wouldn't move.

Gentlemen didn't want to talk about the things she thought were interesting. They didn't want to talk about panning for gold or imports from Hawaii and China. They certainly didn't care about the works of Hawthorne or Longfellow. When she tried to discuss the troubles in Kansas over slavery and the problems of slave states and free states, she got blank looks—except from the Marquess of Richfield.

He would talk with her about all of these things. He wasn't bored by such topics. No indeed. He seemed to delight in bringing up the very subjects dear to her so he could take the other side of an argument and try to make a fool of her. The snake.

And he kept doing it. Kate would go out of her way to avoid him so she wouldn't have to argue, especially after that scene in the kitchen garden. She spent hours closeted with Mr. Poggs, yet when she came out of a meeting, there Alexis would be, walking past her door, or out on the courtyard playing with his dog. She took a book to a secluded corner of the castle grounds; he came strolling by on a supposed inspection of his trees and plants. The man was a nuisance.

He didn't play fair, either. He provoked an argument and then accused her of unladylike quarreling when she defended herself. After four days of this treatment, Kate was ready to send to California for a posse and a rope.

It was on the fourth day that she gave up all hope of understanding Alexis de Granville. She'd taken great care in selecting a hiding place in which to read. He'd found her when she'd gone to the Red Drawing Room, the Cedar Drawing Room, and the armory. This time she took refuge in the Clocktower.

The tower was a fourteenth-century construction with over fifty rooms. It stood just inside the massive barbican, the outer fortified gate house in front of the drawbridge. She selected a deserted chamber stuffed with medieval furniture and sporting a fireplace big enough for a man to stand in. What attracted her was the tall, diamond-paned window that let in the morning sunlight. The brightness streamed in and reflected off the whitewashed stone of the tower walls.

She dragged a heavy walnut chair over to the open window, then curled up in it and opened the book she'd brought with her. Her view was of the turquoise sky and a single, thin wisp of a cloud that hung like a bride's veil spread by the wind. What sounds there were came from the stirring of the pages of her book when a breeze caught them. She gradually sank into a world of bright light and beautiful words.

"Aaarrrroooof."

Kate jumped. Her knee hit the arm of her chair, and she yelped. There was a scuffling of paws, then the door to the chamber slid open under the weight of Iago's shoulder. The spaniel bounded forth. He sprang and landed with his front paws on Kate's thighs and barked again.

"Iago!" she heard Alexis call, his voice sounding too innocent.

"Damn," she said, and shoved Iago off her lap. "Go away, doggie."

Iago burrowed his head in her skirt. She got up and began pulling the dog by his collar.

"Come on, Iago. If you don't get out, he'll find me."

She was pushing on the beast from behind when the marquess stepped into the room.

"There you are, old fellow," he said. "Kate, this is a surprise."

"I don't see how. He's hunted me down three times now."

"I know. Odd, isn't it? We set out on a walk, and he comes to fetch you right away."

Iago barked, patted his paw at Alexis, and bounded out of the room.

"Now where's he going?" Kate asked. She tried not to sound annoyed.

The marquess threw up his hands in mock disgust. "I don't know. Sometimes I think he consorts with pixies so he can disappear and appear at will. What are you reading?"

Before she could stop him, he snatched the book from the chair where she'd left it.

"Le Morte d'Arthur," he said. "I didn't think you'd read such romantic stuff. Knights and damsels and chivalry. Do you like romance, Miss Grey?" He didn't wait for her to answer. "Shall I read to you?"

Again he didn't wait. He started reading while leading her back to her chair. Kate frowned at him as he sank down at her feet. He was so close he almost touched her knees. She'd never had a man read to her. She was so surprised that he would want to, she let him. At first she was uncomfortable, but the sound of his voice lured her into forgetfulness. It was a low, soft voice infused with feeling and vibrancy, and it set her insides tingling in the strangest way.

The tingling made her forget the words. She listened to the sound of his voice alone. When he rested his arm on the seat of her chair, she moved so that he would have more room.

He glanced up at her and smiled. Without looking at the book, he recited. " 'Then Sir Mordred sought on Queen Guinevere by letters and sounds, and by fair means and foul means, for to have her to come out of the Tower of London; but all this availed not, for she answered him shortly, openly and privily, that she had liefer slay herself than to be married with him.' "

Kate looked down at him. Inside she felt a small shiver of excitement. His voice wove a spell. It shot out magical tendrils that combined with the cool, bright air, the smell of old wood, and the warmth of his body, suffusing her in charm. She paused, balancing on an enchanted strand of faerie web between his spell and her own caution. He was looking up at her still, but his eyes changed. They became liquid metal. She started when he put his hand on hers and lifted it to his lips.

"If I were Malory," he said, "I would have Guinevere have firelight hair and skin like the glaze on ancient porcelain. She would have earth-brown eyes and little hands that disappeared when I covered them with one of my own."

His hand slid over hers. She looked to remark that it did vanish, and when she did, he was there. His mouth came up to meet hers, and she opened her own as if it were the only thing to do.

It couldn't be helped. She wanted to kiss him, so she did. Hesitantly she put her hands on his chest. As if it were an invitation, he wrapped her in his embrace and plunged deeper into her mouth. She felt a hand sweep down her arm and then up her rib cage to rest on the side of her breast. That simple touch called forth an ache in her body that made her press against him.

Suddenly she was lifted and laid on the rug that covered the floor. He rose over her, his face and body blocking out the light, and she opened her mouth to object.

"Shhhh." He nipped at her lower lip before devouring her mouth once more.

It felt too good, having his body cover hers. All reason, all thoughts of propriety were meaningless when set against the pressure of warm, straining muscles and the smooth-rough texture of a male cheek against her own. When Alexis's hand pushed at her thigh, she let him shove it aside. The resulting contact of hip against hip and groin against groin fed the burning ache that was driving her insane. The more he did, the more she needed. That was why she had to have his mouth on her neck. It was why she allowed him to free her breasts and touch them. It was why she didn't scream when he sucked a nipple and tugged at it with his teeth.

Kate heard her own breathing. It was loud and rough. It went with her burning skin. In the grip of her first full arousal, she touched his face and found it hot. The knowledge that he was as frenzied as she stirred her even more. The tingling pain in her loins escalated, and she arched her hips upward. As she moved, Alexis let out a curse and tore at her skirts. With sharp, jerking movements he nearly ripped them in his haste to bare her legs. She felt cool air on her calf and thigh, then something warm covered her knee. It was his hand. She gave a little start as that hand stroked up farther and farther, until it reached the juncture of her thighs.

The feather-light touch there was what broke the spell. It was too much. The feelings were too much. His pump-

ing hips and sucking mouth were too much. Kate made a
small sound of protest. Alexis ignored her. She wriggled,
and he pressed his weight down on her, settling his hips
directly on hers. She tried to pull her mouth free of his.
He let her, immediately shifting to kiss one of her breasts.
She gasped for breath while he unfastened his trousers.
She uttered a "no" that came out a dry, hoarse whisper
that was cut off by his mouth. Panic chilled the throbbing
in her loins when he covered her with the hot fullness of
his own. The touch of his genitals was the impetus she
needed.

Kate tore her mouth free. "No!"

He stared down at her. His face was beaded with
sweat, and his gaze almost frenzied. He closed his eyes
and arched his back. She felt a burning tumescence slip
between the folds of her own flesh. He was going to put
himself inside her.

"Alexis, stop," she whispered.

"No. I can't. Dear God, I can't."

She grasped two handfuls of black hair and pulled
hard, so that his head snapped backward. "Yes you can.
You have to."

He growled. He fastened his hands on her wrists, forc-
ing her to release his hair, and lifted his hips from her.
The hatred in his face made her heart jerk.

"Damn you to hell," he said. "You castrating little
tease, I ought to—" He stopped, studying her face. His
hands loosened their bruising grip on her wrists. "You
don't know what I'm talking about, do you?"

The staccato hammering of her heart settled down.
"No, no."

In a second Alexis was standing over her. He turned
and adjusted his clothing. With his back still turned to her
and bracing himself on the arms of the medieval chair, he
ordered Kate to cover herself. Confused and feeling as if
she were somehow guilty of torture, she complied. When

she was finished, she sat with her legs tucked under her, staring at Alexis's back as she waited. He remained with his face averted for long minutes. The only sound was his uneven breathing. At last he spoke.

"Are you finished?"

"Yes."

He faced her with his hands gripping the back of the chair. "Not since I was fifteen have I been so completely unnerved. You twist my guts on a spindle."

"I'm sorry," Kate said. She ventured a question. "Are you all right?"

"I'll recover."

Wetting her lips, she tried not to blush while she tried to explain. "It felt so good. I didn't know I'd get scared, and I didn't know I would hurt you."

Soft, masculine laughter filled the room, but she wasn't offended. He had lifted his eyes to the ceiling and was shaking his head.

"I realized your ignorance too late. It was my fault. I mistook intellect and poise for sexual experience."

"I should have known, though."

He rested his forearms on the back of the chair and smiled at her in disbelief. "How could you know?"

"Patience told me. It was a while ago, but I should have remembered. She said men get so . . . so—I don't know what the word is, but she said when they get that way, they hurt terribly. I forgot and I'm sorry. Are you crying?"

She jumped up, rushed over to Alexis, and put her arm around his shoulders. His head was buried in his arms and his body was shaking.

He lifted his head, and she saw that he was laughing again. She grinned back.

"Upon my honor," he said, "you will have me in Bedlam before the month is out. I feel as if my soul has been stripped out of my body and minced for a pie."

"That sounds awful."

He touched the tip of her nose with his finger. "No, I don't think it is. In fact, I can't remember when I've ever felt so alive."

"Does that mean you're not mad at me?"

He kissed her cheek. "Yes, my ignorant wise one."

She smiled at him, but she couldn't think of a reply. He'd battened on her weakness, her ignorance of sexuality and sexual love. She wasn't about to let him know it. She didn't understand what had just happened, and she was afraid he did. What she needed was a distraction.

"Alexis, you never did let me tell you I changed my mind."

"About what?" he asked as he fished under the carpet for her discarded book.

"Your sick soldiers. I decided to let them stay in my house. Don't you think we'd better find an architect and get started making it ready for the men?"

He bounded to her side, his look of triumphant satisfaction giving her pause.

"Thank you, little savage." He took her hand, opened it, and kissed the palm.

At his touch, Kate forgot his odd reaction to her news and let him escort her from the Clocktower. As they walked out into the barbican, it suddenly occurred to her that Alexis de Granville wasn't such a snake after all. Though, come to think of it, he did have a wonderfully tight ass.

Chapter Nine

The de Granville ancestors, the male ones, were probably laughing at him. He'd let her go. Not only had he let her go, he'd escorted her to the library so she could write to her damnable Mr. Poggs. Striding through the great hall, Alexis passed a tapestry showing a warrior smiting helpless Saxons. That savage, Norman Phillipe de Granville, wouldn't have stopped until he'd rutted the girl five or six times. Hunching his shoulders, Alexis hurried by the tapestry as if he feared to see the black-haired lord sneer at him.

God, he was paying for his idiocy. He was still hard as a helmet, and it was all he could do to reach his sitting room before his control slipped. He slammed the door behind him. His lips pulled back over his teeth in a snarl. Rushing to his desk, he scooped up the books and papers there and hurled them to the floor.

He stood amid the mess, fists working

open and closed, and ground his teeth together while he searched the room for something breakable. He spotted a Greek vase and headed for it. At that point, the unfortunate Meredith knocked and entered, holding an envelope.

"Duck, Meredith!"

Meredith dropped to his hands and knees barely in time to avoid the vase. The pottery crashed and splintered against the wall. Meredith didn't spare it a glance. He picked himself up, rearranged his cravat, and put himself between Alexis and a glass figurine. Thwarted, Alexis came to a stop with murder seething in his eyes.

Meredith ignored the look and handed him the envelope. "My lord." When Alexis snarled at him, the valet turned the envelope over so that Alexis could see the handwriting on the address.

Alexis snatched the envelope from him, tore it open, and read the enclosed note. Turning his back on Meredith, he drew in a deep breath and let it out in a long, groaning sigh.

"I shall be riding to Heppleton immediately, Meredith."

"I have laid out your costume, my lord."

"Good." He handed the note and envelope back to his valet. "Burn it as usual. I'll be along soon."

Meredith pocketed the note and walked toward the door that led to Alexis's bedchamber.

Alexis braced his arms on the desk and closed his eyes. "Meredith."

"Yes, my lord."

"Thank you."

"Fealty, my lord. There is a responsibility inherent in the position."

Feeling transparent and a bit like a porcupine with sore quills, Alexis allowed Meredith to get him ready to leave. A day or two could change a person fundamentally, he thought. He should have known that, for Balaclava had mutilated his soul as well as his mind. However, he felt like a molting parrot after his short acquaintance with Miss Katherine Ann Grey. The note from Carolina proved that to him, for suddenly he couldn't abide the thought of going to the woman. He had to, though, for it was an obligation. He had a duty to her.

Ophelia had replaced Carolina Beechwith. Not that Carolina had known it. He'd gradually been easing away from her before he'd been sent to the Crimea, but she had refused to take hints. She lived on expectations of a re-union, waiting for a chance to resume what he'd already ended in his own mind. This was the first time since he'd been well that she'd found a chance to see him.

Alexis wasn't certain how he got there, but he was soon walking toward the portcullis and drawbridge, beyond which a groom waited with his horse. He entered the darkness of the vaulted tunnel formed by the two towers of the gate house. Sunlight at either end made the black-ness more complete. Alexis slapped his riding crop against his thigh and glanced up at the murder-holes above his head. He always looked up at them, expecting to see a medieval sergeant ready to pour boiling oil down on him.

Ahead he could see Theseus munching carrots sup-plied by the groom. Two people rounded the corner and stepped into the passageway. Fulke and Hannah. Lovely. Fulke would decide to take his wife for a stroll on this particular day. Alexis fixed a neutral smile on his face and greeted the two. As he'd expected, Fulke got rid of his wife before she could say a word.

While Hannah retreated in a flutter of ribbons, net-ting, and lace, Fulke stood still, blocking Alexis's way out. The spiked teeth of the portcullis hung behind him like the jaws of a beast.

Alexis faced Fulke. "She only exists for you when she's in your presence, doesn't she?"

Fulke pulled off his gloves, not bothering to look at his

departing wife. "Who? Hannah? Remember the words of Paul. 'Wives, submit yourselves unto your own husbands, as unto the Lord.' It is for her to interest herself in me, not for me to concern myself with her."

"Fulke, you are starving her."

"Forget Hannah. We've got on well for a long time, and you're trying to distract me. Valentine tried to challenge Cardigan this morning."

Alexis tapped his crop against the side of his boot. "Only tried?"

"I stopped him. You were to keep him away."

"He was supposed to be at the Dower House."

"He was stalking the earl," Fulke said.

"I'll see to it." Alexis tried to walk past Fulke, but the older man held out an arm to stop him.

"I know where you're going. Mrs. Beechwith came back from London without her husband last night."

"How did you know? I only found out just now."

"Servants, of course. 'Abstain from fleshly lusts, which war against the soul,' Alexis."

"My, you're preachy today. You'd think you had enough on your hands playing nanny to the Queen's pet soldier. Or has having to spend twenty minutes with your wife made you bilious?"

Alexis was unprepared for Fulke's attack. His cousin snatched his riding crop from him and lifted it. The weapon paused high over Alexis's head. Alexis ignored it in favor of goring Fulke with his eyes.

Fulke let the crop sink down to hang loosely at his side. "You make me forget you're not a boy anymore. Chastisement will have to come from the Lord, it seems."

Alexis held out his hand, and Fulke relinquished the crop. The darkness of the tunnel closed in around Alexis as he remembered those first days after his father's death, when Fulke had tried to comfort him while everyone else was preoccupied with his brain-fevered mother.

"I keep expecting Him to smite me at any moment," Alexis said. "I've been waiting a long time for the Lord's punishment, even tried to help Him along, but— What are you doing?" Alexis tried to back away, for Fulke had seized his arm in a fierce grip.

"When will you believe me?" Fulke asked. "You were hysterical, but you led me to your father and Thalia. You didn't hide like one guilty of murder. I've told you hundreds of times. You're not capable of something that unspeakable."

Shaking his head, Alexis pried his cousin's hand from his arm. "You don't know that. If only I could remember. I can't recall anything before I saw Thalia hit the . . . and then Father went down under his horse. The next thing I remember is holding him. He was so heavy. The dead are very heavy, Fulke."

The memory pulled at him, but before he could be swallowed up by it, Fulke touched his cheek.

"My dear boy, I know you better than anyone in this world, and I can assure you that you could no more plan such a crime than you could run a bayonet through a kitten." He patted Alexis on the shoulder. "You were better when you were in the cavalry."

"I was either too tired from drills or distracted by the spectacle of other people's blood."

"Before they died, you were so different," Fulke said. "No, listen to me. You don't remember how it was. Oh, there was fighting. All families quarrel. But you were always thinking of ways to please your parents. I remember you spending the whole of six months' allowance on a shawl for Juliana."

"Stop." Alexis winced at the way his voice boomed in the tunnel. "Don't you see? No matter what I did, I couldn't make her love me. She loved Father and had no room in that pea-size heart of hers for me, or for Thalia."

He leaned against the stone wall. "When I was five or

six, Father let me ride by myself for the first time. Not far, not for long, but I was proud. As soon as I got off that pony, I ran to Mother's room to tell her. She wouldn't listen." Alexis ran his hand over the cold stone that supported him. "She was angry, you see. Angry because Father had taken time away from her to teach me how to ride. She said he should have left it to the grooms. She said no father should play games with his son or teach him things best left to servants. Too much familiarity, she said. And the older I got, the less she seemed to be able to tolerate me. That's how it is with our kind, isn't it, Fulke? We live our lives trying not to be familiar."

"You know I don't agree. That's not how it was when I had charge of you."

Alexis pulled himself upright and smiled at his cousin. "No, you were good to me, even when I didn't want you to be. What I don't understand is why you can't be good to Hannah."

"I am."

"Dear God, I think you mean that. You should give women a chance, Fulke. They make this world worth living in. I'm off. There's a lady waiting for me."

This time Fulke didn't try to stop him. Instead, he called out as Alexis strode into the sunlight.

"Miss Grey is no more suitable than Carolina Beechwith."

"Go to hell, Fulke."

It took almost an hour to get to the Beechwith house outside Heppleton. Ezra Beechwith was an immortal old county man with enough wealth to buy a young and lovely wife, but not enough sense to know he shouldn't buy one. Ezra had interests in the city that took him to London constantly. Alexis suspected that Ezra's absences were the result of a deliberate blindness to his wife's unmentionable needs and the method by which she chose to satisfy them.

The Beechwiths lived at Lonsdale Hall, a baroque manor surrounded by yews. The house was deserted except for Carolina's maid. The girl ushered him down a white-plastered vaulted hall and into the state bedroom. Carolina had a penchant for sinning in grandeur.

The room was made black and gold by the absence of any light save that given off from the fireplace. Carolina was waiting for him at the foot of the crimson damask state bed. One hand clutched a bed curtain while the other was held out to him.

He heard the door click shut behind him. Knowing he was going to seem as fickle as an heiress with her pick of suitors, he hesitated just inside the room. Carolina said his name, but he kept himself busy by disposing of his hat, gloves, and riding crop.

Carolina waited, unfortunately, and he was forced to go to her. He bowed as she held out her hand again, and so he wasn't prepared when she grasped his clothing and started tearing it away. He saw her mouth aiming at his.

"Wai—mmmmph!"

Before he knew it, she had backed him up until his legs hit the side of the bed. He fell backward with her on top of him.

"Blast you, Carolina, wait."

Further complaints were impossible because Carolina savaged his mouth. As she unbuttoned his jacket, he tried to sit up, but she pressed him back down on the bed. She tore his shirt open and sank her teeth into the flesh of his shoulder, and he went rigid. He dug his fingers into her hair and pulled free of her teeth.

"Stop it."

She paid him no mind. Digging her nails into his skin, she began to suck on his mouth, then tried to eat his neck.

He got his arms beneath him, ready to shove. "Damn and blast you, Carolina, wait. Ow!"

"Sorry." She kissed the wound on his neck.

He turned his head away from her questing mouth and his arms fell to his sides. Biting his lip, he stared at the shadows cast by the fire, trying to think of a polite way to get this woman off him. At the same time, he wondered how long he would have to wait to have Katie Ann.

A pair of lips sucked at his. He tore himself away and wriggled out from under Carolina. When he was free, kneeling on the bed next to the confused woman, he pounded the mattress with his fist.

"Bloody hell!" Why shouldn't he enjoy himself after what Kate had done to him? He didn't need to keep thinking about her. Was it the crimson damask? Did it remind him of her hair? God, he had wanted it to be her touching him. It was the war, he decided. His ordeal had given him brain fever.

Carolina knelt beside him and traced his lips with her finger. "My lord, it isn't me who is the savage, but you."

He stiffened, gazing up at the canopy. "What?"

"You called me a little savage."

"Everlasting Hades."

He shot up off the bed and retreated to the fireplace. There he puzzled furiously over nothing. Carolina anxiously chirped questions at him for a full minute before he noticed that she was tugging at his hand.

He grasped her by both arms. "I'm sorry. It's— I'm worried about the men at the Dower House. It's not a good day for me."

"You worry too much, Alexis. You try to take care of too many people. No wonder you're distraught."

Rubbing his brow, he groaned. "The people I have to put up with are beyond your imagining." He lifted his head, scowling. "But I haven't changed that much. I won't. Sh—they can't make me."

He grasped Carolina's arm. "Come to the house party."

"But your mother . . ."

Carolina was continually in fear of being put out of Society if her indiscretions were discovered.

"My mother notices only what is convenient for her to notice. She knows better than to cut you. Please, Carolina." He kissed her forehead, her nose, her throat. "Come to me, be with me."

As he intended, Carolina was unable to do anything but obey his wishes.

She'd almost made love to Alexis de Granville in a Clocktower. Over two hours had passed, and Kate still couldn't believe she'd done it. Almost done it. Partially done it. After he'd escorted her to the library, she'd tried to write her letter to Mr. Poggs. Impossible. Now all she wanted was to be free of the ornate stateliness of the castle and avoid anyone related to Alexis. With this aim, she hustled along corridors and through rooms until she found the way to the conservatory. From there she peered outside at the formal gardens of Richfield. Seeing no one, she let herself out and ran.

I don't believe I did that. I don't believe it, I don't believe it, I don't believe it. Mama would be so shocked.

Kate stopped to catch her breath beside a topiary peacock. All around her low hedges formed geometric patterns filled with rose bushes. She was too visible out here. Lifting her skirts and petticoats, she flew toward the shelter of the trees that surrounded the castle. There a marble bench was set beneath a giant cedar of Lebanon. She sank down on it and pounded her fist on the marble.

"I don't believe it." *Pound.* "I don't." *Pound.* "I don't, don't, don't." *Pound, pound, pound.*

Kate wrapped her arms around herself and started

rocking back and forth. How was she to have known that being touched by him wouldn't be like being groped by smelly prospectors? It wasn't fair. He'd changed. He'd changed from a snake to a beautiful incubus, and lured her into feeling things she'd only known about from her talks with Patience. Knowing a thing in one's head and feeling it with one's body were not the same. Patience had forgotten to explain the difference to her. It was Patience's fault that Kate had allowed that charming sensualist to take Liberties.

Liberties must not be allowed. That was a rule. Mama said men don't respect girls who allowed Liberties. Although . . . Alexis hadn't been disrespectful to her at all afterward. He had treated her with deference and gentleness, as though he feared she might take fright. The man was a puzzle, and she didn't know how she was going to face him again. He'd touched her intimately, and she was going to have to meet him, dine with him, speak to him.

"Miss Grey."

Kate sighed and glanced up. Coming toward her from the garden was Hannah Sinclair. She carried a basket half filled with early roses, and a dainty pair of scissors hung from a ribbon around her wrist. Her delicate face was composed, her lips pursed in a decorous smile. They exchanged greetings, and Kate made room for Hannah on the bench. Hannah was full of excitement about tomorrow's arrival of guests for the house party. The Duke of So-and-So was coming, and a German princeling, and Lord and Lady Something were expected. Kate listened while she sniffed at a rose. She touched a blush-peach petal with the tip of her finger.

"Lady Hannah, you're a married woman."

Hannah paused in her list of guests and nodded.

"Do gentlemen fall in love like women do?"

Hannah looked down at the basket in her lap. "I don't think so, Miss Grey."

"Oh."

Kate's disappointment must have shown, for Hannah patted her arm.

"A gentleman's chief interest and goals lie in the world, my dear. In achievements and duties, like those of Lord Fulke in the government, or Lord Alexis in the cavalry. While a woman's existence is for home and children."

"But there must be love."

"Well, my dear . . ." Hannah blushed and fiddled with the roses in her basket. "That sort of thing is to be endured as a duty. Surely your mother has told you." Her voice sank to a nearly soundless whisper. "A duty, for the sake of children. God has not blessed me, but I hope He will soon."

"But that doesn't make sense," Kate said. Her confusion was growing. "God made women as well as men, and if we feel pleasure, surely it's because the Lord meant us to."

"Miss Grey!"

"You can't tell me all the millions of babies in the world were conceived by women doing their duty with teeth gritted and bodies numb."

For once Hannah's voice rose above a breathy murmur. "Please."

"Don't have a hissy, I'm shutting up."

Kate rose. She clasped her hands behind her back and rocked on her heels. Hannah set her basket aside and pulled a useless lace handkerchief from her pocket. She dabbed at her upper lip while watching Kate with apprehension.

"Lady Hannah, would you like to see the new fashion magazine Mother just got?"

"Oh . . . mmmm . . . yes."

Kate linked arms with Hannah and they started walking toward the castle.

"And while we're looking," Kate said, "would you

mind helping me with my dress for the party tomorrow night? I'm not good at fashion, you know. And I want to look especially nice. More than nice."

"You want to look a beauty," Hannah said. Her eyes lit with the gleam of challenge.

"Do you think that's possible?" Kate asked.

"Of course."

They went to Kate's rooms and dug out every dress Kate owned. Sophia joined them, and for once Kate enjoyed fussing with clothes. It wasn't that she didn't like clothes. It was just that fashion dictated that Ladies wear too much of everything. Lace, for example. Hannah wore lace at her neck, on her sleeves, at her hem. Her handkerchief was lace, her cap was lace, her shoes were trimmed with lace. And the ribbons. What wasn't covered with lace dripped with ribbons. Even her cap had ribbons that spilled down her back and ran down the sides. Hannah's voice never reached above a whisper, but her clothing was visual noise. And Kate had to admit that her own mother was just as bad.

They finally chose a dress for the party, and Hannah commandeered it, saying it needed a bit of lace at the neckline. She left to find a seamstress as Sophia fetched from her own room a box of jewels and another containing ribbons and bows.

Kate sat in front of a mirror while her mother held the fripperies up to her face and neck. Sophia hummed a nursery tune as she worked. Kate looked at her mother's smiling face in the mirror.

"You're happy again, aren't you, Mama?"

Sophia paused with a bow in her hand. "Yes, Katie. Although I miss your father when I'm not busy. But all these goings-on distract me."

"But it's more than distraction."

"Yes, I suppose so." Sophia's eyes grew misty. "In

America I never belonged. Everyone thought I was cold and a snob. But they didn't see how difficult it was for me. Americans are so open, Kate. Even your father's decorous Virginia family were much too . . . too free. I'd never been among people who spoke their minds so openly. And California was worse. You don't remember how terrible it was at first. No real civilization. No churches, few books, no schools. Almost no women to talk to. And what few women were there knew nothing of England or what it's like here. I gave up so much to be with your father."

"What did you give up, Mama?"

"Oh, all this." Sophia swept her hand around to indicate the castle. "I was so young. I didn't know how much I loved Society. The house parties and balls, the calls, the hunts. I'd grown up with them, and when I no longer had them, I realized what I'd given up."

Kate sighed as her mother held a string of pearls to her neck. "You're so good at having fun. You can stay up until two in the morning and not fall asleep. You even enjoy calls. I bet Papa is smiling at you in heaven right now."

"Your father never had much patience with Society."

"Papa was the most sensible man I've ever known," Kate said. "Unlike some men of my acquaintance, who want humbling."

"Now I understand this sudden interest in dresses."

Kate lowered her eyes. "I don't know what you mean."

"My little girl is going to be a belle, as they say in Virginia." Sophia squeezed Kate's shoulders. "Just wait until tomorrow night. Mind, though, you'll have to refrain from being too clever. As lovely as you are, you still can't make a gentleman feel ignorant and expect his admiration."

Kate picked up a bow and stuck it on the top of her head like a crown. "I won't say a sensible thing the whole evening."

As it turned out, Kate didn't have to worry about saying anything too intelligent. She was so pinched by the corset her mother made her wear, she could only talk in short, breathy sentences. She had balked when presented with a crinoline, though. Remembering Ophelia's trials, she refused to wear it. Mama was placated by the substitution of several stiff petticoats.

Such discomforts topped off hours of strain. Guests had been arriving all day, until every chamber from the Queen Anne Bedroom to the Yellow Boudoir was filled. Juliana introduced Kate to each guest, and Kate promptly forgot the person's name. As the evening wore on, however, she had occasion to remember a few of them.

Cinched into a black silk evening gown—she was in mourning for Ophelia and didn't have to bother with a choice of colors—Kate picked her way through the eleven courses of dinner. The meal was given in the state dining room. It was the first time Kate had seen the place, and when she walked in, she'd nearly disgraced herself by gawking at the white-and-gold paneling, the twelve-foot ceiling with gold-painted and molded plaster, the life-size paintings in ornate frames sporting winged cherubs. She was sure the picture at one end was of Charles I. At the other end of the room was a Rubens.

Juliana kindly had asked Val Beaufort to escort Kate in to dinner. To her dismay, they sat near three Honourables, the three Honourable Misses Dinkle to be precise. The young ladies were daughters of some viscount or baron, Kate couldn't remember which. Merry and Cherry Dinkle were twins. They competed with each other to see who could be the most vapid and had the habit of twirling in unison the little bouquets they carried.

The Honourable Miss Georgiana Dinkle wasn't much

better. She walked on tiptoe and was always saying "ain't" in an affected way that made Kate want to ask her if she was from Texas.

Midway through dinner Kate had managed to fix the names of several more people in her head. There was what she referred to as the "great beauty" contingent—the Countess of Landsborne, Mademoiselle St.-Germain, and Lady Fiona Churchill-Smythe. Kate didn't like any of the three. She decided her antipathy arose from several causes. None of them had corsets that creaked, they all could walk in their hoops without getting stuck in doors, and each wanted to monopolize Alexis de Granville.

Alexis, Kate noticed, was adept at skirmishing with the various females who made forays at him. He flitted from one to the other, dodged the Honourable Dinkles and Mama Dinkle, and spent most of his time with a woman named Carolina Beechwith. Everyone seemed to like Mrs. Beechwith, but Kate hadn't had a chance to talk to her.

As it happened, she was saved from having to talk much at dinner anyway, because everyone wanted to hear about the Crimea from the Earl of Cardigan. Kate listened to the man's recounting of the charge of the Light Brigade while keeping an eye on Val. To her surprise, the young man kept his gaze on his plate during the whole story. When it was over, she began to relax her vigilance, but Val lifted his eyes and looked at the earl. If there was an opening into hell, it was in those blue eyes. They held lakes of fire, the rack, howling fiends, and the lust for blood. Kate put her hand over Val's. He blinked and lowered his gaze.

"Don't worry," he said. "Alexis has set a watch on me. Colonel Maude and Sir Humphrey. I can't get near Cardigan without one of them pulling me away."

"Good," Kate said.

"And since the guests have arrived, he's been surrounded by women. I don't understand it. They love him.

Always have. Did you know he's been cited for criminal conversation?"

"What's that?"

Val laughed without humor. "That, Miss Grey, is what the legal man calls seducing another man's wife."

Kate took in the simpering faces of the women near the earl and lifted an eyebrow.

"Yes," Val said. "It almost rivals the de Granville charm, doesn't it?"

She switched her attention to the head of the table where Alexis held court. It was disgusting, she thought. Lady Churchill-Smythe kept leaning toward him and hanging on his words as though he were the Archbishop of Canterbury. Mademoiselle St.-Germain cast hot-wax looks at him that he returned with composure, and the Countess of Landsborne actually touched him. Kate was glad when it was time for the ladies to remove themselves. If she had to watch those women cavort in front of Alexis much longer, she would need a glass of port herself.

The ladies' retreat was held in the Red Drawing Room. Kate stepped into the chamber and at once felt as if she needed a pair of spectacles with dark lenses. The room got its name from its red lacquer paneling. Finished with gilding, draped with red Italian silk curtains, furnished with red damask couches and chairs, the place was as much a shock as the gold dining room. She walked a circuit of the room with her mother. Sophia's step was quick and her smile bright with contentment at being among what she called the Cream of Society. Kate couldn't adjust to the red room.

Facing a mirror that reflected the hue of her surroundings at her, she winced and spoke to her mother.

"Think somebody likes red?"

"Kate, hush. This room is almost three hundred years old. That painting is a Raphael, and Lady Juliana told me that table once belonged to Marie Antoinette."

"It's red."

Sophia twisted the lid on her scent bottle. "Oh, Kate, do be quiet."

Kate submitted to being tugged into a corner beside a china cabinet. "You must be on your best behavior. Lady Juliana is furious."

"But I haven't done anything. Lately."

"Not at you. At the marquess. He brought Her."

"Her?" Kate said.

"Her," Sophia repeated in a frightened-doe voice. She nodded in the direction of the three Dinkles.

"The Dinkles?"

"No, Her."

Following the direction of Sophia's gaze, Kate spied the generously endowed figure of Carolina Beechwith.

"Mrs. Beechwith?" Kate's hands and feet lost sensation, and it seemed as if she were looking at the room through a window.

"Yes, that Beechwith person." Sophia edged closer to Kate and turned her back to the woman they were discussing. "She's his, his . . . And he brought her to his home. It's an insult. You mustn't speak to her. Avoid being in her presence."

"Criminal conversation," Kate said.

Her mother kept talking, but Kate didn't listen. For the first time, she really looked at Carolina Beechwith. The woman had thick chestnut hair that shone in any light, and her lips were naturally pink. She had a squarish face, but her eyes were so large and round that one didn't notice. And those eyes were almost night-sky blue, the kind of blue that made one think of tropical birds and lapis lazuli.

Mrs. Beechwith and Alexis. Mrs. Beechwith lived in Heppleton. Mrs. Beechwith had an elderly husband, an absent husband. Mrs. Beechwith also had Alexis.

Kate felt sick. Her corset was too tight. The food she'd

eaten was stuck somewhere between her throat and her waist, and it was going to come back up.

She even had taste, this Mrs. Beechwith. She wore a gown of pearl gray satin with none of the fussy tucks, frills, or tiers worn by the other women in the room. Worst of all, she was clever enough to wear a more modest neckline. Kate looked down at her own chest. Hannah had insisted that shoulders and bosom were displayed at evening affairs. "I feel like one of the figures on the prow of a ship," Kate had muttered.

Mrs. Beechwith had the right idea. If everyone else went about jiggling and bouncing, one would gain more notice by covering up.

"Mama, did you say Lord Alexis invited Mrs. Beechwith? When?"

"I don't know," Sophia said. "But Lady Juliana didn't know she was coming until yesterday."

"Yesterday." That was the day he'd come to her in the Clocktower. The day she almost let him—

The men burst into the room, their tenor voices cutting across the prevailing soprano hum. Black tailcoats streamed forth, and Kate found herself surrounded by three of them. Lady Juliana introduced a scholar from Cambridge, a clergyman, and a lord. Juliana remarked on Kate's interest in literature, and three pairs of eyes lit up. To her surprise, she was drawn into a real conversation. It was regrettable she was too hurt to enjoy her first taste of popularity.

There was nothing to be done but talk. So she talked about Blake and Dryden and Wordsworth, about Thackeray and Trollope and Dickens. All the while she watched Alexis de Granville work his way from Dinkle to Dinkle to Dinkle to Countess to Mademoiselle, all with the intent of cornering Mrs. Beechwith.

Her nausea returned. Because she was watching the lovers, she was startled when the Earl of Cardigan swept down on her little group and sent the scholar, the clergy-man, and the lord skittering away. The earl offered his arm and escorted her to a settee. With her permission, he sat beside her. Kate wondered if he'd chosen the small sofa on purpose. There was room only for the two of them. Hellfire. She couldn't see Alexis and that woman from where she was sitting.

She fished in the pocket of her skirt for her black-bordered handkerchief. Twisting it in her hands, she wished it was Alexis de Granville's beautiful neck.

The Earl of Cardigan bent toward her and touched her skirt with one finger.

"What?" Kate asked.

"I asked if you have been avoiding me, Miss Grey."

"Of course not, my lord."

"I thought perhaps you didn't care for soldiers."

She dragged her attention back to the earl. "I don't have a thing against soldiers."

Cardigan's glance oozed down her face and took a sleigh ride all the way to her feet. Kate had to stop herself from hunching her shoulders forward to make her chest seem smaller. Annoyed with herself for acting like a schoolgirl, she deliberately smiled at the earl. He had an elegantly trimmed mustache and soft curls at his temples.

"Miss Grey, I hope you will allow me to spend more time with you. If I may be permitted a small liberty, I would like to say that your beauty makes me wish I had been born an American gentleman instead of an English-man."

Never having had much practice at accepting compli-ments, Kate had no idea how to reply. At least she didn't blush and giggle. She settled for a calm thank you. The admiring inclination of his head told her she had made the right decision.

Success with one compliment evidently called for more of the same in the earl's estimation. The blandishments kept coming. Kate began to feel like a rum cake being doused with glaze. Discomfort gave way to astonishment when the man captured her hand and kissed it, then replaced it in her lap so quickly, she almost thought she'd imagined the touch. At the same moment she saw a movement across the room and was transfixed by the wrathful gaze of the Marquess of Richfield.

He was angry. What did he have to be angry with her about? The snake. He'd taken up a post beside the liquor cabinet and was watching her and the earl. She stiffened her spine and favored Cardigan with another smile. When she next looked at the liquor cabinet, Alexis was handing a glass of wine to Mrs. Beechwith.

"Hellfire," Kate said.

The earl laughed. "What an expression."

She was saved by Lady Juliana. They were all to ascend to the curtain wall of the castle to view the surrounding landscape by moonlight.

The earl offered his arm. Kate took it, and they followed Lady Juliana with the rest of her guests. As they donned mantles and capes and progressed like lords and ladies in a court procession, the earl leaned down and whispered in her ear.

"I confess, Miss Grey. It isn't the landscape I long to see by moonlight."

Chapter Ten

Alexis had thought himself clever to seek the company of the dean and old Lady Wickworth. He'd maneuvered it so that the three of them were in step behind Cardigan and Kate. The bastard wasn't going to seduce that particular female, even if Alexis had to throw him in the dungeon.

From the moment he'd seen Cardigan approach Kate, Alexis had been thinking of his dungeon. When the earl's lips had touched her hand, Alexis had felt his composure warp like a portcullis assaulted by a battering ram. She had smiled at the slavering animal, and Alexis had begun to review the various torture instruments gathering mold in the dungeon.

Thumb screws were too tame. There was the iron chair used to lower a victim gradually into a blazing fire.

The earl put an arm around Kate's

waist to help her up the stairs to the curtain walk.

He could use the boots. High leather boots were put on a victim's feet, then boiling water was poured over them. It penetrated the leather and ate away the flesh. Still too tame. Anyway, Cardigan's feet were too small.

He searched his memory. Hot pitch. Hanging with two-hundred-and-fifty-pound weights. Now that sounded promising.

Cardigan whispered something in Kate's ear that made her laugh.

He could throw the bastard in the oubliette—that small, black hole in the bedrock below the dungeon, where there was only enough room for a man to lie down. After the hue and cry of the search died down, he could put Cardigan to the rack.

Lost in his fantasy, Alexis forgot to keep up with the dean and Lady Wickworth. He emerged upon the curtain wall in a rage that would have gratified the savage Phillipe de Granville. Cardigan had attached himself tick-wise to Kate and wasn't letting go. Alexis veered around a countess and the master of the local hunt, aiming at his intended victim, and was brought up short by a covey of Dinkles.

"Ooooooo, my lord, do point out the best views for us," said Miss Cherry Dinkle.

Alexis started to retreat, but he was surrounded. In a trice there were Dinkles to the left and right of him, and one—a twin—hovered in front of him twirling her bouquet. Georgiana Dinkle filched his right arm and wouldn't give it back. Merry Dinkle blocked his escape route to the left by dropping her bouquet so that he had to pick it up for her. As he righted himself, his free arm was captured. There was nothing for it but complete surrender.

He became a guide. He pointed out the constellations, the mountains on the moon, the distant hills, and suffered paroxysms of irritation at the gushing ooooo's and aaaaah's his statements elicited. If he hadn't tried at the same time to keep an eye on Kate and her stalker, he wouldn't have been duped into showing Miss Georgiana Dinkle the Watch Tower.

They entered the tower from the wall walk. A priest at the funeral of a child couldn't have been more somber as he conducted the young lady down the winding stone stairs. He showed her munitions rooms, guardrooms, storerooms, but the Dinkle seemed to be interested in a bedchamber.

Shoving open an oak door, she rushed into a fifteenth-century room outfitted with dark paneling, Tudor period portraits, and a small bed.

"Oh, how clever of you to have a little room like this so near, Lord Alexis."

The self-preserving instinct that should have been working all along suddenly resurfaced. Since he was fifteen he'd been the object of feminine traps. He could smell one. In this case, it smelled of lemon verbena. It was a skinny Dinkle with fingers like the legs of a spider and the flat body of a ten-year-old boy.

He deserved the breach of promise suit he saw galloping toward him, and cursed himself for his preoccupation with Kate.

Alexis was standing in front of a clothes chest at the foot of the little bed. The Dinkle had positioned herself between him and the door. It was half closed. Through it he could hear a faint metallic whine, the call of Mama Dinkle. Alexis took a step toward the door. A musket ball in satin and lace whizzed at him. He stumbled backward onto the clothes chest with Miss Georgiana Dinkle on top of him.

"Oh, my lord, oh, oh, oh, oh." The oh's got louder and louder. Mama Dinkle's bleating drew near.

Spitting out a mouthful of petticoat, Alexis pawed his way out from under yards of satin. "Not again."

"Oh no, oh no! Please, my lord!"

Alexis heaved the girl to the side and jumped up. Miss Dinkle landed on the floor with her skirts over her head. Alexis bounded out of the room. He scrambled back up to the wall walk, but heard Mama Dinkle howling nearby.

"Georgiana, my deeeeeeeeear, where are you?"

Alexis raced across the walk in the opposite direction from which the Dinkle horn blew. The terriers had his scent, but this rat wasn't going to get caught. The entrance to another tower loomed in front of him. He threw himself into the doorway and down the stairs, heedless of the twists and turns. His long legs took the steps three at a time. He grasped a wooden rail and swung himself down and around a sharp bend, head low. He hit something, something hard. He heard a little cry as he fell back holding his forehead with one hand. A little figure in black collapsed at his feet on the stairs just below him and moaned.

"Kate."

"Uuuuuh."

He grasped her arms and lifted her. She had a hand on her forehead just as he did. They both slumped against the wall and held their heads. Alexis was the first to recover, and he helped her stand upright. Once on her feet, she made a fist and poked him in the stomach.

"You hurt me." She twisted around and peered back down the stairs. "He's coming!"

"Who?"

"The earl. I've got to hide."

"Me too." He grabbed Kate's hand and plunged back up the staircase. At the top, he stopped and flattened himself against the wall. Inching around the corner, he made sure the wall walk was clear before hauling Kate after him.

He ran back the way he'd come. The Dinkle Hunt would be spreading out in search of him.

In the Watch Tower, near the bedchamber of the Dinkle trap, was a storeroom. Alexis darted into it, dragging his accomplice. When he released her hand, she closed the door and listened at it.

The room was filled with crates of tools, chains, and boxes of nails. Alexis shoved a few of these aside and knelt on the floor. Using an iron rod from one of the crates, he lifted a flagstone and hauled it back to reveal a black hole. He stuck one leg into the hole, and his foot met a step. Glancing back at Kate, he held out his hand.

"This is a way outside."

"Are you sure?"

He caught her wrist and pulled. She sailed toward him, and he lifted her down into the hole. He could hear her breathing as she waited for him to replace the flagstone. Then, in complete darkness, he edged his way down the stairs with her clinging to his arm.

"I hate this," she said.

"When I was a boy, I used to hide in here to escape my tutors. It's most convenient."

At last they gained the foot of the stairs. Alexis's groping hands found the door and shoved it open. Peeking out, he saw the expanse of courtyard lawn outlined in silver moonlight. He slipped outside, pulling Kate behind him. Above their heads he heard a male voice furtively call Kate's name.

"Damn and blast," Alexis said. "Come on."

He gripped Kate's hand again and ran. Keeping close to the wall, they shimmied around two towers, then ran for the farthest structure in the castle, the keep. Once inside, they both leaned against a wall and breathed.

Alexis recovered first. "The keep's under reconstruction. They won't think to look here."

"Did you know that one of your strides is equal to more than two of mine?" Kate asked.

He smiled into the darkness at the little puffs that kept coming from her direction.

"Next time I'll go slower. There are lamps in here somewhere."

He felt his way around until he encountered a table. He lit one of the lamps on it and came back to Kate.

She was still leaning against the wall beside the door, and Alexis came to an abrupt stop when he held the light near her. Her hair tumbled about her face and shoulders in fiery destruction. There was a bruise on her throat, and the sleeve of her gown was torn.

Drawing near, he touched a curl. She shied away from his touch.

"I will kill him," Alexis said.

"Nonsense."

"You don't realize what this means. I have to call him out."

She tried to pull her sleeve back up to her shoulder, but it kept falling. "I've already taken care of the earl."

"What did you do?"

"I punched him in the nose."

Alexis lowered the lamp so that he held it in both hands. "Dear Lord in heaven."

"My hand hurts."

"Let me see."

He drew her to the table. Setting the lamp down, he took Kate's hand in his and examined it. The skin over the knuckles and fingers was red, and the flesh was swollen.

"Can you move your fingers?" he asked. The small digits wiggled at him. "Your hand will be sore for a few days, but it's not broken. We must soak it in cold water. While you're doing that, I'll deal with Cardigan."

"Deal with Mrs. Beechwith," she said. "I can put Cardigan in his place."

"How did—You shouldn't know—*Nom de Dieu*. The extent to which you are informed about my affairs is most improper, Miss Grey. No wonder you're unmarried. A woman of breeding at least pretends ignorance. Look at Hannah."

Alexis would have gone on, but Kate gave him one of her lower-than-a-worm-at-my-feet looks and sneered at him.

"Ha!"

"What do you mean 'Ha'?"

"I mean 'Ha.' Lady Hannah refers to table legs as 'limbs' and covers them with little skirts because she thinks they're obscene. She pretends women don't have bodily functions or those 'limbs' she's so disgusted with."

A long curl of hair had spilled down her neck and across a white expanse of chest to nestle above the space between her breasts. Alexis didn't know which made him more angry, her scorn of poor Hannah or the fact that he couldn't touch that curl.

"We were discussing why you let Cardigan undress you," he said.

Alexis had imagined Kate losing control many times since he met her. Standing on erupting volcanoes, pirouetting on the edge of a cliff, and similar brushes with death came to mind. He was fooled when she made a little hissing sound and planted herself across the table from him, her hands braced on its surface.

"Let me explain something to you," she said. "I don't like you. You seduced my cousin. She was flighty, and maybe she did think too much of your position, but she had a heart bigger than California. If you hadn't insisted on coming to her that night, maybe she wouldn't have fallen asleep and knocked that candle over and died."

"What?"

"I'm not finished. She's dead, and now you're trying to seduce me. I may not be a proper Lady, but I'm not a fool.

You flutter about like a butterfly, lighting on a tulip, dipping into a rose, landing on an iris. Don't try landing on me, sir. I'll rip your wings off."

Alexis was still stalled on her first remark. "I wasn't with Ophelia the night of the fire."

"Uh-huh."

"Miss Grey." He drew himself up to his full height. "No one has ever had cause to doubt my word."

"Well la-di-da. Get used to it."

"Don't wear such a pleased look. It isn't me whose word is about to be doubted."

"What are you talking about?"

He folded his arms and smiled at her. She was glaring at him with her hands on her hips, which gave him an excellent view of her figure.

"You've been gone from the others for a long time. So have I. The Dinkles couldn't have planned a better method by which to compromise themselves." He strolled around the table and edged up close to her. "The whole castle knows we're missing by now, and you can bet one of your precious gold mines they'll never believe that you and I spent the whole time talking."

To make his point he captured that enticing curl. The backs of his fingers brushed against her breast, and she jumped away from him. He kept hold of the curl until she yanked it out of his fingers. He grinned at her in triumph.

She snatched victory from him. "Sorry to disappoint you. I don't care if they think I entertained a whole regiment."

"You'll be put out of society."

"Never wanted to be in it."

He stepped closer to her. "You'll be ruined."

"Dresses get ruined, cakes get ruined, sometimes cities crumble into ruins, but women survive, my lord. You'll be comforted to know I can live quite happily knowing that half of England thinks I'm a Fallen Woman."

He cursed in a whisper, thinking quickly. " 'De l'audace, encore de l'audace, et toujours de l'audace,' ma petite. You may not care, but your mother does. If you keep on as you are, she'll never kiss hands at court."

The understanding that swept across her face made up for the shocks she'd dealt him. Almost. He couldn't stand the unhappiness in her eyes.

"There's nothing I can do," she said. "You said yourself it's too late."

He couldn't resist taking her hand, but he was surprised she let him keep it. She probably hadn't noticed.

"I'm sorry," he said. "I should have warned Cardigan off, but I was detained."

"The Dinkles."

"They laid a trap. God, I'm weary of fighting. Mademoiselle St.-Germain tried to twist me into a ring and put me on her finger. In French, of course. She thought I'd be more defenseless in a foreign language. During the war one of the infantry commanders' daughters put herself in my tent. We were in the Crimea, for the love of God." He groaned. "There have been too many women in my life."

Kate heaved a long sigh. "The earl came after me even though his nose was bleeding. If he's ruined me, I'm going to ruin his face."

They studied the lamp in companionable misery. Alexis suddenly laughed. Kate scowled at him as he turned to her and clasped her by the shoulders.

"Little savage, would you like a great big helping of revenge?"

"I'd love it."

Stepping back, he bowed over her hand, then held it to his heart while gazing into her eyes in an enraptured manner.

"Then do me the honor of betrothing yourself to me, my dearest."

The little hand was snatched from him. "Toad."

"Only for a few months. For protection, for your reputation." Her hands were on her hips again. "For your mother."

"For Mama?" Kate's shoulders drooped. She rubbed her head where his had bumped it. "A few days."

"Months."

"Days."

"Three months."

"Weeks."

"Think of Mama," Alexis said. "It's only a temporary arrangement."

"Six weeks."

"I bow to your wishes."

"Somehow I find that hard to believe. What are you doing?"

Alexis had taken advantage of her distraction to pull her into his arms. He put his hand on the back of her head and lowered his mouth to hers. Before he kissed her he spoke.

"I'm sealing our bargain."

The kiss went straight to his groin. He'd been trying so hard to keep from watching her all evening, only casting surreptitious glances at her face and breasts. Each furtive view whetted his appetite, churned his gut. He was done with looking. His hand belonged on her breast, so he put it there.

Before he could understand what was happening, the soft mouth and breast were torn from him. He felt as if someone had ripped the skin from his body. He fell back from her to lean against the table. After a moment he opened his eyes, aware that he'd been sprawled there with his eyes closed, heaving and flushed like a randy school-boy. To cover his lapse, he grinned at Kate. She had retreated to the shadows beyond the glow of the lamp, and he couldn't see much of her.

"I'll take you back to the castle," he said. "You can't join the others looking like that."

She tried to push her hair back into place, but with no success. "I know."

"I'll have to tell them why we've been gone so long. I'll say you're so overcome that you've retired."

"Me? Overcome?"

He narrowed his eyes. "I take it you're not overcome. Pretend. As a courtesy to me. You can't go about treating me as if I had leprosy if we're engaged."

He gave her his arm, and she took it with all the enthusiasm of a child facing a tooth extraction. *By the Queen's ancestors,* he swore silently. He still ached with sexual tension, and she was as frigid as a mountain lake.

They emerged from the keep, and Alexis covered the hand that rested on his arm so she couldn't withdraw it. He had six weeks, perhaps longer. Before those six weeks were over, his little savage was going to forget railroads and gold mines, Mr. Poggs, and even Mama. When he was finished with her, she would cling to him the way Carolina Beechwith did. She would wait for him, study his moods and his pleasure. Especially his pleasure.

It was seldom that he bothered to exert the power he knew he possessed, for using it meant enduring tiresome infatuations, as had happened with Carolina. However, enslaving Kate Grey wouldn't be the same. She was as quick as a hornet and so unconsciously sensual. He wanted her to desire him. After all, it was only fair for her to suffer as he was suffering.

Chapter Eleven

Kate untied the ribbons of her bonnet and lifted it from her head. She hoped the action would convince the physician who blocked her way that she wasn't going to leave. She'd tracked the marquess to the Dower House, and no pompous old grouse was going to stop her from seeing him.

"You might as well tell me where he is," she said. She put her bonnet on a side table and tossed her gloves into it. "I'll go through every room if I have to."

"Miss Grey, the marquess is with a sick man who may not live through the day."

"Oh."

Having satisfied himself that she was properly chastened, the man left her standing in the entryway and disappeared up the main staircase. Kate hesitated while two doctor's assistants walked by and a maid dusted the banister. She'd

come to light into Alexis de Granville for exposing her to
the ire of thwarted females. There wasn't a woman in the
castle—except Mama and Lady Juliana—who didn't hate
her after Alexis's announcement last night. Mrs. Beechwith hadn't come out of her room all day, and one of the
Dinkles had tried to kick her. The kick was what had sent
her looking for de Granville.

He was with a dying man, though. Somehow she'd gotten the idea that the marquess ran the Dower House from
afar. It never occurred to her that he would interest himself in the individuals under his roof. Kate glanced casually
at the maid. The girl was bent over a railing, dust cloth
rubbing madly. There wasn't anyone else around.

On tiptoe, Kate sidled past the stairs and cracked open
a pair of sliding doors. Before her lay a room lined with
windows and full of single beds. Set close together, each
bed contained a patient. Several women dressed in black
with white aprons moved among the rows. Kate slipped
inside the room, closed the doors, and bumped into a
woman carrying a stack of linens.

"Excuse me," Kate said in a low voice. "The marquess?"

The woman craned her neck to see over the linens.
"Oh, Miss Grey. His lordship is in that alcove."

Following the woman's nod, Kate spotted a recess at
the back of the room. She thanked the woman and approached the alcove slowly. Most of the men she passed
were asleep. Some tossed and turned; some watched her
with curious eyes. She smiled at them and crept close to
the single bed set in the alcove.

The occupant was young, hardly more than a boy. His
face was the color of dough and beaded with perspiration.
Where his legs should have been, there was only sheet. He
lay still with his eyes shut, but he was whispering to the
marquess. Alexis was sitting on the bed beside the young
soldier, on the side opposite Kate. His head was in profile

to her, and she could see that he was having to lean close to hear what was said.

She wedged herself behind one of the supports of the archway that separated the alcove from the rest of the room. The soldier's voice was weak, and his breathing uneven.

"My wife and the baby."

"You shouldn't have sent them away," Alexis said.

"Didn't want her to see me like this. Half a man. Less than half." The soldier's eyes flew open. He drew in a wheezing breath that ended on a cough. Alexis helped him sip water from a glass. "Didn't want her to see me go, my lord. Didn't want her to know I'm afraid."

"You're not going anywhere," Alexis said.

He was interrupted by a spasm of coughing that would have doubled the soldier over if he'd been strong enough to move. Alexis braced the young man while holding a cloth to his mouth. When he withdrew it, blood stained the white linen. Alexis tossed the cloth aside and called the soldier's name as the patient collapsed in his arms.

A thin hand grasped Alexis's jacket and attempted to pull the marquess closer. Alexis bent down to hear the whispers of the dying man. The hand that was twisted in the lapel of his coat suddenly became heavy. The whispering lips stilled.

Kate almost went to the two men, but couldn't make herself take a step. Alexis remained bent over the dead man, bound to him by that leash of a hand.

" 'If I take the wings of the morning,' " he whispered, " 'and remain in the uttermost parts of the sea; / Even there also shall thy hand lead me, and thy right hand shall hold me.' "

Drawn by the catch in his voice, Kate emerged from her hiding place. Alexis made no sign that he knew she approached. When she gently disengaged the dead man's hand from his jacket, he said nothing. She put her hands on his shoulders. Still no reaction. Kate called to a nurse. After asking the woman to take care of the dead man, she grasped Alexis's arm and shook it. He looked up at her without surprise. There was a pale line about his mouth, and his eyes were bright with tears held at bay.

He smiled at her. "I don't quite think that our allies, those Turkish sons of Allah, are worth it. Do you?"

"Hellfire," Kate said. She pulled at his arm, and he stood up. Relying on his gentleman's instincts, she put her hand on his arm. Immediately the arm came up to support her, his other hand covered hers, and he began to walk. They were crossing the lawn when he stopped.

"What are you doing here?"

He had recovered.

"I . . . uh . . . the antiques dealer and the draper will be here soon to take orders for Maitland House. I thought since your men will be living there, you might want to have a say in what is ordered."

"I can't. I'm going for a ride."

"A ride?"

"Yes. Right now. I'm going to ride."

She perused his rigid body and expressionless face. "You mean one of your gazelle-chased-by-a-lion rides?"

"I mean a ride, Kate."

"Why do you—"

"Where are your bonnet and your gloves?" He shook a finger at her. "You're engaged to me now. I won't have you tripping about without the proper dress."

"Is that so?"

"Definitely so. And another thing. You're going to have to stop deliberately shocking my family and friends with your bluestocking opinions and mannish ways. You're stuck with the form of a woman, Miss Grey. Leave the business of being a man to those equipped for it."

She was about to take a slice out of his gut with her tongue, when she noticed the way he held his body, so stiffly, and how his face was drained of color. Still, her irritation got the better of her.

"I know you're upset about that boy dying, but you don't have to try to make yourself feel better by insulting me."

"Damn."

He jerked his arm free and turned away. With his back to her, she couldn't tell what he was thinking. He veered around and snatched her up in his arms before she could react. He kissed her. It was a hard, furious kiss, and he lifted her off her feet. As abruptly as he began, he dropped her back to the ground and cursed again.

"Unless you want to risk me dragging you back to the Clocktower, I suggest you allow me to go on my ride."

Turning on his heel, Alexis stalked off. Kate watched him go, then returned to the Dower House to get her bonnet and gloves. Her lips still tingled from the kiss. Hellfire. He'd made her want him with little effort on his part, and she already knew what happened when he took the trouble to exert himself.

She should have gone with him to the Clocktower. She wanted to, but she couldn't. She'd only just discovered that she liked the man. She wasn't used to liking him. She was used to thinking of him as half snake, half satyr. And what was worse, she was very much afraid that she had too many feelings for Alexis de Granville. Disturbing feelings, some of them were. Like desire. She wanted to undress him and press and squeeze his muscles, run her hands over his smooth skin.

The desire had been tolerable as long as she had disliked him, but he was shedding his snake's skin bit by bit. He was a loving friend to Val. He cared for the suffering of others. He was intelligent, courageous, beautiful, kind. Maybe kind wasn't the right word. Compassionate.

And he hadn't been with Ophelia the night of the fire. Alexis de Granville might be annoyingly domineering, but she was sure he wasn't a liar. Besides, she had since learned that the marquess had stayed up late talking to Fulke on the night of her cousin's death. Altogether, it was most frustrating to find that one's enemy possessed virtues.

He was a rich man. He could have financed his soldiers' home through underlings and not involved himself personally at all. He could have spared himself constant pain. Instead he gave his own strength, and after seeing him with the young soldier, she believed he gave too much of it.

"I'm going mad," she muttered. "One kiss and I'm as daft as a whiskey-drunk billy goat."

She tied her bonnet ribbons, tugged on her gloves, and set out for the castle. He'd be furious if she sent a groom to follow him. Not that any of the staff would dare such a thing. Why did he do it, ride so recklessly? He was bothered by something, hounded. The strangest events would send him hurtling across fields and jumping hedgerows. A fight with Fulke was a sure harbinger of one of Alexis's rides. Kate listened to the tap of her shoes on the drawbridge while she thought. The more she thought, the less she could make sense of Alexis de Granville. This being in love was more difficult than translating Latin.

She stumbled over her own feet, then stopped, lifting her gaze to the teeth of the portcullis. In love?

In love. Hellfire. What was she thinking?

In love. With that aristocratic, magical irritant.

There were no grammar texts on love. No tutor could give her a set of mathematical theorems that would prove whether she was in love or not. Kate thought about all the stories she'd read about love while she ran up the steps of the castle.

Romeo and Juliet was little help. Infatuation at first sight didn't work, as she well knew. As a matter of fact, too many famous lovers died. Anthony and Cleopatra, Hamlet and Ophelia. Best not pursue the thought.

She was once more removing her bonnet, pondering love, when a man's voice distracted her.

"I beg your pardon, Miss Grey."

It was the Richfield butler, Hazelton. He always managed to disconcert her. Perhaps it was because he more resembled a cabinet minister than a servant. She smiled and nodded to him.

"Two gentlemen have called," he said. "A Mr. Mungo Fettiplace and a Mr. Osbert Snead."

"Drat. It's the draper and the antiques man. Where are they?"

"In the small drawing room, miss."

The interview with Fettiplace and Snead lasted until almost teatime. Most of it was spent curbing the desire of both men to stuff Maitland House with unnecessary accoutrements. At last she followed the two to the door of the drawing room, watching them struggle under the weight of samples and sketchbooks.

"And remember," she said, "not one antler on the walls. No stuffed birds under glass. No doilies. No skirts on table legs. I want lots of light, a few paintings, which I will pick out, some mirrors." She raised her voice as they turned a corner. "And no geegaws."

Fettiplace swiveled his head around to her. "Geegaws, miss?"

"Feather flowers, wax fruit, seaweed pictures. Dust collectors, Mr. Fettiplace."

"As you wish, Miss Grey."

Fettiplace vanished, and Kate released the giggle she'd been holding back.

"You have style, Kate. Simplicity and elegance are to be commended."

Kate put her fingers to her lips to suppress her laughter. "I didn't see you, Lady Juliana."

Alexis's mother approached with her entourage of canine and feline retainers. The marmoset bounded around a corner and skittered into the drawing room.

"I must speak with you, my dear."

Juliana closed the drawing room door after Kate and sat beside her on a sofa. "This engagement."

"I know you're surprised. I'm not English, and I wasn't born into a noble family."

Juliana patted Kate on the shoulder. "Hush, child. I have a great affection for you. And I thought we agreed about my son. That's why I can't understand this engagement."

"I guess I changed my mind."

"You shouldn't." Juliana's gaze slid away from Kate. It flitted from object to object around the room as she talked. "Your original opinion was the correct one, but I see you've been exposed to Alexis's corrupting ways for too long. That's why I must tell you the truth."

"Yes?"

Juliana stared down at her hands. They were clasped tightly in her lap, and she rocked back and forth.

"My son is worse than Cain."

Kate shook her head, but Juliana wasn't looking at her.

"Do you know why my son rides as if the hounds of hell were after him? It's because they are. They have been since he murdered my husband and daughter when he was twelve."

"No."

Juliana's rocking speeded up. "It's true, though it was never proved. He fought with both of them, then went out and strung fishing line between two trees across the path they were to race on. Thalia's head was severed from her body, and my husband's horse fell and crushed him. The only person to see it was Alexis—because he was the one who laid the trap." Juliana stopped rocking and lifted tortured eyes to Kate. "He says he doesn't remember what happened before they died, or what happened after. Nothing could be proved, and the authorities weren't about to arrest a boy who had suddenly inherited the title and one of the greatest fortunes in England."

It was impossible, Kate thought. Compassionate, phoenixlike Alexis a murderer? She tried to picture the man she knew as a monster child who could plan such a horror. Ridiculous. The act went against his nature.

"But nothing was ever proved," she said. "Someone may have put the line there for another reason, or someone else might have wanted your husband dead."

Kate's words petered out under the unblinking stare of the woman beside her. Juliana went on as if Kate hadn't spoken.

"My husband was my reason for being on this earth. When he died, I became a living wraith. Alexis may not remember what happened, but he still believes he did the murders. I think he went into the cavalry hoping to die. And then there are the women."

"Lady Juliana, I don't think you should be telling me this."

"There was a mistress. When he was quite young. She vanished, and no one knows where she went. Another died in a carriage accident that wasn't an accident. The wife of a general in the Horse Guards became his mistress two years ago. It was well known that she liked young, handsome cavalry officers. She especially liked them in her stables at night, on the floor of a stall, my dear. One morning she was found in a stall with her head kicked in by a stallion."

"Stop." Kate sprang up and faced Alexis's mother. "It's impossible. Alexis couldn't have done all those things."

"He is evil, my dear. And clever. Nobody believes me. I could never convince Fulke either, but I must make you understand. It is dangerous for you to fall into his hands."

"You say Lord Fulke believes the marquess innocent,"

Kate said. "Lord Fulke is one of the most Christian men I've ever met. If he's sure Alexis is guiltless, I am too."

Juliana rose. She picked up her marmoset. Two cats and three poodles scurried to the door. "You're shocked. I'll give you time to adjust, my child. The good Lord knows I've had long enough to get used to the idea."

The dowager left her alone, and Kate kicked at the rug that lay beneath the sofa.

Absurd. Impossible. If he liked killing, he would have loved the war. Nobody harbors that much evil in his soul without giving some clue to it in his behavior.

Not satisfied with kicking the rug, she aimed at the sofa. The tip of her boot hit a cushion. Juliana must have conceived this terrible idea long ago, and it had corrupted her mind. After all, the woman was a bit strange. All those pets. No telling how many there were. And sometimes forgetting who was dead and who wasn't. Then there was her sleeplessness. Mama had learned that the woman lay on a couch most nights while a maid read to her. Sometimes she would wander from room to room while the maid followed, still reading, until it was time to dress in the morning.

No, Juliana's opinions weren't to be relied upon. The woman needed someone to blame for her misery, and it seemed that the person she wanted to blame was her own son. No wonder Alexis went on death rides.

Tea was a disaster. Alexis wasn't present, and Kate was thankful for that. Juliana kept giving her sorrowful looks. Fulke was as testy as a wet cat; he didn't approve of her engagement to his blue-blooded cousin either. The Dinkles clustered together, feeding their shared hate, and Mrs. Beechwith kept sniffling into her handkerchief.

Val scowled at the Earl of Cardigan from various observation points in the room. Cardigan eyed Kate as if he were an osprey and she were a fish he'd like to catch in his talons. He was furious with her and wanted revenge. This knowledge made her even more uncomfortable than she was already.

She took advantage of a maneuver by Mademoiselle St.-Germain that distracted the earl and slipped out of the drawing room. Unfortunately, he still followed her. She sped on ahead of him and took refuge in the great hall. To her chagrin, Cardigan opened the doors not a minute after she shut them. He came at her at a slow, menacing walk.

"Uncivilized witch," he said.

"Now, earl." She started walking backward and tried not to smile at Cardigan's swollen nose.

"I had to tell everyone I fell down the stairs."

Kate put a long table between herself and the earl. "Better to be known as clumsy than tell everyone I punched you?"

"You want mastering, and I'm going to do it."

He vaulted over the table to land beside her and grabbed her arm.

"Let go of me, you varmint."

"An uncivilized vocabulary as well." He pulled her close. "You ran away from me and accepted de Granville's suit. Has he tamed you? I think not from the way you're squirming. I'll do him a favor and best you before you're married."

As she struggled to keep her temper under control, Kate stopped trying to get away from the earl. He was much too strong for her to oppose him directly. Letting her body go limp, she allowed him to pull her closer. She read surprise on his features that soon gave way to lust. Cardigan lowered his mouth to her neck and fastened one hand on her buttock. While he nibbled at her flesh, Kate lifted her skirts and fumbled for the knife she'd decided to wear since their first disagreement.

Cardigan was groping at her breast when she pulled

the knife free from the sheath strapped to her calf. She jumped away from him, and before he could recover, she shoved the knife in front of his eyes. He gawked at the blade and then at her.

"Leave me alone, earl, or you're going to find out just how uncivilized I can be."

"By God, you mean it," he said. "Damn me."

It wasn't fair, she thought, staring at him. He wasn't furious; he was intrigued. She lowered the knife in astonishment as the earl began to smile. He took her hand and bowed over it.

"I cry quits for now," he said. He straightened and put his fingers under her chin. "I do so love the chase. Everyone will tell you I'm the best hunter in England. You've made me take quite a few jumps already, and one fall. But I'll run you to ground and enjoy doing it."

Before she knew what he was about, Cardigan kissed her lightly on the lips and disappeared. Kate stared after him, debating as to whether the man had brain fever or not. Eventually she consigned him to the ranks of the incomprehensible, along with woman-starved miners, drunk gamblers, and Alexis de Granville.

As she was still standing there, she heard the voices of Cardigan, Juliana, and her mother. She replaced her knife in its sheath. Unwilling to meet the earl again, she tiptoed across the hall, trying not to let her steps echo as they had when Lady Juliana had found her there. It was quite a walk down the length of the hall, and it seemed as if the room were inhabited because of the numerous suits of armor that stood against the walls. At the end of the hall stood the parade armor of a sixteenth-century Alexis Phillipe de Granville. It was damascened with gold and silver, all embossed and sculptured, and as she stared at it, Kate forgot about the earl.

She touched a raised figure of a beast done in silver and gold that projected out below the left flange. She was measuring her hand against one of the gauntlets when she heard a door slam. Glancing around, she saw Fulke approaching her, and he still looked as though he'd caught someone playing cards in church. Positioning himself between her and the nearest exit, Fulke spoke his mind without introductory remarks.

"Miss Grey, I didn't think you were like the rest of those greedy title hunters. I insist that you break this engagement. It is nothing less than picking and stealing."

"But I—"

"I was fooled by your American manners, I suppose. I should have remembered how loose American women can be. That's what has Alexis rearing like a stallion, your harlot's ways. Going about in split skirts and improper dress."

He raised an arm and pointed an accusing finger at Kate. He was so tall and quivered with such righteous fury, she felt guilty without thinking.

" 'All wickedness is but little to the wickedness of a woman,' " he continued. "You seduced Alexis with your obscene flaunting and fornicating tongue."

Kate blinked at Fulke. "Fornicating tongue?"

"I repeat, release that boy from your talons."

Rapid footsteps echoed through the hall. Fulke was hauled away from Kate, and she got a view of the marquess's lithe body before Valentine Beaufort hurled himself between Alexis and his cousin. Alexis permitted Val to stop him from going for Fulke, but Kate suspected it was only out of consideration for his friend's weak state. The two cousins dueled with their eyes instead.

"You forget yourself, sir," Alexis said. "And you dare much when you say such things to my fiancée."

"It's my duty to protect you from sin," Fulke said.

"If you speak of Kate and sin in the same breath again, I'll stuff you into that suit of armor."

Fulke ran a hand through his black and silver hair. "I

don't understand, Alexis. You've never let your appetite run away with your judgment before."

"By God, sir, I will teach you to respect the delicacy of my lady if I have to take a whip to you."

Fulke wasn't at all perturbed. He shook his head. "You're upset. We'll speak of this when you're calmer."

"Come back here, Fulke." Alexis started after his cousin, but Val detained him by thrusting an arm in his way.

"Let him go. He's never made sense where women are concerned. *Damnant quod non intelligunt*, my friend."

Kate laughed and translated. "They condemn what they do not understand."

Alexis's bearlike expression melted into a smile. He took Kate's hand. "I find this small barbarian a trifle difficult to fathom myself. And speaking of barbarians, I saw Cardigan. He appeared to be looking for someone. Was it you?"

"Yes, but don't worry. I have taken precautions."

"One hesitates to ask the nature of these precautions," Val said.

"Nothing much," Kate said. "Only a little knife."

Both men looked at her dress.

"You can't see it."

Val cleared his throat and bowed. "I shall excuse myself before I say something that will get me stuffed into the damascened armor."

Chapter Twelve

As Val left the hall, Kate turned back to the damascened armor. She grasped one of the metal fingers of the gauntlet and bent it back and forth.

"Where is the knife, Kate?"

She started and whirled around to face Alexis. "Strapped to my leg." Her attention wandered back to the armor. Her hand crept up to the visor, the front of which projected like a snout.

"Katie Ann!"

She looked at Alexis. He was still in his riding clothes, but showed none of the signs of exhaustion that signaled a death ride.

"Leave the armor alone," he said. "I am overcome with foreboding at the thought of what you intend to do with a knife."

"Nothing much." She deemed it wise not to mention her latest conversation with the earl.

Alexis took two menacing steps toward her.

"I'm only going to scare him if I need to," she said quickly.

"No."

"But I thought you'd like the knife better than my revolver."

"Dear Lord." Alexis rubbed his temple as if he were getting a headache.

"I can get my revolver," she said.

"No, no." He chewed his lip as if in thought. "I don't suppose you'd consider allowing me to protect you."

"Certainly," she said.

"But you're not giving up your knife."

She shook her head and grinned at him. "Want to see me throw it?"

"Did you know that my cavalry troops were easier to manage than you are?"

"Thank you."

Alexis didn't respond. He grasped her arm and conducted her to a scarred settle. He sat beside her on it and took her hand. Kate watched her fingers disappear inside his palm. The warmth of his flesh sent a river of heat up her arm. She felt the first quivers of excitement begin in her stomach.

"I must apologize for my cousin," he said.

"You don't have to. You aren't responsible for his bad manners. And anyway, I almost laughed at him. To think he considers me a Jezebel."

"Why would you laugh?"

She lowered her eyes. "I'm hardly the kind of woman men find irresistible."

She saw a movement, and without warning a pair of lips were fastened over her own. She kept her eyes open for a moment and caught a glimpse of thick black lashes and the shadow of shaved whiskers. Her eyes snapped closed at the feel of his mouth sucking on hers. Then he released her. He ran the tip of his tongue over her lips before moving back to look at her. Cupping her face in one hand, he pressed his thumb against her lips.

"Let me explain what obviously you've never been told," he whispered. "Your face is a perfect oval. Your eyes can be like those of a bewildered foal, then change instantly to volcanic glass. It is all I can do not to sink my hands in your hair when the sun turns it to silken fire. And I can no longer remember the number of times I have had to stop myself from hauling you into the nearest bedchamber and trying to— Well, perhaps I'd best not complete the thought." He touched the tip of his finger to her nose. "You really don't understand, do you?"

She put her hands on his chest and leaned away from him. "You didn't think I was so wonderful when we were first introduced."

"There was a fire, my innocent. Even I cannot court a lady while a building burns down in front of me."

"No, last year. Ophelia gave a ball, and you said you'd hurt your leg and couldn't dance with me." She was afraid to look at Alexis, but he was silent for so long that she had to. He was staring down at her, his brow wrinkled.

"I was very white and my hair was pulled back," she said.

"Oh." He thought for a few more moments, then gasped. "Was that you under all that powder? Don't tell me. Ophelia told you to put it all over your face, I know it." He sighed. "I did say I couldn't dance. I was rude."

Kate nodded. She wasn't about to tell him she'd seen him dancing with another woman after refusing her. She was afraid to trust him with her hurt.

"I was furious, and I let my anger strike out," he said. "Unfortunately, you were in the way. I wanted to throw Ophelia in the nearest pig sty."

He released Kate, and she craned her neck to see him

as he stood up. He dropped to one knee in front of her and took both her hands.

"You won't let me apologize for Fulke, but you have to let me do so for myself."

Kate studied the floor. "You were mean," she said, then shot a look at him.

He gave a quick, delighted smile. "You're an honest little thing. Can you forgive me for being an ass?"

Her face hot, and unable to hold her head up, Kate nodded quickly. Alexis laughed again and kissed her on the cheek. He ducked his head so that he could see her eyes.

"It is I who should be embarrassed," he said. "The fault was mine."

Once she had to look at him, it wasn't so bad. He was far less threatening when he laughed. Kate's mouth curled up at the corners. Alexis stopped smiling. She watched his expression change. He stared at her, unblinking, then he swallowed and closed his eyes. When he opened them again, she was assaulted with green heat that made her think of the desert, of the air turned liquid with the sun's rays, of clusters of palm trees and the bright, dangerous tension of a lion in the sand. The images brought recognition to Kate. He was aroused.

Why didn't he say anything? He just kept still and poured the burning oil of his gaze over her body. She wanted to touch his lips as he had touched hers. If he didn't say something, she was afraid she was going to put her hand on his leg and dig her fingers into the muscles of his thigh. It was something she had to do. Her fingers twitched, and she shot to her feet in alarm.

Nipping past Alexis, she avoided his arms and began to chatter.

"I really must write a letter. If I don't attend to my correspondence, Mr. Poggs takes it into his head to deal with my advisors on his own. And tomorrow I'll ride over to Maitland House."

Alexis had risen and was standing with his back to her and his head bowed. Taking a deep breath, he turned around.

"That reminds me," he said. "We still haven't settled the question of your provoking behavior. Everyone needs improving, Kate, and you're no exception. I would appreciate your modeling your conduct after that of Lady Hannah."

Kate flushed. "I never said I didn't have faults."

"Nevertheless, you explode at the smallest hint of criticism. If ever gentlemen have found you unattractive, it is because of your unmaidenly behavior and not because of your appearance. The gods know there's nothing unattractive about that."

"If you don't like me—"

"You see. This is what I am talking about." He paced back and forth in front of her. "I like you, but an English lady's conduct reflects upon the man who has charge of her. To the world I am your fiancé. I am therefore soon to have the responsibility of guiding you, in caring for you and your worldly possessions, and in seeing that your manner reflects well upon the honor of my name. I won't have you outraging the sensibilities of half the county."

Kate said nothing. She was too shocked. He made her sound like a puppy that needed housebreaking. Afraid that she would burst out with one of the colorful swear words Patience had taught her, she turned her back on the Marquess of Richfield and marched out of the great hall.

Angry as she was, Kate paid little attention to her own progress. When she did, she found herself upstairs in the wing that contained her own rooms and those of her mother. From Sophia's sitting room she heard her mother singing. Kate knocked and went in.

In her present mood, the room was more of an annoyance than usual. Its furniture was covered with a dull brown fabric that depressed her, and the tables were of black marble with ornate gilded legs fashioned in the shape of fat rams standing on their hind legs. Being old and expensive didn't make things less tasteless.

Sophia was embroidering on a love seat near a window. She rose and kissed Kate on the cheek.

"My little girl. I'm still in a tizzy thinking about how my little girl caught a marquess."

"Don't count your coronets," Kate said. "I'm thinking about throwing my catch back in his stagnant pond."

Sophia regarded Kate for a moment before answering. "You're upset. Has something happened?"

Kate plumped herself down on the love seat. Leaning forward, she rested her arms on her knees.

"He keeps pestering me. Worse than flies on a cow pie. Sorry, Mama."

Taking up her embroidery, Sophia sat beside Kate. "I know it's hard being in love, but if you have troubles, my dear, you should talk to Alexis, not run away from him."

Kate turned to stare at her mother. Hearing someone else speak of her feelings for Alexis somehow made them more real. Mama thought she loved Alexis.

"How did you know you were in love with Papa?"

Sophia put the last stitch in a knot and took up her sewing scissors. She smiled. "I didn't know for the longest time. Your father was most annoying. He teased me, incessantly. And we quarreled, though I tried not to."

"You quarreled with Papa?"

"Only when I was forced to. Neither of us wanted to be the first to admit our feelings, and naturally it was up to him as a gentleman to take the lead."

"I'm glad you quarreled. I mean, that is, you see . . ."

"You don't feel quite so alone?" Sophia asked.

Kate grinned, then slumped back in the love seat. "But

I'm not sure. Love isn't something you can learn from books, and getting experience at it hurts."

Sophia let her sewing fall to her lap and nodded. "I remember the feeling."

"How did you know?" Kate asked.

"It took me a while to decide, and I don't think I ever worked out a method. That's what you want, Kate, a method like you and your father used to solve those awful mathematical problems. There isn't one."

"Oh."

"I did ask myself a question, though."

Kate perked up. "What question?"

"I asked myself whether I could face the rest of my life without your papa. What would I do if he went away, back to America, and I never saw him again? I couldn't bear the thought."

Sitting up straight, Kate rested her chin in the palm of her hand and unleashed her imagination. She thought of herself going home, back to San Francisco, to a big house, to the family businesses. There would be no mysteriously tortured, black-haired chimera to alternately entice and criticize her. No more verbal jousts, no more kisses and touches, and never, never, never would she be able to pull him close and try to merge her body with his as she longed to do.

Never see him again.

"What am I going to do?"

Sophia patted her hand. "What is it that you quarreled about?"

"He wants me to be like Lady Hannah."

"Ah."

"What is that supposed to mean?" Kate put her hands on her hips.

"Now, Kate, being stubborn and trampling over conventions hasn't gotten you far."

Slumping forward again, Kate covered her face with her hands and groaned.

"I haven't wanted to interfere," Sophia said. "But if you continue to embarrass such a proud and well-bred young man, you may drive him away. No gentleman wants a wife of whom he's ashamed."

Kate lifted her head and gazed at her mother. "Really?" She clasped her hands in her lap and studied them. "You think he's ashamed of me?"

"I'm afraid so," Sophia said. "This is what I've been trying to tell you for years. You drive men away. Kate, it is a woman's place to bend, to comply with a gentleman's wishes, to make a home where he can retreat from the world and feel cherished. In return, Alexis will give you his love and his protection."

Kate pressed her hands together. "I didn't realize he was ashamed of me. I thought he was being nasty."

Perhaps she had been wrong. After all, so many women believed as Mama did, and men too. A horrible thought occurred to Kate. No one else agreed with *her,* so might it be that she was mistaken, that everyone was right about Lady things and she was wrong? An even more horrible idea came sliding in on the heels of the last one. Was Mama right? Was she driving Alexis away? Her thoughts stopped then, out of fear.

All her life it had been the same. She would do something that came naturally to her, like talking about mathematics. Sophia would react as though Kate had stripped naked in church. When Kate saw her mother's reaction, she would feel ashamed and worthless. She believed Mama's threats about how no man would want her if she behaved in such a manner, and because she believed her mother, she hid her fear behind bravado and hostility. Oh God. She couldn't bear it if Alexis were ashamed of her.

"I guess I'll have to do things a little differently," she said.

"It's the only way, my dear. After all, you don't want him going back to that awful Beechwith creature."

Several days after he'd chastised Kate about her un-maidenly behavior, Alexis stood beside an ivy-covered tree near the ruins of Thyme Hall and scowled at Carolina Beechwith. She'd drawn him away from the others in their riding party. Iago was snuffling at the base of the tree, and Theseus was tethered to a sapling along with Carolina's mare.

Carolina had proved unexpectedly tenacious. Since she'd heard about Kate, he'd endured nearly a week of hysterical reproaches, pleas, and bawling. Now she was going to cry again. When Carolina wept, her face writhed like an insect in its death throes, and her accompanying wails and shrieks put him in mind of banshees, wraiths, and lost souls. Alexis covered his ears with his gloved hands, for it was about time for a shriek.

"Aaaaaaaaaaaaaaaah!"

Iago's head came up. His ears pricked—as much as their great weight allowed. At the onset of another wail, he lifted his nose in the air and howled in sympathy. The horses began to stir. Alexis closed his eyes.

"Aaaaaaaaaaaaaah." (Carolina) "Oooooooooooooo." (Iago)

Carolina was sitting on a ruined wall. She kicked at it with her heels and opened her mouth wide.

Alexis rushed to her and clamped a hand over the beginning of another shriek. "That's enough. You've been crying so long you'll become ill. And you're hurting Iago's ears, and the horses will bolt."

"You *hic* love her *hic*."

"Don't be absurd," Alexis said. He slapped his riding crop on the palm of his hand. "I told you it was a temporary arrangement. I can't marry."

"I don't believe you. A temporary convenience doesn't make a man follow a woman's every move. It doesn't require a man to litter his conversation with a woman's name until he creates the impression of a besotted youth."

Reason wasn't one of Carolina's attributes. Alexis gave up trying to convince her to apply it. Casting aside the riding crop, he yanked her to her feet, intent on leading her to her horse. She opened her mouth, and he could see another bawl coming.

"Shut up, Carolina."

Her mouth snapped closed, but she wasn't startled for long. She threw herself at him, clutching him around the neck.

"You don't want a wife," she said in between nips. "You said so. You want me."

A familiar metal-on-metal whine caused them both to wince.

"Alexis deeeeeeear boy, where are you?"

Now he knew how a damsel in distress felt upon being saved from a dragon. "Mama Dinkle," he said with a chuckle.

Carolina jumped away from him, straightened her hat, and snatched up her discarded whip. Bounding for her mare, she hardly glanced at Alexis until she was mounted. He stood back from helping her and gave her a mocking salute.

"Why the hurry?" he asked.

"Don't be annoying," Carolina said. "We have to rejoin the others from different directions."

"Kate would have invited the Dinkles to sit with her in the ruins."

Carolina looked down at him. "Kate Grey isn't a lady. I am."

Grinning nastily, Alexis watched Carolina kick her mount into a trot. "Oh yes," he called after her. "I forgot."

Iago barked at him, and Alexis dropped to his knees.

The spaniel always perked up when Carolina went away. His nubby tail was wagging rapidly.

"Happy, old fellow?" Alexis sank back to rest on his heels while he stroked Iago.

His campaign to win Kate's favors was progressing more slowly than any he'd ever mounted before. There was an obstacle: her mind. Kate had a busy, frighteningly quick intelligence that never went to sleep. Several times he'd thought he had succeeded in lulling it into a sexually induced doze, only to have it rear up and snap at him. She was responding to his tactics, though.

He'd known from the beginning that asking for her body would be a mistake. It was almost always a mistake to ask. And she didn't like flowery compliments or gifts. Nor would she believe gushing devotion. So he winnowed his way into her affections with language, beautiful, enchanting words designed to arouse and launch the soul into the sky.

Iago lay down, and Alexis sat beside him with his fingers buried in white fur. Few women loved words and images the way Kate did. Oh, they sometimes went into dizzy raptures over Byron or Wordsworth. When he shared a passage with Kate—always under the guise of literary conversation—she would listen quietly. Her gaze became unfocused, her breathing shallow, and he would know that she was inside the images created by the words. It was a world he knew also, a world engendered by language, so real he could almost feel it. Seeing her so transported made him want to give that feeling to her with his body, to show her a place as devastating as the words she loved.

Iago snuffled at him. Alexis put his nose level with the dog's and chanted to him. "'My soul is an enchanted boat,/Which, like a sleeping swan, doth float/Upon the silver waves of thy sweet singing.' She likes that one, old boy."

In attempting to win Kate, he had learned humility
and patience. It wasn't only the pursuit that tried his patience. His equanimity was also tested in his battle to im-
prove her behavior. His admonishments were bearing
fruit, however. During the last few days there had been no
more writing to Mr. Poggs, no unwomanly discussions of
the price of building lumber and designs of clipper ships.

To his surprise, Kate had even put aside her split riding skirts. Yesterday she'd shocked him by wearing a corset
and crinoline. Lace and bows appeared on her dresses. He
wasn't happy with the bows, however. Somehow Kate and
bows didn't go together. It was like putting clothes on a
cupid.

Theseus whinnied. Alexis pulled out his watch, looked
at it, and got up. "Come on, old fellow," he said to Iago.
"It's time to check on my fiancée's progress. I left her with
Hannah, and if I don't put in an appearance, Kate will be
using the poor woman's scent bottles for target practice."

Chapter Thirteen

Alexis found Kate and Hannah in the courtyard, their two figures dwarfed by the surrounding castle walls and drum towers. The women had taken shelter from that enemy of Ladies, the sun, beneath the ancient oak that stood before the keep. As he walked across the courtyard lawn toward them, he saw Hannah wave her hands at Kate. Kate began to walk back and forth in front of her. She took short, hesitant steps and her hands hung limply from her wrists.

Alexis choked on a laugh. Hannah must have objected to the way Kate walked. His young lady moved with decision and confidence, taking swift, driving steps. When she walked, one knew that she was certain of her destination and that she wouldn't let little things like mud puddles and cobblestones get in her way. Where most women cultivated the impression that they had no legs and floated

instead of walked, Kate charged forward without bothering to try to hide the sound of her footsteps. No, Hannah
wouldn't like the way Kate walked.

Alexis quelled his urge to laugh again when Kate made
a turn and pitter-pattered back to Hannah. She dribbled
to a halt in front of her tutor.

"Good afternoon, ladies." He included them both in
his greeting, but he was looking at Kate. She spun around.
From her expression he would have thought she'd been
forced to eat tadpoles.

"Hellfire."

Hannah sighed, and Kate put her fingers to her lips.
Alexis ignored her lapse.

"How are you two getting on?"

Hannah floated over to him and gave him one of her
sheer-as-cambric, helpless gazes. "We have been practicing demeanor. Earlier we tried polite conversation. I'm
afraid Miss Grey knows so little of Society that it was necessary to lecture rather than converse."

"I don't know any of those people," Kate said. She was
squirming inside her corset, but Hannah frowned at her
and she stopped. "Not only that. I can't draw or sing or
play the piano."

Alexis went over to Kate and took her hand. "Don't
look so unhappy. You can learn to sing."

"Only if you like to suffer."

Trying not to grin, he thanked Hannah and suggested
that the lessons be suspended for the day. Hannah agreed;
she always agreed with him. Offering her limp hand for
him to kiss, she poured a glutinous smile on him. He knew
he was supposed to notice the difference between Kate's
brash healthiness and her languor and delicacy.

"Thank you," she said. "I find myself quite fatigued,
and I know I shall have to spend the rest of the afternoon
on my sofa in order to be fit for dinner."

When they were alone, Alexis offered to show Kate the

keep. She agreed happily, and they strolled across the lawn and inside the old tower. With walls fifteen feet thick, and the only light the little afforded by arrow slits and windows set high above the ground floor, the keep was chilly and black inside.

They entered a great vaulted chamber. Windows were set behind the second-floor gallery at the end of deep cone-shaped passages, giving the whole place the look of a sanctuary. The keep was the oldest tower at Richfield; the rest of the castle had grown up around it.

Threading his way through workmen's toolboxes and saw horses, Alexis led Kate to the center of the keep. Beside them was a circular fireplace set in the floor. He pointed up at the wooden gallery barely visible in the faint light that struggled through the recessed windows. Beneath the gallery and spreading out toward them, was a massive pile of armor and weapons. Axes, staves, and pikes jutted from the pile at all angles.

"I'm having the gallery beams shored up or replaced," Alexis said. "It's not safe to walk around up there anymore. That's why all the armor and things have been shoved out of the way." He gestured toward a spot on the gallery lit by one of the windows. "Before a battle, the lord of the castle would stand there and speak to his men, who gathered below, where we are now. My ancestors hung thieves and murderers from a gibbet on the roof."

"I think I would have preferred hanging from the keep like a battle pennant to being tossed into the oubliette." She shivered, and Alexis took her back outside. They waited a moment to let their eyes adjust to the sunlight.

Alexis bent down and whispered in Kate's ear. "You're the only woman I've ever met who could wear mourning and not look drab. Black makes your hair shine and turns your skin to snow."

She turned to him, and his heart jerked at the sight of her smile.

"I think you're pretty too," she said.

"Pretty!"

She nodded. "If you went to San Francisco you'd have all the ladies panting after you, and that's saying a lot since there are hundreds of men for every woman. I think it's because you look like you belong in one of your pictures."

"What?"

"Like the one in the great hall. That one of the prince who was killed. He's wearing a sword and riding a giant black horse. When you walk into a room, everyone looks as if they're going to fall on their knees or bow."

"I think you're imagining things."

She shook her head and swept an arm around her. "You take all this for granted, but I think you must have absorbed dignity and authority from the castle's stones or something."

"You make me sound like a doddering archbishop."

She shook her head. "You don't understand. I come from a city that was a village of less than two hundred people before the gold rush. The oldest building in San Francisco couldn't have been standing more than ten years. But this place . . ."

They walked on, and Kate looked around at the curtain walls, the towers and battlements. Alexis looked too. Her excitement was catching.

"In this place, I can feel time," she said. "Sometimes, when I walk up one of the stone stairways, the ones that dip in the middle, I think of all the feet that must have gone up those same stairs throughout the centuries to wear away the stone like that. And I wonder, are we as different from them as we'd like to think?"

He turned to her and grasped her forearm. "That's the way I feel. No one else cares whether the older parts of the castle fall down, or if the keep needs new beams, or if the Saxon and Norman manuscripts in the library disintegrate."

"They ought to care." She poked his chest with her finger. "People didn't just arrive in this modern age all on their own. What we have is built on the experience and knowledge of centuries."

"Exactly what I told Val the other day. Do you know what he said?"

"No."

"He said we'd all be better off living in tribes like the American Indian."

"I don't know," Kate said. She glanced at the moss-covered keep. "I like it here."

"This is wonderful. At last I have someone I can tell all the grisly stories about my family. Would you like to see our Ghost Tower?"

She started tugging on his arm. "Show me now. Right now."

He took her hand, and they walked together to a drum tower in the east wall. He shoved a door open to reveal a narrow stone staircase. Kate hesitated and glanced down at her crinoline.

"You'll have to help me squish all this so I can get in."

It wasn't easy, but together they mashed the hoop down so that Kate could get up the stairs to the top of the tower. By the time they reached the chambers at the summit, both of them were winded.

Alexis opened a door set in the last turn of the staircase, and Kate squeezed through it. He had to duck to get inside. Kate was walking into a long, arched recess that ended in a diamond-paned window. She tried to get near enough to see out, but the bulk of her petticoat-padded crinoline made it almost impossible. She stepped back.

"Damnation! Ooops. I mean, oh dear."

Alexis chuckled. "I think for the moment we must cast aside fashion. Shall I turn my back?"

She bobbed her head with such enthusiasm, he smiled and turned to face the dark paneling. Hearing the swish of fabric, he couldn't help glancing over his shoulder. Kate was flushed with the effort of gathering the yards and yards of her skirt to her waist, and was now trying to see over the mountain of material to untie the tapes that fastened the crinoline. He snapped his head back around as she lifted her eyes.

"Alexis."

"Yes."

"Would it be terribly improper of me to ask you for help?"

God was kind. "I shan't tell anyone."

"Then could you get this hellish, I mean awful contraption unfastened?"

"I think I could do that."

He was careful not to touch her body, but after he loosened the knots, dragged the awkward contraption down past her hips, and helped her step out of it, his hands were shaking. It didn't matter that stockings, a shift, and petticoats separated his hands from her flesh. He could make out the outline of her legs and buttocks. It was at that moment that he decided he wasn't going to stop at removing the crinoline.

With carefully studied negligence, he allowed her skirts to fall into place while he rose and put his hand on her waist. She looked up at him in surprise, but he guided her to the window seat. Helping her kneel on it, he opened one of the panes. They stuck their heads out. Below was a sheer drop made longer by the fact that the tower was built upon an outcrop of rock. Moss crawled up the face of the rock and invaded the stone of the tower. A breeze whipped Kate's hair free, blowing a strand across his face. He twined his fingers in it and crushed its softness into his palm. She pulled back into the room, and he let go of the curl.

"This was one of my first projects," Alexis said. He helped Kate settle herself on the window seat. "The room needed new roof timbers, new plaster. And the furniture hadn't been seen to since James I died."

"It all looks uncomfortable."

He smiled as she surveyed the chairs made of heavy, dark wood. There wasn't a cushion in sight.

"I must admit," he went on, "the bed took some refinishing. It was the one the lovers died in. The ropes were rotted."

Kate was instantly up and trotting toward the bed. "What do you mean the lovers died in it?"

He strolled over to stand beside her. "This is sometimes called Lettice's Tower." Leaning against a bed post, he studied the wild curls that cascaded over Kate's shoulders. "Lettice was the only daughter of Sir Richard Hopwelt, who got the castle when my family was dispossessed for fighting for the Yorkists against Henry Tudor. She was spoiled, but left alone much of the time while Sir Richard was at court."

Kate tested the mattress. "And being bored?"

"She entertained herself with her father's young, well-endowed steward. That's Lettice's portrait over the fireplace. As you can see, she would have no trouble seducing a man. Anyway, the poor fellow would meet her in this room late at night. He knew he risked death, but he was so besotted he didn't care."

Kate climbed up on the bed and sat, her legs swinging. She looked down at her feet, then bent closer to peer at the floor. "Alexis, there's a stain."

"Yes."

Her eyes grew as big as plums, and he quickly sat beside her and put an arm around her shoulders. He lowered his voice to a whisper.

"One night Sir Richard came home and found them asleep in this bed. He went mad and ran the steward through with his sword. Impaled him to the mattress.

Then he dragged Lettice from the bed and threw her on the floor. Right there. And he stabbed her to death."

Kate pursed her lips. She leaned over to study the faded bloodstain. He leaned with her. They leaned back. She looked at him, their faces close together.

"I wonder if she thought having him was worth it," Kate said.

Brushing her cheek with the tips of his fingers, Alexis kissed the corner of her mouth. "When you desire someone, not having them is so painful that it becomes an obsession."

Her brows went up. "Really?"

"Really. 'Mad in pursuit, and in possession so,' my dear."

While she was thinking about the words, he was absorbed in the redness of her lips. He was about to kiss her again when she spoke.

"Is it like that? Madness?"

He didn't have to ask her what "it" was. "A little. Pleasure fills the senses until there is no room left for anything else."

Putting one arm behind her, he rested his weight on it, and she leaned back as he eased toward her. He caught her with his free arm so that she wouldn't fall. When her back met the mattress, he followed her down into a kiss.

Her cheeks were hot, and she wasn't protesting. Afraid to speak, he kept up the assault until she was breathing as rapidly as he was. It was almost impossible to keep his head. In spite of the damned corset and the thickness of her bodice, he could feel the pliancy of her breasts. His fingers tangled in curls of fire as he unfastened the buttons at the back of her dress. He didn't want to give her time to think, so he pulled a breast free of the bodice and fastened his mouth on the nipple. To his surprise, she wrapped her arms around him and pressed herself into his mouth.

Expecting a fight, he was disconcerted by its absence.

In his surprise, he lost the reins by which he'd been guiding his passion. He was lying beside her, and he inched his leg up until it lay across her pelvis. It wasn't enough. Giving in to the lust that was driving him, he swept skirt and petticoats upward and burrowed his way between her legs.

"Oh, hellfire."

He lifted his head. "Did I hurt you?"

She didn't seem to hear him. She was staring up at the canopy that covered the bed. He watched her eyes close, then she thrust her hips into his. Alexis sucked in his breath and knew a dread that made him want to scream. He put his cheek to her breast. She was thinking again.

"I can't stand it," she said. Her voice trembled. "I've decided, Alexis. I'd rather have the madness than the pain."

His head shot up, and he stared at her flushed face in disbelief. She had decided to have him. After all his plotting and attempts at sensual disarmament, she had removed the choice from him and taken it for herself. He had no time to pursue the thought, for Kate pulled his face down to hers and started nipping at his cheeks and lips.

"God," he said in between kisses. "I can't stand this either."

He got rid of her clothes. Refusing to let her become embarrassed, he lay down on top of her as soon as she was naked. He teased her nipples, pressed his fingers into the soft flesh of her breasts, and ground his hips against hers. One thrust was enough to tell him that he had to get his trousers off or burst through them.

A little hand worked its way beneath his jacket. It invaded his shirt and stroked the skin of his breast. Another hand joined it. They tugged impatiently at the shirt.

"Aren't I supposed to see you?" She sounded so unsure and so disappointed, he smiled.

"I didn't want to frighten you."

He pulled his jacket and shirt off while he kissed her face and breasts. Boots and socks vanished, and he freed himself from the imprisoning trousers. Again he didn't give Kate time to panic. He came back to her, shoving her legs apart, and lowered his body to hers once more. His loins were burning and swollen. When they touched hers, she jumped. He murmured words of assurance, and she quieted.

He had planned the seduction of Kate Grey down to the last kiss. Those plans vanished the moment he moved his hips. As his rigid flesh pressed into the moist triangle, he felt her small hands knead the skin on his back, and then—incredibly—they sought his buttocks and squeezed.

She wanted him! She enjoyed him as he enjoyed her. A fierce exultation and pride rushed through him. The underpinnings of his soul came loose. Frightened, he sought escape from the feelings in arousal.

He moved so that he could run his tongue from her breasts to her navel. Kate's hands fluttered, seeking to restrain him. He caught both of them in one of his and wouldn't let go. She made a sound of protest, but he kissed his way down her abdomen until he reached the curls between her thighs. He kissed them, and she gasped. Her hands writhed in his. She tried to press her legs together.

"Hush," he said. "This is the way to madness, and I'm going to show you now."

He held her open and pressed his mouth to her. She sucked in her breath, but she let him continue. He raked his tongue over her, separating the lips and seeking out the small bud of flesh. Finding it, he suckled gently. Kate's whole body relaxed. Her hips thrust up, and he gathered them in his hands.

Relentless, he teased and stroked rhythmically. He quickened his pace as Kate began to pant. Her body was covered in a thin film of perspiration, and his hands slid over her skin. The wetness drove him to take another risk. Slowly he eased his hand to the opening that lay below the place where he worked his mouth. He circled the entrance with his finger, then inserted it. Her muscles jerked and spasmed about his finger. He moaned into her flesh and sucked hard. Kate cried out in the frenzy of orgasm. He felt her body convulse, grow rigid, then subside.

That feeling of pride returned briefly before he succumbed to his own lust. Hugging her small body to him, he spread her legs with his knees.

He rained kisses over her face and neck. Her cheeks were damp from tears, but she smiled at him.

"Wonderful," he said. "Like female Cognac. Little savage, give me the madness of pleasure."

She spread her hands out across his back and kissed him.

"Be still," he whispered, "and relax."

He put his hand on her hip, then gradually slid it lower to cover her loins. When he parted her flesh, she ducked her head and buried her face in his neck. To him the rest of the universe dwindled until it focused on the tip of his phallus where it lodged at her entrance. He pressed forward. Living flesh quivered about his muscle, and he lost all control. As he felt his will give way, he stabbed with his hips. He burst through a thin barrier, and at the same moment, Kate whimpered.

He had never given a woman pain before. He had never taken a virgin, never wanted one.

"Oh no," he said.

He gritted his teeth and prepared to withdraw. He lifted his hips, but Kate grasped his buttocks and pulled him back to her. Losing his balance, he came to rest inside her again. All he could do was groan and begin his painful retreat once more. As the tip of his penis reached her entrance, those torturing hands came back to thrust him inside again.

"No," he said. "I hurt you."

Kate was panting. Her face was tense, but she refused to let go of his body.

"I want to feel your madness," she said. "The hurt isn't bad, and there's pleasure too."

She lifted her hips, swallowed him, and Alexis gave up. He began to pump back and forth. The feel of her hands on his back and buttocks increased his passion. His universe shrank again and stayed shrunk. He thrust gently at first, then harder as sensation crawled up his shaft, into his loins, and back down. Over and over he pushed in and withdrew until he felt himself swell and pulsate. As he began his explosion, the blessed cavern of muscles that held him contracted. For the first time in his life, Alexis gave a small roar at the moment of his climax. He drove his penis to the mouth of her womb. Arching his back, he held himself rigid and endured the spasms of painful pleasure.

At last he collapsed on Kate and breathed heavily. Her arms came up to embrace him, and he smiled. "Was I mad enough for you?"

She squeezed him. "Yes. Your surrender was most pleasing."

He lifted his head and let out an indignant curse. She grinned at him. Noticing her flushed skin and wild hair, he smiled too.

"And your surrender brought me great joy as well." He eased to her side and drew her into his arms.

Stroking his left arm, Kate whispered, "Thank you."

"For what?"

"For not demanding a one-sided surrender. You gave yourself to me as much as you asked me to give myself to you."

"I had no idea I was so . . . so . . ." He gave up trying to find the words. "Kate, it isn't always like this."

"You mean I won't always like it?"

"I mean with others there isn't the same feeling of giving. Damn."

"I know."

She sounded sympathetic, and he realized she was as taken aback as he.

"I'm going to have to think about this," he said.

"So am I."

She put her hand on his thigh and sank her fingers into the muscles.

"But not right now," he added.

"No, not now."

He held himself still, intrigued by the look of curiosity on her face. Her hand slipped to his inner thigh and squeezed. He began to swell. He remained motionless and held his breath as her hand explored him. She touched his penis, and his hips jerked.

"My love," he said. "You can't do this again."

"But I want to touch you. I don't have to wait for that, do I?"

He gave a pained laugh. "I should have known better than to expect you to play the hysterical virgin." The adventurous hand left him. "No! You misunderstood. I'm overjoyed."

Taking her hand in his, he placed it where he needed it to be.

Chapter Fourteen

Alexis was on his way to Carolina Beech-with's apartments. It was after midnight, and he was tired, but he'd promised Carolina. Even if he hadn't, his last encounter with the woman had convinced him of the need to rid himself of his old obligation. After that afternoon's sensual cataclysm, he could delay no longer, especially considering Kate's remarks as they were winding down the tower stairs.

She had been following him with her skirts gathered in both hands while he'd transported the blasted crinoline. As he rounded a turn, he noticed that the little footsteps behind him had ceased. He looked back over his shoulder. Kate was perched several steps above him, skirts lifted. She was staring at the mortar between two stones that formed part of the wall.

"Is something wrong, my love?"

Turning her head slowly, she looked

down at him. He had the feeling she was surprised to see him there.

"No," she said. "I'm not sure, but I think I'm a Fallen Woman now."

His jaw went slack, but only for a moment. "You are not."

"Oh yes I am. Mama has been most adamant about virtue, you know. I am definitely a Fallen Woman."

"Now see here—"

Kate went on as if he hadn't spoken. "But I couldn't help it. The thing is, Alexis, we've made a mess of things."

"I don't see how."

"I can't be a Lady anymore. After all, Ladies don't make love to gentlemen unless they're married. And since you want me to be proper and decorous and all those kinds of things, it appears to me that I can't touch you anymore."

It was her brain, dammit. If only she weren't so bloody intelligent. Alexis propped the crinoline against the wall and went up to her. She was giving him a puzzled examination.

"You hate it when I'm improper," she said.

He backed her against the wall and started nuzzling her temple. "This is an exception." He kissed her. He couldn't help thrusting his hips against hers. Instantly in flames, he tried to squish her body between his own and the stones behind her.

She tore her lips free. "This is hypocrisy."

Bracing his hands on the wall, he pushed away from her and met her eyes.

"You're right, little savage. But if I went around openly flaunting my personal relationships, it isn't I who would suffer. Like you, I can do without the approval of people with minds like little biscuit tins. However, Fulke and Hannah and my mother cannot."

Kate bit her lower lip. "Neither can my mother." She narrowed her eyes at him. "Neither could Ophelia."

Bending to her, he kissed the tip of her nose. "Ophelia would not give up. Her heart was set on being the mistress of Castle Richfield, and she had such persistence."

"It runs in the family." Kate stiffened abruptly. "Shhh."

She poked her head under his arm and listened.

"What?" he asked.

"I hear Dinkles."

"Lord deliver me."

"Quick! To the curtain wall. We'll run to the next tower."

"Anything to avoid an infestation of Dinkles."

Alexis's own chuckle woke him from his reverie. He looked about and found that he'd taken root in the Long Gallery, which connected the family apartments and guest rooms. Set with tall windows and paneled in oak, the hall was lit by twenty silver candle sconces bearing the family arms. He began to walk again, passing portrait after portrait.

Sighing, he faltered beside a study of Charles II and addressed it. "It has to be done, Your Majesty. You should understand the duty owed to one's mistress."

Charles stared out at him with regal nonchalance. Alexis sighed again and continued on into the hall that led to Carolina's apartments. He stood in front of her door, put his hand on the knob, then withdrew his hand.

Contemplating the door panels, he felt his mood grow blacker and blacker. There was something wrong with him. The thought of fending off Carolina—and even possibly succumbing to her—alarmed and annoyed him, and he kept remembering how innocently puzzled Kate had looked on the Ghost Tower stairs. He remembered her calling herself a Fallen Woman.

"Better not," he said to himself.

He turned on his heel and retraced his steps. He was opening the door to the long gallery when it hit something solid.

"Bloody hell," said Val.

His friend backed up into the light of a candle sconce as Alexis entered the gallery. Val held a heavy, long sword. Its blade gleamed in the candlelight, but was subdued compared with the brightness of gold hair and hate-kindled eyes.

"What are you doing with that sword?"

Val lifted the hilt in front of his face in a salute. "Mademoiselle St.-Germain is a lady of peculiar tastes."

Alexis folded his arms over his chest and waited.

"Oh, all right. Tonight seemed a good time to rid merry old England of a festering pustule by the name of James Brudenell, Earl of Cardigan."

Holding out his hand, Alexis remained in Val's path. Val glared at him, but relinquished the sword.

"The only reason I'm giving it to you is because you're unarmed, and I don't want to hurt you in a fight."

"Certainly," Alexis said. "Never mind the fact that you're tired from carting it all the way from the great hall. Your hands are shaking. Come along."

He placed a steadying hand on Val's arm, and they started back to the private wing.

"You never spied on your men," Val said.

"Of course not."

"He did. And he tried to court-martial an officer for ordering the wrong wine at mess. He had the most expensive regiment in the Horse Guards. All the officers had to furnish themselves with the finest Thoroughbreds—for the hunt, you know—and the best cuisine, the most fashionable tailors."

"But he doesn't deserve to be killed for being a prima donna."

They had reached Val's rooms. Alexis crossed the sitting room and dug in a cabinet for a decanter of port. He gave Val a glass, but he refused it. Alexis propped an arm on the mantel and watched Val wander from armchair to desk to sofa to window. He stayed longest at the window, looking out into the darkness.

"Your hatred is consuming your health," Alexis said.

Val jerked his head around and glared at him. "You were wading in blood that day too."

"That's why I want to know the truth, Val." He was presented with the back of a golden head.

Alexis set the glass down and walked up behind his friend. "Tell me."

"No."

Val placed the flat of his hand on a windowpane. Alexis knew that hand would be as cold to the touch as the glass beneath it.

"Then I'll tell you what happened," he said. "It took twenty minutes to ride down the valley of death. One and a half miles of cross fire riding straight into artillery. All you saw at first were swords in the air. Pistols fired in all directions. Everyone was slashing about, cutting away. All around you, round shot, mortar fire, and rockets exploding, and the longer you rode, the more men fell, until the ground was covered with human bodies and horses."

"Stop." Val dropped to the window seat and huddled there.

"You were covered in blood when I found you, lying half under your horse."

Val exploded. He sprang at Alexis, fists flying. Alexis dodged and caught him. Falling forward, he deposited his friend back on the window seat, then grabbed the flailing arms. He forced them behind Val's body, then resumed his soliloquy while fighting to maintain his hold.

"Remember the sounds of the artillery? Innocent little fizzes and whirrs that cut off a man's head, blow away his legs and his cock, or maybe only sheer away an eyeball or a jaw."

"God, Alexis, no!" Val heaved up, gave a long cry of anguish, and collapsed. Turning his face to the cushion of the window seat, he began to shudder.

Alexis shook him. "Tell me."

"Tell you?" Choking back sobs, Val turned his wet face to Alexis. "Damn your soul. I'll tell you just to make your nights as horrifying as mine. I was riding back. I could hardly see ahead for the smoke, but I could see the ground. I was riding on a carpet of bodies, the bodies of my friends and my men. Atherton was beside me, but a musket caught him in the chest and he fell. I tried to go back, but others were coming up behind and blocked the way. I was swept on, but I heard him call my name."

Val paused. He was oblivious to the shivering that racked his body. Alexis released his arms, but he didn't move.

"He called to me," Val said, "begged me to help him. But I couldn't see him. I wasn't hurt, not until I was almost out of it. I should have been able to see him. He screamed my name, again and again, and I finally spotted him. I was turning my horse to go back, but something hit me. If only I could have stayed conscious."

"But you tried to go back."

"They told me part of his spine was blown away. I could have saved him before he was hit that second time. Every night after that he would come to me in dreams, screaming, screaming, screaming." Val began to chuckle. "But I've outwitted old Atherton. I don't sleep anymore. Don't you think that's clever of me?"

Val's chuckles rose into laughter. Alexis sat back on his heels and watched his friend shake with unhappy mirth.

He reached out and slapped Val once, lightly. Val blinked at him.

"You want to have a row, Alexis?"

"You feel guilty because you're not one of the hundreds that died. It wasn't your fault. And no one could have saved Atherton. If you had turned back, you both would have been killed."

"Both?" Val shook his head. "No, I would have saved him."

"What makes you so sure? Everyone else was dying."

"But I could have saved him."

Alexis snatched Val's arm and hauled him upright. "You could have done what? His horse was gone. You could have carried him back double? All that way? You were already hurt. You would have been killed too."

Val stared at Alexis as if he were a boy learning a lesson from a tutor. "I would have been killed too."

"Say it again, louder."

"I would have been killed too."

Alexis pulled Val into his bedchamber. He stuffed him into bed, then fished around in a side table for a bottle. After pouring a glass of water, he measured out a few drops from the bottle.

He held the glass out to Val. "Drink this."

"I don't want any laudanum. You know I don't take it."

"If you don't drink it willingly, I'll have to make you."

Val drank, shoved the glass back at Alexis, and sank into the pillow in a huff.

Alexis stood over him. "Tell me again."

"Go to hell. Oh, very well. I would have been killed too."

"And?"

"And there was nothing I could have done, damn you."

"And?"

"Bastard. All right! I have nothing to blame myself for."

"Good." Alexis headed for the door.

"It's all his fault."

Alexis groaned. "Once you get hold of an idea, you cling to it like one of those Australian koala bears hugs its tree. Good night, Valentine."

"Night, tyrant."

Alexis was back in his own room quickly. Shedding his clothes, he reached for his dressing gown, then paused as he caught sight of his own hand against the crimson satin. It was shaking. The last few minutes had brought back unwanted nightmares. He wasn't going to be able to sleep for a while. Dragging the gown after him, he went to the glass doors that led to his balcony. He opened them and stepped out. The night was unusually warm and still.

Looking out, he could see one or two lights in other parts of the castle. The pennants on the Watch Tower hung limp from their staffs. Taking in a deep breath, Alexis wondered if he should have taken some laudanum himself. He hated the stuff more than Val did. It reminded him of the Crimea, and of the time after Father and Thalia died when Fulke gave it to him.

No, he wasn't having any laudanum. He shook out his dressing gown and was about to put his hand through an armhole, when he glanced to his right. Across the distance of three apartments lay Fulke's rooms. A figure in white was standing on the balcony. Hannah.

She was in darkness. Alexis lowered his arm. The dressing gown slithered in folds of material around his legs. He could feel her eyes on him. She didn't move, didn't speak, just kept watching him. He turned so that all she could see was his profile, then put on the garment, slowly. The silk was cold against his bare skin. He tied the sash at his waist and stepped back inside his room without looking at the woman. He didn't have to. He was sure she was still there, a silent white hawk watching its prey.

As he walked to his bed, Hannah faded from his

thoughts. To his dismay, he found himself thinking of Kate. Kate, Kate, Katie Ann. The name chimed in his brain and brought forth the memory of her body. An hour passed, and another, and still he lay awake. She was nearby. She was sleeping in his house, and he couldn't rest. He'd thought that having her would be like slaking his thirst after a death ride. But having her was like taking opium. He wanted more.

He watched the clock on the mantel, but he could barely make out its black hands by moonlight. They seemed frozen in place, yet the clock ticked. With each tick, his arousal grew. He could feel himself swelling in rhythm with the sound. *Tick, tick, tick, tick.* He bit the inside of his cheek. The pain didn't help.

"Bloody everlasting hell."

Alexis threw back the covers. Pulling on his robe again, he slipped out of his room. Soon he was facing Kate's door. He opened it silently. Instead of darkness, he was met by the glow of a single candle. Kate sat in the middle of her bed turning the pages of a book. As he watched, she sighed and stopped thumbing the pages.

"Kate."

She jumped and stared at him openmouthed. Drawing the book to her breast, she hugged it. Alexis drew near the bed, all the while expecting her to curse him and throw him out. He stood beside her watching the candlelight turn her hair to fire, then he whispered to her.

"Katie Ann."

She squeezed the book tighter to her chest and looked up at him with frightened eyes. Holding her gaze with his, he grasped the book and pulled it out of her hands. He dropped her shield to the floor, then placed his hand on her cheek and felt her shiver. A niggling doubt assailed him. She was so inexperienced, and he wasn't giving her any choice. Not really. He'd set about her seduction deliberately, and then found out that, all along, he hadn't been as clever as he'd thought. He had trapped himself.

Kate turned her face to his palm and kissed it. Alexis drew in his breath, and all compunction fled. He'd found a treasure, and he wasn't about to give it up. Not yet.

He placed one knee on the bed, then the other. Kneeling before her, he pulled at the belt to his dressing gown. He opened it while bearing her down beneath him to the mattress. She was wearing something diaphanous, and it was in his way. He braced himself on one arm while pulling the hem of her nightgown up to her waist. All the while, Kate said nothing. She kept staring at him as though she couldn't look away. When he lowered his hips to rest on hers, she finally closed her eyes. At the same time she opened her legs to accommodate him, and he buried his face in her neck.

"I can't sleep for thinking of you," he said. He sucked at the flesh of her throat. "I want you so much the pain is killing me. I shouldn't press you so soon, but I can't bear the pain. Help me."

She brought his face up so that she could kiss him. Catching his lower lip between her teeth, she nipped it gently. "I think you've decided to help yourself."

He licked his way down to the material that covered her breast. Suddenly, he hated that cloth. His hand swept up her body, twisted in the fabric, and tore it.

"You're right," he said. "I will help myself."

He fastened his mouth over her breast and sucked. Her hands linked at the back of his head and pressed him to her flesh. He drew on her nipple, and she arched into him. His hand slid down to her hip, then between their bodies to lie at the juncture of her thighs. He pressed down.

"Open," he said. "Open to me. Wider. Wider." He slid a finger inside her. His groin ached, and he was beginning to twitch. He thought of the clock. His finger began to imitate its beat as he thrust it in and out. She was straining against his hand, driving him mad. Her hands squeezed his buttocks, and she tried to pull him into place.

"No, not yet."

He eased down until his lips were pressed against the moist nest where his hand played. Again Kate tried to lift him back between her legs. To stop her, he kissed the most sensitive part of her body.

"No," he said. "Spread your legs wider." He urged her thighs apart with his hands and kissed her again. He flicked his tongue over her, and he felt her try to close her legs. "Relax. That's it. Feel what I'm doing to you. This is what I want."

When he had her so aroused that she was bucking in response to his caress, he laughed. "At least I can get you to obey me in this."

He should have kept his mouth shut, for Kate surged up, reached for him, and caught his penis in her hand. He almost yelped at the feel of her squeezing his overripe flesh. She stroked him once, and it was enough to make him throw her back to the mattress and cover her with his body. His dressing gown was still hanging from his shoulders. He could feel her nails dig into his back through the silk.

"The gown," he said between gritted teeth.

She ripped the garment from him as he spread her legs. He sank deep into her, then pulled out until he was almost free. She took a deep breath that caused her muscles to contract. Alexis broke. He thrust back in and began pumping, over and over. Incredibly, he heard her demand.

"Faster."

"Damn you," he said.

He writhed and circled his hips in revenge, then pierced her deeply. She bit her lip and shivered beneath him to her climax.

He rammed into her. "Yell for me, Katie Ann. Scream. I want to hear you scream."

He got a long, furious moan, then another, then Kate reared up to meet a demanding thrust and screamed. Alexis let himself go at the sound. He pumped and ground his way to a release that shattered him like glass hurled against steel. He collapsed on top of her while he struggled to regain some awareness of reality.

That awareness was long in coming. His self-control lay scattered, as did his will. He buried his face in Kate's hair and admitted something to himself. He had wanted conquest, and he'd gotten it. Only the battle was so raw, so filled with ultimate pleasures. And it was Kate that made it so. He had seduced women before and felt nothing but momentary satisfaction. It was Katie Ann herself, this little savage who tortured him, who spun him on his head, who transformed him from a civilized man to a barbarian.

He sighed and lifted his upper body so he could see her face. She was running her hands up and down his back. Oblivious to his turmoil, she smiled at him and kissed his nose.

"I wanted you to come to me tonight," she said. "I wanted it so badly, but I was afraid to ask. I'm glad you succumbed to temptation."

"By the time I reached your door, I think I would have killed to have you."

Stunned by his own words, Alexis cursed. He shouldn't have admitted his need. And now she was smiling at him as though he'd given her diamonds. Dear Lord, she was moving her hips again. "Kate, no. You're new to this. Dammit, stop."

He squeezed his eyes shut as she wrapped her arms and legs around his body and rotated her hips. He felt her muscles suck at him, and his protests died. Burying his hands in her hair, he moved back and forth inside her and succumbed to his own incomprehensible madness.

. . .

Kate was supposed to go with Hannah, the countess, and the Dinkle trio to rub the noses of the poor in her wealth. Hannah called it Christian charity. Kate suggested that providing training in a skill would be more constructive. Hannah didn't like that idea. It would involve organization, mixing in the affairs of businessmen. A Lady was above such worldly matters, and, at the same time, too light-minded to comprehend them.

Kate wasn't in the mood for charity. She wanted to find a secluded hiding place and think about Alexis and how he'd made her feel in the Ghost Tower the day before, and in her own bedchamber last night. After sending a note to Hannah with an excuse, Kate put on a stuffy riding habit with a trailing skirt—not split—and rode into the woods near Castle Richfield.

She left her horse to graze in a clearing a few yards from her goal. On a previous excursion she'd found the ruins of Thyme Hall. Buried in the forest, the house had been built by one of Alexis's ancestors for his mistress. Cromwell's men had burned it during the Civil War. Though only a moss and ivy-covered shell, the house had been built originally in red brick. Crumbling lumps of the stuff lay scattered around, and she trod on several while picking her way over to the structure. There was a stretch of grass beneath one wall where she liked to sit and read.

Since she'd decided to try to become a Lady for Alexis, most of her enjoyable reading had to be done in secluded places like Thyme Hall. This time, instead of burying her nose in the book she'd brought along, she propped her back against the wall and gazed out at the tangle of brush and wildflowers that threatened the ruins.

She was feeling guilty about not feeling guilty about making love with Alexis de Granville. Her old trouble was back again. Society had rules, and she didn't agree with them. They were illogical. If Alexis could have sex, she didn't see why she couldn't as well. Another source of irritation was that all the proper, moral people she knew said women loved home and family and didn't enjoy the physical side of a relationship. Thank the Lord she'd met Patience when she did.

Patience had set her right. It was mighty low of everyone to keep a girl ignorant of such an important fact as a woman's ability to experience pleasure. Not that Patience found pleasure with her customers, but she had assured Kate that a man could give a woman as much excitement as a woman gave a man. Ever since Alexis had first kissed her, Kate had suspected that Patience had been telling the truth. Now she was certain.

She fished in the pocket of her riding habit for the small book she'd brought with her. She opened it, but didn't read. There was only one answer to her dilemma, she decided. She would have to make Alexis love her. They were already engaged, and her efforts at decorum and propriety had brought his approval. She would make him love her so he wouldn't want to end the arrangement. If she showed her love by making herself into a Lady and by making love to him until he dropped with exhaustion, he would end up giving himself to her permanently.

A quiver of excitement shot through her. She was sure Alexis loved her a little already, though he hadn't realized it yet. She didn't see how he could have done those things to her yesterday and not feel some love. It wouldn't be logical. And last night he had been magnificent, and as wild as she.

Her thoughts drifted to the beauty of Alexis's body, and she relaxed against her wall in a near doze. The warmth of the sunshine, the smell of the moist earth, and the stillness of the air all lulled her to sleep. She started when the whinny of a horse awakened her.

Hearing Alexis's voice, she smiled. He had followed her. She would remain where she was and make him look for her.

She heard rapid steps. The crunch of a boot heel on pebbles, the soft thud of a footfall on grass, the impatient tap of riding crop against thigh. Kate grinned. When in a temper, Alexis always slapped his crop against one body part or another. She started to stand to reveal herself, but his sudden harsh voice made her sink back down.

"Are you mad? Sending me that note was an act of insanity, Hannah."

"You've been home for months and not spoken to me once," Hannah's voice said.

Alexis's tone was low and strained. "I speak to you every day."

"In front of others. Polite emptiness. You haven't touched me in all the years since we parted."

Mouth dry, hands cold with tension, Kate snuggled close to her wall and peered at the two through the ivy that spilled over her hiding place.

Alexis was standing in a patch of sun. Suffused in brilliant light, he held himself erect, his eyes like cold, green water, his expression revealing nothing except a vague distaste.

"Don't treat me this way," Hannah said, walking closer to him. "You look at me as if I were a lazy servant in need of dismissal. Oh, don't bother to protest. You know that dignity of yours is intimidating. When I try to speak to you, I feel as if I'm a subject daring to seek intimacy with my king."

"This conversation is distasteful to me," Alexis said. He started toward his horse.

Kate's spirits lifted with each step he took away from Hannah.

"Fulke hasn't changed," Hannah said. "He never touches me."

Alexis stopped with his back to her.

"I need you, Alexis."

Facing the woman, Alexis shook his head. "I'm not a fifteen-year-old virgin anymore. I never should have let you touch me. I betrayed Fulke once, but I won't do that again. I've committed too many sins in my life already. Don't ask me to repeat one of them."

"I need you."

"Why me? Surely there have been others."

Hannah smiled and fluttered her hands in one of her helpless gestures. "You were such a beautiful, sweet creature, and so close. Every day I saw you at fencing practice, learning to shoot, riding. I even saw you swimming once. You had flung off your clothes and jumped into the lake. That evening at dinner your hair was still damp. I imagined your whole body damp and warm and ready. I had to have you."

"Shut up."

Hannah rushed at him. Kate almost left her hiding place when the woman clutched his jacket, attaching herself to him like the ivy hugging the Thyme Hall ruins. Alexis attempted to pry her loose, but she stuck fast. He gripped her hands as they crushed the material of his jacket and pushed against her so that she had to leave a space between their bodies.

"I want children," she said.

At her words Alexis stopped trying to free himself and went motionless. "*Christ.* What kind of monster do you think I am? I won't do it."

"He won't be able to say anything. What will he do? Say the child couldn't be his because he hasn't made love to his wife in years? He won't admit that to the world, because then he'd have to admit he's only half a man because of his parents. Did you know they beat him for showing the least sign of affection for females?"

"Stop it," Alexis said, attempting once again to separate himself from Hannah. "Fulke can't help what happened to him when he was young."

"But what about me?" Hannah shook Alexis by the shoulders. "My beautiful child, you look so much like him, no one would ever know the baby is yours."

"Except Fulke."

Kate winced as Alexis thrust Hannah from him with such violence that she fell to the ground. Her sympathy was short-lived, for Hannah was up and chasing after Alexis at once. He was almost to his horse when she caught him. Snagging him by the coat sleeve, she dug in her heels. Alexis veered around and slapped her hand away. Unfortunately, he made the mistake of not looking at what was behind him. He took a step backward, and another, and came up against the trunk of a tree.

They were too far away for Kate to hear what they were saying. She moved an ivy leaf aside so that at least she could see them. As Alexis stumbled against the tree, Hannah closed in. She caught his face in her hands and kissed him. Alexis stiffened. He grasped her shoulders and began to shove. In response, the woman slid one of her hands low between their hips. Alexis's head snapped back. His mouth formed an O, and Kate could almost hear him gasp. For a suspended moment he stayed pinned against the tree, then Hannah dropped her other hand to his groin. This time Kate did hear him.

"No!" He tore her hands from his body. "By God, there are too damned many women in my life."

He had dropped his riding crop when she touched him. Snatching it up, he slashed it through the air as Hannah reached for him again. Then he mounted Theseus and vanished into the forest, leaving Hannah to fend for herself.

Kate watched the woman bury her face in her hands and weep. It was some time before Hannah recovered and was able to leave the ruins. When she did, Kate braced her arms on the top of the wall and pushed herself to her feet. Her legs were stiff and cramped.

The bitch. Hypocritical, scheming, deceitful bitch. No, Hannah couldn't help it. Fulke was the monster. No, Hannah was. She'd seduced Alexis when he was fifteen. Fifteen, dammit.

"Oh, hellfire." Kate scooped up her book and started pacing.

"How many women does he have?" she asked the trees. "Let's see. There is Mrs. Beechwith, the countess, Lady Churchill-Smythe, the Dinkles, Mademoiselle St.-Germain, and now Hannah. And there was Ophelia. The man could earn his living as a stud."

What an intimidating thought. Kate sank down on top of a crumbling wall and sighed. Why would he want her when he had so many lovely and eager women pawing him? Another, even more melancholy thought occurred to her. Alexis was used to being sought after, pursued, courted.

Before Papa had discovered his gold, she had thought how wonderful it would be to have lovely, expensive clothes. When she got them, it had taken only a few months for those wonderful satins and silks to become as ordinary to her as cotton. If diamonds were as numerous as sand grains, no one would want them.

Women scattered themselves at Alexis's feet like grains of sand, so he couldn't be expected to treat them like diamonds. Poor Hannah, poor Mrs. Beechwith and Ophelia.

Poor Kate.

Oh no, not poor Kate.

Launching to her feet, Kate headed for the clearing where her horse waited. "Watch out, my lord marquess. This is one grain of sand who is going to turn herself into the biggest, fattest diamond you ever saw."

Chapter Fifteen

Considering the provocations to his temper, Kate wasn't surprised when she returned from Thyme Hall to learn that Alexis had visited his estate room, tongue-lashed his secretary, and taken himself off to the Dower House. She went to her room to change and to hide her book. Since she had decided to alter her ways, she'd hidden all her interesting volumes. Only approved religious tomes were left, and poetry.

Wordsworth, for example, was allowed. Kate hated Wordsworth. All that gushing about daffodils and budding twigs and clouds. Nature herself would grow nauseated if she had to listen to such driveling raptures. "O Cuckoo! Shall I call thee Bird,/Or but a wandering Voice?" Kate gritted her teeth. She could still hear Hannah's hushed voice lisping that line.

She was stuffing her book under her mattress when her maid came in with a

letter. Half an hour later she was running downstairs with
the letter and her reply in hand. She sailed down the last
few steps, skirts flying. She hit the carpeted floor and
dashed around a corner, then was suddenly caught and
spun around.

"Kate?"

"Hellfire."

Kate bit her lip. It was Alexis, and he'd seen her running. He was with the Earl of Cardigan and Lord Sinclair,
and he was frowning at her in that detached way he had
when he was furious and couldn't show it because there
were witnesses.

"Is there something wrong, my dear?" he asked.

Propriety and convention forgotten, Kate burst out
with her wrath. "That idiot Poggs has gone and fired my
ship designer."

If she hadn't been so angry, she would have taken a
warning from Alexis's tense jaw and Fulke's frown. She
didn't, and went on.

"I don't care if Wainwright does drink bourbon and
keep three harlots in his house. He builds the fastest clipper ships afloat, and he's going to build them for me."

There was a choked whoop from the earl. Fulke excused himself and took the amused Cardigan with him.
Kate glanced at Alexis and bolted. He caught her again
and dragged her into a room near the stairs. Slamming the
door shut, he towered over her.

"You're a disgrace."

"I'm sorry, but Poggs—"

"I don't care about Poggs. You embarrassed yourself
and me. Again. In front of Fulke and Cardigan, no less.
Fulke already thinks you're fast. Now he'll be sure you're a
degenerate."

"But Poggs—"

"To the devil with Poggs. How many times must I ask

you to act as if you deserved the honor of being the mistress of Castle Richfield?"

Humiliation washed over Kate. An awful heat spread up her neck and into her face, and she swallowed the thick lump that had formed in her throat. Alexis was still talking, but she didn't hear him, so overwhelming was her misery. She was going to cry, and she couldn't stop the tears.

Dear God, don't let me cry. She swallowed again. Her eyes filled. She closed them in hopes of holding back the tears. She would have succeeded if Alexis hadn't suddenly lunged at her.

Without warning she was lifted off her feet. He carried her to a couch and sat down with her on his lap, hugging her to his chest. That hug released the tears. All she could hear was his soft, low voice whispering apologies while she sobbed.

"I didn't mean it, little savage. I'm sorry. Don't cry. Don't cry, I said. Kate, stop crying." He snapped at her. "Stop it at once. You're making me feel like a hound."

She sniffled, then hiccupped and chuckled. Alexis drew in a breath. Placing his hands on either side of her face, he tilted it up. He kissed her wet cheeks, her eyes, and finally her mouth.

Drawing back, Kate touched his lips. No longer drawn and stiff with anger, they were one of the few soft parts of his body.

"I'm sorry," he said.

"Me too."

"It's just that you are so unexpected. You rage like Medusa, but if I get angry with you, you crumble like damp sugar."

Kate blushed and studied the toes of her shoes. Her feet couldn't touch the floor when she was in his lap.

"My sweet."

"Mmmm."

"You don't cry often, do you?"

"Hardly at all."

"That's probably why." He pulled her close again and pushed her head against his shoulder.

"What do you mean?"

"Hannah cries all the time. So does Georgiana Dinkle and the twins, and most of the women I know. You never cry, so when you did just now, I could have cut out my tongue for being the cause."

"Don't do that." She lifted her head and looked into his eyes. "I like your tongue."

That remark got her kissed most thoroughly. Before she realized it, she was on her back on the couch and Alexis's hands were roaming beneath her skirt. He was so quick, she had only gotten the first word of a protest out of her mouth by the time he was lodged between her legs. The rest of her objection drowned under his mouth. He lifted his hips. She heard the rustle of fabric, then in a single movement he was inside her.

She didn't understand how it could happen so quickly. He pulled almost all the way out of her, then thrust deeply into her. Lifting himself on his hands, he pushed against her so hard, she wanted to scream. She forgot to be shocked. She didn't care about anything but what he was doing. He arched his back and rocked back and forth faster and faster. Her loins tingled, and a pressure built at the center of her pleasure. The more she sought to feed it, the more overwhelming the sensations became. Finally she cried out and jerked against him frantically. In the last throes of her own climax, she felt him spasm and explode with release.

Kate held Alexis as he throbbed inside of her. He lifted his head, and they exchanged a look of complete bafflement.

"What happened?" he asked.

"We forgot everything, everything. Oh, Alexis, do you think we're depraved?"

"You aren't," he said. "You aren't the one who made sure to lock the door even though he was furious."

"I didn't care if the door was locked."

He grinned. "That is the greatest compliment a woman has ever given me."

She giggled. Alexis drew in his breath and stiffened, then he kissed her and withdrew. Feeling the warm stickiness of his seed on her thighs, Kate quickly pulled her skirt down while Alexis refastened his trousers.

"Oh dear," she said.

"Yes." He handed her his handkerchief. She blushed, and he turned his back. "I'm sorry, my love. You're not used to this at all." He came back to her and sat down. "We have to think."

"Yes, we do."

"I don't usually rape virgins, you know."

"You're scared too."

"Out of my silk underwear."

She slipped her hand into his. "I was hoping you would know something about it, seeing that you've had so much practice."

"None of it seems to matter when I get near you." He squeezed her hand. "I must be losing my wits."

"Mine are already scattered from here to the next county."

She allowed Alexis to help her up. He kissed her and unlocked the door.

"I must leave you before I make a rutting monster of myself again." He went out into the hallway. "I will escort you to dinner, if I have recovered by then."

Kate smiled. As he started walking away from her, she heard him mutter to himself, "I'm going to have to do something. This can't continue."

Frowning, she opened her mouth to ask him what he meant, but he was gone. She ignored a feeling of foreboding and looked around the room for the papers she had dropped when Alexis had picked her up. It was almost time for dinner, and though some of the guests had left, it would be another terribly formal event. She would need time to wash and dress. And she needed to rest. Being with Alexis was more tiring than washing five tubs of miners' laundry.

Rest proved an impossible goal. She lay down, but kept seeing lines of women dropping at Alexis's elegantly booted feet. Ophelia led the parade, followed by Hannah, the countess, and several beautiful but unnamed victims. In her vision, Alexis did nothing but stand in a cloud of vapor and accept homage. Until she approached. Her he grabbed and pulled beneath him. They disappeared into the mist.

Kate groaned and sat up in bed. In spite of the resolution she'd made at Thyme Hall, she'd acted like a grain of sand again. Her only consolation was that Alexis was as confused as she was.

She was tired of being confused, though. It was time to corner her elusive love and get a few things sorted out. She wanted to know how he felt about her; she wanted to ask why his mother accused him of crimes Kate knew were against his nature to commit. And most of all, she wanted to know if he still considered their betrothal a farce.

Of course he didn't show up to escort her downstairs. Kate was of the opinion that he sensed a showdown and was avoiding it. He made a habit of irritating her anyhow. Why should tonight be any different?

She went down to dinner with her mother instead. Everyone was assembled in the State Dining Room when they arrived, including Alexis. Juliana greeted Kate and Sophia, and the woman's air of martyrdom irritated Kate. Ever since the betrothal announcement, Alexis's mother periodically warned Kate of her impending doom. Juliana went about in a state of melancholy even more dramatic than usual. It was especially at odds with the frantic enthusiasm of her poodles and marmoset.

Alexis went to Kate as soon as he saw her, and spared enough time to talk to Mama. Then he was gone. He chatted with the dean. He cast showers of compliments on the Dinkle covey. He coaxed a silent and grave Valentine into a flirtation with Lady Churchill-Smythe. He exchanged hunting stories with the Earl of Cardigan. He affectionately insulted Fulke. To Kate it was clear that he was willing to spend time with anyone as long as it wasn't her.

As a result, Kate couldn't eat. When dinner was over and the gathering moved to the Red Drawing Room, her despondency fermented into anger. How dare he ignore her? She wasn't the one who couldn't control her passions. It wasn't her fault that whenever they were together, they ignited like an oil-fed fire. After all, he was the one with the artist's model body and erotic walk. It was all his fault.

Kate sat on a crimson damask couch and pretended to listen to Juliana talk about the Queen and Prince Albert. Alexis was slinking over to a window, alone for once. Kate scowled at him, but he wasn't looking at her. He was looking outside. He leaned closer to the window. Without a word to anyone, he scooted around the room made crowded by the ladies' crinolines and slipped away.

It took her a little while to get to the window, but she made it. Looking out, she at first saw nothing but blackness. As she scanned the lawn below, a movement caught her eye. It was a skirt. She cupped her hand against the glass, blocking out the light from the drawing room. Beside the skirt was a leg encased in black, a leg well-muscled from riding and too long to be anyone's but Alexis's or Fulke's. Fulke was in the drawing room.

"Hellfire." Kate clamped her arms down to keep her crinoline where it belonged and sailed out of the room. She gained the lawn, but not in time to see where the two went.

"The snake," she muttered as she scanned the lawn. "The worm. Two-faced, rutting ass. Tries to make me into a human rug to wipe his feet on and then goes about sticking his unmentionable into whoever is close enough to make it stiff."

She set off toward the Ghost Tower. "If he's in Lettice's room, I'll take a pair of scissors to his lordly gifts. And I won't cry. Maybe later, but not until I tell him where to put this engagement."

They weren't in the Ghost Tower. Kate didn't want to think of what she would have done if they had been. Not giving herself time to contemplate, she searched a few more rooms. Finally she walked out onto the lawn again. Picking up a twig, she started breaking it into little pieces as she paced back and forth in front of the Ghost Tower. The castle was too big to search. Hellfire. She wanted to catch him with his pants down. What she needed was a whip. There might be one in the keep. She headed for the old tower. The door was unlocked, and she stepped inside.

Lost in blackness, she felt her way through the entry, past a gap that was the foot of the stairs that led to the gallery and upper floors, heading in the general direction of the table she'd seen when Alexis had brought her there.

Above her head there was a rustling sound, then two thuds, a small one and then a louder one, and finally, a long scream. At the first sound, Kate had searched the darkness around her, seeing nothing. The scream brought with it a loud crash. Metal clanged against metal, stone, and wood. Something rolled past her feet. Kate stayed put, trying to decide where the crash came from.

At the same time, a light appeared from the direction of the stairway. A lantern floated toward her held by Alexis, his tie undone and his shirt open. Behind him was a hard-breathing Mrs. Beechwith.

"Kate?" Alexis stopped in front of her. "What have you done?"

"Don't go accusing me, you Sybarite. The noise came from over there." Kate pointed.

"What are you doing here?" he asked.

"Shut up and give me that lantern." She snatched it from him and walked into the darkness.

Weapons were strewn all along the path toward her destination. Pikestaffs, axes, swords, shields, maces. Kate kept walking until she reached the great pile of armor and weapons Alexis had shown her. In the light of the lamp, the old metal gleamed dully. She held the lantern higher, and its glow spread upward over the pile to illuminate cuirasses, helmets, lances.

The light also revealed drops of liquid dotting the metal. Red splashes became a trickle which led to a hand. Kate's own hands trembled, and she put both of them on the lantern. Barely aware of Alexis coming up behind her, she stood gaping at the body on top of the hillock of weapons and armor, impaled on a boar spear and a halberd.

Alexis rushed past her. "Hannah?"

There was a retching sound behind Kate. Carolina Beechwith gagged, doubled over with her hand to her mouth, then fled.

Kate swallowed hard herself. She felt her head swim and her arms become light. *Stop it. It's not the worst you've seen. Remember that man the Indians caught out by himself in the Carson Desert.*

She watched Alexis lean toward the grotesque pile, stretching across the weapons to grasp Hannah's wrist.

"Don't bother," Kate said. "She's dead."

"But how?" Alexis asked. He shook his head and straightened. He kept shaking his head as if in denial of what he saw. "Dear God. Poor, poor Hannah."

Kate knew she had to do something besides look at the dead woman's open eyes and mouth. She tugged at Alexis's arm.

"She fell. Hold the light up. I'm not tall enough."

As Alexis's arm stretched high, the glow of the lantern revealed a hand and arm hanging from the gallery floor above them. Without a word he raced for the stairs with Kate behind him.

On the gallery he halted. "Be careful. There are rotten boards."

They walked slowly toward the spot directly above Hannah. Lying face down, one arm hanging over the edge, was the Earl of Cardigan. The railing above him was broken where Hannah had fallen through it. Alexis handed the lantern to Kate. He touched Cardigan's head and turned the man over.

"He's been hit from behind." Alexis looked around and picked up a mace lying nearby. "With this, probably."

"I don't understand," Kate said.

They remained beside the earl in silence. Alexis bent over the man to check his breathing, then stood straight, his body rigid. He stared into the dark emptiness of the keep.

"Val."

Kate's heart started fluttering. "Oh, no. The earl probably took liberties and Hannah panicked."

"And hit him with the mace she always carries with her?"

"It could have been here all the time. She could have hit him and lost her balance."

"But why would she be here at all? With him?" Alexis ran a hand through his hair.

"Maybe she wanted a more willing stud to father her child."

It was a nasty blow. She knew it. Alexis started and looked at her as if she had struck him with one of the glaives. He said nothing for a long time, merely stared at her.

"Are you going to ruin her reputation after she's

dead," he asked finally, "or just make Fulke desperately
unhappy?"

"Neither," she said.

"Then go for help. Get my steward and don't speak to
anyone else. Carolina has probably fled to her room, and I
know she won't tell anyone."

Kate left, and for her the next hours passed in a numb
fog. The earl was carried off to his bed and a doctor summoned. Servants removed Hannah's body while Alexis
broke the news to Fulke. Officials came and went. Kate
talked to them, as did Alexis, and it was sunup before she
crawled into her own bed. In spite of her shock and unhappiness, or because of them, she slept until almost sunset.

She woke to find that Juliana's guests had gone, and
the earl had been questioned by the head of the constabu-
lary. Cardigan could remember nothing. He had been
standing on the gallery with Lady Hannah when someone
hit him. He passed out, then he woke up. That was all.

Sophia recounted all the events to Kate, and it was
during this recital that Kate got her first taste of English
justice tempered by aristocratic privilege. The investiga-
tion had been conducted quickly. Police had swarmed un-
obtrusively and left.

"They questioned Lord Fulke," Sophia said, "and Mr.
Beaufort, too, for a long time. But Lord Alexis wouldn't let
them take him away."

"Who?" Kate asked.

"Mr. Beaufort, of course. You know how he detests the
earl."

"But there's no proof."

Sophia nodded. "Exactly what Lord Alexis said. Mr.
Beaufort was supposed to be in his room resting after
dinner. Lord Alexis said there were too many people
roaming about who could have killed Hannah. He said

there were other officers at the Dower House who hated the earl. He wouldn't let them take Mr. Beaufort."

"And what does Valentine say?"

"Oh, he made the marquess furious. They almost came to blows."

"Mama, what are you talking about?"

"You see, the marquess was protecting Mr. Beaufort from the superintendent. But Mr. Beaufort told both of them that he knew the difference between a lady and a fool, and that if he had set out to dump the earl onto those awful spears, he would have made short work of it, and no mistakes either."

"Oh no."

Sophia bobbed her head up and down. "Lady Juliana was spying on them and she told me about it. She said the marquess told Mr. Beaufort to be quiet and then asked the superintendent to leave. So there it is. Poor Lady Hannah is dead, and no one knows who did it or why."

Kate said nothing of her own suspicions. Val could have tried to kill the earl and struggled with Hannah, but she couldn't see the young man choosing to attack with a lady present. From Sophia she knew that Fulke had absented himself from the drawing room shortly after she, Kate, had left. Fulke. Could he have found out about Hannah's infidelity? Perhaps he'd known all along and had been waiting for a chance to kill her. Also, there was the possibility that one of the recovering officers might have tried to kill the earl and fumbled it.

"But you haven't heard the worst."

Sophia's voice interrupted Kate's musing.

"What, Mama?"

"Lady Juliana accused the marquess of killing Lady Hannah. Right in front of those police people. In front of everyone."

"That's absurd."

"That's what Lord Sinclair said. Of course, they all

knew that you had been walking with him, along with that Beechwith creature. It was all quite clear, but Juliana didn't care. She kept telling the constables to arrest the marquess, and dear Lord Alexis just stood there and let her accuse him. If Lord Sinclair hadn't taken Juliana away, I don't know what would have happened. It's all so confusing and terrible."

"So she humiliated him, and he didn't defend himself?"

"Well, you know how Lord Alexis is with his mother, all closed up and frozen. I don't understand it."

Kate made for the bedroom door. "Where is he?"

"Asleep. Meredith finally got him to bed an hour ago."

Slowing, Kate resigned herself to a wait. But she was going to face down Alexis de Granville, dead Hannah or no.

Chapter Sixteen

Kate emerged from the Watch Tower onto the wall walk. It was almost sunset of the second day following Hannah's death, and she knew from Meredith that Alexis was up on the curtain wall. He was standing between two merlons with his arms propped on an embrasure. In profile his face was outlined with the gold haze of the setting sun. There wasn't an unclean or bulging line to complain of in that visage, and its perfection made her all the more angry. He might have forgotten Mrs. Beechwith, but she hadn't. Marching up to him, she stopped beside a merlon. It was pierced by an arrow slit.

"I won't be a grain of sand."

Alexis whipped about to face her. "Everlasting hell. You shouldn't sneak up on a man."

"I didn't sneak. You were daydreaming."

He came close to her. "I was thinking of you."

She threw out a warning hand. "Don't bother to be nice. You won't feel like it for long, because I have a few things to say to you."

Sighing, he leaned on the merlon, folded his arms, and cocked his head. Kate scowled at him.

"I hear you managed to protect Valentine from justice, spare Fulke the knowledge of Hannah's infidelities, and save your mistress's reputation all at the same time."

"It's a talent I learned from having the keeping of dozens of regimental officers whose sole object in life is to play havoc with the Queen's peace."

Balling her hands into fists, Kate summoned up her courage and plunged ahead. "So you've put everyone's house in order. How considerate. The only problem I see is that you don't give me the same courtesy."

"You aren't making sense."

"You're a little dollop of butter, my lord, and you spread yourself over too many pieces of toast."

"Your metaphor is giving me nausea."

"I'm trying to explain something to you, de Granville. And I'm trying to be ladylike about it." She poked her finger in his chest. "When I was walking hundreds of miles across the American continent behind starving oxen and growing up in houses with canvas walls, I learned one important thing—if you don't demand respect, you're not going to get it. And by God, sir, you'll respect me, or I'll string you up by your generous endowments."

Alexis gaped at her, then blinked rapidly. "You're mad."

"If you mean that I'm angry, you have grasped my point. I'm through with our engagement. You can go back to the lady with the hot-air balloons on her chest."

Kate turned on her heel to leave, but Alexis grabbed her arm and swung her around. If she hadn't been so angry, she would have been frightened at the rage in his eyes. He pushed her against the merlon and placed his arms on either side of her to block her escape.

"I will decide when to end our betrothal, you presumptuous little witch. And I'm not ready for that yet."

Scowling up into glass-hard eyes, Kate said, "I'm not a convenience like indoor running water. You may run Val's life, and most everyone else's, but you don't run mine. It's a wonder to me that you belly up at your mother's feet like you do. But then I forgot. She has even less respect for you than I."

He grabbed her shoulders and lifted her off her feet, then just as suddenly, he dropped her. Kate's ankle gave way, and she stumbled. Alexis caught her around the waist and held her steady.

"She told you," he said. His hands dropped away from her.

"Told me what?"

"About my murders."

Kate furrowed her brow. His anger was gone. No, it had changed somehow. Alexis stood over her with one arm resting on the top of the merlon. Beneath the sleeves of his jacket she could see the bunching of his muscles. When he spoke his voice was no longer raised. It was quiet but resonant with suppressed emotion.

"Aren't you afraid to be alone with me now that you know?"

"Did you kill your father and sister?"

He closed his eyes and whispered, "I must have."

"You mean you don't know?"

"I remember them dying."

"Don't you remember setting the trap?"

He shook his head.

Kate slipped away a few paces, then turned to face him, her hands on her hips. "I didn't believe your mother when she told me. After we announced our engagement she told me you'd murdered them and every mistress you ever had."

"What?"

Kate nodded.

"But only one is dead besides Ophelia," he said, "and she was killed in a carriage accident when I was with my regiment two years ago."

"Then why does your mother tell these stories? To behonest, Alexis, I don't think she's, well, healthy in her mind."

He laughed. "It's not that. She hates me for killing Father and Thalia."

"Stop that. You aren't capable of such evil."

"You don't know that. Like Macbeth, 'I am in blood stepp'd in so far, that, should I wade no more,/Returning were as tedious as go o'er.' " He turned away from Kate and looked out at the clouds on the horizon. They glowed with volcanic intensity as the sun set. "But regardless of my sins, we will continue as we are until after Hannah is buried and things have settled down. We should be rid of each other in a few weeks."

"Oh no."

"And then I'll find some perfect Lady whose head is stuffed with goose down, marry her, and get an heir. A Lady who won't ask questions to which she doesn't want the answer."

The morning after Kate confronted him with his supposed infidelities, Alexis sat in the small dining room, a plate loaded with eggs and ham in front of him. He contemplated the blobs of white sprinkled with pepper while he thought of Hannah and Cardigan, and Val. Worry over his friend, sadness for Hannah, and bewilderment about Kate caused his stomach to do one of Iago's somersaults. He shoved the plate away and tried to force tea down his throat. He was unsuccessful, because at that moment his mother came in on Fulke's arm.

Placing the cup back in its saucer with great care, Alexis nodded to Juliana. He expected no greeting from her and got none. Fulke murmured something to him.

"How are you?" Alexis asked.

"I'm fine," Fulke said. "It's hard to believe she's gone."

Fulke sat down beside Alexis and toyed with his napkin. Alexis studied his cousin's face. Since Hannah's death he'd been withdrawn, but calm.

"I'll find out what happened," Alexis said.

"I know what happened. Like all women, she succumbed to her evil nature at last. She went out to fornicate with her lover and in her crazed lust, she lost her footing and plunged to her death."

Alexis clenched his hands into fists and looked away from Fulke's righteous expression.

"Oh, Fulke, no," Juliana said.

"Please," Fulke said. "Do me the favor of avoiding the whole subject. It is painful to me."

Alexis tried to lift his teacup again while Juliana and Fulke talked about the weather. He managed a nod to several questions directed to him by Fulke.

"By the way," Fulke said. "It seems your repairs to the keep weren't extensive enough. Part of the upper wall is falling down."

"But it was fine," Alexis said.

"Not this morning. I was walking on the lawn and noticed several stones and some mortar at the foot of the keep."

"I'll look into it after I finish my meal."

"Your food is cold," Fulke said.

Before Alexis could protest, Fulke ordered hot food for him. Under his cousin's badgering, he managed to eat, but only after Juliana excused herself. At last he escaped

Fulke's brooding presence under the pretense of his concern for the damage to the keep.

Once out in the courtyard, he wandered along the perimeter of the lawn until he came to the old tower. At its base lay several broken stones. Crumbling mortar spattered the grass, and one of the stones had torn a deep gouge in the turf. Alexis kicked a rock, then bent back and looked up at the top of the wall, shielding his eyes with one hand. As Fulke had said, part of it was collapsing. He could see two stones, one beneath the other and each the size of his chest, that had collapsed on each other so that they rested at a tilt. Perhaps the mortar between them had given way with age.

Alexis looked at the stones on the ground again. One had fresh chip marks in it, probably from being struck by another rock. He bent, grasping it in both hands. As he did so, he heard Iago bark. Dropping to one knee, Alexis looked up and saw the dog bound across the court after Val. His friend waved, and Iago raced in circles around the limping man. Alexis scowled at Val. He was still angry at the fool for scoffing at the superintendent. Alexis turned back to lift the rock.

"Alexis, move!"

The words themselves wouldn't have produced his instant reaction. What caused Alexis to dive headlong away from the keep was Val's tone. It was the one he'd used in battle, the one that commanded his men to charge, to wheel, to retreat, an officer's shouted order. As Alexis hit the ground he felt a heavy weight glance off his shoe. There was a thud and then the sound of pebbles and sand falling. He landed on his stomach. Iago romped over to him, barked, and stuck his muzzle in Alexis's neck. Alexis cursed and shoved the dog away.

"Good boy, Iago. Not now."

Val hurried up to him. "Are you all right?"

"Yes, just covered in dust and feeling stupid." Alexis brushed mortar from his hair.

Craning his neck backward, Val examined the crumbling wall. "What possessed you to stand beneath those stones when they were obviously about to tumble down?"

"You're standing under them."

Val stepped away from the keep. "It would be ironic to survive the Crimea and get smashed by your own house."

"I'll have someone build a barricade and get my foreman to look at the damage."

"Mmmm. I want to talk to you."

"That's a change. It wasn't long ago that you had nothing to say to me."

"Not about Hannah and Cardigan," Val said. "About Kate."

"What about Kate?"

"What have you done to her? She's moping around like a puppy who's lost its mother."

"Stay out of it," Alexis said.

"I like her. And don't think I haven't noticed you and that Beechwith woman. Don't hurt Kate, Alexis. She's a sweet little thing underneath all that determination."

Alexis looked up from brushing dirt off his coat sleeve. Val was so angry, the gold in his hair seemed to catch fire. Alexis slowly straightened to his full height, his gaze fixed on Val's.

"Don't try shriveling me with that lord-of-the-castle stare," Val said irritably.

"Then don't presume to interfere."

Val stabbed his cane into the grass. "Someone has to stop you from tossing your own future into the latrine. When are you going to forget the past?"

"That's the trouble," Alexis said. "I've forgotten my past too much lately."

Val made an impatient and rude sound. Turning from Alexis, he called to Iago and stalked away. Alexis watched the two leave before returning to his examination of the keep. There was a hole at the top of the tower now, where the fallen stones had been. He would need to see his foreman immediately. After he'd done that, perhaps he would visit Carolina. He should, if only to prove that he could do as he wished, prove it to himself and to a presumptuous snippet named Katie Ann Grey.

Several days of misery passed for Kate. She spent much of her time sitting in her room crying, or simply befogged by melancholy. She had lost. It was her own fault for being so jealous that she had berated a proud man as though he were a dog. All it had gotten her was an Alexis who avoided her, a cold, princely man who treated her with impersonal respect and insulting politeness. He didn't even protest when she stopped wearing a crinoline.

She was sure he was seeing Carolina Beechwith. Val said he wasn't, but Kate was sure those long rides of Alexis's ended in that woman's bed. Val said she was wrong. He seemed sure his friend wasn't bedding Carolina.

"It's what he wants you to think," Val had said. "He's trying awfully hard to make you hate him. Don't let him, Kate. He needs you."

She was in the kitchen garden early one morning thinking about what Val had said when Alexis appeared. She hadn't talked to him in days. The first sign she had of his presence was hearing his riding boots crunch on the gravel outside the kitchen door. He stopped when she looked up from the hole she was digging. Dressed in riding clothes tailored to enhance the near perfection of his body, tapping his crop against his thigh, he looked too much the sophisticated aristocrat. He frowned at her in silence.

She stabbed the dirt with her spade. "I hear your castle is falling down on top of you."

"It was nothing serious."

"Not unless you consider how many accidents have happened in this neighborhood in the past few weeks."

He walked over to her, stopping so close that his polished boot knocked dirt back into the hole she was digging.

"My house is centuries old," he said. "Parts of it are always falling down."

She sat back on her heels and glanced up at him. "That may be, but when was the last time some of it decided to fall on you?"

She was startled when Alexis dropped to his haunches beside her. His gaze traveled over her face, and he cast aside his riding crop. Pulling off one of his gloves, he touched a finger to her chin.

"You've been working hard," he said. "You're all tousled, and those tiny wisps of hair on your forehead are curling again."

"You're not listening. I think you ought to be worried."

He was staring at her neck. Kate remembered that, along with rolling up her sleeves, she'd undone the top buttons of her gown when she started to dig. She refused to clutch at the open bodice like a guilty serving maid.

"Alexis, you're not listening."

Her irritation rose when he failed to answer a second time. He was beginning to make her nervous. She could smell the soap he used—its aroma was like wood and clean air—and feel his body heat. Even when he was kneeling his height and the bulk of his shoulders made her feel like an ant.

It wasn't easy to move away from him while she was sitting on her skirt. Kate managed to put a few inches between them, but the effort was wasted because Alexis moved closer. She put out a hand to stop him, and he caught it. His thumb stroked the back of her hand, and her agitation increased. He wasn't going to answer her at all. The snake was content to let her babble while he examined her as if she were a jewel he was considering purchasing. She tried to pull her hand free, but he wouldn't release it. He turned it over and opened the curled fingers.

"A grubby little paw." He pulled at her hand until she was resting against his chest. "You're all hot and sweaty, Katie Ann. I like you hot and sweaty."

"Let go."

He grasped her wrists and held them down at her sides, then he kissed her ear. His breath tickled her neck, and she shivered as his teeth raked gently down her throat. Her whole body vibrated. Her nipples and the ends of her fingers and toes began to tingle. Her concern about the accidents faded when Alexis released her wrists and fastened his hands on her buttocks. He brought her up against his body and began to flex his hips. The steady thrust of those talented hips warned her. If she didn't say something now, he wouldn't stop. Already his eyes were burning with sexual tension. Once he'd made up his mind, he wouldn't give quarter.

She pressed her hands against his chest. "No."

"Yes."

"I said no."

"And I said yes." He leaned over her.

Kate bent backward to avoid more contact with his body, but he kept leaning. She lost her balance. Catching herself with her hands, she realized that he'd forced her back to the ground and was on his knees straddling her body. She tried to get her legs under her, but he lowered himself on top of her. Smothering the beginnings of an objection with his mouth, he pressed his body down until her breasts flattened against his chest.

She pulled her mouth free of his and said the one

thing that kept her from unleashing her own passion. "What about the Beechwith?"

Breathing hard, Alexis lifted his head and glared at her. "Forget Carolina."

"I'm not a pliable English miss. I don't forget my lover's mistresses. I won't let you touch me and then go to her."

Alexis held Kate's arms to either side of her head. He favored her with a smile that sent a tremor of dread through her body. Lowering his lips to the exposed flesh of her chest, he whispered to her between kisses.

"I'll have you, here, in the dirt of my garden, and there will be no need for me to go to her. My Katie Ann."

She felt his tongue slide beneath the edge of her gown. Arousal warred with her instinct for self-preservation. She wrenched her arms free, grabbed the hair on the back of Alexis's head, and yanked.

"I told you. I don't share."

Alexis cursed and jumped to his feet. "No woman orders me about." He picked up his discarded glove and crop.

"I don't want to order you about," Kate said, standing too. "I only want you to treat me as if—"

"As if you were a Lady?"

She shook her head, but he ignored her.

"You're lying to yourself. You're a hot-blooded little savage who takes pleasure in arousing me and then putting me in the stocks."

Putting her hands on her hips, Kate raised her voice. "You came after me. I did nothing."

"Nothing! You could give lessons to a king's mistress." He tugged on his glove with sharp, jerking movements. "I'm not through with you, Katherine Grey. Take the warning. I'm not through with you, and your demands and your pride won't help you the next time I want you."

He turned his back and walked away. Kate uttered a

cry of rage, then stooped to pick up a clump of dirt and threw it. The lump splattered against the outside wall of the kitchen as the door slammed behind Alexis. She picked up another dirt clod, intent on hitting Alexis even if she had to follow him into the castle. Her reason returned before she got out of the garden. As satisfying as it would be to hurl mud in the face of that snake, she wasn't foolish enough to think she could do it and escape without reprisal. No, upon examination, hitting the Marquess of Richfield with a handful of dirt before dozens of his servants was not a good idea.

Kate dropped the lump of dirt and wandered back to the spot where she'd been digging. Val was wrong. Alexis didn't need her, not as she wished to be needed. Alexis wanted her, like he wanted Mrs. Beechwith. She would think that after being the object of lust himself so many times, Alexis would know she needed more from him. Wiping the sweat from her forehead, Kate sighed. She wasn't doing anything right, not anything to do with Alexis. Confused, that's what she was. Confused.

After their fight in the kitchen garden, Alexis alternately glared at Kate and ignored her. Kate either glared back at him or pretended she didn't care that he snubbed her. While she was feeling sorry for herself, the Earl of Cardigan was recovering from his head injury. A week after Hannah's death, he asked Kate to walk with him. He promised to make no advances. Since she was tired of sulking in her room and she didn't much care how she spent her time, she agreed.

She was waiting for the earl outside the castle walls on the lawn before the "back door" drawbridge. Down the path that led to the stables, two men came toward her, Cardigan and Alexis, their voices raised in argument.

"He should be in gaol," Cardigan said.

"He didn't do it."

The earl halted and stared at Alexis. "You're protecting him, de Granville. Harboring the man who tried to kill me. If you had any honor, you'd hand Beaufort over to the authorities this moment."

"You question my honor, sir?" Alexis asked. "By God, I've had enough of you. We can settle the matter in the usual way."

"Tomorrow morning, before I leave."

"Done."

Kate had been staring at the two men. At last she found her tongue. "That's ridiculous."

Alexis tossed his head. "Women know nothing about a man's honor."

"I know about honor, and I know about stupidity, and facing off with dueling pistols is stupid."

Ignoring her, Alexis inclined his head to Cardigan and left them. Cardigan took her arm and guided her away when she continued to glare after the marquess. They took a path through the woods. Kate waited until her own temper had cooled before speaking.

"Dueling is against the law."

"My lovely Miss Grey, I refuse to speak of it."

"Men. All right, let's talk about what happened in the keep. Are you sure you didn't see who hit you?"

Cardigan pursed his lips. "I was preoccupied."

Kate forbore from asking the nature of his preoccupation. The bastard had probably been kissing Hannah.

The path was beginning to wind into an S curve. Cardigan stopped beneath the heavy limbs of a tree whose trunk was so wide, it had to be several hundred years old. He took Kate's hand and kissed it. She pulled her hand away.

"Miss Grey, it is obvious to me that you aren't happy in your engagement to de Granville."

"Ha!"

He edged nearer to her. The earl was shorter than Alexis, but still taller than she. A slim man, he moved with a quick grace that she assumed served him equally well in the cavalry and with women. Beginning to feel nervous, she tried to edge away from him, but he kept coming, and she found herself back up against the old tree.

"You promised to leave me alone," she said.

"You're afraid of me. Do you still carry that knife?"

"I am not afraid of you, and, yes, I still carry it."

He stopped so close to her that his breath stirred the fine wisps of hair on her forehead. "Prove that you aren't afraid."

Kate narrowed her eyes. She was about to say something mutinous, but the earl interrupted her thoughts.

"A lovely girl like you should be worshipped, my dear. You are glorious, and de Granville is a fool to let you out of his sight."

He darted at her and Kate, caught off guard, stood still with her eyes open while he kissed her. His lips were strange to her, for they weren't Alexis's. And since they weren't Alexis's, she didn't want them on her mouth. She put her hands on the earl's chest and shoved.

She had forgotten how experienced he was. He countered by fastening his arms around her and squeezing her between his body and the tree. His hand rubbed her neck, then caressed its way down to her breast and squeezed.

Cardigan lifted his mouth from hers. "Oh no. I'm not about to let you get to that knife." He kissed her again.

Kate tore her mouth free and stomped down hard on the earl's foot. The yelp he let out was most satisfying. She watched him hop on one foot for a moment as she straightened her clothing.

"Ass," she said. "You're lucky I used my foot instead of the knife."

Without giving the earl another glance, she swept back toward the castle.

"Stupid man," she muttered. "All men are idiots. Groping, rutting fools." Realizing Cardigan was coming after her, she broke into a trot.

She hadn't gone far when she heard another yelp. She listened, and there was another cry. It was Cardigan. Was the man trying to get her back by pretending to have hurt himself? He was capable of such a trick. After checking to make sure her knife was in place, Kate ran back the way she had come.

Veering around a turn in the path, she almost ran into the earl. He was standing with his back to her. Opposite him stood Valentine Beaufort wielding a Scottish dirk she recognized from the armory.

"Val?" Kate started forward.

"Stay where you are. No, move away from the earl, Kate. Farther. That's good." Val's hand flexed on the handle of the dirk. "I thought you were gone."

"I heard a shout."

"The coward," Val said. "He won't stand his ground."

"You're mad," the earl said. His eyes bulged wider every time Val moved the dirk.

Kate held out her hand to the younger man. "Now, Val, you don't want to do this."

Val laughed. He lunged at the earl, then jumped back. Cardigan yipped and scuffled out of the way. Val circled his prey, taking swipes at him and taunting him. As the play continued, his breathing grew labored.

"Everyone thinks I killed Hannah in trying to get you."

He jabbed at the earl's stomach.

"So I decided I might as well be hanged for your murder too."

The earl dodged a backhanded slice. Val stepped away and lowered his weapon. He was sweating and his eyes never left Cardigan. To Kate he seemed oblivious to anything else but the man he wanted to kill.

Val hefted the dirk. "It's time for your execution, my

lord hero. I wanted to hang, draw, and quarter you, but I'm not strong enough." He ran his finger along the edge of the blade. "My men were smashed like raw eggs thrown at a stone wall. They burst open, and their insides spilled out and ran all over the ground. Now I'm going to cut you open and spill your guts like theirs were."

As Val talked, Kate noticed a movement beyond his shoulder. Around the last turn in the S curve came Alexis. Since Cardigan was speechless, she had to keep Val's mind off killing long enough for Alexis to reach him. She licked her lips and clasped her hands in front of her. "Oh, Val, please don't do this. I couldn't bear it if you were hanged for murder."

At her desperate tone, Val finally turned his gaze from the earl and looked at her. "Why would it matter to you? Your eyes are filled with the beautiful Alexis."

"He doesn't want me anymore, and I . . . I've come to admire you." Kate thought smoldering thoughts about Alexis and stared at Val. Wetting her lips, she took a step in his direction. "Please, Val."

As Kate moved, Alexis threw himself at Val. The two hurtled to the ground, and the dirk flew across the path. Cardigan shouted. Backpedaling away from the fighters, he drew a small pistol from his coat. The barrel of the gun waved and dipped as he tried to get a clear shot at Val.

Kate skittered away from the rolling and grappling men and stopped behind the earl. She saw the gun bob first in one direction and then another. Alexis and Val were wrapped around each other in a vicious hug. She heard the click as the earl cocked the pistol. Kate hauled up her skirt, palmed her knife, and threw it. The blade sank into the earl's biceps.

Cardigan shrieked and dropped the gun. At the earl's cry, both Val and Alexis froze. They looked up at the wounded man as if he'd suddenly turned into a blue pig. Motionless, they watched Kate retrieve her knife from the earl's arm, wipe it on his coat, and replace it in the sheath strapped to her calf.

Cardigan sank to his knees, his fingers pressed against the wound. Blood spilled out over his fingers and he moaned.

Alexis loosened his grip on Val and helped his friend rise. Val's gaze was fixed on the earl's arm. Kate went to him and put her hand on his shoulder.

Val's attention never wavered from the wound. Suddenly he turned his head away. "I thought I wanted to see his blood. I was wrong."

Alexis threw his arms around Val as his knees buckled. With Kate's help he lowered the man to the ground. "No more blood, Alexis," he said, his eyes fluttering closed. "I'm sorry."

Kate put her hand to Val's cheek. "I think he's fainted from exhaustion." She glanced up to find Alexis's furious gaze boring into her.

"Do you always expose your legs to strange men?" he asked. "Do you make a habit of declaring love to one man while betrothed to another? Fulke was right about you, wasn't he? I have made myself ridiculous by linking my name with yours."

Kate rose and bit her lip to keep it still. "Then by all means, my lord, unlink our names. I won't stop you."

She ran away. It was the only thing she could do to keep him from seeing her cry.

Alexis closed the door behind the physician and returned to Val's bedside. It had taken all his influence to keep Cardigan from having his friend arrested. The reprieve was temporary, though. The earl had been persuaded to leave the matter in Alexis's hands for only one week.

After pulling the covers higher on Val's chest, Alexis

sat down in an armchair and rubbed his face with both hands. One bloody disaster after another, he thought.

He'd managed to make Kate hate him. It was the passion that had done him in. No woman should mean that much to him, no woman like Kate. She was such a brilliant and ingenuous little creature. Funny how she was blind to his great transgression and yet battened on a little fault like Carolina Beechwith. She kept insisting he was incapable of killing. But she hadn't been with him in the Crimea.

If only she hadn't made him so angry. In his entire adult life no woman had ever boxed his ears so thoroughly as Kate had on the wall walk. And the silly part about the whole thing was that he was more or less innocent.

Oh, he'd been tempted to make love to Carolina that night, but only out of spite. In the keep, Carolina had been as insistent as ever, but he'd only been able to think about Kate. His mind had persisted in showing him pictures of her—Kate hiding her tears when he hurt her, Kate attempting a maidenly walk, Kate sitting on his lap and swinging her feet. As he'd made himself kiss Carolina, he'd heard Kate calling herself a Fallen Woman. He'd pulled away from Carolina after that kiss, an apology on his lips. That was when he'd heard the scream.

At his side, Val stirred. He opened his eyes and groaned. "You sat on my ribs."

"Unfortunately I didn't break any."

"I didn't kill her." Val closed his eyes again.

"I know that, you young ass."

Val smiled, but Alexis could tell he was drifting off to sleep already. Leaving his friend to the ministrations of his valet, Alexis went to his own rooms where Meredith had a hot bath waiting. He soaked in the steaming water until his skin was uncomfortably wrinkled. He almost fell asleep, but Meredith got him out and into a dressing gown.

It was nearing time for dinner. His shoulders ached,

and his elbows and knuckles were bruised from fighting with Val. He didn't want to face Kate. He knew that if he didn't speak to her soon, he would never be able to convince her to forgive him and let him make love to her. And if he couldn't see her and love her, he didn't think he could face living. He thought of the death ride. More and more, he found himself preferring her company to riding like a demon. When he was with her, he was either too fascinated or too angry to succumb to his guilt.

"Meredith."

"Yes, my lord."

"Am I ready?" Alexis examined his black evening trousers and jacket. He tugged at his cravat.

Meredith shoved his hands away and put the tie back the way it had been. "Yes, my lord. Shall I tell Lord Sinclair that you and Miss Grey will be down a bit late?"

"I won't ask how you know what I'm about. Yes, thank you."

He was knocking at Kate's door in five minutes. He cleared his throat and tried to smile as it opened. Kate's mother stood in the threshold dabbing a handkerchief to her eyes. She didn't look surprised to see him. His smile vanished.

"She never would behave like other girls," Sophia said. "She wouldn't listen."

"What are you talking about?"

Alexis pushed past the woman. Striding across the sitting room, he entered the bedchamber. Petticoats, shoes, and dresses were strewn everywhere. The doors of two armoires were open. Alexis picked up a transparent chemise and stood looking at it.

Sophia came to stand beside him. "She cried for over an hour, and then she started packing. She wouldn't listen to me. She took a carriage and her maid."

"But why?"

"My little girl has great courage. But something or

someone has frightened her more than Indian savages or drunken miners ever did."

He watched Kate's mother leave, then stepped over a pile of dresses and sat on the bed. He landed on something hard. Rising, he fished beneath the mattress and pulled out a book on paleontology. He sat back down, only to get up again and throw back the mattress. There was a layer of books under it. Picking up a volume of Voltaire, he noticed something sticking out from under the bed. The corner of yet another book.

Curious, Alexis opened a drawer in a bedside table. Nothing there but handkerchiefs. He picked up the cushion of a chaise longue. More books. Books beneath petticoats, inside hats, in the compartment of the window seat. Letting the lid of the seat fall, Alexis perched on it and opened a worn volume bound in gilded leather. There was an inscription.

> To my little Hypatia. Let knowledge light your soul, and don't get caught by the Christians.
>
> Your loving, Papa.

Alexis turned the flyleaf. It was a history of astronomy. Hypatia. She had been a lovely and learned scholar of Alexandria who had been attacked by a Christian mob, dragged into a church, and scraped to death with oyster shells. Closing the book, Alexis ran his hand over the cracked spine and gazed out at the sky. It was taking on the deep azure glow of twilight. The castle battlements grew dark in contrast, and the merlons looked like stubby teeth in a giant mouth.

"Have I been scraping you to death with oyster shells, my little savage?"

Dropping the astronomy book, Alexis shot to his feet and ran out of the bedroom. She could have given him a chance to apologize. Didn't she think he was man enough to face his mistakes? The little menace. She stabbed the earl, then left Alexis to patch up the wound and clean up the mess. He was the one who should be angry, but no, she had to rush off in a dudgeon and leave him feeling guilty. She did it on purpose, and he wasn't going to stand for it.

He pounded downstairs to find Meredith waiting for him with a cloak.

"This habit of reading my mind is frightening," Alexis said, turning so that Meredith could drape the cloak over him.

"Yes, my lord. I spoke to Mrs. Grey's maid. Miss Grey will be staying the night in the village of Thistleborough, the Fox and Hound Inn."

Alexis rode Theseus as though his demons were chasing him, only this time he was the one doing the chasing. Thistleborough was a good three hours' ride away. It boasted a railway station. If he didn't catch her that night, Kate would most likely take a train to London and vanish. He had no doubt she could disappear so that he would never find her.

When he reached the village, the only light in the whole place came from the Fox and Hound. He clattered into the staging yard and roused a groom. It was after eleven o'clock by the time he'd found the proprietor and intimidated him into revealing Kate's room. He took a moment to catch his breath in the hall, then knocked. Not waiting for an answer, he opened the door and stepped inside.

Kate was curled up in a chair with a book open in her lap. She didn't look up.

"All right, Maisy," she said. "I'll get ready for bed, but I won't sleep."

"Let me help you take your clothes off."

Chapter Seventeen

The book sailed off Kate's lap and banged on the floor. She jumped up and took refuge behind her chair.

"Get out," she said.

"Young ladies don't order peers of the realm about." Alexis stooped and picked up the book. "You ran away, you little coward."

He glanced at the book in his hand.

"It's Roman history," she said. "Unmaidenly, I know, but I haven't come down with brain fever from overstraining my mind yet."

He was feeling guilty again.

"What's unmaidenly," he said, "is your traveling without a chaperone. And you had the temerity to leave me like a pregnant bride on the altar steps. You will make us the subject of common gossip."

"If you've come to drag me back to save your own reputation as a rake, you can turn right around and go back to your castle full of mistresses and murderers. Our engagement is over."

"It isn't over until I allow it." He heard his voice raise and saw Kate give a little start. A thrill shot through him when he detected the glint in her eyes. It reminded him of the gleam of a bayonet in sunlight.

"I don't care what you want!" she shouted at him. "I'm tired of being an embarrassment. I'm tired of pretending to be a well-bred Lady, and I won't do it anymore." Her hands worked open and shut on the back of the chair. She lowered her voice. "Don't you see? I'll never be a proper gentlewoman. And don't you dare interrupt me. I'm going to tell you the truth, and you're going to listen and find out what I'm really like."

She left the safety of her chair and stood in front of him. Alexis held his breath. He didn't want to risk a distraction that would stop her from telling him what was making her voice choke and her hands tremble.

"How can you expect me to concern myself with lace patterns and wax flowers? When I was sixteen I shot a prospector who was trying to rape me. I've washed dirty underwear for strange men. I've doctored whores and served meals to men who'd be put in prison here."

She cursed and wiped tears from her eyes, then fished in her pocket for a handkerchief. Alexis handed her his, but kept silent.

"Go away, Alexis." She stopped to dab furiously at her eyes. "Damn. Don't you say anything. Just because I'm crying doesn't mean I'm not thinking clearly. I'm just mad. Go home. You don't want me. Not the real me. And I can't pretend to be anything else."

He stepped out of the way as she attempted to shove him aside. She collapsed in the chair again, and he watched her try to cry without making a sound.

"You're crying," he said. He shrugged off his cloak and let it fall to the floor.

"I am not," she said, then gave up and let out a great, long sob.

"Hell and damnation." He dropped to his knees and tried to take her in his arms. She stiffened the moment he touched her.

"Don't touch me, you sanctimonious, blue-blooded prig."

She struggled, got an arm free, and aimed at his chin. He captured her fist and tucked it between their bodies, then saw her open her mouth. Knowing her, he wasn't surprised when she tried to bite him. He dodged her teeth while fighting to maintain his hold on her. Burnished curls swung at him, and his face was soon obscured by a fine curtain of hair. She bit him through it.

"Ouch!" He grabbed the back of her neck and shoved her face into his shoulder. "Stop it, damn you. I'm trying to apologize."

Kate went still. He relaxed his grip, and she lifted her head to gaze at him, unsmiling.

"I've been thinking and thinking," she said before he could continue, "but it doesn't do any good to try to find answers to feelings with logic, so I gave up. Then, tonight, as I was reading, a thought just bubbled up from somewhere inside me."

Leaning back, she stared into his eyes. "All of us, Mama, Hannah, Ophelia, even Mrs. Beechwith, all of us women are taught from childhood to lock our real selves away in a little prison in our heads, because we learn what the world wants us to be like. Most of us try so hard to be Ladies, to be what everyone says we should be. But all the time there's this other self inside somewhere. Locked up in chains, suffering, hurting from being told she isn't wanted. Most of us just don't listen to her."

Kate sighed and turned her head away from him.

"Maybe that secret part of us dies from neglect," she said. "Me? I'm turned inside out. All the parts nobody wants are on the outside, and I can't seem to shove them inside and out of sight where they belong."

"Oh, God, Katie Ann."

"I accept your apology. Now please get out."

"No." He kept one arm around her and brushed aside her hair with the other hand. "I listened to you, so you have to listen to me. We've arrived at the same conclusions by different paths. I've been scraping you with oyster shells." He heard her catch her breath, but he rushed on. "I've been scraping at what you call your outside since we met, trying to peel away your layers of gold to find a nice, comfortable surface of tin, when all the while it was the gold I wanted."

She was quiet. When she didn't speak, the fear that had sent him riding out into the night to find her returned.

"If you leave me, I don't think I will care about what is happening to my family, or my wounded at the Dower House, or fixing my castle. If you don't love me, I might as well jump into my own oubliette."

He was afraid to look at her. During his little speech, he had addressed her clasped hands. Assembling his courage, he lifted his gaze to the woman who had turned his life into a carousel full of music, brightly painted horses, and joy. She was watching him with eyes framed by damp lashes. Her lower lip was caught between her teeth, then her pink tongue shot out to moisten it.

"I'm a Fallen Woman."

Alexis took his final risk. "Not if you're married to the evil ravisher of your innocence."

"Are you sure, Alexis?"

He was tired of talking. He made a kiss his answer. Kate was quiescent at first, as if she didn't quite believe he knew what he was about. As he deepened the kiss, she made a little gasping sound and wrapped her arms around his neck.

Later neither of them could remember how her gown

got ripped or at what point his trousers ended up dangling from the bedpost. Alexis did remember tunneling beneath the covers and coming to rest on top of a deliciously soft body.

He ran his fingers through the long, copper tresses that shone against the white of the pillows. He spent an eternity kissing her, and another caressing her breasts and nipples. He was curling his tongue around a hardened peak when Kate slipped her hand between them, and he felt it close around him. The little devil had known her hand was cold. Alexis cried out at the icy touch and arched his back. He shot forward, deeper into her grip, and she squeezed him. He felt blood churning in his groin and tried to pull away, but she wouldn't let him. He laughed.

"All right, all right. Together."

After their lovemaking, he fell on top of Kate's moist body and panted. His face burned. He could feel her hands still roving over his back and buttocks. Exhausted, he made no protest when she reversed their positions. She straddled him, then laid her head on his shoulder and licked his neck. He wriggled, and she laughed. She kissed his lips, snuggled back down on his shoulder, and sighed.

"Have to get married," he said, his voice slurred, "before my seed takes root like a weed in a vegetable patch."

Kate didn't say anything, and he thought she'd fallen asleep. He was drifting off when he felt a hand on his thigh. Fingers dug into the muscles. They traced a path to his inner thigh and caressed. His eyes flew open at the resurgence of life in his groin.

He grinned at her. "You're going to marry me for my title and then pleasure me to death, aren't you?"

Again there was no answer. The exploring fingers reached the top of his thigh and then darted to his groin. Alexis whooped with amusement and pounced on Kate. She was smirking at him. He forced her legs apart and caressed her with his erection.

"I warn you," he said as his hips began to move. "I'm going to defend myself with every weapon I have."

She closed her eyes and squeezed his bottom. "That was the whole idea. I wanted to see all your weapons."

She would have a fairy-tale life if it weren't for all the people who were mad at her. Kate returned to the castle with Alexis to find that Mama was angry at her for running away without explaining why. Lady Juliana was furious because when they got back, they told everyone they'd decided to marry in three weeks.

And Fulke. Fulke had taken the news worse than he had his wife's death. He exploded at Alexis, and the two men had to be separated by Val and the butler.

After that incident, Kate avoided her detractors by making visits to Maitland House and surveying the renovations. During that time, even after the Earl of Cardigan left, Alexis was busy with official men in black suits who kept showing up and questioning servants, the family, and especially Val.

All that questioning dug beneath the fluffy layers of her happiness with Alexis, prickling her nerves. Hannah had died by someone's hand, and that person was still unknown. And the more she thought about Hannah's death, the less Ophelia's seemed an accident. Kate couldn't bring herself to believe that her cousin wouldn't wake if her room caught fire. Yet nothing indicated that Ophelia had died other than by misadventure. Then there was that incident of the stones from the keep almost falling on Alexis. Two deaths and a near death, and no one thought the amount of ill fortune remarkable.

Kate made the mistake of confiding her suspicions to her mother. They were visiting Maitland House, inspecting newly arrived drapes. As soon as Kate mentioned that there were too many deaths at or near Castle Richfield, Mama launched into a vapor.

"Oh dear," Sophia said. "Ohdearohdearohdear!"

"What now, Mama?"

"You're making trouble again. After nearly creating a scandal by running away, after shocking practically the whole of county Society with your behavior . . ."

Kate listened to her mother's complaints, but this time something was different. This time she was aware of a feeling of repetition. Alexis. Alexis had criticized. Mama criticized, but Mama had been criticizing for as long as Kate could remember. She heard Mama say the word "ashamed" and her mind and heart burst into flames.

"Shut up, Mama."

Sophia put a gloved hand to her throat as her mouth opened and shut. "Oooh."

"I mean it, Mama." Kate felt her throat go dry, but she was determined to finish what she'd begun. "I'm sick of being criticized. Do you know how much that hurts? Do you even care? If it weren't for me being unladylike, you wouldn't even be here. In fact, you just might be dead."

Kate could feel the anger she'd held back for years ramming against the shield of her control. "Don't try to interrupt, Mama. I'm going to say this, so that we understand each other from now on." She swallowed while Sophia stared at her. "You aren't willing to take the responsibility of doing all these things you criticize me for doing, like looking after the family business, but the only reason you have the luxury of pretending you don't know anything about such tawdry things is because I do it all. But you're quite willing to spend the money I have to guard, aren't you? Well, if my unladylike behavior upsets you so much, why don't you do some of the work so I can be delicate and ethereal like you?"

"Oh! To think that my child—"

Trembling, Kate couldn't help shouting. "Your child?

You don't want me for your child. You'd rather have somebody like Hannah or Ophelia. Well I'm sorry. You're cursed with me instead, and I'm tired of apologizing for being myself. Why don't you love me for myself, Mama? Am I so awful?"

Not waiting for an answer, Kate ran out of the house and down the road to Castle Richfield. She was crying so hard she couldn't see the road, so hard she missed the rider trotting toward her until he was upon her.

"Kate," Val said. "Kate, what's wrong?"

He dismounted and caught her by the shoulders. Rubbing her eyes and face, Kate tried to stop her tears. When Val put his arm around her shoulders, she burst into renewed sobbing. Unlike Alexis, Val let her cry without trying to stop her. In a few minutes, she was able to blow her nose on his handkerchief and sigh deeply.

"Can I help?" he asked as he removed his arm from her shoulders.

"No, thank you." She gave him a little smile, but it disappeared as she heard the rumble of a carriage.

He glanced over her shoulder. "It's your mother. Would you like to ride with me?"

"You're a smart man, Valentine Beaufort."

"Not really. I just know how impossible it is to please one's parents. I offended my father simply by being born."

Kate heard Mama call to her.

"Damn."

"My horse is fast," Val said, grinning.

"I have to face her sooner or later. Might as well get on with it."

Saluting her, Val mounted and turned away, cantering off in the direction he'd come as Sophia's carriage pulled up beside Kate.

Placing her hands on her hips, Kate looked up at her mother. Nose and eyes red from weeping, Sophia held out a hand to her.

"My little girl, I'm so sorry."

"Me too, Mama."

"No, no, I'm the one to blame. I'm the mother. I should have realized how much of a burden I was shoving onto you. And about me trying to make you into a Lady, although I thought I was doing what was best for you, I hurt you, and that was wrong."

Wiping her forehead with the back of her hand, Kate managed a smile, though she was about to start crying again.

"Thank you, Mama."

"I do love you, Katie Ann. Just as you are."

This time she did cry. Standing in the dusty road, in full view of the coachman, she cried. Sophia wrestled with the carriage door, then stumbled out and gathered Kate into her arms.

"Shall we try to be kinder to each other, my little Katie Ann?"

Kate snuffled into Val's handkerchief and nodded.

"And you know something?" Sophia said as she patted Kate's head. "If you're right, we should be careful around the castle. I do wish Maitland House was ready."

"So do I, Mama. So do I."

Several days after the fight with Mama, Kate was waiting for Alexis with her usual impatience. He was closeted with Val, who was composing a letter of apology to the Earl of Cardigan. Alexis said he would put Val to the rack if he didn't write the damned thing. The talk of racks piqued Kate's curiosity, and she told Alexis to meet her in the dungeon when he was finished.

She took a lantern with her into the courtyard, then descended a flight of narrow steps that disappeared underground. Blackness surrounded her except for the patch of light cast by her lantern. She heard dripping water, and a moldy smell made her nose wrinkle. As she stepped down onto the floor, something slithered past her foot. She shrieked and jumped. In the careening light, she caught a glimpse of a rat.

Perhaps she'd wait for Alexis. No, he would tease her for being a coward. She held up the lantern. Before her was a large chamber, empty except for a few chains hanging on the walls and suspended from the ceiling. She tiptoed farther into the room and beheld an open iron grille that separated her from another room. In it were iron cages, a wooden trestle that must be the rack, a table full of evil-looking instruments, and what looked like a forge.

Kate shuddered and lowered the lantern. The light swept across a small door set in the floor. Discarding the lantern, she grabbed the iron ring mounted in the wood and heaved. It took all her strength, but she got it open. Taking up her light again, she peered into the hole. It was like looking into the neck of a bottle. The hole was long and narrow, barely wide enough for a person to fit in it. About fifteen feet down it widened into a tiny egg-shaped chamber.

"They used a pulley."

Kate screeched. She dropped the lantern, and it was caught by the speaker. Panting like a frightened puppy, she rounded on the man who had crept up on her.

"Hellfire, Fulke."

He lifted the lantern high and pointed at the ceiling. "You see the pulley? A prisoner was lowered into the oubliette with it. The door was shut, and the poor soul was left to starve to death in complete darkness."

"I'm glad they're no longer used."

"We have substitutes. They're called mines." He set the lantern down between them. "You can't marry Alexis. You will corrupt him."

"Me?"

" 'All wickedness is but little to the wickedness of a

woman.' You ensnared him with lasciviousness and have stolen his purity."

"Purity? Are we talking about Alexis de Granville? Anyway, you're repeating your quotations."

Fulke muttered something under his breath. With a suddenness that made Kate jump, he shouted at her.

"You will not marry him."

She began to wish Fulke wasn't between her and the stairs. They were facing each other with the lantern between them still, but Fulke was closest to the light. The glow yellowed his face and turned his eyes to black hollows. Already furious, he grew more so by the minute.

"If he marries you, it won't be for convenience. He won't adopt purity after he gets an heir." Fulke stepped around the lantern.

Kate edged backward, but kept her eyes locked with Fulke's. "Don't you think you should let Alexis decide his own future? We all have different needs, Fulke."

" 'For the lips of a strange woman drop as an honeycomb, and her mouth is smoother than oil:/But her end is bitter as wormwood, sharp as a two-edged sword.' "

As she took another step away from him, he reached for her. Kate hopped back. She stumbled and put her foot back to catch herself. It met emptiness. As she fell, she heard a shout and a clatter on the stairs.

She landed with one leg in the mouth of the oubliette and one on the dungeon floor. Fulke loomed over her. A shadow leaped at him and knocked him aside. Alexis bent down and lifted her to her feet. She was caught in a bruising hug.

"Are you hurt?"

"Eh!" She pawed at his back, and he loosened his hold. "I'm fine, but you're going to smother me."

With lightning movements, Alexis released her and whirled on Fulke, who was standing behind them. He jabbed the older man in the stomach. Fulke grunted and doubled over. Alexis stood over him for a moment, then stooped and grabbed Fulke's cravat to jerk him upright. As he pulled back a fist, Kate swatted it with the flat of her hand.

"Hitting him won't settle anything," she said.

"It will make me feel better." Alexis drew back his fist again, but met Fulke's gaze. He hesitated, then released his prey. "Don't come near Kate again."

"Very well," Fulke snapped. "Next time she's going to fall in the oubliette, I'll let her."

Alexis looked from Fulke to Kate.

Kate flushed and put her hands behind her back. "I'm afraid I wasn't looking where I was going."

"It's his fault you were careless. Get out of my sight, Fulke, before I lose what's left of my temper." Biting his lip, Alexis stopped, then swore. "I'm sorry, Fulke. Please, you know I hate fighting with you."

Rubbing his stomach, Fulke said, "I know, boy." He squeezed Alexis's shoulder and walked slowly to the stairs. He was halfway up when he let loose his final shot. "She has no breeding, Alexis. 'As a jewel of gold in a swine's snout, so is a fair woman which is without discretion.' You will regret taking her to wife."

Alexis growled, but Fulke was gone before he could say anything. Kate looked at his tight mouth and the working muscles in his jaw. She giggled, and he looked at her as if she were addled.

"I think old Fulke just called me a swine's snout."

She was rewarded with a smile that would have made Cleopatra swoon with rapture. Alexis grabbed her and swung her in a circle, laughing.

Kate hugged him while he still held her in the air. "I can imagine old Fulke as the evil lord of the castle," she said, "throwing helpless peasants into the oubliette."

"Haven't you heard about Alexis Phillipe, the one with

the armor? He's the one I resemble, and he's the one who most liked to use the dungeon."

Alexis set Kate on her feet. She smiled up at him, but he assumed an expression of cold, haughty evil and looked her up and down.

"A fine piece, you are, my lady. By God's teeth, deny me not, for I'll have you. Here, now, in my dungeon."

Startled at the change in Alexis, Kate felt her smile waver. He took a step toward her, and she backed up. He kept coming, and she kept retreating.

"It will do you no good to run."

Kate had backed away from the lantern now, and his words came to her from a figure cast into darkness with its back to the light. The figure lunged, and she felt arms sweep her up and pin her against a wall. Alexis pressed his body into hers and put his mouth on her neck. A terrible growl came from deep in his chest.

"I'm going to ravage you."

"Alexis?"

"Grrrrrrrrr." He lifted his mouth from her neck and kissed her nose, quickly, three times. "I'm a ruthless, lusting savage."

She squealed as he tickled her ribs while popping the buttons at the back of her gown. By the time she stopped laughing, he had pulled her bodice down to expose her breasts. She felt his mouth travel from her neck to her breast, leaving a trail of moisture and goose bumps. The stones at her back were cold, but her skin was on fire. She managed to whisper his name.

He transferred his mouth to her other breast and started pulling her skirt up.

"Alexis, this is a dungeon."

He silenced her by kissing her while he trailed his fingers from her knee to her inner thigh.

"We can't," she said.

"Yes we can," he said in between kisses. "I can, and I will."

She opened her mouth again, but he pressed her hard against the wall, and air rushed out of her lungs. He whispered to her while he unbuttoned his trousers.

"Sweet, sweet Katie Ann. Stop thinking."

She did as he asked, and gave her body up to pleasure. When they were calm again, Alexis collapsed against her, pressing his hands to the dungeon wall.

"Dear Lord," he said. "I've sealed my own doom."

"Are all Englishmen so wild?"

"Must be our Viking ancestry, or that of my conquering Norman forebears. Somehow you strip away all the years of breeding in between, little savage. I'm not like this, not with—"

She grinned up at him. "A wise point at which to stop. Tell me, did your ravaging ancestors happen to make another way out of this dungeon, or are we going to parade past the whole castle staff in our present condition?"

He made a courtly bow to her and took her hand. "Come, wench, your lord will show you to your room by a privy way, but beware. I'll have you again soon."

"And I suppose next time it will be in the gate house, or on the tower stairs."

"What a difficult choice."

"Not at all, my lord. Next time I want a bed." She thought for a moment. "Or perhaps a chair, or an ottoman."

"Thank you, God, for sending her. Thank you."

Kate woke early the next morning, and the second she opened her eyes, she was madder than a scorpion trapped in a basket. Dinner had started out beautifully the night before. There were no Dinkles gushing over Alexis. No Mademoiselle St.-Germain to make her feel as attractive

as a diseased moose. She had had Alexis to herself, and he
had spent the evening bathing her in a gaze as blistering as
the sun on the Carson Desert. She'd wanted to drag him
into a closet and maul him.

And then Juliana had ruined it all. The woman had
grown more and more despondent as the evening progressed with Kate and Alexis almost oblivious to everyone
else. Her ill humor eventually erupted into active malice,
and as always, she directed it at Alexis. Fulke jumped to
his cousin's defense, and he and Juliana were squabbling
before anyone could stop them. Val, Sophia, and Kate listened in shocked silence as the two fought over the marquess. Alexis did nothing, even when Juliana called him a
murderer.

Fulke dropped his fork on his plate and glared at Juliana. "Control yourself. We've been through this time and
again. Alexis is incapable of such evil, and anyway I saw
him leave to join them, and he wouldn't have had time to
set that horrible trap."

Kate paid no attention to the argument. She watched
Alexis instead. He sat quietly and contemplated his uneaten food. He had about him an air of hopeless resigna-
tion. When he lifted his eyes to hers, she felt as if she were
looking at a soul condemned to hell.

She didn't believe in putting up with idiocy, so she
threw her napkin down, got up, and walked around the
long table to stand at his side. The arguing stopped as
everyone stared at her. She held out her hand to Alexis.
"Would you take me for a walk?"

They got out of the dining room, but Alexis excused
himself as soon as they entered the garden. She tried to
speak to him, but he shook his head and directed an absurd quotation at her.

"You made a mistake accepting me. 'I am very proud,
revengeful, ambitious, with more offenses at my beck than
I have thoughts to put them in, imagination to give them

shape, or time to act them in. What should such fellows as I do crawling between earth and heaven?' Good night, my love."

Kate kicked back the bedclothes. "What rot."

She dressed and took breakfast with Sophia in her rooms. She was about to go for a morning ride when her maid brought her a small envelope. It was a note from Carolina Beechwith.

"I'll be damned." Kate opened the note.

Carolina was heartbroken. She couldn't live without Alexis. Please, could Kate meet her at once at the ruins of Thyme Hall.

She glared at the note. "What does she think she can do? Make me hand him back to her? Probably expects me to share him."

She didn't want to go, but knowing Mrs. Beechwith's determination where Alexis was concerned, Kate decided to face the woman. Slipping the note in a book on the table by her bed, she shrugged. Might as well fire a warning shot at her. It would save a fight later on.

She reached Thyme Hall before nine o'clock. It was a bright day, and the air was heavy with the moisture of the previous night's rainfall. Water drops hung from the pointed leaves of the ivy and ferns. She heard the trill of a dove in some tree.

Carolina hadn't arrived, so Kate pulled a book from her pocket. Settling on a rock in the sunshine, she attempted to distract herself. Her luck was bad, for she had mistakenly picked up Wordsworth. She groaned and eyed a poem. That awful meter. Ta *da,* ta *da,* ta *da,* ta *da.* Ta *da* ta *da,* ta *da.* Kate cringed. And the rhymes. Bower/flower, earth/birth, orchard plot/Lucy's cot. Bleh!

She was scanning a stanza of particularly sickening sweetness when a shadow cut across the whiteness of the page. Before she could look up, something hit the back of her head. She felt an exploding pain in her skull, then nothing.

She couldn't have been unconscious long, because when she surfaced, her feet were bumping over the old bricks of Thyme Hall. She wanted to vomit. Her head had become a giant balloon, and the pain at the back of it was so great, she couldn't summon the strength to open her eyes for long. When she did, she caught glimpses of dirt, grass, and the eroded flagstones inside the ruins. Someone was dragging her into Thyme Hall. Her body tilted, and she was swallowed by darkness. Since she was still awake, she guessed she was being hauled down some hole. Her feet bumped on several steps until they hit stone again. The jolting made her lose her tenuous hold on consciousness.

When she woke once more, she was alone, lying on cold rock. She moaned and sat up. Cradling her head, she concentrated on breathing and on not vomiting. Soon she was able to lift her head. Whoever had done this to her had left a candle burning near her. By its meager light she could see that she was in a narrow cell. There were no windows, only a wooden door set with a peephole. Dank air flowed under the door, making her shiver.

Struggling to her feet, Kate lurched over to the door. There was no knob on this side, and the lock was newly cleaned and oiled. She pounded on the wood. If she shouted, her head would split open. She didn't have to shout, though. The small door to the peephole opened.

Kate cried out and jumped back. A hooded face peered at her. Black material completely shrouded the head of her captor. There were slits in the mask for eyes, but they were so narrow she couldn't see into them.

"What are you doing?" Kate asked.

The mask was silent.

"Let me out. The marquess will come looking for me."

A raspy voice came from the hood. "Such a shame. What am I to do with you? You aren't like the others."

The peephole door snapped shut. Kate leaped at it and pounded.

"Come back! You can't leave me here. Please."

She pounded until her fists were bruised and her skin broken and bleeding. The hooded figure never came back. Finally exhausted, with stinging bolts of pain shooting through her head, Kate sank to the floor and burst into tears. Crying made her head hurt worse, so she stopped. In spite of her fear, she lay down, cradled her head on her arms, and closed her eyes.

Chapter
Eighteen

Alexis had been closeted with Fulke and
his estate manager all morning. It had
been an uncomfortable few hours with
Fulke brooding at him like an eagle
whose chick preferred to walk rather than
fly. And now he couldn't find Kate. Neither Sophia nor Val nor his mother had
seen her. Her maid said she'd gone riding
that morning, and he'd tried to find her
on horseback with no success.

Cursing her independent nature,
Alexis resigned himself to doing without
her until luncheon. She wasn't back at
one o'clock. He ate to the accompaniment
of Val's teasing and his references to lovesick Romeos. A message arrived from the
head of the county police asking for an
interview the following day. Already put
out, Alexis's mood deteriorated. To make
matters worse, he had to go see Carolina
and tell her he'd set the date for his wedding.

His irritation reached new heights when he arrived at the Beechwith residence and found old Mr. Beechwith returned from London. Concealing his foul disposition, Alexis spent a polite half hour in the company of his former mistress and her husband.

He arrived back at the castle to find that Kate hadn't turned up. Assembling the household staff, he initiated a small hunt and spent the rest of the afternoon tearing around the castle looking for his missing fiancée.

Alexis grew more and more worried as the day progressed. By five o'clock the search had taken to horseback. He sent one party to cover the woods, then took another group to ride across pastures, fields, and the valley where Kate had caught him riding Theseus. He returned home well after dark to find Val waiting for him in the stable.

"No luck in the woods," Val said. "I even had someone search Thyme Hall."

Val had wanted to ride on the search, but Alexis had forbidden it, backed by two doctors, Fulke, and Juliana.

"When I find her, I'm going to . . . to . . ." Alexis couldn't think of a punishment drastic enough.

"You'll sweep her into your arms and moo at her like an enamored bull."

"I will not."

Val stumbled, and Alexis caught him by the neck of his jacket.

"Sorry," Val said. He smiled at Alexis, but it was obvious that he was tired.

"You haven't rested as the doctors instructed," Alexis said. "You've been scrambling about the castle looking for Kate, haven't you?"

"I'll be fine. What I need is food."

They joined the search party in the great cavern that was the Richfield kitchen. From Meredith, Alexis learned that Sophia had taken to her bed, hysterical with worry. Juliana had comforted the woman, given her laudanum to keep her quiet, and retired for the night. She'd left word with Fulke that she would direct another search of the castle first thing in the morning.

Fulke delivered Juliana's message while Alexis picked at the crust of his steak-and-kidney pie. Beside him Val had finished eating and was trying to keep his eyes open.

"She's run off," Fulke said.

Alexis shoved his pie away uneaten. "She has not. She's had an accident."

"She's run off, probably to Cardigan."

Alexis slammed to his feet, reached across the table, and grabbed Fulke's collar. "She loves me." He shoved Fulke away. "Besides, Kate isn't the type of woman to flit off leaving silly notes behind confessing undying love for some fop."

Val had his head down on his arms. From this pillow came his sleepy voice. "Didja look for a note?"

"Her maid said she went for a ride this morning and didn't come back," Alexis said. "There wouldn't be a note."

Val yawned. "Shoulda looked anyway."

Alexis contemplated his friend's wheat-colored curls for a moment, then strode rapidly from the kitchen with Fulke close behind.

He found the note tucked inside Kate's book almost immediately. He read it and handed it to Fulke. His cousin snorted and tossed the paper on the bed.

"Alexis, we searched Thyme Hall."

"I'm going to search it again." He tried to step around Fulke. "Let me by, cousin."

"I tell you, she's run away."

"Go to hell."

Alexis tried to pass Fulke again. This time the older man got in front of him and shoved him in the chest. Alexis was thrown back, but kept his footing.

"I don't have the patience for this, Fulke. Get out of my way or I'll move you."

"You're exhausted. You can't go racing around in the dark. Your horse will trip in a hole or stumble on a log."

"Step aside, Fulke."

Alexis started walking, but Fulke grabbed his shoulder. Alexis caught Fulke's arm and gave it a quick twist. Fulke gasped and fell back. Alexis raced past him, but when Fulke called his name, he turned back to face his cousin. Fulke was pointing a pistol at him.

"Come here," Fulke said.

Warily eyeing the gun, Alexis retraced his steps until he stood a yard away from Fulke.

"You are pointing a pistol at me, Fulke."

His cousin nodded slowly. "God made a mistake when he created women. They are the source of all corruption, and I won't have your chance for purity ruined by that harlot. Don't move!" Fulke darted at Alexis, put the nose of the gun to his throat, and wrapped his free hand around Alexis's neck.

Alexis let Fulke draw him closer. "I don't feel as you do. Even if I'd never met Kate, I wouldn't adopt celibacy. Look at me, Fulke. Can't you see that this fear for her is driving me past reason? Let me go."

"It's all her fault."

"Have you done something to her?" With effort, Alexis kept his voice calm. "By all that's sacred, if you've hurt her— Have you?"

"No. God answered my prayers and made her succumb to her own lusts. She's probably in Cardigan's bed by now, and you're staying here."

Alexis grasped the barrel of the gun and dared Fulke with his gaze.

"Is this how you're going to keep me saintly and pure, by killing me?"

"I'm going to keep you here where you'll be safe."

Alexis shook his head. "You'll have to shoot me to keep me from leaving, right now, because I'm going to find Katie Ann if I have to do it while I'm bleeding to death."

There was a slight relief from the pressure of the gun barrel at his throat. Alexis held his cousin's gaze while he yanked the gun from him and tossed it away, into a chair. Fulke's hands dropped to his sides.

"God has made you too trusting when it comes to women."

Alexis threw himself at Fulke, landing on top of the man as he hit the floor. Pinning his cousin's arms, he swore.

"By all the demons in hell, Fulke, I'm giving you one last chance. Swear by Almighty God that you don't know where Kate is."

Fulke tried to heave Alexis off him, but Alexis pounded him back to the floor.

"Swear," he said.

"You're addled by a whore's tricks."

Alexis fastened his hands on Fulke's neck. "Swear!"

"I swear, damn you."

Springing to his feet, Alexis snatched up the gun as he left.

Fulke shouted after him. "She will get you cast out of the Garden of Eden."

"We'll make our own Eden."

Alexis rode to Thyme Hall with only Iago for company. Everyone was tired, and he didn't expect to find Kate anyway. He walked around the shell of the house with a lamp held in one hand. Iago disturbed a wild cat, and Alexis had to keep a stranglehold on his collar to keep the dog from chasing after it. When Iago settled down, he resumed his wandering among the crumbled walls. He ran into vines hanging from saplings, then stubbed his toe on a small boulder sitting in the middle of what was once the library. Weariness overtook him. Putting the lamp on the ground, he sat down on the rock. Iago lay down beside him.

Alexis had known fear like this before. It was a helpless, blind fear that came only when someone close was threatened. He'd last known it when Val disappeared into a cloud of mist, blood, and steel in the charge of the Light Brigade.

What was he going to do if he never found her? What if she had fallen from her horse and was lying dead in some field?

Don't think about it.

Alexis leaned forward, bracing his forearms on his thighs, and stared at his feet. Amid the noise of insects and rustling leaves, he could hear Iago sniffing. The spaniel lifted his head and craned his neck, sweeping the air with his nose. From that sensitive instrument came the dog's characteristic snuffling sound. It was a sound he made when he'd caught scent of something.

Iago stood up. The snuffling grew louder, and Alexis sighed. The dog was going to find an animal trail and disappear again. The sucking motions of Iago's jowls and nostrils increased. Suddenly the dog's head dipped. He snorted at the ground in front of Alexis's feet. Then, to Alexis's consternation, the animal began to whine and paw at the ground.

"What's the matter, old fellow?"

Iago barked once, then started to dig, only he couldn't. His claws scratched through a layer of dirt and hit something hard.

Alexis rose and stomped on the ground. Metal. Moving the lamp, he dropped to his knees and shoved dirt aside as Iago snuffled frantically. Alexis's hand hit a ring. It was a handle. Standing up, he shoved the rock he'd been sitting on aside. It moved easily, as though it had been moved before. He kicked away dirt, leaves, and twigs, then grasped the ring and pulled. Dust flew in his face and pebbles hit his cheeks as a trapdoor sprang open and back.

Drawing Fulke's pistol from his belt, Alexis ducked into the hole revealed by the door, taking the lamp with him. Iago bounded after him. At the foot of a steep staircase lay a black chamber much like the dungeon at Castle Richfield, only smaller. Set in one wall were three doors with peepholes. Alexis flung the first one open. The door banged against a wall. Nothing.

He was about to open the second door when Iago threw himself at it and barked. Pounding came from the other side.

"Kate?"

"Alexis! Open the door."

He stuffed the pistol back in his belt and opened the door, and Kate threw herself into his arms. He hugged her and buried his nose in her mass of tangled hair. Iago sprang in the air, yipping at them.

"Little savage."

"Someone locked me in."

He felt her tremble and stroked the back of her head. "What happened?"

"Mrs. Beechwith wrote me a note."

"I know."

"And when I got here, somebody hit me and dragged me down into this cell."

Kate lifted her face. Her cheeks were smudged and her lashes were wet. Alexis kissed her, gently, and then, as he remembered his fears, he hugged her to him so hard that she gasped. She cried out something, and her hands clawed at his back. He smiled and began to release her. He heard Iago growl and then yelp, but before he could turn, something hit the back of his head and he collapsed.

• • •

Alexis heard someone groan. He frowned, trying to figure out where the sound was coming from. There it was again. He couldn't open his eyes to see who was making that pitiful noise.

"Alexis, don't move," said Kate's disembodied voice.

"Noise," he said. He could barely hear his own voice.

"Shhh."

"Who's makin noise?"

"Hush. It's you. That bastard hit you, but he's gone now. Are you all right?"

Still unable to open his eyes, Alexis tried to bring his hand to his face. He couldn't. Neither hand would move. As his senses returned, he could feel a great weight tearing at his hands and arms. They were suspended above him and he seemed to be hugging a wall. Grinding his teeth together, he pulled, and found that his wrists were bound by chains.

"What?" he mumbled.

"I can't see very well," Kate said, "but I think he's chained you to the wall. He hit you and Iago with a rock and shoved me back in the cell before I could stop him. Can you get free?"

Alexis tried to ignore the stinging and pounding in his head and managed to straighten from his slumped position. The pain in his arms eased somewhat, but he could do no more than strain helplessly at his bonds. At last he opened his eyes. They focused on his own shoulder. On the floor beside him, Iago lay motionless. Nearby he spotted his coat and, lying on top of it, Fulke's gun. He pulled at the chains again.

Kate shouted encouragement to him, but her words stopped as, to his right, the trapdoor sprang open. Someone came down the stairs holding a lamp. It was a figure in

black, dressed in dark boots, trousers, and a cloak. Alexis
strained to see his enemy's face.

"Mother?"

"Lady Juliana!" Kate cried.

Juliana walked over to Alexis and set the lamp on the
floor. Stooping, she picked up the gun and stuck it in her
belt.

"Mother, what are you doing?"

"She ruined it all," Juliana said.

"I don't understand."

Juliana shoved the cloak back from her shoulders and
glared at Alexis. "She ruined it all by making you happy. I
was punishing you. I had it all planned, years of suffering,
losing the ones you loved, as I lost my husband."

Closing his eyes for a moment, Alexis cringed away
from his mother.

"You know," he said. "You know what happened that
day. Have you known all along? Oh God, why didn't you
tell me? I'd rather know for sure that I killed them."

Juliana raised her fist. Alexis turned his head and met
her eyes. She was breathing rapidly and glowering at him.

"It was worse than that, you fool. He died instead of
you, and it's all your fault."

Alexis held his breath, then let it out while his tortured
thoughts assembled themselves. "My fault. What did I
do?"

"Don't you remember? You and Thalia were to go riding together that day. If you had, the right ones would
have died, and I would have had my dear Phillipe all to
myself again."

"Mother?" He sounded like a hurt child. "Tell me the
whole of it."

"I suppose it won't matter, although you deserve to be
kept guessing. I got back from arranging the trap and
found all of you gone. It was already too late when Fulke
told me Phillipe had gone riding with Thalia and that you

were chasing after them. You monster. If you hadn't quarreled with Thalia, you would have been the one to die instead of Phillipe."

His legs were shaking. His whole body trembled, and his head was going to split open with the pain. He heard Kate calling to him, but he couldn't answer. He was seeing himself quarreling with Thalia over luncheon. His father's furious voice sent him to his room. Then he was riding, riding, riding, and Thalia was falling, her head toppling to the ground. Father's horse screamed.

"Stop," Alexis whispered to himself. He lifted his gaze to his mother once again. "The reason I don't remember putting that wire between the trees is because I didn't do it. And you let me think I killed them. All these years. Why? Why do you hate me so?"

"Because you stole his love!" Juliana screamed. Her face distorted by rage, she continued shouting at him. "Before you and Thalia, we didn't need anyone else. But he loved you, especially you. He would tell me how proud he was of you, how brilliant you were. God, I was sick of seeing the two of you laughing together and sharing things. And then one day he told me I was ill."

Her rage vanished abruptly as if it had never been, leaving no trace of emotion in her visage. When she spoke again, her voice was calm.

"He came to me and said that I was getting sicker and sicker, and that was bad for Thalia and you. He was taking both of you away with him." Her voice rose again, taking on the high, querulous tone of a child. "Phillipe said I would have to stay in a new place with doctors. He said I was getting much worse, and he was afraid."

Her mood switched once more without warning, and she snarled at Alexis. "He was especially afraid for you. He'd seen me watching you. Seen me. It was your fault he turned against me."

"Mother, he loved you," Alexis said. Juliana wasn't listening to him.

"I knew then that I had to get rid of you. If you were gone, he would love me again. You were his son, and a male, and you could ride like he did, and soon you would hunt, and go to clubs and shoots, and accompany him to all the places I couldn't. You'd stolen him from me at last, and I wanted him back."

"But he died instead of me."

Juliana looked at him, smiling. "Yes, and I nearly died too, but I lived because I wanted you punished with years of suffering, losing the ones you loved as I lost Phillipe."

"Did you ever love me, or Thalia?"

"At first," she admitted, sounding frighteningly rational. "But you killed my love over the years. It took me a long time to realize you were stealing my Phillipe, you see."

Alexis felt a tearing at his heart, as if something inside it were dying. "You said you punished me. Dear God in heaven, Mother, what have you done?"

Juliana laughed.

Behind him Kate called out, her voice sounding thin and strained.

"It was her," Kate said. "She visited Ophelia the night of the fire. It was she who set the fire. It was you, wasn't it, Juliana?"

"She wanted to please me, to make me like her," Juliana said, turning to speak to Kate. "It was easy to get her to meet me secretly. She thought we were going to make a plan to capture Alexis for her. I drugged her wine and set the fire. Only . . . only Alexis wasn't hurt enough when she died. Not nearly enough." Juliana's voice wavered. Her eyes strayed from Kate to Alexis, then back to Kate.

"I was going to kill Carolina Beechwith, but you arrived, and then I found out about Hannah. You were at

Thyme Hall that day too, when she begged Alexis to impregnate her. Hannah was one I missed."

Alexis lowered his forehead to rest on his arm. "Don't say any more, please." He lifted his head to plead with his mother. "You're ill. Let me go so I can take care of you."

"Oh no. Your final punishment is about to begin. I've decided since you won't die when I want you to, you'll be punished for that as well."

Alexis stared at his mother's twisted face. Reeling inside from her last words, he could say nothing. Juliana suddenly reached toward him. He felt her hand at the neck of his shirt, then she ripped it from his body. The violence spurred his tongue.

"The keep."

She dropped the shirt and sneered at him. "Yes, the keep. Your guardian angel Valentine ruined your death for me. After I had worked so hard to loosen those stones and made sure Fulke noticed them, your stupid friend came along and warned you."

It wasn't believable. After all she'd confessed, Alexis still couldn't accept her hatred. He was aware that his mother was still talking, but he couldn't seem to hear her. Her mouth was moving. He watched her lips pull back from her teeth. She stopped talking, and he was jolted back to awareness when she turned from him.

She disappeared from his sight and returned holding a whip. He looked from the whip to the woman's face, then shook his head, murmuring a denial. She couldn't. Mothers didn't use whips on their children. He almost laughed at himself. He bit down on his lip, using the pain to ward off hysteria.

Juliana yelled at him, calling him a monster. Then she vanished. He tried to twist his neck far enough to see her, but she was directly behind him, and far away.

A hissing crack ripped through the air, and a line of pain etched itself from his shoulder to his waist. His body arched. Confused and disbelieving, Alexis blinked his eyes. Another blow tore at his ribs. The leather dropped from his flesh and slithered on the floor. He gripped the chains at his wrists as pain crawled over his back.

Kate was shouting at Juliana. His beautiful Katie Ann hurled threats and curses at Juliana, and it was the sound of her voice coupled with the knowledge that she was in danger that cleared his mind. He had to endure, survive. For Kate.

Kate was hoarse from screaming at Juliana. She beat at the door of her cell as the woman raised the whip again. She shouted Juliana's name, and the woman turned to her.

Juliana had been handsome. Her silver hair and thoroughbred height commanded attention, and she shared with her son an almost royal dignity. All had vanished from the being that confronted Kate. The hair was still vivid, but it was tangled and matted with leaves and snarls. She crouched like a shrike hovering over a dead insect, her shoulders hunched forward and her body curled into itself. Even her nails seemed to lengthen and curl into talons.

Juliana whirled away from Kate. Her arm flexed, and Kate heard a snap. The movement was impossible to follow, but the results were plain. Alexis jerked and cried out. Another red line appeared on the flawless skin of his back.

"No!" Kate screamed her fury at Juliana, and her voice cracked.

Juliana paused again and looked at Kate. Her chest heaved and spittle had gathered at the corners of her mouth. Kate shouted, but her voice was drowned in the pounding of boots on the stairs. Fulke hurled himself down the last step, racing toward Juliana. She raised the whip, but he ripped it from her hand. Howling, she grabbed for it, but Fulke threw the whip into the shadows and ran to Alexis.

Frustrated at her impotence, Kate pounded at her cell door. Fulke pulled at a ring set in the wall to hold the chains that bound Alexis. The chains loosened, and Alexis fell to his knees. Fulke helped him rise, supporting him while shooting questions at him.

"Don't wait!" Kate yelled. "She's mad, and she wants to kill him. Get him out of here."

Fulke's head came up. He shot a startled look toward Kate. Someone else was running down the stairs, but Kate paid no attention.

"She's dangerous, I tell you. Where did she go?"

Alexis lurched toward Kate's voice, but Fulke pulled him back. Val sailed past both of them and fumbled with the key in the lock of her cell, then collapsed against the door frame, out of breath. Alexis struggled with Fulke, cursing at him. As Kate shoved the door of the cell open, Juliana darted out of a shadowed corner. In her hand was Fulke's gun, and she aimed it at the two wrestling men.

Everyone moved at once. Alexis threw himself in front of Fulke. Kate and Val sprang at Juliana. Kate tackled the woman's feet, jerking them out from under her. She heard a shot, but her face was smothered in the folds of Juliana's cloak. A heavy weight landed half on Kate and half on Juliana. Feet jammed into Kate's stomach, and she doubled over while an unseen struggle took place beside her. Another shot robbed her of her hearing for a few seconds. She unwound herself, shoving her hair back from her face, and peered across the floor. Alexis was bending over Val, lifting his friend off a black bundle on the ground. Val moaned.

"Did she hurt you?" Alexis asked.

"Kicked me in the chest. The gun."

"It went off," Alexis said.

Kate got to her feet and rushed to Alexis. Wordlessly

he held out an arm. She fastened her arms around his waist, and he held her to his side. They looked down at Juliana. She lay on her back, eyes open and staring at them. The bullet had entered her head beneath the chin and gone out the back of her skull.

Kate closed her eyes against the sight of spattered blood and tissue. Alexis left her to kneel beside the still Iago. As he cradled the dog's head on his lap, Iago groaned, then a pink tongue snaked out and licked Alexis's cheek. Alexis laughed.

"You always did have a thick skull, old fellow."

Val approached and held out his arms for the dog. Alexis relinquished Iago and took Kate's hand.

A groan came from beyond Juliana's body. Kate turned to see Fulke crawling on the floor.

"What happened to him?"

"He tried to stop me from helping you," Alexis said.

Fulke was rubbing his jaw. "You could have been killed."

"Dammit, Fulke, you're going to have to stop protecting me. I'm not a child anymore, and Kate could have been killed."

"And me too," Val said.

Kate interfered before Fulke could answer. "Can we get out of this place?"

Alexis put his arm around her and led her to the stairs. He asked Fulke to precede them with the lantern, and Val was instructed to seal the trapdoor until a party could return for Juliana's body. Noting the grim whiteness of Alexis's face and the tense strength he exerted to keep himself erect, Kate didn't bother him with questions.

Once outside, Alexis helped her mount Theseus. Clutching at the stallion's mane, she settled into the saddle. Alexis mounted behind her.

Fulke came up to them with Alexis's jacket. Alexis started to take it, but Kate stopped him.

"You can't," she said. "You won't like taking it off."

He nodded and kicked gently at Theseus. The stallion set off at a gentle walk. Kate tried to sit straight and hold herself away from Alexis so that he wouldn't have to support her body. His two arms crossed in front of her, though, and pulled her backward. She sank against Alexis's chest and sighed.

"I'm sorry about your mother."

"I don't want to talk about it."

Kate chewed on her lower lip. "You know you've been innocent all along."

"Be quiet, my love. I said I don't want to talk about it."

As far as she could see, that was the trouble with the de Granville family in the first place. All the wrong people got to do the talking, and the innocent ones kept their mouths shut.

In his bedchamber, Alexis lay on his stomach with his face resting on his forearm. His body burned with fever, and the lacerations on his back stung and throbbed. Kate held a cold, wet cloth to his cheek while he tried to forget his mother's death. Had it only been that night? It seemed he'd been on fire forever. Yet the writhing of his soul caused greater pain than any wounds or fever.

Kate pitied him, and he couldn't bear her pity. Every time he looked at her she smiled and said something kind. He'd rather she hated him.

"Kate, get some rest."

"I'm not tired," she said. "I want to be with you. I want to take care of you."

"I'm fine."

"You are not. Don't you think I can see that your mother's treachery is eating at your gut? Talk about it, share the pain with me."

He curled his fingers into the bed sheets and turned his face away from the cloth she held to his cheek.

"Can't you understand that I need to be alone? Please. Don't argue with me. I need to be alone."

He heard her dress rustle as she stood up. "All right. But I'll be back tomorrow morning, and I'm sending someone to check on you once in a while. The doctor said I should."

He waited until she was gone before he lifted his head. Slowly he raised up and took a glass of water from the table beside the bed. Draining it, he put it back, then eased down again. It was late, past twelve, and everyone else had gone to bed.

He'd relived the horrors at Thyme Hall until he was drained of emotion. There was no hate any longer, no revulsion or remorse. The only feelings left were shame and fear. He experienced both when Kate was with him— shame that she knew what his mother was, what he came from, and fear that she would pity him.

God, he was tired. He shifted so that his arms were spread out. His face was turned to the side. With Kate gone, he could sleep.

Grateful for the lassitude that crept over him, Alexis drifted into a state of half-sleep. As he lay there, tendrils of memory curled around his brain until he found himself standing in the woods watching a boy run past a headless corpse and a struggling horse. The boy threw himself down beside a man. His father. It was as if Alexis was looking over the boy's shoulder. The youth lifted the man's head, and for the first time since the day he died, Alexis saw his father's face.

Alexis was jolted into the body of the boy, and they became one. He struggled with the weight of his father's body as he called to the man. Phillipe de Granville opened his eyes. They were green, like his own, but full of pain.

"Alexis . . . Why?"

Alexis lurched with the sudden shift of weight as his father's head fell back. "Father, no. Wait. It wasn't me. Father?" The body was too heavy, and it was slipping from his grasp. Alexis screamed. "Father, no, listen to me! You have to listen. Father, I didn't do it. Father!" He gripped his father's coat and shook the limp body while he wept. "Come back. You can't go away. Do you hear me? I didn't do it."

Alexis's eyes flew open and he shoved himself up off the bed. "Come back!"

Someone grabbed his arms and turned him, and Alexis stared at his cousin. Fulke had one knee on the bed and gripped his upper arms. Alexis kept still while he fought his way back to the present.

"It was only a dream," Fulke said.

"It was a memory." Alexis fastened his hands on Fulke's arms. "I remembered Father's death. Fulke, he died thinking I'd set that trap. He asked me why."

Alexis squeezed his eyes shut and lowered his head. Fulke shook him.

"That can't be. What did he say? Exactly."

"Only that one word," Alexis said. "Why."

"Then you're wrong. Look at me, Alexis. I knew your father. Phillipe loved you, and he knew you loved him. You've always made more of that little squabble with your sister than there actually was. It was a quarrel between brother and sister. All brothers and sisters fight. Phillipe knew you'd both outgrow your differences. He told me so. He would never believe jealousy would make you harm him or Thalia."

"But he asked me why."

Fulke shook him again. "It's time you looked at what happened with the eyes of an adult. Phillipe was dying. Suddenly, without warning, when he was still young. He knew he was dying. He knew he was leaving you alone.

Don't you see, Alexis. He wasn't asking you why you killed him. He was asking God why he had to die."

Alexis gazed into his cousin's eyes until his own blurred. Tears overflowed and spilled. He stiffened and tried to pull away from Fulke, but his cousin held onto him.

"Give in," Fulke said. "You haven't let go since she died. How much can you take before you rip apart? Give in, Alexis, before you break."

Pulling his knees up to his chest, Alexis buried his head in his arms and tried to stifle a sob. It was no use. The strain, the fever, the pain, they all combined and fed each other. Another sob threatened to explode his chest. This time he released it and surrendered to the tears.

When he was able to lift his head, Fulke was still with him. The older man was sitting beside the bed pouring a glass of water. He held it out. Alexis ignored it.

"Thank you."

"You are welcome," Fulke said.

"Does madness run in families?"

Fulke sighed and shoved the glass at Alexis. "Don't be absurd. You're as sane as I am."

Alexis tilted his head to the side and regarded Fulke with a faint smile.

"Don't," Fulke said. "Don't smile and let those silly ideas rattle about in that head. Here, drink this. I put laudanum in it."

Alexis shook his head and laughed. His skin was burning, and there was a fire in his mind as well. He jumped when Fulke's fingers curled around the back of his neck. The cold edge of the glass touched his lips.

"Drink. You're a stubborn boy, and you need rest."

The tainted water rushed into his mouth, and Alexis swallowed. He finished the whole glass because Fulke kept it pressed to his lips until all the liquid was gone. When he was released, he lowered himself onto his stomach, his burning cheek pressed to the mattress, and gazed at his hand as it lay beside his head. Fulke sat down again.

"Fulke."

"Be quiet and don't torture yourself."

"I couldn't have survived without you. I want you to know that. You took Father's place, cared for me when she wouldn't, made me study, go to church, helped me grow up. I'll never forget."

"You were my son."

Alexis glanced at Fulke, understanding what neither of them could put into words. He smoothed his hand over the sheet that covered the mattress.

"Still," he continued, "I have to face the past, and the truth."

"But not tonight."

"Maybe not."

Alexis closed his eyes and listened to his own breathing and Fulke's. Facing the past was something he might be able to do. Facing Kate was another matter altogether.

Chapter Nineteen

Kate paced up and down the wall walk. Three weeks. Three whole weeks of being avoided as if she were one of the Dinkle sisters. It was going to stop. Alexis de Granville was going to learn that he couldn't deal with problems by not dealing with them.

First there had been his fever. He hadn't wanted to talk, and he'd been ill. Then there were what he referred to as "the formalities." As far as Kate could determine, "the formalities" included using the de Granville influence to conceal Lady Juliana's crimes. The woman had murdered Ophelia and Hannah, and had tried to kill Kate and Alexis. Still, a public revelation would have done no one any good.

Other formalities were Juliana's quiet funeral and Val's exoneration. Two endless duties were accepting visits of condolence and corresponding with Sovereign, family, and friends. All these kept Alexis busy from sunrise until midnight. To Kate and Val had fallen the responsibility of the Dower House soldiers and the continuing renovation of Maitland House.

Kate hadn't realized Alexis was trying to elude her for almost a week, for she could understand that he would be grief-stricken and bewildered at the revelation of his mother's sickness. After another week, her patience ebbed. She knew Alexis had never been close to Juliana; his grief was for a love of which he'd been robbed. She didn't see why he couldn't console himself with the love he did have.

For three days now she'd been trying to talk to the man. He wiggled out of her grasp each time and vanished into the bowels of the castle. But she'd found his lair. He'd made the Ghost Tower his refuge, and she was about to invade it. How dare he hide from her in the room where they first made love?

Kate pounded her fist on an embrasure and winced. The flesh of her hands was still tender from beating at her cell door under Thyme Hall. She turned when she heard a man chuckle and saw Val walking toward her from the direction of the Ghost Tower. His health was improving fast. His step was swift and loose-limbed, and he was carrying a full wineglass.

"He is exasperating, my dear," Val said as he neared. "It comes from holding the title from such an early age, I fear."

"Hellfire."

Val laughed and offered her the wineglass. "Fulke will tell you how difficult it was to control him. Half the time he was trying to ride himself to death, and the other half he spent charming anyone who came near."

"He hasn't spent too much time trying to charm me lately." Kate took the offered glass and set it in the embrasure.

"Ah, but you're the only one of whom he is afraid."

Her mouth dropped open. "Me?"

"Indeed. I find you quite scary myself."

Crossing her arms over her chest, Kate eyed Val. He gazed back at her without smiling, but when she continued to stare at him, his lip curled, and his throat muscles convulsed.

"You inane puppy." She snatched up the wineglass and took a sip. "Never mind. Did you lock the door?"

"Of course. I got most of a bottle of Bordeaux down him. He was jousting with the cork of a new bottle when I slipped out."

"I hope he's not asleep when I get there."

"Not a chance. A cavalry officer isn't allowed to join a regiment unless he proves he can hold at least three bottles and still perform in a dress parade."

Kate grinned and kissed Val on the cheek. He took her hand.

"*Bon chance, ma petite.* He needs you so very much."

"Thank you."

She squeezed Val's hand, then walked on to the Ghost Tower. She tiptoed the last few steps and listened for sounds of an angry nobleman. There weren't any. Turning the key in the lock, she let herself in and relocked the door from the inside.

Alexis was standing in the window embrasure. One arm was draped on the open window, and his head was resting against the glass of another.

With his eyes shut, he spoke. "You shrank with fear at the thought of my anger and thus came to release me. That was well done, Val."

"I didn't come to let you out," Kate said. "I came to let myself in."

His eyelids rose slowly, and Alexis gazed at her with a lazy detachment. "Begone from my presence, devilish sprite."

"Alexis, watch."

She held up the key so that he could see it. Then she pulled at the neck of her gown and dropped the key inside. Alexis abandoned his relaxed posture. He flew from the window and landed before her bristling like a harassed falcon.

"A much-used trick, unoriginal and useless. Hand me that key."

"It may be an old trick, but I happen to value some traditions."

"If you don't give me the key, I'll take it."

She put her hands on her hips. "I thought you might."

He cursed and put his own hands behind his back as he moved away from her.

"You're going to weasel out of our engagement," she said. She began walking toward him, and he eased away from her again.

"Haven't you seen enough of my family to know why?"

"I love you."

"My mother was insane."

"I love you."

"Then there's Fulke."

"I love you."

Alexis shook his head. "I couldn't bear waking up one day and seeing hatred in your eyes."

"Coward. Alexis, you are a brilliant man, but you are set in your ways." She scooted around a chair and followed him to the window.

He dodged away when she reached for him. Walking over to the portrait of Lettice, he touched it with the tip of his fingers. "Brilliant, you say. Then you agree with me. 'Great wits are sure to madness near alli'd,/ And thin partitions do their bounds divide.'"

"Nonsense," Kate said. She joined him by the portrait. "You're as sane as I am."

She gasped as he grabbed her by the shoulders. He shook her until her hair came loose from its pins.

"My mother killed people. Fulke thinks women are God's mistake." He began to shake her with each word. "You have to leave me alone."

Kate felt her gown tighten and heard a rip. Disoriented from being shaken, she could only cling to Alexis's arm while he groped between her breasts. He found the key and thrust her to the floor. She heard the lock click while she was still fighting her way clear of her hair. Alexis was standing on the threshold, regarding her with a cold stare. Tossing the key on the floor beside her, he smiled.

"I thank you for the offer of your body, but I'm afraid I have already promised mine to Carolina Beechwith. She tells me she wants a child, like Hannah. And this time I've decided to oblige."

Kate stayed on the floor long after Alexis left. Too shocked to cry, she held the shreds of her bodice together and tried not to hate Alexis de Granville.

Alexis swirled brandy in a snifter and stared into the flames in the fireplace without seeing them. He didn't hear Fulke leave the drawing room. He didn't hear Val come in until his friend spoke.

"You know she's gone."

"I know."

"You're a fool," Val said.

"I don't wish to discuss Kate with you."

"You're going to unless you care to fight. I'll gladly do either. Now that I think of it, I'd rather sink my fist into your gut." Val stepped farther into the room. "Come on. I'm feeling much stronger, and I promise not to mess up your pretty face."

Alexis put his snifter on the mantel, then leaned on the

mantel himself, resting his chin on his arm so that he could stare at the brandy.

"Well?" Val asked.

"I won't fight you, and I'm not going to talk about Kate. What I did was best for her."

"What you did was run away. By God, Alexis, it's beyond me how you can face Russian bayonets and dance your horse through mortar fire, and yet lose control of your bowels at the sight of that bundle of contrariness and fascination."

Alexis whirled on his friend. "Shut up. For the last time, I'm telling you to leave it. I won't give her a heritage of perversion. There are plenty of women who are blinded to all else when they catch a whiff of my position or my money."

Val marched over to a sofa and sat on it. He was grinning, and Alexis didn't like it.

"So!"

"What does that mean?"

"So," Val said again. "It's as I said, old school chum. You're afraid of her. Because she isn't blinded, to use your own word. She doesn't see a marquess when she looks at you. She doesn't see Richfield and all that it means. No, she sees Alexis, and you're not used to that. You're afraid that once she sees all of you, she won't like what she sees."

"Enough!"

Alexis grabbed the brandy snifter and hurled it at the fireplace. The glass shattered; brandy made the fire spit. Shards flew back at him and buried themselves in his tail-coat. He lifted his hand to brush droplets of liquor from his sleeve. He was bleeding. He was still staring at the blood when Val took his hand and wrapped it with a handkerchief.

"It seems that one of us is always patching up the other," Val said.

"I'm sorry."

"Don't apologize to me. But I wonder how you're going to feel."

"What do you mean?"

Val continued winding the handkerchief around Alexis's hand. "When Cardigan or some other man tries for her. Don't look so appalled. You saw how that bastard drooled over Kate. She's gone to London, and in London she's bound to meet him again. And then there's Lord Snow, recovered nicely from his dysentery and hot for a woman, by all accounts. And of course there are the artists and writers and musicians. They will adore Kate, and she will adore them. Where are you off to?"

"Somewhere where you can't get at me," Alexis said. "It won't work. Let her bed Cardigan, or Snow, or a musician, or all of them. And damn you to hell, Valentine Beaufort."

After Val's scolding, Alexis tried to avoid his friend. He hated the way Val smiled at him as if he enjoyed Alexis's suffering, as if Alexis deserved the pain of losing Kate. He threw himself into the renovating of Maitland House and stayed with his wounded soldiers for hours. Sometimes, when a man died, perhaps, he could forget one source of pain for another. He kept himself so busy he didn't realize that over a week had passed.

On the tenth evening after Kate left he was too exhausted from work at the Dower House to dress for dinner. He had some food brought up on a tray, then bathed and donned a dressing gown. Huddling on the rug in front of the fireplace, he took long swigs from a wine bottle and sulked. That afternoon Fulke had congratulated him on escaping the temptations of Adam.

Behind him he heard his door close and looked over his shoulder. Carolina Beechwith was sweeping toward him. She wore an evening gown that barely covered her breasts, and diamonds nestled in her cleavage.

"I invited myself to dine," she said, "but you weren't there." She knelt on the rug beside him.

"I was tired."

"You haven't come to me."

He took another pull on the wine bottle. "My mother is dead. I'm in mourning."

"Then let me comfort you."

For once Alexis didn't care one way or the other. He let Carolina kiss him, and found within himself a strange detachment. She took the wine bottle from him and slipped her hands inside his dressing gown. She caressed his chest and kissed him again.

Alexis felt as if he were a god looking down upon two foolish mortals. He could see them touching, see the woman pull the man's robe apart, lean over him, press him to the floor. The woman cupped the man's genitals in her hand.

He was jolted back into his own body by Fulke's shout. His cousin slammed the door behind him and bawled at Carolina. Carolina scrambled off Alexis, tripped on her gown, and went sprawling onto her back. She lurched to her feet, sputtering at Fulke.

Alexis raised up on his elbows. He didn't bother to cover himself while he listened to Fulke's wrath. He watched Carolina wrestle with her skirts and snarl at Fulke at the same time. Both of them shut up when he began to laugh. He lay back, chortling at the ceiling.

"It's no use, Carolina," he said when he could talk. "My virtue is defended by a hulking duenna who spouts Scripture. He'd fit me with a chastity belt if he could." He laughed again.

"Oooooooooooh!" Carolina tried to kick him, but her long skirts got in the way.

Fulke was trembling and red faced. He pointed a finger at Carolina. " 'For they that are after the flesh do mind the things of the flesh; but they that are after the Spirit the things of the Spirit./For to be carnally minded is death . . .' "

"He's found you out, Carolina. You're carnally minded."

Carolina bent down and slapped him. Alexis leaped to his feet so swiftly, his dressing gown flapped out behind him. He grabbed Carolina by the hair and headed for the door. Along the way he grabbed Fulke's arm and hauled his cousin with him. Snatching the door open, he shoved both intruders into the hall, then slammed the door in their faces. He locked it as he yelled at them through the wood.

"I'm not in the mood to be raped nor to be scourged, so you can both take your nasty desires to bed with you, preferably as far from me as possible."

This time he hadn't come after her.

Standing on the deck of the clipper that would sail for America in the morning, Kate hugged her shawl closer to her shoulders and walked toward the prow. It was evening and there were few crew members about.

Mama had advised forgiveness and perseverance, but Kate was too hurt. She had offered her love and her heart, delicate, sparkling jewels suspended on the fragile necklace of her trust. Alexis had thrown all of them into the hypocaust of his guilt and watched them burn into ashes. And it had happened in less time than it took to pour tea.

Val came on deck from taking his leave of Mama and joined her at the prow. They watched the moon turn from gray to silver and white.

"Stay a few more days," Val said. "I'm sure he will come."

Kate grasped the railing in front of her and stared at her hands. "I don't want to be hurt again."

"But it's only been a couple of weeks, my dear. And

Alexis has dug a monstrous deep hole this time. It will take him a while to get sick of standing at the bottom and staring up at the light."

Wetting her lips, Kate asked the question she'd wanted to ask since Val came to say good-bye. "Mrs. Beechwith?"

"I'm sorry. Alexis can be intimidating when he doesn't want to be cornered, and I'm afraid he is playing the grand seigneur. I don't understand it. There's something in his character that enables him to make one feel like a squire who spilled wine on the king's mantle, and do it without saying a word."

"You should have kicked him."

Val smiled and took her hand. "If he doesn't come to you, I will."

Bowing, Val kissed her hand. Kate stood on tiptoe and kissed his cheek. He whispered a farewell and left her.

Kate stayed at the prow listening to the sound of ropes scraping against wood, of water lapping at the sides of the ship, of beams creaking. There was so much to do, she thought. Correspondence had to be read, reports on shipments and profits had to be checked. Work had been piling up since she'd gone to Maitland House all those weeks ago, but there was a deadness inside of her that kept her from attending to it. She would stare at a column of figures and see a sinuous body and luminescent black hair.

A clammy breeze invaded her shawl, and she retreated to her cabin. Donning a high-necked nightdress and a dressing gown, she settled into bed, opened a book, and tried to read by the light of one lamp. In the past weeks, she hadn't fallen asleep until well after midnight.

Her eyes were fluttering closed when a rumbling sounded on the deck above. Kate blinked and looked up at the ceiling. The rumbling skittered across the deck, down below, and into the passageway. There was a loud crack, and her door crashed open.

Kate gawked at the sight of Val being propelled into

her cabin by a furious Alexis de Granville. Once inside, Alexis hurled his friend to the floor. Val sailed toward Kate; hit a chair, and landed under it near her bed. He grunted as he shoved the chair off his chest, then he laughed. Kate found her tongue.

"What do you think you're doing? Get out. Go settle your little-boys' quarrels somewhere else."

Alexis was out of breath. He charged across the cabin to stand over Val like a circuit preacher over a sinner, and pointed at him.

"He's not sailing tomorrow. I'm taking him to France where I will challenge him and put a bullet through those bright curls you like so much."

Kate folded her hands in her lap and examined Alexis from head to toe. He was beginning to remind her of the marauding Phillipe de Granville. "You're babbling nonsense."

"Uh." Val sat up and touched his fingers to his bleeding mouth. "It's no use, my little mouse, I wrote Alexis the truth. It was the honorable thing to do."

"Little mouse?" Alexis growled and reached for Val.

"Stop that," Kate said.

He turned on her. "Mouse, is it? If he has touched you, I'll kill him. I'll take his head in my hands and snap his neck, as I would a mouse's." He shouted at Val. "All the time you were jibing at me about Cardigan and God knows how many other men, it was you I had to fear."

Kate got to her knees on the bed and put her hands on her hips. "Do you have brain fever, or do you always plunge about imitating Othello?"

"I am not imitating Othello." Alexis jabbed a finger at her. "No man would stand his best friend making off with his fiancée."

"Your fiancée," Kate said, her voice rising to a raven's cry. "You presumptuous, tyrannical, conceited man, can't you see Val tricked you?"

Alexis had been glowering at Kate. He now transferred his ravaging scrutiny to Val. There was a sudden quiet in the room, and Kate joined Alexis in studying the man on the floor.

Val adopted a grave expression as he maneuvered himself to his feet and limped to a chair near the door. Two pairs of eyes followed his progress. Fishing in his coat pocket, he brought out a handkerchief and dabbed at his bleeding mouth. Something dropped into his hand, but it was too small to be seen.

Alexis broke the silence. "You haven't much time to explain before I stuff you in a sea chest."

Val stood up and began folding the bloodied square of cloth. "Ah, well. *Varium et mutabile semper femina,* my friend." He held a key up before their eyes and chuckled.

He was through the door and slamming it shut before either Kate or Alexis could move. Alexis swore and launched himself at his friend too late. Hitting the closed door, he jerked at the knob as the lock clicked. Alexis pounded at the wood and yelled.

"Val, you miserable excrescence, open this door."

"Good night," Val said over the noise. "The crew have orders from Mrs. Grey not to let you out, so don't bother yelling."

Alexis rammed his shoulder into the door and bounced off it. He kicked it, and Kate covered her ears.

"Stop it!"

Hopping on one foot, Alexis glared at her. "Bloody everlasting hell."

"You won't get out without a key."

He limped to the chair near the door and groaned while he nursed his foot. Sighing with exasperation, Kate got out of bed and went over to him. She caught hold of his ankle.

"What are you doing?" he asked.

"Taking your boot off, simpleton. Your foot is going to swell."

"Leave my boot where it is."

She put one hand on his chest and shoved him back in the chair. "Mulishness isn't one of your endearing qualities."

She took hold of the boot and pulled hard. It came off, and she threw it at Alexis. It landed on his chest. He grunted and dropped it on the floor. She ignored him. Padding back to her bed, she sat on top of the covers, folded her arms, and scowled at him.

"What did Val say?" he asked.

"He said 'Woman is ever a fickle and changeable thing.' Ha!"

"Ha, yourself. He was right." Alexis pulled off his other boot and tossed it in a corner.

Kate clenched her fists. "Do all women a favor, Alexis, and adopt celibacy as Fulke wants."

He stood and shed his topcoat. Hurling it to the floor, he stomped over to her.

"You plotted this ruse between you. You wanted revenge. It wasn't enough that I was alone, you wanted me to think of you together, making love."

A keg of blasting powder went off in Kate's head. Springing up off the mattress, she brought her fist around and punched Alexis in the stomach. He doubled over her arm, making an *oof*ing sound. She raised her other arm, but he dodged out of reach.

"Damn," he said. Puffing twice, he rubbed his stomach.

"Don't say anything. Just don't say anything." She went to the end of the bed, opened a chest, and pulled out blankets. She tossed them at Alexis's feet. "I don't set out to hurt people, Alexis. That's your favorite pastime, so keep your mouth shut. Maybe that way we can get through this night without killing each other."

She got into bed again and tried not to watch Alexis as he took off his coat and socks. Rummaging in the covers, she found her book and bent over it. Her hair fell in a russet screen between her face and the man across the room. Why didn't he find a place to lie down? He was standing there in the yellow glow of the lamp, facing her. She could see his bare chest and the scar that ran down one side of his ribs. The waistband of his pants rode low, and she could see the indentation of his waist.

He moved, and she fastened her gaze on the book. When the light shifted, she looked up. Alexis was standing beside the bed with the lamp in his hand, staring at something beside her head. She turned to see what he was looking at, but saw nothing. A look of wonder transformed his angry features. His eyes lost that hard, snarling-wolf expression and softened. Confused, she watched him raise the lamp and bring it near to her. He slowly reached out with his free hand and touched her hair.

"Like copper ingots cast at the sun," he said in a whisper.

She scooted away from him. "You see? I'm not the one who's fickle."

He dropped his hand. "No, you're not." He put the lamp back on the table beside the bed. "I was coming to get you when Val's letter arrived."

"I don't like you anymore, Alexis. And if you liked me, you would never have treated me like fool's gold." She shook her head when he tried to speak. "I don't want to talk to you."

Kate got under the covers, turned away from Alexis, and closed her eyes. The red blur against her eyelids disappeared as he blew out the lamp. Tears stole from the corners of her eyes. She wiped them away with her fingers while she listened to Alexis spreading his blankets. The tears kept coming, and she resorted to dabbing her eyes with the edge of a sheet. A sob welled up in her throat.

Desperate to keep silent, she fumbled with the sheet and buried her face in it.

Something landed on her back. She sucked in her breath and pulled the sheet from her face. Warm lips were pressing kisses to her ear and her wet cheek.

"Don't cry, little savage."

His breath tickled her ear and neck, and the tremor it set off in her body snapped her control.

"G-go away," she wailed.

She tried to curl up in a ball, but the sheets and blankets grew wings and flew away. She was gathered in the hollow of Alexis's body. His arms wrapped around her, and she couldn't push them away. He ducked his head, found her lips, and assaulted them with little nips that spread to her chin and throat. In between pecks he whispered pleas and threats.

"Don't cry, don't. Forgive me, please. Dammit, I forbid you to cry. Please. You will forgive me. You have to."

The demands sounded so bewildered and so helpless, she felt a fluttering in her belly and chest. The fluttering turned into a giggle, which escaped her at the same time that Alexis decided to put his tongue in her mouth. She felt his lips curl into a smile. In the darkness, she could hear his amusement.

"I sound as mad as I once claimed to be."

"I feel a bit daft myself." With no light in the cabin, she had to feel her way up to his face. "Your cheek is wet."

"You cried all over me. If you hadn't stopped when you did, I'd have needed an umbrella." He took her face in his hands. "I will not allow you to hate me."

"I'm afraid."

"Will you still be afraid if I give you a promise?"

"What kind of promise?"

"I give you my word never to try to drive you away again, and never to lie to you."

"Lie?"

He hugged her to his chest. "I haven't been seeing Carolina."

"Good." She pulled her arms from between their bodies and wrapped them around Alexis. She heard him sigh with relief.

"Thank God," he said.

They exchanged lung-crushing squeezes.

"Do you know when I came to my senses?" he asked.

She shook her head.

"It was the night Fulke congratulated me on getting rid of Carolina. He started at me about purity and chastity topped off with port. After a few glasses, I found myself actually listening to him. He ranted about sin and iniquity, something about 'He that toucheth pitch shall be defiled therewith.' I nodded like an old dowager at matins. And then we progressed to a catechism. You know, 'renounce the devil and all his works, the pomps and vanity of this wicked world, and all the sinful lusts of the flesh.' And then Fulke held up his glass to me and said, 'Give not thy soul unto a woman.' And I laughed."

"You laughed?"

"Yes. Because at that moment I realized that Fulke was too late. I had already given my soul to a woman, and she was about to take it across an ocean with her."

"Oh."

Kate lost interest in Alexis's soul, for his hand was sliding beneath her dressing gown and nightdress and slithering up her leg. It pinched gently at her waist before traveling on to cup her breast. He squeezed, and she arched her back. She couldn't see him, but his face nuzzled at the neck of her nightgown, and she felt the heat of his skin and the rapid pace of his breathing.

His excitement reached out and trapped her in a web of eroticism. In turn, she tried to memorize his body with her hands. After only a few moments, Alexis both laughed and cursed while pulling away to snake down her body.

She felt a wet mouth on her ankle. It hopped up her leg and slithered along her torso. Shivering, she giggled and lunged for him. She wrapped her arms around his chest and heaved, catching him unaware. She twisted her body, bringing him down beneath her, and trapped his arms against the mattress on either side of his head.

"Katie Ann, let me go."

"Never. Not ever, ever, ever." She bent down, guided only by the sound of his heavy breathing, and found his mouth. Feasting on it, she heard no more objections.

Soon his hips began to thrust in a blind quest, and he pulled his mouth free. "Katie, my love, my mistress, my master, have pity."

"Poor, poor marquess, has he suffered?"

"Agonies." He arched his back, lifting her from the bed.

"Without relief?"

"My only solace took herself off." He groaned, then swore. "I need you, Katie Ann. Now."

"And I need you, my sweet, beautiful lunatic."

Encircling Alexis with her arms and legs, Kate gave up teasing. He rolled her beneath him, and the cabin filled with whispers and small gasps, the rustling of sheets and finally cries of pleasure. After spending several hours in happy sin, they at last surrendered to exhaustion. Kate woke again before dawn when Alexis began twirling one of her curls around his finger.

"I do love you," he whispered into the darkness. "I love you so much, I am filled with it to overflowing. I think I am more besotted than Romeo, Mark Anthony, and Othello all put together."

Kate tried not to grin foolishly. "It's all right," she said, hugging him. "We'll be besotted together. And think of how much fun we will have irritating Val and Fulke with our lovesick sighs and yearning glances."

She felt Alexis's chest bounce and heard him chuckle.

He gave her a kiss that landed on her nose. The second found her mouth. He put his lips to her ear.

"You can trust me with your love."

"Ah, you have decided that you deserve me after all."

"Yes."

"Good, because by the time I got home, I probably would have decided to have you abducted and spirited to me on one of my ships."

"We shall marry and sail to San Francisco for our wedding trip."

"Yes, my lord."

"Insolent, teasing peasant girl."

"Despot."

He nudged his hips against hers, and she giggled.

"Very well," he said. "We won't go to San Francisco. I shall lock you in the Ghost Tower and ravish you whenever I wish."

Digging her fingers into his buttocks, she wiggled against him until he groaned. "I tell you what. Let me abduct you and carry you off to the wilds of America, and I will let you steal me away and ravish me in the Ghost Tower."

"It shall be as my lady desires. Now shut up. I need to practice my ravishing."

Kate heard a loud growl, then Alexis caught her to him and rolled back and forth across the bed. She shrieked and wriggled free. Their laughter echoed in the blackness of the cabin, and neither of them worried about who would tell of the criminal conversation between Miss Katherine Grey and Alexis de Granville.

If you enjoyed *Lady Hellfire*,
be sure to watch for Suzanne Robinson's
next historical romance,

Lady Defiant,

on sale in hardcover from Doubleday in September 1992 and in paperback from Bantam Fanfare in December 1992.

Set during the tumultuous Elizabethan era in England, *Lady Defiant* tells the story of Blade, first introduced in *Lady Gallant*. The disarmingly handsome Blade, now one of Queen Elizabeth's most dangerous spies, is given the task of romancing a clever young beauty named Oriel. She unknowingly holds a clue that could alter the course of history—bringing Mary Queen of Scots to the throne of England. Unfortunately, Blade has already met Oriel and did not exactly make a favorable impression on her. For a tantalizing glimpse of this wonderfully entertaining romance here's the first meeting between these two unforgettable characters.

Northern England, December 1564

Since young noblemen had always looked through her as if she were a window, Oriel couldn't stomach them regarding her as they would a fat rabbit now that she was an heiress. She had spent the last eight of her twenty years as an orphan cast into the lair of two aunts and dependent upon their mercy. Aunts were one of God's plagues.

In order to avoid the plague, on this bright and icy morn on the last day of December, Oriel had taken refuge with Great-Uncle Thomas in his closet, where he kept his papers, books, myriad clocks, and other instruments. Oriel had burst in upon him, out of breath from running as usual, and caught him directing the hanging of his newest picture, a portrait of Queen Anne Boleyn.

She smiled at him when he glanced at her over his shoulder. He sighed, for he always knew when she was hiding.

"Little chick," he said, "how many times have I admonished you not to gallop about. Such unseemly haste befits your dignity and degree."

"Aunt Livia searches for me," she said as she wandered over to examine a model of a printing press. She picked it up, feeling its weight in her hands. "Uncle, why do you suppose things fall down instead of up?"

Sir Thomas waved his servingman out of the room while he straightened the portrait. "Is this a new riddle?"

"Nay. I just bethought me of the question."

"You're always thinking of unanswerable questions. You won't find a worthy husband if you're too clever."

Oriel glanced at the likeness of Anne Boleyn. "She was clever, a great wit, so you say, and she married King Henry the Eighth."

"And got her head cut off."

Sir Thomas subsided into his chair, groaning as his body met the cushions. His great age was a marvel to Oriel, for he had seen more than sixty-one years. Walking-stick thin, his skin almost transparent, his hands shook, yet he could still set quill to paper and produce a fine Italian script. He had taught her Greek and Latin in her girlhood and had given her solace when Aunt Livia cuffed her for answering back or Aunt Faith made fun of her wildly curling hair with its auburn hue.

"God's toes, Uncle, I won't get my head cut off."

From the ground floor came the sound of a bellow honed by years of shouting at hapless grooms on the hunting field.

Sir Thomas lifted his brow at her. "Get your ears boxed, more like."

"She wants to put me in a farthingale and stomacher." Oriel wrinkled her nose and looked down at the scandalously comfortable wool gown she wore. "And she wants me to put on a damask gown, so I told Nell to give out that I'd gone riding. I think another suitor comes today, but I'm not certain. Uncle, I hate suitors."

"You must be patient. Some girls come into their beauty late. The young men won't ignore you forever."

Oriel looked down at her hands. She was twisting her interlocked fingers. "Did you—" She gathered her courage. "Did you know that I'm twenty and no one has ever tried to kiss me? I think there's something wrong with me."

Uncle Thomas held out his hand, and she went to him. He took her hand and patted it. "It must be quite terrible to fear being unwanted."

Oriel nodded, but found she couldn't reply.

"I think you're pretty."

"You do?"

"Upon my soul I do."

"Even if I don't wear brocades and silks?"

"Even without the brocades and silks, but you could do with some new gowns," Thomas said. "Look at that one. It binds your chest, girl."

Oriel knew how to avoid chastisement. "Tell me about your new picture. You knew Queen Anne long ago, didn't you?"

"Aye." Thomas rested his head on the back of his chair and gazed at the portrait. "You can't tell from the portrait, but she was all wildness and courage, was Anne Boleyn. And our good Queen Bess takes after her. It was her wit and fey courage that captured old King Harry's heart."

Thomas sighed and glanced at Oriel. He seemed about to speak, but didn't. After a short silence he continued.

"He never captured hers, though. It had been taken, and Henry Percy had it always, may God rest his soul."

"How so?" Oriel asked. This was a story she'd never heard.

"I forget. Have I told you about that Italian fellow da Vinci?"

"Ohhh—ri—el!"

"God's toes, she's coming."

Oriel bounded for the door, threw a kiss to Uncle Thomas, and scurried through his chamber, the withdrawing chamber, a short passage, and down a side stair. Hugging herself, she scampered along the frost-ridden lawn beside the east wing of Richmond Hall, through the gardens, and back into the house.

She crept into the Old Hall and stood at the base of the main stairs looking up. Aunt Livia's stiff skirts disappeared above her, so she tiptoed after the woman, her own skirts lifted to her ankles. Stealing into her own chamber on the third floor, she snatched up her new cloak lined with squirrel fur and dashed back downstairs. As she went, she could hear Livia's booming voice in Great-Uncle's closet. Someday Livia would have a fit from her own choler.

Aunt Livia wanted her to don a farthingale and a gown as stiff as cold leather. Oriel couldn't remember why at the moment, but Livia's reasons never made sense anyway. Proud of her stealth, Oriel hurried to the stables. She must go riding so that Nell wouldn't be caught in a lie.

She returned to the hall an hour later. Having galloped the last few leagues, she was flushed and damp with sweat when she entered Richmond Hall once more. Livia was waiting for her. Oriel paused upon seeing her aunt, then gripped the carved stone newel post. Livia descended upon her from the first landing. A tall woman, she had the bulk of one of her hunting horses and a habit of flaring her nostrils like one of them as well. Though Oriel matched her in height, she did not in weight. Once she would have shrunk away from Livia in anticipation of a slap. No longer. Oriel lifted her chin and her shoulders and met Livia's gaze.

Livia came to rest on the last stair and swore at her. A fleshy hand twitched, and Oriel glanced at it, knowing how much damage that beringed fist could do. Then she stared at Livia. The woman swore again and put her hand behind her back.

"You strain all courtesy, girl. Would God I had the chastening of you still."

"No doubt."

"None of your clever retorts," Livia said. "Have you forgotten that Lord Fitzstephen comes this day with his son? A match with his heir is above you, but Lord Andrew knew your father and has asked to meet you for some passing strange reason of his own."

"Not so wondrous, Aunt. I'm an heiress now, or has your memory failed you? Grandfather saw to the matter."

"You're the one with the unfit memory. Why, your aunt Faith and I took you in—"

"Who did you say was coming?"

Livia vented a storm of a sigh. "How haps it that you remember French, Italian, Latin, and Greek, but fail to remember the names of your suitors? Yesterday you even forgot to come down for supper."

"It's another suitor," Oriel said with a long-suffering sigh.

Each visit from an eligible man increased her suffering. Grandfather had been dead only a few months, but Aunt Livia and Aunt Faith couldn't wait to rid themselves of her. Thus she had been forced to entertain the suit of every likely man in the county. For Oriel, the business was an ordeal. Never a great beauty, left with but a poor inheritance by her parents at their death, she'd spent most of her time at Richmond Hall with her great-uncle reading or riding.

Her cousins Agnes and Amy were too young to provide companionship, while their sisters Jane and Joan harbored a spiteful resentment toward Oriel. Why this was so remained unclear, except that Jane and Joan were as plain as their names and bore spite toward anyone even the slightest bit more presentable than themselves. Livia's sons were much older, except for Leslie, and even he was away much of the time.

"My lady!" The steward came bustling toward them, his chains of office clinking as he moved. "My lady, Lord Fitzstephen and his son are riding here."

"God's mercy." Livia shoved Oriel up several steps. "Get you gone until I send for you. And put on a suitable gown, you addled goose."

Oriel bolted upstairs, but stopped on the landing of the third floor and looked over the rail. The stair took right angles several times, and as she looked down to the bottom floor, she saw the swirling edge of a black cloak and heard the scrape of a sword sheath and ching of spurs.

She heard a voice. The voice of a man, a young man. Low, soft, and vibrant with tension, it caught her attention, trapped it, tugged at it. Hardly aware of her actions, she reversed her steps following the voice as it floated up to the second floor and then faded toward the Great Chamber. Oriel darted after it, hovering on the landing, her upper body bent toward the sound.

What was it that drew her? She listened and heard the voice respond to her aunt. There was something different about this voice, something beyond the lure of its deep, quiet tones. Ah! An accent.

This young man spoke with an accent. Barely perceptible though it was, it gave the voice a distinct character. The r's blurred, and sometimes the vowels stretched out. A French accent. How did the son of a border lord come to have even the slightest of French accents? Aunt Livia had spoken to her of the visitors, but she hadn't listened.

Oriel cocked her head to one side, but the voice was

muffled now that its owner had entered the Great Chamber. She stole along the gallery with its mullioned windows and walls lined with paintings until she neared the doors to the Great Chamber, where all noteworthy visitors were entertained.

Livia was speaking. "Are you certain you wouldn't like to retire for a while? I've sent for my niece, but your comfort is my greatest concern, my lord."

"Thank you—"

"But we must needs make our visit a short one," the accented voice said. "I take ship for France soon."

"A pity," Livia said. "Though I understand that you must attend to your holdings there. Your dear mother was French, and through her you hold a title?"

"Aye, my lady. I am called the Sieur de Racine. But at home I am called Blade."

Oriel peeped around the open door and saw her aunt standing beside the fireplace. An older man stood nearby, and both were looking at a man standing with his back to them. All Oriel could see was a tall figure made even taller by a soft cap and feather, the sweep of a black cloak, a silver sword sheath, and a pair of mud-splattered boots.

The young man spoke again and, as he did, turned to face his hostess. Oriel beheld a pair of gray eyes so bright that they seemed silver. Straight brows echoed the dark brown-black hair beneath the cap. Now that he faced her, his body framed in the light of the windows, she could see the line of his mouth with its full lower lip and contained tension. His hand rested on the hilt of his sword, and a heavy gold signet ring surrounded the third finger.

He walked toward the two by the fireplace, and as he came near, one of his brows arched. She caught the impression of much-tried patience, of skepticism and barely concealed mockery, all smoothed over by a grace of manner that spoke of the French court rather than the border castle in which he was born.

All at once he threw his cloak back over one shoulder and rested his boot at the base of the marble chimney-piece. Oriel cocked her head to the side, fascinated by his smooth movements. He moved as if he were dancing in a masque. She was staring at a long leg, tracing the knot of muscles in a thigh, when he suddenly looked past Aunt Livia and saw her. His eyes widened, and he faced her without speaking.

Drawn by that unwavering silver stare, Oriel came out of hiding. She barely heard her aunt's admonishments. She spared Lord Fitzstephen not a glance. Her whole attention fastened on this dark, graceful creature with the alluring voice and argent eyes. They stood opposite each other without speaking, and Oriel found herself trying to memorize the Sieur de Racine with her eyes. He met her gaze with a puzzled stare of his own, but soon, when she remained silently gawking at him, one corner of his mouth twitched.

"Mistress," he said.

The sound of his voice broke the spell and wove another just as compelling. This was a suitor from whom she wouldn't hide. When she didn't reply, he glanced at Livia in inquiry.

"Oriel!"

She jumped. Livia's brassy voice shattered her reverie, and she came to herself. What had she done? She had entered unannounced and stalked a young man like a huntress pursuing a deer. For once Oriel cursed her forgetfulness. She had to say something.

"I—I . . ." He looked at her again, and she noticed a smooth cheek, the sharply angled line of his jaw, those startling eyes. All her wits scattered. "What was your name?"

This time both brows arched, and that arresting mouth drew down. "Marry, lady, do you forget the names of all your guests?"

"Oriel!" Livia hurried to them and gripped Oriel's arm. "I marvel greatly at your lack of courtesy. Look at you. Your gown is besmirched, and you're flushed. And your hair. Have you never been taught the use of pins or caps? Jesu Maria, come with me."

Livia nodded to both men. "We will see to the bringing of wine and bread, my lords. Pray rest yourselves here awhile."

Shutting the Great Chamber doors, Livia rounded on Oriel. "Worthless girl, your head is stuffed with learning and no sense. I'm going to the kitchens. Be off to your chamber and prepare yourself."

Livia stomped downstairs, leaving Oriel to rush to her chamber and call Nell to aid her in changing her gown. Never had she imagined that her aunts could produce a suitor she would care to meet at all. But this one—the mere sound of his voice and sight of his body had dashed her prejudice asunder. This man she could imagine touching, an act she had so far avoided when confronted with the countless others her aunts had dragged to Richmond Hall.

As Nell laced and buttoned her into a gown and fussed with the small ruff at her neck, Oriel shuffled her feet with impatience. She was afraid the man would vanish, and she had forgotten his name in her obsession with his person.

What was it, that name he'd said. Blade, that was the name. At last Nell was finished, except for her hair, and Oriel dashed back down to the Great Chamber. One of the doors was half open, and she couldn't stop herself from peeping around it to catch sight of the young lord again.

They had been served wine and bread. The father was sitting before a table laden with a flagon, wine cups, and a tray with a loaf on it. His son, however, prowled about the Great Chamber, his cloak still about his shoulders and swinging with his strides. He stopped abruptly by the fireplace and glanced back at his father. The older man tore a chunk of bread from the loaf and began eating.

"May God damn you to the eternal fires," Blade said.

Oriel had been about to push the door open, but paused as she heard the young man speak. The father said nothing. His mouth was full and he chewed calmly.

"This is the fourth girl you've dragged me to see, and the worst. She's also the last."

"Clean her up and she'll be worth looking over. Jesu Maria, did you see that wild hair? Almost black but with so much red to it there must be a spirit of fire in her to match."

"I care not. Did you think to buy my return to your side with a virgin sacrifice?"

"It's your duty to stay by my side and produce heirs."

Blade crossed his arms over his chest and purred at the other man. "It's my duty not to kill you. That's why you're alive, dear Father."

Lord Fitzstephen slammed his drinking cup on the table, and wine splashed out. He stood, rested his hands on the table, and glared at his son.

"I haven't raised a hand to you since you took up with that foul thief Jack Midnight."

"Nay, Father, you're wrong. You haven't raised a hand to me since I was sixteen and big enough to hit back. I haven't forgotten those lashings, or how you left me bleeding and locked in a bare stone chamber when I was but fourteen."

A fist pounded the table so that the flagon and cups

clattered. "My heir should bide in England, not France. You still fear me, or you wouldn't run away."

"You always did twist the truth to suit your illusions," Blade said. "As I told you, I'll come back when you're dead. There's nothing to keep me here now that you've driven Mother to her grave."

"Your mother was a weakling, and you're a coward, afraid to marry a feather of a girl like that Oriel."

"God's breath!" Blade took several steps toward his father, then halted and cursed again as he tried to strangle the hilt of his sword with one hand. "I won't do it. I won't marry her. She has eyes like dried peas and a pointy little face like a weasel, and she can't even remember my name."

"It's Blade." Oriel pushed the door back and stepped into the Great Chamber.

It had taken all her courage not to run away. His disdain had been so unexpected. He'd said those words so quickly, she hadn't understood their meaning immediately, and then she realized that while she had been enraptured, he had been offended by her and her appearance. All the years of encountering youths and men who paid her slight notice came thundering back into her memory. The evenings spent watching while others danced, the hunts spent pursuing a deer or fowl while other girls were instead pursued themselves, these had driven her to seek comfort in learning and solitary pursuits.

Until today she'd scorned to seek the favor of men, for there lay the path to great hurt. She had forgotten herself and her fear this once, for the prize entranced her without warning, danced before her in the guise of a dark-haired lord with eyes like the silver edge of a cloud when lit by the sun behind it. She had forgotten, and now she paid the price.

When she spoke, both men had frozen. Neither spoke as she entered, and now Blade approached. Oriel held up a hand to stop him, and he hesitated.

"If it please you, my lord, let there be no pretense between us." Oriel stopped and swallowed, for her voice trembled. "I see that you like not my person and have no time or desire to make yourself familiar with my character. Likewise, I find myself unable to countenance a suitor with so ungentle a manner, be he ever so handsome and endowed with a goodly estate."

"Mistress, my hot and heady language was the result of being near my lord father."

"Whatever the cause, I have no wish to deal with you further. Good day to you, my lords."

Oriel turned her back on Blade and made herself walk slowly out of the Great Chamber, down the gallery to the staircase. She lifted her skirts and was about to dash upstairs in a race to beat the fall of her tears when she heard Blade's voice calling to her.

He was at her side before she could retreat. His cloak swirled around her skirts, and his dark form blocked out the light from the gallery windows. She could smell the leather of his riding clothes. He put a hand on her arm, and she sprang away, shaking it off.

"Mistress, stay you a moment."

"I have work, my lord." She must gain her chamber before she betrayed herself with tears.

"I swear to you, my words were hastily spoken and ill-reasoned on account of my anger at my father. A meanness of spirit overcomes me when I'm in his company for long, and this time I struck out at him and hit you instead. I would take an oath before God that none of my insults are true."

"Ofttimes we speak our truest feelings when our words are least guarded, my lord."

She brushed past him and mounted the stairs with as much dignity as she could summon. When she was half-way up, he was still looking at her from below.

"Lady, I go to France soon and would not leave this kingdom without your forgiveness."

Oriel looked down at Blade. Even from this height he appeared as tall as a crusader tower and as beautiful as a thunderstorm in July. In a brief span she had been enthralled and rejected, and if she didn't get away from him, she would throw herself on the floor and weep for what she had lost almost before she knew she wanted it.

"Of course. As a good Christian I can hardly withhold my forgiveness, and you have it. It seems to be the only thing in Richmond Hall you want. Once again, good day to you, my lord."

Suzanne Robinson

loves to hear from readers. You can write her at

the following address:

P.O. Box 700321

San Antonio, TX 78270-0321

Loveswept

FREE MYSTERY GIFT • FREE BOOK • RISK FREE PREVIEW

Open your heart to soul-stirring tales of love by best-selling romance authors through our Loveswept at-home reader service.

- Each month we'll send you 6 new Loveswept novels before they appear in the bookstores.

- Enjoy a savings of over 18% off the cover price of each book. That's 6 books for less than the price of 5—only $13.50 (plus S&H and sales tax in N.Y.).

- Each monthly shipment of 6 books is yours to examine for a 15-day risk-free home trial. If you're not satisfied, simply return the books...we'll even pay the postage. You may cancel at any time.

- The exclusive Loveswept title LARGER THAN LIFE by Kay Hooper is yours absolutely FREE. The book cannot be found in any bookstore because we have published it exclusively for you.

- THERE'S MORE...You will also receive a mystery gift. This beautiful and decorative gift will be yours absolutely FREE simply for previewing Loveswept.

YES! Please send my 6 Loveswept novels to examine for 15 days RISK FREE along with my FREE exclusive novel and mystery gift. I agree to the terms above.   41236

Name _____

Address _____ Apt. No _____

City _____ State _____ Zip _____

Please send your order to: **Loveswept,**
Bantam Doubleday Dell Direct, Inc.,
P.O. Box 985, Hicksville, N.Y. 11802-0985

Orders subject to approval. Prices subject to change.   RBBA1